THIN PLACES,
A Supernatural Thriller

BOB LAURENT

Illustrated by,
Christopher Laurent

ISBN 978-1-63525-778-6 (Paperback)
ISBN 978-1-63525-780-9 (Hard Cover)
ISBN 978-1-63525-779-3 (Digital)

Christian Faith Publishing, Inc.
296 Chestnut Street
Meadville, PA 16335
www.christianfaithpublishing.com

Printed in the United States of America

This book is yours, Braden Hartman. You're the reason the two boys within these pages are brilliant, funny and wise beyond their years. They're just like you. I hate that cancer kept you from reading this story on earth. But I know you're enjoying it now. I miss you.

"'Thin places,' the Celts call this space,
Both seen and unseen,
where the door between this world
and the next is cracked open for a moment,
and the light is not all on the other side.
God shaped space. Holy."

—Sharlande Sledge

"Don't run from the sun," the bluebird said,
"Or your feet will unravel, leaving nothing but thread."
"Then come with me," I said in reply,
And we'll fly to a place where the shadows don't lie."

—Olivia Autumn

PROLOGUE

"The pleasure of remembering had been taken from me,
because there was no longer anyone to remember with."

—John Green, *The Fault in Our Stars*

CHAPTER

one

Zach Keegan and Liz Ryder met in their eighth grade homeroom at Wright Brothers Middle School in Dayton, Ohio. That was twenty-two years and five children ago, and she still thought he was the funniest boy she'd ever known. He could make her laugh even when she didn't want to. But today she wanted to.

It was their son's tenth birthday, and Ben got to choose the restaurant for his party. "You're a big ten-ager now," Zach had told him after church. "It's time for you to make really important decisions—like where we're all going to *eat! soon!* Pick somewhere close. *I'm starving!*"

Ben smiled and made his choice.

On the way there, Liz was pretty sure she knew why Ben chose Chuck E. Cheese. He could coax a crazy number of reward tickets out of those arcade games—like turning on a gushing faucet. But mostly, she knew he would lead with his heart, and this was where his siblings would have the most fun.

He was always looking out for his seven-year-old sister, Kate, who was back to wearing an eye patch on her stronger right eye to help correct her lazy left eye. The thicker lensed glasses made her look like an intellectual, kid pirate, and Ben loved that she had a sense of humor about the whole thing.

"Ahoy, matey," she quipped when he came home from school one day last week and saw that the patch was on again.

"Shiver me timbers," he responded. "Jack Sparrow, eat your heart out."

That same afternoon, he stole into her room and used a rubber band to rig a makeshift, cardboard eye patch on her favorite stuffed animal, Rags, the sock monkey. He heard her coming and dove to the hidden side of her bed just as she walked into the room. She took one look at her beloved, tattered primate, fired off her notorious machine gun laugh, and ran out of the room yelling, "Benny, you are so going to get it!"

But if anyone else dared to disparage her about her eyesight, Ben was quick to shut them down. Katie was his best friend, and everybody knew it. After all, he'd bought Rags for her in the first place.

Together they doted on their four-year-old twin brothers, Gabriel and Michael. Although whenever they introduced the mischievous pair to visitors at home or at the church where their dad was pastor, they immediately added, "But they're no angels!"

That left baby Rose, Annabelle Rosewater Keegan, that is. She was as beautiful as her name, with oversized olive-shaped eyes and a smile that would melt the heart of Cruella de Vil.

The Keegan tribe, along with Zach's parents from Fort Wayne, Indiana, noisily descended on Chuck E. Cheese for the party. "Grandma K" was there to help Liz with Rose, and "Grandpa K" was there to "tickle some ribs" and pay for the afternoon.

After two and a half hours of munching three pepperoni pizzas, rolling scores of skeeballs into the ten point hole, and redeeming countless tickets for twelve mini-Tootsie pops, a plastic puddle of fake vomit, a bracelet with an estimated life span of two hours, and a fluffy, pink dinosaur for baby Rose, the family was ready to leave for home.

"I've got the birthday boy," said Ben's Grandpa. "We'll follow you guys."

With that, the family loaded up and pulled out of the parking lot. Finding the sign for I-75 North, both vehicles merged onto the highway that would take them the seventeen minutes to their home in Vandalia.

When they got up to speed, Zach decided to settle in behind a red, Peterbilt 387 hauling a load of pharmaceuticals from Nashville to Toledo. He probably would have passed the truck if his parents and son weren't following him.

The driver of the eighteen-wheeler, Manuel Gutierrez, was alert and capable, but he had one major problem. He didn't speak English. Earlier that year, he'd paid a bribe to obtain a commercial driver's license in Tennessee. Now he couldn't understand the CB chatter from his fellow truckers. They'd been warning him all afternoon that a piece of his rig—a thirty-pound bracket that holds one of the truck's mudflaps in place—had broken loose.

The bracket hit the highway just five miles south of where the Keegans would have exited a few blocks from their house. By the time Zach saw the piece of metal, he couldn't avoid running over it. The bracket punctured the SUV's gas tank and dragged like a matchstick along the road's surface. The spray of sparks detonated the gasoline, and the van exploded into a flaming ball of fire hurtling down the highway at a mile a minute.

For Ben, it was a macabre scene that would play out in slow motion nightmares for years. There was no time or reason for hope. He and his grandparents watched the decelerating inferno that engulfed his family swerve off the road and crash into the concrete embankment of the Route 12 overpass. Feeling the shock blast of the explosion, Ben cried out,

"No, God! No!" Then softer, surrendering to despair. "No, God. No."

It would be the only prayer and last words he would speak for three years.

PART ONE

"The difference between genius and stupidity is: genius has its limits."

—Albert Einstein

CHAPTER

two

Just outside the Nuclear Structure Laboratory on Notre Dame's campus, Babe Hightower sat on a forest green bench under an eighty-foot white pine and waited for her twelve-year-old son, Jackson. Home-schooled through the seventh grade, her oldest child was two hours into what was always a grueling one-on-one examination. The Wechsler Adult Intelligence Scale is the gold standard IQ test, and Dr. Jurgen Volheim, an eminently trained psychometrist, was the best at administering it. He knew how to humble the most egocentric doctoral students and leave them shaken by his prolonged face-to-face mental interrogation.

Finally the doors to the Jordan Hall of Science opened, and out walked Jackson Jazz Hightower, his red ball cap slightly crooked over his curly black hair, an inscrutable Mona Lisa grin on his face. Middle names are usually invisible to classmates and even relatives, so Babe and Gurney decided early on to give their children middle names that people would remember—even if they heard them only once. Their singular criterion was to choose names that made them happy without trying very hard. That's why Jackson's sister was named Carrie Sunshine.

Since Babe's recent pregnancy, Gurney had been lobbying for the baby's middle name to be "Discretion," as in the phrase, "Discretion is my middle name." Babe's response to the suggestion was terse: "Fat chance, Millstone," which was Gurney's middle name, suggested, no doubt, by his father, Maxwell Jubilation Hightower. Everyone called him Jubal.

A moment behind Jackson was Dr. Volheim, who paused at the door to watch "Jacks" and his mother embrace. He was always moved by the way the Hightowers cared for each other. He knew they had as many problems as any other family—maybe more since Ben came to live with them three years ago. Babe's sister's son, the boy was still mute from the traumatic accident that had taken the lives of his entire family in Ohio.

Liz had stipulated in her will that if she and Zach died prematurely, Babe and her family would get custody of all the children, emphasizing that the kids were to be kept together "as a family unit." As things turned out, there was no family to keep together, and Babe's attempts to fold her nephew into her family had not been easy.

Dr. Volheim felt honored to be privy to all of this story and more. Middle-aged and a curmudgeon by nature, he was privately grateful that the family trusted him with their grief and regularly included him in their gatherings.

There was no question that he would waive the 550-dollar fee he normally charged to administer the IQ test. Gurney had done so much for him since taking a position at the university. As a confirmed bachelor with no living relatives who would brook his irascible nature, he surprised himself five years ago by accepting Gurney's invitation to spend Christmas day on the Hightower "farm." He hadn't missed a Christmas with them since, and even made it to a few Thanksgivings. Besides that, he figured the fee was nothing compared to all the gluten-free cookies and cupcakes he'd consumed in Babe's kitchen.

Because the WAIS-IV was a computer-generated exam, the results were available immediately, and Dr. Volheim was anxious to talk with Jackson's mother about them. Ever intuitive, Babe understood that and said to her son,

"Do me a favor, sweetie. Go over to *La Fortune* for a SINGLE-dip. 'Doc' and I need to talk."

"Sure, Babe. How long do you need me out of the way so you guys can talk about me?" He'd always called his mother the only name he'd ever heard his father call her, and she liked it that way.

Not biting on his playful sarcasm, she said, "Not long. Then we'll pick Carrie up at gymnastics and go home."

When the boy walked away, Dr. Volheim sat down by Babe. He stared after Jackson for a moment, shook his head and opened with,

"I knew he was smart. Hell, I knew he was brilliant!" Catching himself, he apologized.

"Excuse my French. I'm just a profane man."

"You're a wonderful man, Jurgen, and you don't need to apologize. I believe in hell. Now, what were you saying?"

"That I knew Jacks was brilliant, but I wasn't prepared for this." He held up a computer printout of the results.

"May I look at that, Doc?" asked Babe.

"Of course," he said, handing her the paper. "But you may not understand the numbers."

She scanned the sheet and saw scores for Verbal IQ, Performance IQ, and several other subsets.

"You're right. This doesn't make a lot of sense to me. What does it mean?"

"The short answer is that Jackson has an IQ approximately forty points higher than Stephen Hawking's."

A short, high-pitched laugh burst from Babe, which she quickly stuffed back inside with her hand over her mouth. She lowered her eyes and smiled, followed by,

"I guess I'm not surprised."

"Well, you should be, crazy lady! You should be apoplectic!" shouted the doctor, waving his arms for emphasis.

"Do you realize that of the ten highest IQs in history, only five are alive today and only one of those lives in the United States? Your son makes that a grand total of two!"

"So that would put his IQ somewhere around two hundred, right?" asked Babe.

"'Somewhere around 200' is exactly the way to put it. His Full Scale IQ is between 200 and 225, and scores over 200 are referred to as "unmeasurable genius.""

"But, Doc…" interjected Babe.

"I'm sorry," he countered, "but there's more. Jackson answered all sixty questions—not only accurately, but contextually! And several times after his answer, he then asked *me* questions that naturally arose from the topic. He had me sweating! We could have been out of that room an hour ago!"

"I know. I know. He does that to Gurney and me all the time at home."

"I'm glad you brought that up," said Jurgen. "I don't want to be rude, but home-schooling isn't going to be productive for him much longer. He could matriculate at Notre Dame right now. Hell…" he paused, nodding at Babe. "I know. You believe in it. What I'm saying is that he could test out of many of our courses this semester."

"That's not going to happen, Doc. He'll be attending public school this year."

"Why would you want him at IUSB?" he replied, referring to the South Bend campus of Indiana University.

"First of all, IUSB's a fine school, but that's not where he's going. He and Ben will be attending an age appropriate school. They'll both be eighth graders at Rockne Intermediate when it opens in a week."

"But, Babe, there's nothing this boy couldn't be. There's nothing he couldn't do. He could help us understand dark energy and the mysteries of the universe. He could help us get to the stars someday. He could be president of the United States!"

"That last one's unlikely; he's way too smart for that," she teased.

"Then he could be the next Da Vinci, for God's sake!" Doc insisted.

"If he is, it *would* be for God's sake, trust me," said Babe. "Jurgen, my friend," she spoke softly. "Da Vinci didn't start with *The Vitruvian Man* or *The Last Supper*. His first painting was a monster spitting fire. We need to let Jackson be a boy," she said. "At least for a little while longer," she whispered, staring aimlessly past Jurgen into a future she couldn't see.

"But don't you want him to fulfill his limitless potential?" asked Jurgen, knowing he was losing the battle.

"Before I answer that loaded question, I have one for you. Will you keep your promise not to disclose the exam results to anyone, especially not the media?"

"But that was before I realized who he is."

"Who is he, Jurgen?"

"I'm not sure…" his voice trailed off.

"He's my son and that's enough for now. My job is to make sure that all of my children have the opportunity to be children."

"It just seems like such a waste," countered the professor.

"Of course—as does reading Tennyson or Yeats to most physicists, or signing an autograph gratis to most professional athletes, or dealing in truth to most politicians, or choosing to give birth to a Down's Syndrome baby to most abortion doctors. 'There are more things in heaven and earth, Horatio, than are dreamt of in your philosophy,'" sallied Babe. "I think what you call 'waste' is what I call 'life.'"

"I always learn something when I lose an argument to you," he replied.

"What can I say? I'm a K-12 teacher. We're inerrant!" she laughed.

Then Babe's brow furrowed, and she said,

"You mentioned his limitless potential. We really aren't surprised by this exam." She still held the printout. "And we've laid out all the options we could think of for him to consider, including early college enrollment. In the end, fulfilling his potential will be his choice, just as going to middle school next week with Ben was his choice."

One of the world's foremost psychometrists knew when he was beaten, but he had one last question.

"Then tell me: what can I do for him, Babe? I really don't think you and Gurney realize how difficult it will be for Jackson to thrive or stay hidden among classmates of average intelligence."

"You might be right," said Babe. "But that's a bridge too far for now."

"I'll tell you what I *can* do," said Jurgen. "If he chooses an area of study he's passionate about, I'll get resources to him that will take him as far as he wants to go in that direction."

"Because I trust you, I have no objection to that." She looked at him with the affection that only a parent can feel for someone who loves her child.

"You're such a phony, Doc. People who don't know you're the kindest man in the world don't know you."

"Let's make a deal," he replied. "You keep that private and I'll guard the exam results with my life. Now tell me what he loves the most: Science? Math? Philosophy? What?"

"That's easy," said Babe. "People. He loves people."

At that moment, Babe looked up and saw Jackson running across the campus green, trying to get two rapidly melting vanilla cones to them. Five months pregnant or not, if she'd known what was coming before the year was out, she'd have eaten both of them.

CHAPTER

three

Visitors were usually surprised when they turned off Kintz Road into the Hightower driveway to find such a bucolic setting just a short walk or really long football pass from the Notre Dame campus. The twenty-three-acre farm made for a pastoral scene that Thomas Kinkade might have painted if he'd recently visited Galadriel in Lothlorien. The roadside was lined with soft maples that brandished fiery crimson leaves in the fall, while the lane to the house was bordered on both sides by flowering crabs and pear trees that threw a party of pink and white every spring.

In five well-spaced areas of the three acre, fenced-in yard were multi-colored garden beds redolent with the summer flowers that made the Midwestern winter worth surviving. There were evocative assemblies of annual snapdragons, petunias and dinner-plate dahlias flirting with panoplies of perennial asters, larkspur and practically indestructible day lilies. Anchoring every bed were generous clusters of chrysanthemums patiently waiting for September.

Babe's favorite flower though, perhaps because it was her father's as well, was the bright, daisy-like zinnia. She called it the "queen of neglect" because it didn't mind poor soil or hot and dry conditions. She offered it the perimeter around the front of the house so that it surrounded her whenever she took a good book to the wicker love seat on the porch.

Finally, outside the yard's morning-glorified gate, platoons of happy-faced potentilla shrubs marched along the two-acre pond's south side while brigades of black-eyed Susans claimed the north. The whole scene accomplished the family's goal of making visitors feel they were entering a safe zone where the cares of the world outside weren't forgotten, but somehow diminished.

The weathered sign post at the redbrick driveway's entrance announced in black letter print, *"Rivendell,"* and under it were the words, *"Speak 'Friend' and Enter."* Unintentionally, the sign had come to serve as a way for the family to recognize people who "got them" immediately and those for whom it might take an effort. If a guest had a visceral connection to *The Lord of the Rings* lore, no explanation of the sign was needed. If not, no explanation would have mattered.

Inside the ruddy, clapboard house with white trim and shutters, Ben sat alone on his bed in the upstairs room he shared with Jackson. With his laptop before him, he was reading Yahoo Answers to a question he hadn't asked his computer for over seven months: "What is the best way to kill yourself?"

CHAPTER

four

Benjamin Jonathan Keegan came to live with the Hightowers two weeks after he lost his family. He remembered almost nothing about those weeks. He knew he was staying with his grandparents in Fort Wayne and that they drove him on a rainy day to the funeral in Vandalia. But he didn't look at the faces in attendance or listen to their words.

His father's parents might have been aware he hadn't spoken to them for the duration of his stay, but their own grief had been so profound his silence went unchallenged. Besides, their behavior wasn't that different from his; they only spoke when remembering became unbearable. And then their words were intentionally vacuous.

When they dropped him off at the farm in South Bend, his grandmother remarked, "He doesn't talk much. We've gotten used to it."

And there is a sense in which a home does get used to it. Nothing grows like silence in a family—especially after that family tried everything they could think of in the first year to break it without effect. Psychiatric visits. Cognitive Behavioral Therapy. Counseling appointments. Earnest one-way talks met with determined muteness.

They learned from the doctors that diagnosing Ben's condition was an inexact science. "PTSD," said one. "Selective Mutism," said another. "Intellectually disabled," a third. "Horse hockey," said Babe finally. "This boy needs a loving family."

In the end, they made a tacit decision to make room for his quiet ways. There was never any discussion about sending him away. He was now one of them come heaven or high water, and his future would be theirs. They became the lifeguards of their own gene pool and determined not to let him drown in his sorrow. So they settled into a routine that surely would have seemed odd to outsiders, but for them was the new normal.

When he first arrived, he rarely made eye contact and simply seemed shy and sad, though not anxious or uncomfortable. That he wouldn't or couldn't talk to them didn't mean they wouldn't talk to him. They talked to him all the time. The Hightowers were a verbal bunch and never met a word they didn't like. But Ben made it clear that he wouldn't respond to their questions or comments—not even in writing. Gurney bought him a small white board and markers at Costco's, but he would only use them to answer academic questions during home schooling sessions, at which he excelled.

The family never took his silence personally, so he was easy for them to love. A classic mesomorph, there was nothing stiff or awkward about him. Like his father, he'd always been tall for his age and moved with an athlete's grace. Thick, honey-wheat hair casually framed the face he got from his mother: high cheek bones, wide-set, chocolate brown eyes and a sturdy chin. He'd won the genetic lottery, and it showed.

To those outside the family, his striking attractiveness was more than offset by his perpetually blank expression and reluctance to smile whenever he was around them. But to the Hightowers, he was golden, and they viewed his presence with them as a holy thing, and his silent suffering as a cross they wanted to help him carry.

From the moment Ben entered their home, Jackson became his voice. He'd always felt close to his six-month-older cousin, who was given the top bunk in his bedroom, and now he didn't require verbal cues to tell him he was needed. His patience with Ben's moods and unresponsiveness seemed limitless. He often felt he could pick up on the other's inner thoughts and was fearless in revealing them when it seemed helpful.

On their first Sunday morning as roommates, the boys heard Gurney yell from the hallway, "Up and at 'em, men. Breakfast in ten minutes; we leave for church at nine." Every other morning that week, Ben, unlike his cousin, had gotten up without delay. This time he pulled the covers over his head and turned his face to the wall.

A few minutes later, Gurney's voice was back at their door.

"It's five minutes to pancakes, boys. Last call, and I mean it."

Jackson moaned, rolled over and sat up on the edge of his bed, rubbing the sleep out of his eyes and yawning. Ben was usually done in the bathroom by now, so he was surprised when he realized his cousin was still in bed. He stood there looking at the shapeless lump in the upper bunk and decided not to say anything.

When he arrived at the breakfast table, Babe said, "Good morning, sunshine." As usual, Carrie chirped while chewing cheerios, "Momma, that's *my* name." Gurney lowered the sports page and asked, "Where's Ben?"

"I don't think he's coming down for a while," replied Jackson.

"But he'll be late for church," Gurney frowned.

"I think that's his plan," said the boy.

"I don't get it, Jacks. What's going on?" he said, then turned to Babe. She shrugged her shoulders and Jackson spoke carefully.

"It's okay, you guys, if you expect me to go to church. But I don't think you should force Ben to go. He's got his reasons, and we should respect him."

"But his father was a pastor," said Gurney.

"That's one of his reasons," answered Jackson.

CHAPTER

five

Ben didn't go to church that Sunday, or any other time the family attended. The new normal meant that either Babe or Gurney would stay home with him and follow the service on-line. They took Jackson's advice and respected whatever reasons he had for not going. One of the things they loved most about God was his light touch, and they weren't going to get heavy-handed with anybody about their beliefs. They figured if their faith was the real thing, Ben was smart enough to recognize that and might someday change his mind. But change or not, he was a full member of what they liked to call their "famn damily," and nothing could change that.

Any family with people in it is dysfunctional. The Hightowers accepted that and life moved on. Even a damaged heart can have a predictable rhythm to it, and such were the next two and one-half years.

Babe was in charge of homeschooling the kids, and she was gifted at it. A *summa cum laude* teacher education graduate of Bethel College in Mishawaka, Indiana, she'd intended from her first philosophy class to homeschool her children someday. It was in that class that "I fell in love with two men," as she liked to tell it: C.S. Lewis and G. M. Hightower. She used to watch Gurney walk in late to the lecture every Monday, Wednesday and Friday morning in a hooded sweatshirt and jeans with the hood partly covering his longish, curly brown hair and still-sleepy, bespectacled blue eyes. He always slouched in the very back row of the multi-leveled room while she sat upright and alert in the front. They may never have met if they hadn't been assigned to the same C.S. Lewis study group that second semester. One evening an argument broke out in the group over Lewis's words:

"The homemaker has the ultimate career," he wrote. *"All other careers exist for one purpose only—and that is to support the ultimate career."* Those words struck a chord with Holly Dawn Gossman, her name before Gurney christened her "Babe" later that semester. Of the six students in the group, four considered Lewis's idea to be anachronistic, unreasonable, out of touch, and anti-women. *"On the contrary,"* said the cute mouth under the royal blue hood, *"I think he's got something."* From that moment, though he wasn't aware of it at the time, Gurney had something as well: Babe's attention. They married in the summer before their senior year.

After being certified and licensed to teach elementary grades (K-6) and exceptional children (K-12), Babe taught English Literature at a local high school while achieving her Master's in Reading at Western Michigan University in Kalamazoo. At the same time, Gurney was matriculating at Notre Dame in their doctoral program in theoretical physics. It was a crazy period in their lives and they longed for the day that their souls would catch up to their bodies. With their diplomas in hand and some of their sanity returning, Gurney accepted a position with the university, and the day after Jackson's arrival, Babe chose "the ultimate career." In doing so, she found her sweet spot, her reason for being. That Ben joined her classes ten years later simply energized her and kept her up nights dreaming about ways to reach him.

Babe knew homeschooling wasn't right for everybody but never doubted it was right for her children. Her goal never wavered: she would provide each of her children with materials and hands-on experiences to stretch their abilities and expand their interests. And she had a sixth sense about how to teach each of them. Carrie was an auditory learner who loved to have Babe read to her and later studied best with music in her earphones. When Jackson wanted to pursue areas his mother couldn't teach him, she tapped other resources outside the home, including many of Gurney's Notre Dame colleagues.

She learned early on that Ben's pathway to learning was losing himself in the dimensionless world of books, so she got him a library card and took him there every week. On the way home, she usually didn't speak to the quiet boy who was already entering the Shire and learning hobbits had hairy feet, or crash landing in the Canadian wilderness with thirteen-year-old Brian Robeson in every boy's favorite book, Gary Paulsen's *Hatchet*. Babe understood her wordless child desperately needed the romantic worlds of Richard Adams, Mark Twain and Orson Scott Card to escape, if just for an hour, the prosaic world of loss that haunted him daily. When he was with ten-year-old Ender fighting the ant-like, alien Formics to save the future of mankind, he was actually pushing back the darkness and silencing the Voices that tormented him—especially in the night.

The guilt that he felt for being the only one to survive that fateful day on I-75 North was compounded by him sometimes forgetting the faces of his parents and siblings. Now the only time he could see them clearly was in a nightmare replay of the crash. Jackson, in the lower bunk, often heard him whimpering and moaning in his fitful sleep and knew his cousin would soon awaken in a cold sweat. Then would come the click of the flashlight under his covers where Ben would read until he finally fell asleep from exhaustion. It was almost a nightly ritual.

After his morning classes with Babe and then lunch at the window seat in the kitchen, Ben could usually be found in two places for the rest of the day. His desire for routine and dislike of changes led him first to the homely, russet barn bordering the north side of the fenced-in yard.

There in the paddock adjoining the barn stood a six-year-old strawberry Appaloosa roan named Pockets, waiting for an apple or carrot or whatever Ben had secreted in his blue jean jacket. Next to Jacks, she and Bear, the family's yellow lab, were most responsible for him still being alive. But even the gentle mare and affable dog had never heard his voice.

Pockets got her name the day Gurney found her through a Horse Rescue website. That same afternoon, the family drove their used trailer over to Elkhart to get a closer view of the abused filly.

Four-year-old Carrie took one look at the cornsilk white horse with a red patch on each side and yelled, "She's got pockets!" The name stuck.

By evening, she was bedded down on a comfortable layer of pine shavings on the floor of the only clean stall she'd ever seen. The next day, her new name was hung over the door, and by the week's end, a sign was nailed to the outer wall of the stall "If you want a stable relationship, get a horse."

Whoever first said that a dog is man's best friend never had a horse. When Ben showed up at the barn on his first morning in South Bend, Pockets took to him like a mare protecting her colt. Babe saw it as a God-thing, an answer to a heartfelt prayer. She told Gurney Pockets could sense the gaping hole in the boy and gave all of her heart to him as only a sentient animal could.

The best he could, the damaged boy tried to repay her in kind. He found a book at the library that explained how to groom a horse and took it to his second favorite place on the farm: a behemoth, forty-five-year old weeping willow that held court down by the pond. Old Man Willow, as Gurney had named it, gave Ben the option of several enormous and not uncomfortable, horizontal limbs he could sprawl out on with his book of choice. The family got used to seeing him, midafternoon, leave his grooming session with Pockets and slowly walk toward his perch in Old Man Willow. These were the years when the boy read books like most people breathe oxygen: to stay alive.

Babe would often look out the kitchen window and see Ben's silhouette up in the tree. It never failed to produce an ache in her heart. More than once, she tearfully prayed, "Lord, we need a miracle."

That miracle came two years later.

CHAPTER

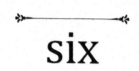

six

"You were supposed to be in that van," the Voices whispered. *"Why are you still alive?" "It can all end. All the pain can end."* The boy tossed and turned, and seldom felt rested when he awoke.

It's possible to sleepwalk through life. People do it all the time. They might be physically awake, but they're living unconsciously—without purpose or self-awareness. By his third year at the farm, Ben had taken this to another level. He would rise in the morning from a slow wave sleep stage to a state of low consciousness. Though he was always polite, his behavior became more and more perfunctory. Even with his eyes open, his expression was often dim and glazed over. Babe and Gurney were getting very worried.

The only time he seemed engaged was when he was riding Pockets, always counter-clockwise around the meadow, and the colder weather was about to bring that to an end. Ben assumed he alone knew the Voices were getting louder at night, and were now spilling over into the day.

"You've waited long enough." "You can join them all." "They're waiting for you."

By mid-December, the boy had lost what had never been a healthy appetite. He sat at the table and picked at his food, paying little attention to the family conversation and giving up all pretense of hearing any comments directed at him.

The Hightowers seldom got sick. Babe worked hard to serve up meals low in sugar and gluten and high in probiotics. In spite of her efforts, Ben went to bed two days before Christmas with a bad sore throat. In a way, he had contracted type A-2 influenza three days earlier because of Harper Lee. *To Kill a Mockingbird* was always on the waiting list at the Francis Branch Library, and Ben was the next one to be called. Alex Hess, a local college golf coach and recent flu victim had returned the book an hour earlier. After the assistant librarian handed Ben's card and the book to him, she wished him a good day and habitually pumped a generous dollop of disinfectant on her hands. When the boy got to the car, buckled the seat belt over the book in his lap and rubbed his eyes with his knuckles, he was doomed. The incubation period had begun.

CHAPTER

❧———————☙

seven

An hour before dawn on Christmas Eve Sunday, the pernicious virus was swatting Ben back and forth like a toxic tennis ball between drenching sweats and shaking chills. The sudden urge to vomit yanked the boy out of his troubled sleep, and he lunged over the edge of the top bunk, thumping awkwardly to the floor. Jackson woke to the noise of his cousin retching over the porcelain bowl in the next room.

He stumbled into the bathroom and placed his hand gently on the miserable boy's shoulder. "I'm so sorry, Ben. Get it all out," said Jacks, feeling the heat under the sweat-soaked pajamas. "I'll wake Babe."

After she'd cleaned Ben up, Babe walked him back to his bed and helped him get under the covers in Jackson's lower bunk. She'd already told her son he was officially up for the day. "You wash your hands now, Jacks, and I'll see you in the kitchen shortly." It was Babe who'd noted once that "Mom" was the middle word in thermometer. Now she inserted a digital one under Ben's tongue toward the back of his mouth. "Press your lips over it, dear," she said tenderly. A moment later she read the result: 101 degrees.

"The best thing you can do for the flu is to sleep. Close your eyes now, and I'll check in on you later."

Later came sooner than she'd hoped. The rest of the morning was a series of depressing trips to the commode. He'd eaten so little the day before that mostly he was dry heaving. His head pounded, his whole body ached, his skin was hyper-sensitive to touch, and Babe was monitoring his temperature.

Babe had already decided that if Ben's temperature reached 104, they were taking him to the E.R. She spent the afternoon sponging him down with hand towels soaked in cold water. Gurney lowered the temperature of the entire house, while Jacks did his best to keep him hydrated. At one point, Carrie showed up at his bedside with a cherry popsicle. When he showed no interest, the little girl knew what to do with it.

After Babe took his temperature again early in the evening, the digital thermometer had soared to 103.5. "Close enough," she announced. "Gurney, get the car warmed up. We're leaving now."

"Just a minute, Mother," interrupted Jackson, who never referred to her by that name. Surprised, she turned to him.

"We need to hurry, Jacks. What is it?"

The boy closed his eyes and pursed his lips for an instant, then replied,

"I think God wants me to pray for him right now."

"But we've been praying all day."

"I know, Babe, but this feels different."

She looked over at Gurney who had paused at the door to listen to this conversation. He shook his head "yes" and unbuttoned his winter jacket.

The three of them walked up the stairs and silently entered the boys' bedroom, dimly lit by the hallway light. Ben lay exhausted on his back with a lukewarm, wet wash cloth on his forehead. He looked like a cyclone had taken him for a bad ride and dumped his broken body on the lower bunk.

Babe and Gurney knelt to Jackson's left and watched their son place his right hand on Ben's damp, disheveled hair while he lifted his left in prayer.

"Father, you know I love you, but right now I'm angry... and confused. I mean, how much can Ben take? This is too much." He paused for a moment, looked down at his cousin, brought his left hand to the boy's chest, and continued.

"Maybe you've got a plan we just don't understand ..." he paused again. Then he rose higher on his knees, took a tighter grip on Ben's hair and prayed, *"... but I'm asking You to abort that plan! He's had enough, Lord. Please...fix him now."* Then, completely spent, he lowered his head to the edge of the mattress and wept softly.

Babe realized Jacks was praying for more than physical healing for Ben. These past few years had been hard for her son who shared more than just a room with his cousin. Although her instincts told her to move over and embrace Jackson, on another level she knew what they were watching wasn't finished and that this was their son's time.

Meanwhile, Ben, who was still unconscious, had been dreaming from the moment Jackson touched him. In his dream, *he was buried deeply under the snow and though he knew he was close to dying, he had a strange sense of peace. Impossibly, he even began to move his arms and legs to build up body heat and fight off hypothermia. Just as he was down to his last trace of oxygen, he heard a dog barking.* Then Ben woke up.

The boy was immediately aware that someone had a hand on his head, and two people were kneeling by his bed but not looking at him. He also recognized that nothing about him was hurting—no sore throat, no headache, no nausea, nothing. But a desire to sleep was on him unlike anything he'd known before, and as he began to give in to it, he took one more look at Babe and Gurney. They were still staring at their son with solemn, wondering eyes. About to close his own for the next fourteen hours, Ben turned on his pillow to find Jackson looking tired but smiling at him. He never really knew whether or not he was dreaming again, but just over Jackson's slumping shoulder, he saw a larger than life, incandescent being, who, from a kneeling position, was looking at him with the same sweet smile. As he fell into a deep sleep with that shining face engraved on his mind, he was unaware that his fever had broken and the Voices were silent.

CHAPTER

eight

It happens to parents all the time, but they don't often admit it. Their own children become their heroes. At some point, in some significant way, the child exhibits a character strength the parent realizes he doesn't possess to the same degree. It makes certain parents uncomfortable and others pleased. Gurney was pleased. After Ben closed his eyes and Jackson's head fell to the edge of the mattress again, his father stood up and lifted the weary boy into his arms. He was about to transfer him to the upper bunk when Babe said, "Just a minute, dear." She bent over Jacks and kissed his forehead. It was on fire with fever.

Only Carrie got to open a Christmas present the following morning. The festivities waited for Jackson's dogged flu bug to run its course. Finally on Friday morning, the family gathered around the Christmas tree and exchanged their thoughtful gifts.

Both Gurney and Babe came from families that were big on Christmas. So it was in their DNA to soak up the spirit of the carols, the lights, the cookies, the stockings over the fireplace and everything yuletide. He began the two week project of decorating the yard and the outside of the house on Black Friday morning when she went off looking for deals at the mall. Carrie and Jackson slipped away to their rooms at odd times in the evenings to work on their homemade surprises. She was making two moss terrariums, complete with tiny gnomes, fawns, and toadstools for her parents. And he was stepping up his game with a scratch foam block printing of Notre Dame's most iconic landmarks, including Touchdown Jesus and The Grotto.

What made this Christmas different from the last two was Ben. For starters, he was there for the gift-giving. In the past, he never sat around the tree with the family. The first year, he chose to stay in his room. The family correctly figured that this part of Christmas was just too brutal a reminder to the boy of what he'd lost. Last year, as Gurney was opening his present from Carrie, they were aware that Ben passed along the edge of the family room like a shadow on his way to the kitchen. Jacks noticed he didn't even look in the family's direction at that time.

But this year, Ben actually camped out as close as he could to the fireplace, just to the side of the tree. The boy had no way of knowing he was sitting in Babe's traditional spot, who was always the happiest when she was the warmest. But nobody, least of all Babe, mentioned it.

That first year, the family had left Ben's presents neatly wrapped and stacked at the foot of his bed, to be opened when he got around to it. He never got around to it. The second year they didn't bother to wrap the presents, but discretely placed them in locations where he would discover them in time: a blue, hooded sweatshirt with the Cubs logo on it in the second drawer of his dresser, a pair of khaki pants in his closet; a new curry brush hanging from a nail outside Pockets' stall, a home-made card from Carrie leaning against the computer screen on his desk, *The Hunger Games Trilogy* in the middle of his bed with a personal note from Jacks inside the first book's front cover that read, *"I remember watching you win a junior archery contest when you were nine. If you were ever picked for the Hunger Games, my money would be on you,"* and his Big Gift, a Tucker western saddle for riding Pockets, draped over the gate to her paddock, where the boy couldn't miss it.

So when Babe saw Ben sitting Indian style by the tree clutching a gift he had clumsily wrapped in reused paper from his last birthday, she had some scrambling to do. She asked Jackson to put Bing Crosby on the Bose and assigned Gurney the job of rustling up hot chocolate for the kids, while she tracked down some of Ben's presents to hastily wrap and put under the tree with him none the wiser. Only Babe could pull this off. And, of course, she did.

CHAPTER

nine

Soon everyone had filled in the circle that Ben had begun. The family's excitement over the boy being there was palpable. A beautiful girl, with her mother's auburn hair and her father's pillowy blue eyes, Carrie sat on the other side of the tree from Ben and casually played with the nativity scene. She was waiting for Gurney's annual reading of Luke two. Her love for the Baby Jesus was the stuff of legend in their house. She had started speaking when she was barely a year old. The first thing she said that sounded like a word was clearly, *"gunk."* Gurney believed that it was a baby cuss word because she only said it when she was upset about something.

The second word she spoke came at Christmas time when she did her signature "butt-scoot" across the carpet to the nativity scene. She grabbed up the miniature babe in the manger and distinctly enunciated the word, *"ba-a-abies."* It took the family several weeks to recognize that whenever Carrie saw or heard anything that had to do with Jesus, she would call it, *"babies."* The church, a cross, the face of Jesus, worship music—to her they were all *"babies."*

To prove their hunch, Gurney played a CD of the song, *Hey Jude,* and she had absolutely no response. Then he played Handel's *Messiah.* Her face lit up and she shouted, *"babies!"*

Some six Christmases later, *"babies"* had morphed into the family's best word for anything that touched them deeply. At Jackson's baptism last year, Gurney turned to Babe and whispered, *"babies"* when their son came out of the water. When their father presented their mother with a diamond ring on her birthday that autumn, it was a poignant moment. With Dan Fogelberg singing, *Longer,* in the background, Babe responded to the bling by pulling Gurney close and planting a double lip-lock on his happy mouth. In unison, the kids yelled, *"babies!"* soon followed by, *"Enough already!"* *"You're grossing us out!"* and *"You guys need to get a room!"*

When Babe returned to the family room she was nonchalantly carrying a large, mysterious bag filled with Ben's presents. Luckily, the boy's attention was on Carrie rearranging the nativity scene for the twenty-third time while she comically tried to match Bing's mellifluous baritone singing *White Christmas.* Babe took the opportunity to slip behind the tree and push some of the gifts into random spots to make it look like they'd always been there.

Finally, it was time for Gurney to read the gospel account of the birth of Christ. When he finished, he looked up and warmly spoke the same six words his own father always pronounced at this moment: *"We give—because He first gave."* It was a better phrase than *"Ladies and gentlemen, start your engines,"* but it had much the same effect on the participants. Let the gift-giving begin.

For a child, anticipation is half the fun, but the other half, whether they realize it or not at the time, is simply being remembered—and well-loved. The next hour was a medley of remembering: what some of them had hinted months or maybe just hours before that they wanted for Christmas; what others bought or crafted for those who formed the patchwork quilt of their fondest memories; what one of them needed but never would have asked for—and that was Ben's Big Gift this year. Babe placed the recently-wrapped present at his feet, and Carrie helped him open it: a pre-owned Bowtech compound bow with a twenty-nine-inch draw length and a quiver of thirty-inch Carbon Express arrows. Since his most recent growth spurt, Ben had seriously outgrown his old bow, which he most likely couldn't find even if he were inclined to shoot again.

He was the only one in the room who understood what a lavish gift it was, although a short week ago it would have meant nothing to him. Ben was increasingly aware that something had changed in him since Jackson prayed over him and then battled a serious case of influenza himself. The boy was convinced that his younger cousin had somehow taken on his own infection, an act that had ever so slightly pried at a door that had closed off his heart and set him on a deadly, downward spiral more than two years ago.

He wasn't prepared to analyze it any more than that. Even if he could speak, he wouldn't know what to say about how he felt. The simple fact was he felt something, and that was such an unexpected development that he'd decided to give Jackson a Christmas gift.

The boy had searched through the boxes at the bottom of his closet until he found it. Hidden beneath a stack of *Bone* and *Batman* comic books was an unpretentious leather pouch. He loosened the draw string and pulled out a clear, plastic case. In that case, was his legacy, handed down from his grandfather to his father, and then to him on his tenth birthday, the last day of his father's life.

Some sixty years earlier, his grandfather had laid out 15 cents for a ten-count pack of Topps baseball cards at an A&P near his home in Cleveland. Maybe this pack would have his favorite player in it. He briskly peeled back the layer of wax paper, and stuffed the flat rectangle of pink bubble gum into his mouth as he thumbed through the cards with his other hand. There it was: the sixth card! It read, *Bob Feller: Strike-Out King*. He checked the schedule on his wall. The very next Saturday, the flame-throwing right hander was scheduled to pitch at Cleveland's Municipal Stadium, "The Mistake by the Lake."

Life was safer in those days. Ben's grandfather, ten year old Charlie Keegan, and his neighborhood pal, Joey Blankenship, boarded the late morning bus at the end of their block and took it to the game by themselves. All the way to the ballpark, Charlie had one thing on his mind.

CHAPTER

ten

The Indians' ace walked the first batter he faced in the top of the eighth inning. His player-manager, Lou "The Good Kid" Boudreau, called time out and shuffled slowly in from shortstop toward Feller to give the relief pitcher time to warm up. When "Bullet Bob" ambled off the mound that day, he had a 4-0 lead, had struck out twelve men, and reduced the vaunted Yankee lineup to a sad band of hapless hackers.

Feller, perhaps the greatest right-handed hurler in history, was in a good mood when he was greeted at the dugout by a standing ovation. One of those cheering was little Charlie, holding out his baseball card.

"Hey, Mr. Feller!" he cried. "Howza bout an autograph, sir?" The boy was leaning so far over the box seat railing that he lost his balance and would have landed on his head if the pitcher hadn't caught him.

"My autograph isn't worth breaking your neck for, son" he said. Then he plucked the card from the boy's hand and signed it, adding, "If I win a few more games, this might be worth something someday, kid."

"The Heater from Van Meter" won a few more games: 265 more with three no-hitters, to be exact. Because Charlie was ten when he got the card, he waited until Zach's tenth birthday to pass it on. At that time, it was worth over $500 in its mint condition. For Ben today, it would bring $3200 on the open market.

The silent boy had no need for words to show his appreciation for their lavish gift. The family could see it in his eyes. He turned from the compound bow and looked up at Babe for a moment, and then over to Gurney—as if seeing them both for the first time.

When Carrie had unwrapped the hunting bow and handed it to him, Ben had instinctively set his own gift for Jackson on the floor by the tree. Now he picked it up and didn't seem to know what to do with it. It had no gift tag on it, but ever Santa's helper, Carrie said, "It's for Jacks, isn't it? I'll give it to him for you."

Maybe Ben was having second thoughts, but he released the frumpy little package with too much scotch tape on it to the girl and turned away from the family, and toward the crackling fire. Jackson couldn't have guessed at the history behind or the value of the gift he opened, but a dead frog or a rusty tin can would have sufficed at that moment. It was the significance of the gesture that moved him to walk on his knees across the carpet and throw his arms around his cousin.

"I love you, Ben!" he blurted out, hugging him for everyone in the room. "We all love you!" he added.

Normally the guarded boy discouraged all physical contact and was adept at avoiding any possibility of it. But many things were different today. Jacks met no resistance this time, and neither did his tearful parents when they joined in.

Carrie sat very still, her eyes glistening. Clutching in her right hand the miniature infant from the nativity scene, she whispered, *"Ba-a-abies."*

CHAPTER

eleven

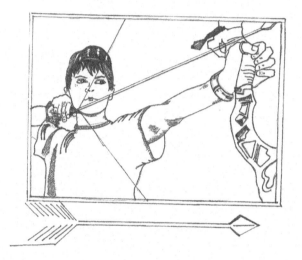

For the next seven months, Ben absorbed the family's love as if it were sunlight. Each month was better than the last. Though he never laughed out loud, it wasn't uncommon to see the boy smiling while he was reading or watching Jacks wrestle with Bear in the back yard. Just like Pockets, the affectionate, yellow lab had taken to him from the first day. Wherever Ben went on the farm, you could be sure Bear was at his side.

One of the places he went was the newly-constructed archery range on the west side of the barn. In late March when the snow had melted, Gurney took three compressed cardboard bales and covered them with black builder's plastic. Then he camouflaged those with shade cloth to make the bales less noticeable. Finally, he mounted sixty-centimeter bull's-eye targets on each of them, and *voilà*, Ben had three durable field targets to practice on.

Always cautious, Gurney also moved the old school bell from the post near the back door of the house to the corner of the barn. There it could do the double duty of calling the kids to dinner and announcing the presence of anyone coming around the south side of the barn into the area of the archery range. They eventually discovered that neither purpose was accomplished very well.

In late spring, the family tabby cat and best "mouser" their barn had ever known, Mr. Meowgi, turned out not to be a mister at all. She had a litter of five kittens, whose antics kept the kids entertained through June. By then, even though Ben still hadn't spoken a word, Jackson was sure he would soon.

One night he said as much to his parents. He was sitting at the kitchen table fiddling with the homework Babe had assigned him for the next day. But it was obvious he couldn't concentrate on it. Every few minutes, he'd get up and check the fridge for something to drink, or go to the doorway of the den to see what Carrie and Ben were watching on TV, or look out the window over the sink where he couldn't see one foot beyond his reflection.

Finally, his parents walked into the kitchen talking about a special IQ exam their friend, "Doc" Volheim at the university, was encouraging Jackson to take. When they saw him at the table, Gurney said, "Let's see what *he* thinks."

"What I think about what?"

"'Doc' wants to find out how smart you are, son," said Babe, "and I'm not sure it's a good idea."

"I, on the other hand, don't know what it could hurt," offered Gurney. "What say you, Jacks?"

"Yeah, sure … whatever," he replied absentmindedly. "Why not? I've got some things I'd like to ask 'Doc', anyway."

The boy paused, looked toward the door to the den, and asked, "Can I change the subject?"

Resisting the impulse to correct his grammar, Babe knew this was an invitation for them to sit down. Gurney pulled out a chair for her and cracked, "As Moses said to the bush, fire away."

"Could Ben talk if he wanted to?" said the boy, abruptly. "I mean, would he have to learn how all over again?"

"No, Jacks, he could talk if he wanted to," answered Babe. "Why are you asking?"

"Because I think he really wants to. Some nights in bed, when I'm talking to him or just saying 'Goodnight,' I feel like he's trying to get the words out."

"With great love comes great loss," said Babe. "Shutting down has been Ben's way of dealing with his unspeakable loss." She was aware someone had just turned the volume up on the television in the other room. She continued, "But, in the end, shutting down only extends the pain. These past few months have given all of us hope we're turning a corner. All talk is heart talk, dear. Ben will speak again when his heart learns to speak again."

"Well, I'm giving God until the end of the summer to make that happen," said Jacks.

Gurney smiled and asked, "Why the time limit? It's been two and a half years. What's the rush?"

"Because, that's when we're going together to public school for eighth grade."

That remark got Babe's attention.

CHAPTER

twelve

Early on the morning of July 12, Gurney and Carrie drove Jacks four hours north to Spring Hill camp for a week of high ropes, watersports, climbing, ziplining and faith-building with a few hundred other twelve- to fourteen-year-olds. It was the highlight of Jackson's summer, and he really wanted Ben to go with him this year. It was a fool's hope, and he knew it. He sensed his cousin's hostility toward anything religious, and yet, he believed Ben was coming to trust his family.

But by the time he worked up enough courage to ask him, registration had already been closed for two weeks. So Ben hung out at the farm, waiting for Jackson's return and becoming more useful every day. Whereas his younger cousins saw chores as necessary tasks to be finished before they could do what they wanted, he seemed to thrive on work and couldn't get enough of it. He'd completely taken over the care of Pockets, a daily regimen of feeding and grooming her, as well as cleaning out her stall.

Gurney taught him how to manage the meadow behind the house. The boy could hook up the antique, sickle bar mower to their John Deere and cut the meadow in five-acre sections from one week to the next. That way nesting birds were given fair warning to move to safer homes. He learned to use a square baler, and after he loaded the bales on a flatbed trailer, how to stack them in the barn so that Pockets would be well fed throughout the coming winter.

Beginning in June, Babe enlisted his help in the apiary on the west side of the pond. Because he had no fear of being stung, he never was, and collected the honey with impunity. He was equally adept in the chicken coop, helping Babe change the bedding twice a month, composting the litter and carrying it to the vegetable garden for fertilizer. Their spring chicks were pullets now, and most of their layers were happy, healthy and cranking out plenty of farm fresh eggs.

Ben was surprised at how loveable and friendly some hens could be. One of Babe's favorites, a Rhode Island Red named Bella, would peck and pull at the cuff of the boy's jeans until he picked her up for cuddling. He actually taught her how to jump up to the perch in the pen so he could pick her up more easily. Eventually, she was up there most of the time just for the attention he gave her.

Some of the things Ben discovered that spring and summer were less productive than his chores, but just as important. He found out Gurney wasn't kidding when he said that the fence around the farm's perimeter was "hot." He learned that if he got stuck in the mud outside Pocket's paddock while wearing his muck boots on a rainy day, it was best to stay put and wait for Babe to rescue him with the four-wheeler. He decided never to crawl under or climb over barbed wire fences again. He discovered that no matter how cute the little mice in the barn looked, if you picked them up, their teeth would make you wish you hadn't.

But most of all, he learned that he could trust Jackson. During the thirty months that he considered ending his life, he'd never had a thought about the future. But now, even though he knew that his life could never be what it would have been if his family were alive, he began to wonder what his future might be like.

There was still so much that he didn't understand and couldn't bring himself to think about, but two things he knew for certain: Jacks was the kindest person he'd ever met, and he was not completely of this earth.

CHAPTER

thirteen

Ben wasn't as sure as all of the doctors had been that he could speak again. But twice in the past month, he had been close to trying it. Both times came at night in his upper bunk. When the urge to speak first came upon him, he was listening to Jackson's voice below. Ben was accustomed to his cousin recapping the events of his day and telling stories of the people in his world. But because Jacks knew no response was coming, he never paused in his narrative to give Ben a chance to answer him.

"It's just as well," thought the silent boy. *"I wouldn't know what to say anyway."*

The second time was less spontaneous and happened on the evening before Jacks went to camp. Ben was waiting for his room-mate to finish his nightly soliloquy and say *"G'night,"* as was his custom. He planned to respond by trying to repeat that word, but as the moment arrived, he felt his heart pounding out of his chest. In the end, he could only mouth the word, and in frustration, turn over on his stomach, press the pillow to the back of his head, and listen to his pulse slow down on its way to sleep.

Jackson had done more than simply pray for Ben last Christmas Eve. He had touched his spirit and triggered in him the dawning of hope. Though still fragile, that hope was beginning to take root, and it showed in his appearance. Thanks to a growth spurt, he was now taller than Babe. Hard work and a healthy appetite added muscle to his frame, and his once-chalky skin, daily bronzed by long hours outdoors, made for a striking contrast with his sun-bleached hair.

On Friday afternoon, July 17, it was a robust, attractive boy in the flower of his youth who stood in the driveway and watched Gurney pull up to the house with Jackson in the front seat. It touched Jacks that he was there to help him with his backpack, sleeping bag and suitcase.

At the dinner table that evening, as the whole family listened to Jackson's camp stories, Ben seemed to hang on every word. Later, Babe insisted she saw him nod his head a couple of times and almost laugh out loud.

"It's the happiest this family's been for a while," she thought. And then, *"Better that my baby will be born this year and not last,"* patting her growing bump.

The fact was that at the moment she had that thought, something had already happened over 6500 miles away that would have a shattering impact on her family.

If history has taught us anything it's that diminutive dictators with overblown egos will go "postal" more often than not, and people are going to die because of it. Pol Pot, Mussolini, Stalin, Hitler and Hirohito all averaged just under five feet, seven inches—the exact height of one of the most dangerous men on the planet: Vladimir Putin. Once an agent of the nefarious KGB, a criminal institution with a record more bloody than that of the Nazi SS, Putin showed his colors and invaded Crimea. Then, on July 17, funded, supplied and encouraged by the ambitious, little egomaniac, pro-Russian terrorists sat waiting for a Boeing 777 to enter Ukrainian air space. They fired a surface-to-air missile at the unarmed, commercial plane on its way from Amsterdam to Kuala Lumpur, the capital of Malaysia. Flight MH17, filled with 298 innocent, international civilians, many of them on vacation, exploded at 33,000 feet and plunged toward the ground in a fireball, clawing a trail of black smoke across the steel gray sky.

As their meal was ending, Gurney received a text message from "Doc" Volheim. It read simply: "Turn on the news." The family heard the beep of the incoming message and watched him read it.

Gurney looked up and said, "Something's going on. 'Doc' thinks we should see it."

Jacks was the first one to the remote, and a few seconds later, they all sat in stunned silence at the horrific scene before them. "What you are looking at," droned the anchorman, "is the wreckage of the deadliest airliner shoot down in history. The crew were all Malaysian, but two-thirds of the passengers were from the Netherlands."

"Kids," said Gurney, "it's your turn to clean up the kitchen. I want you to do that *now*."

Jacks understood and scurried Carrie out of the family room. Unknown to Babe and Gurney, Ben remained motionless behind them in the shadows, riveted to the screen.

The commentator continued, "At least twenty families were on board the aircraft. Eighty of the passengers were children, and three were infants. In fact, whole families of children were killed in the disaster. Here is a picture of three Australian siblings who were on their way home, trying to get back to start school on time. They were traveling only with their grandfather so their parents could have a few more days in Holland."

Ben stood transfixed by the image of the three beautiful, dark blonde-haired Maslin children: Mo, twelve, Otis, eight, mugging for the camera, and lovely Evie, ten. Hearing each name, he saw the faces of his own siblings: the twins, his baby sister, and his best friend, precious Katie, who would be ten years old now, just like the girl in the picture.

The boy doubled over in pain, as if he had just been kicked in the stomach. He wanted to turn away from the images, but found he couldn't.

Without commentary, random snapshots of the plane's wreckage began to appear on the flat screen: a group of local miners picking through the site, searching for bodies, an open suitcase draped by a child's t-shirt that read, "I HEART Amsterdam," a young artist's notebook still opened to the half-finished drawing of an airplane. Each picture hit him like a physical blow. The final image held the screen's attention for several poignant seconds. When Ben saw it, the hope that had been slowly growing within him for months vaporized. A rifle shot couldn't have thrown him against the wall more forcefully. Lying there in the wreckage outside the sleepy, little village of Grabove, Ukraine, framed by disheveled comic books and scattered playing cards, was Katie's beloved sock monkey, Rags.

CHAPTER

fourteen

Babe heard Ben bounce off the wall. She turned to see him leave the room in a rush and take the stairs three at a time to his bedroom. The door slammed behind him.

"O, Gurney!" she cried. "He was in here the whole time! I should have noticed."

"Don't blame yourself," he answered. "If anybody's to blame, it's Putin, not us."

They left the family room and walked into the kitchen, where Jacks was washing and Carrie drying. The boy turned and saw his parents looking discouraged. He was aware of what had just happened, and his words gave voice to their thoughts:

"We lost some ground tonight, didn't we?" he said.

Actually, they lost more than they knew at the time. When Jacks entered the bedroom late that evening, Ben was already turned against the wall in his upper bunk. He lay there in the dark until past midnight with his eyes wide open. There were no tears, or anything that resembled brokenness. If he could have cried, it likely would have helped him. If he could have released the fury of his rage at God for the senseless death of children, it might have led to a struggle with truths he'd never considered before. But he was still only thirteen years old, and he chose the familiar path of silence.

Dante was right when he imagined that the lowest level of hell was ice and not fire. That's because indifference is the nadir of the human soul. Cold indifference will always be farther from the heart of God than hatred of God is. And fewer things in life are more destructive to a human being than frozen anger, but the enemy makes the alternative seem impossible. Ben no sooner closed his eyes than the Voices returned. Had they ever left?

"This isn't your family; your family is dead."

"You were a fool to hope again."

"Death is the door to your real family," they hissed.

If Ben had rolled over and opened his eyes, he might have seen a magnificent being almost nine feet tall standing in the corner of the room—a silent sentinel who had never left him since birth, and who now chafed at the evil that murmured in the dark.

"Freedom of will is His most dangerous gift," thought the iridescent messenger, who was eager to fight but often helpless to do so on his own.

CHAPTER
fifteen

Gurney

Four weeks passed and Jacks was worried. Public school would start in about a week, and he didn't see how that was going to work for Ben. His cousin had walled himself off again, and, if anything, seemed more distant than before Christmas. Jacks sensed if he didn't do something soon, worse things than being told he couldn't go to school were going to happen to Ben. He had to come up with a plan.

Gurney was thinking the same thing at the breakfast table that morning, when Babe walked in, later than normal, stretching out her arms in an epic yawn that made her puffy eyes water.

"Of all the women, in all the gin joints, in all the world, you walk into mine," he quipped in his best Bogie imitation.

"*Don't* play it again, Sam," she answered. "I was awake most of the night, and I've got a beautiful migraine renting a duplex in my head."

"Sit down, my love. I'll pour you a cup of joe."

"I *wish*," returned Babe, testily. "You know I don't do coffee with the baby coming."

"Sorry," said Gurney, getting up as she sat down. "Old habits are hard to break. Let me help you with that headache. First you're going to need some water," he said, filling a glass from the dispenser on the refrigerator. "Now drink as much of this as you can. It'll flush out the toxins I'm about to release."

With that, he moved behind her and using his three center fingers, gently applied steady, firm pressure on the sides of her head, just behind the eyes, holding it for ten seconds. Then he deftly massaged both temples in a circular motion while Babe tilted her head back. Finally, he worked on her neck muscles, ending with a massage of the base of her neck, moving his fingers slowly out towards her ears for the coup de grace.

"Now you know why I keep walking into your gin joint," said Babe, feeling some immediate relief. "You still have the magical touch."

"If you finish your water, I won't send you a bill," he smiled and walked to the window that opened onto the back yard. Leaning against the sill, he turned serious and said, "It wasn't the baby that kept you awake last night, was it?"

"No, it was Ben. You don't think…I mean, he would never…uh…you know …"

"Hurt himself?" finishing her sentence for her. "Only God knows the answer to that. It's a bit of a miracle he hasn't already tried."

Babe abruptly brought her hand to her chest and raised her eyebrows. "Why didn't you tell me you were thinking that?"

"We've all been thinking that—for some time. At least you, Jacks and I have."

"Then why haven't we talked about it?" she asked.

"That's a good question—maybe because we subconsciously feel if we talk about suicide, we increase its chance of happening. I don't know. What I do know is that what's going on here is very unusual."

"What are you saying?" asked Babe

"That it's almost impossible for most people to sustain a tragic mood. That Ben has sustained his for three years is rare and an indication of the depth of his grief. The poor kid. He's a brave one. It takes far more courage to suffer than to die." He paused, looked out the window and saw the lone boy walking slowly toward Old Man Willow.

"The majority of us are born with a phoenix quality of the mind," he continued. "It's a part of our will to survive. We humans seem to be able to grieve only for a time. Then we usually pull out of it—or descend into some form of madness. Suicide is one of those forms."

Babe rose and joined Gurney at the window. She saw Ben stop by the pond and stare intently at it—as if he were plumbing its depths.

She turned to her husband and said, "I don't like this, Gurney. I don't like that he won't let us in. And I hate that he chooses to be alone."

"But you know we can't force ourselves on him, Babe. If we tried to, trust me, you wouldn't like the results."

"Well, how could it be any worse than this?" she burst out.

Gurney was wise enough not to answer that question. Besides, he knew that she wasn't finished.

For a long moment, they stood side by side at the window, watching Ben at the pond and wondering what he was thinking.

Finally, Babe broke the silence. "I used to believe loneliness is just a temporary thing, a cry for friendship." Keeping his eyes on the boy, Gurney put his arm around Babe's shoulders and drew her closer to his side.

"Loneliness squeezes you like a vice grip. It twists simple things and plays evil tricks on your conscience. It strains at your nerves and twangs them with false alarms, never letting you forget no one cares and no one is coming to your rescue—even when there are many who would if you'd just let them."

"The enemy is clever," responded Gurney. "He seduced Judas the same way he did Cain. He got them to go it alone against their brothers. Now Ben feels alone again, a frightened part of no whole, and there doesn't seem to be much we can do about it."

"We can pray," countered Babe, grimly.

"Yes, we can pray." And so they did—holding each other tighter and opening their hearts to heaven. "Please, God. We're scared for Ben, and we need your help." Immediately the forces of evil went on high alert. One of the most powerful instruments for good on the planet, a wife and husband praying for their family, was engaged in a frontal assault on darkness. They had the enemy's attention, and the enemy was shaken.

Later that day, Babe would take Jacks to his IQ test at Notre Dame, while Ben stayed at the farm, contemplating the height of the willow tree and the depth of the pond.

CHAPTER

sixteen

Walking to the car after the IQ exam, Babe worked on keeping up with a melting ice cream cone while listening to Jackson talk about his two hours with Dr. Volheim. It was obvious he was less interested in the exam and more in the examiner.

"Doc is a really cool guy. Why do you think he never got married? You suppose he's a misogynist? No way, he *loves* you and Carrie."

Babe was comfortable with Jackson's way of debriefing an experience by firing off a salvo of questions that didn't require the listener to provide any answers. His stream of consciousness flowed on.

"There has to be a market in South Bend for brilliant, balding bachelors. I mean, don't you think in our church alone there must be dozens of eligible women who would have mad love for "Doc" if they could see past his bow-tie?"

Babe laughed, then paused to make sure he was inviting her into the stream. She answered,

"I know you don't want him to be lonely, but I doubt 'Doc' is interested in mad love right now. He's always been pretty much married to his research. Besides, I think you've got something other than Doc's love life on your mind. Let's have it."

"All right, then," Jackson stopped on the sidewalk outside Siegfried Hall and turned to face his mother, who, at five feet eight, stood at least four inches taller than her son. Guileless as ever, his aquamarine eyes shining with resolve, her freckle-faced philosopher exclaimed,

"I've got a great idea! Today during the examination, I had a chance to ask 'Doc' some questions."

Babe thought, *'You had him sweating, and I had him swearing,"* but she said,

"I know. He told me you had him sweating."

"That's just it," the boy said. "I'm not sure he knew *why* he was sweating, but I think I do. His cynicism is eroding, and it's got him rattled. You and Dad have been listening to him—I mean, really listening to him for years now. I've seen him change—not that he'd ever admit it. What I want is the same chance with Ben."

"It's hard to listen to someone who never speaks, isn't it, dear? What's your plan?"

"Okay, here it is. If Ben won't talk, maybe he'll text. And I think I know how I can get him to do it."

"Wait a minute," interrupted Babe. "Is this a sneaky way to get a cell phone?"

Undeterred, he pressed on. "It's time, Babe. We all saw a difference in him after Christmas. That difference is almost gone." Knowing more than he was revealing, he added, "And his dark moods are back."

His open face closed in a frown for a moment and he looked older than his years. "Something has to change right away." He took a deep breath and let it out slowly. "I've got a bad feeling if he doesn't talk very soon, he probably never will again."

"I agree, Jacks," said his mother. "We're banking on you being right about this public school thing. It could be the stimulus Ben needs. After three years of silence, how much can we lose?"

"Don't worry, Babe. I'll take care of him."

"But who will take care of you, my little man?" thought Babe.

"So what about the phones?" Jackson asked.

"It may take some convincing for your father to free up the dollars from our budget."

"Easy-peasy, lemon-squeezy," said the boy. "There's one word I've never heard Dad say to you."

"Oh, yeah. What's that?"

"No."

The two boys were added to their family's phone plan the next morning. The cell phones were charging in their bedrooms the following day. It was five days before school started. And Jacks was about to risk everything.

PART TWO

"Past is not present; did is not does; was is not is"

—Chauntecleer the Rooster to
Jonathan Wesley Weasel in *The Book of the Dun Cow*

CHAPTER

seventeen

While Babe and Carrie were combing the aisles at Target for back-to-school specials, the boys were home poring over their iPhone instruction booklets, each for his own particular reasons.

For Jacks, learning how to use the phone and adding free apps to it was an exciting and buoyant exercise, partly because he loved connections and had never been taught to fear the world, but mostly because he had a specific goal for the phone in mind. For Ben, who had no interest in the world, crafting a playlist and using the Apple's earbuds as the perfect excuse not to have to interact with anyone, was the extent of the phone's appeal to him.

Wednesday evening was family movie night at the Hightower home during the summer months, and Babe had purposely found a classic film she hoped would draw Ben down to the family room. Using a streaming internet player to download movies from Netflix, she'd chosen *The Black Stallion*, the epic story of a boy shipwrecked on a desert island, whose only companion was a wild, Arabian horse running free on the beach.

But neither the movie nor the smell of Gurney's special, hot buttered popcorn, lightly sprinkled with parmesan cheese, could lure the boy to join them. He remained in his room, listening to Christina Aguilera on Spotify, and identifying with the lyrics to *Say Something*.

Say something, I'm giving up on you
I'm sorry that I couldn't get to you

Anywhere, I would have followed you
Say something, I'm giving up on you
And I'm saying goodbye

By the time Jacks came upstairs to go to bed, Ben was listening to another Aguilera song, called *Hurt,* and had it playing so loud that Jacks, after turning off the window fan, could easily hear the words in the otherwise still room.

There's nothing I wouldn't do
To hear your voice again.
Sometimes I wanna call you,
But I know you won't be there.

"Why does he do this to himself?" thought Jacks. And then he heard the final line in the song:

Oh, it's dangerous
It's so out of line
To try and turn back time.

"That does it!" he thought, slipping out of his clothes and into the Chicago Bulls gym shorts he always wore to bed. *"Tonight's the night."* Grabbing his cellphone from the dresser top and crawling under the covers on his bottom bunk, he breathed a prayer, "Father, help me."

Aware that his cousin had his phone in the bed above him, Jacks texted a message and hit the "Send" icon. Ben heard his new phone beep and plucked it off the bed to look at it. There at the top of the screen was part of a miniaturized message. He engaged the blue text box and saw it was from Jacks, when a shocking sentence filled the screen.

> I know where your parents are.

Jacks had spoken to Ben thousands of times over the past three years, though not lately. But these words felt very different, and Ben didn't know what to do with them. So he followed his instincts. In anger, he deleted the message and powered down the phone.

School started in four days.

The next night, a second text being delivered sounded in his earbuds. He considered not reading it, but curiosity won out. It read,

> I know where your sister is.

This was too much! His rage rekindled, he considered chucking the phone across the darkened room toward the corner where the waste basket was. But he held back—probably for two reasons, although he couldn't have processed either one. He was confused at his cousin's motives for doing this. And he was torn between his friendship with Jacks and the volcanic anger he felt toward him at that moment.

Ben closed his eyes, and the room's darkness seemed palpable. It penetrated every part of him, like an oily shadow passing through a screen door. Then a disembodied Voice stroked him with words that felt true: *"This family would be better off without you."*

A second voice, seductively close, added: *"And you would be much better off without them."*

School would start in three days.

CHAPTER

eighteen

Friday started out badly. Gurney's phone charge played out in the middle of the night so the alarm didn't wake him at 5:00 a.m. as planned. Instead, it was the interim chairman of his department who roused him by pounding on the front door at 6:00 a.m., the time the two men had agreed to leave South Bend to make it to Purdue University by ten that morning, where Gurney was expected to present his research on *Mathematical Symmetries and Global Terrorism.*

While Bear's frenzied barking was waking everyone in the house, Gurney leaped out of bed, and almost fell headlong down the stairs to get to the door whose hinges were being tested by Dean Oswald J. Stratton. Racing around the bedroom gathering up the things Gurney would need for the day, Babe could hear her husband apologizing to his boss. In the next moment, he was flying back up the stairs with the good dean's distinctive voice nipping at his heels: "We leave your driveway at 6:05, Dr. Hightower—not a minute later."

"You'll make it, honey. Don't worry," Babe whispered to him when he got back to the bedroom. "Here are the clothes you should wear; this is a duffle with your portable razor and everything else you need to get ready in the car. And don't forget your briefcase with your notes in it by the hall closet downstairs."

"What would I do without you?" wheezed Gurney, short of breath from his morning workout on the staircase.

"And don't worry about this new dean, dear. You'll win him over with your charm on the trip down. By the way, his voice sounds like an oboe getting over a cold!"

In spite of himself, he laughed out loud at this remark, hopping on one foot and falling off balance, while trying to get his pants on. "Easy does it, professor," Babe giggled and shot her right hand out to steady him. With her other hand, she held out his toothbrush with the paste already on it. "Brush those pearly whites and get down there, big boy. Dr. Oboe's leaving our driveway at 6:05—and not a minute later."

"It's not his fault, Babe. He's a good guy. I'm the jerk here," said Gurney, hastily tucking in his shirt and missing a loop with his belt.

"Yes, but you're my jerk. She reached up and kissed him, saying, "Now go get 'em, tiger. This is going to be a great day for you."

With that, he scrambled back down the stairs, threw open the door and leaped off the porch to the waiting car. Babe watched them drive away before she closed the door and looked at the clock on the wall. It was 6:05 a.m.

If Gurney's day got better, that certainly didn't translate to his family. Robbed of an hour of sleep by Bear's barking, Carrie and Jacks were cranky and argumentative the rest of the day. Ben seemed even more sullen than usual, and Babe felt the tension in the air between the boys.

Having cleared things in June with the middle school's administration for the two boys to attend there, now she was having real doubts about how that was going to work. Even though Mrs. Smalls, their eighth grade homeroom teacher, had agreed to get the faculty to work with Ben's silence, that was before the boy's emotional downturn and his strained friendship with Jacks.

She'd intended to talk with Jacks that day about it, but the opportunity never came. That evening, she was so exhausted from the morning's odd start that she fell asleep on Carrie's bed after reading her a book and listening to her prayer. By the time she awoke, the boys were in their beds with the lights out.

But they were far from sleep. And what had been brewing between them that day still was.

CHAPTER

nineteen

With Ryan Adam's *To Be Young* pulsating in his ears, Ben was trying to prepare himself for another text message. He knew it was coming, and his anger was percolating.

> *"Oh, one day when you're looking back,*
> *You were young and man you were sad.*

When you're young, you get sad..." the spiky-haired, country rocker wailed.

"Well," thought Jacks, texting with his thumbs in the bunk below. *"This is either going to work or he's going to kill me."* He held the message for a moment, knowing that once he sent it, things were going to change. "Oh, what the heaven!" he said out loud and touched the send icon.

Even though Ben wasn't surprised to hear the beep, nothing could have prepared him for what he read:

> I've seen Katie, and she's worried about you.

He lay there seething for a moment. Suddenly, without thinking, he hit reply and shot three words back to Jacks:

> Go to hell!

Jacks, understanding the significance of what just happened, texted:

> That's not where she is.

There was a long period of silence, and Jacks wondered if that was as far as they were going to get. He also knew Ben was smart enough to recognize that he had just used words to directly communicate with someone for the first time in three years. Jack's heart was beating like mad. He could feel Ben thinking hard. It seemed an hour later that Jacks got a response.

> I don't believe in heaven.

Jacks decided, on the fly, not to waste time crafting his responses. If this door was going to stay open, he would have to text spontaneously from his heart and trust that honesty would win the day. So he wrote:

> You should. Just about everyone you love is either there or on their way there.

Still cautious, Ben answered:

> You can't let anyone know about this. They wouldn't understand. I don't understand it myself.

After what happened at Christmas, Jacks had sensed for months that his cousin wanted to communicate with him, and that if he ever figured out how, the floodgates would open. This was the first sign he'd been right. Their thumbs were about to get a workout.

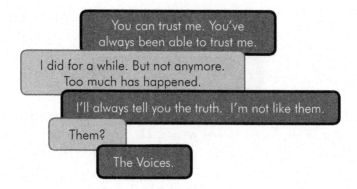

Ben was stunned.

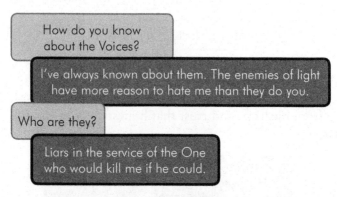

How much should I tell him? Jacks thought—then quickly added:

> Their ancient name is the *Shedim.* I call them the
> Shadows. Most of their power is in their voices, and
> they've been lying to you non-stop for three years.

Considering this remarkable information and remembering the incandescent being in their bedroom at Christmas, Ben asked:

> Who are you?

Jacks paused for the first time in several minutes, and texted:

> It's enough for now that I'm your cousin, and
> that we're your family—and that we love you.

Ben lay there for a while, thinking about everything he'd just read. Finally he wrote:

> Then it's going to have to be enough for you that I've got a lot more questions, and I'm still pissed at you. And don't expect me to talk—to you or anyone. I don't even think I can. This doesn't mean I'm going to church with you either. Not now, not ever.

> You don't believe in God?

> Of course I believe in God. And I hate him.

Both boys had a lot to ponder. It was two days 'til school started.

CHAPTER

twenty

More than falling temperatures or amount of rainfall, it's the steadily increasing length of the nights in late summer and early autumn that triggers the chemical processes in a leaf to begin to change color. The first thing Jacks noticed when he opened his eyes on Saturday morning were the tips of the maple leaves outside his window showing their initial blush of scarlet.

His boyish face pinched and lids narrowed to the sunlight streaking through a morning mist rising from the St. Joseph Valley to his second story room. This wasn't going to be one of South Bend's 293 cloudy days a year, and Jacks was already excited about it for two reasons: though not a verbal one, he and Ben had their first "talk" last night, anticipating another that evening—and today was the first Notre Dame football game of the season.

The Texas Longhorns were invading South Bend for a 3:30 p.m. kickoff, and Gurney had three tickets in Section 9, row 32. After Jacks got a headshake from Ben at breakfast that he wanted to go to the game, the family made their plans. They would walk the half mile to campus at noon with a picnic lunch and a football, and take in all the pre-game festivities: the glee club singing at the Hesburgh Reflecting Pool two and a half hours before game time, cheering along the Player Walk at 1:15 all the way from the "Touchdown Jesus" library mural into the stadium, and the stirring Marching Band Concert on the steps of Bond Hall at 2 o'clock. After that, it was a brisk walk to The Grotto for prayer.

As the Hightowers selected their candles and knelt at the outdoor altar, Ben climbed onto the lowest branch of the gargantuan, 220-year-old Sycamore tree that seemed to be guarding The Grotto. From there, he watched the parade of fans file past the panoply of flickering lights at the holy site, wondering how many of them were praying for a victory. Knowing Jacks would never do that, he then wondered if his cousin was praying for him, surprised that the probability of that didn't offend him.

Leaving the lovely lakeside setting that had once been an Indian hunting ground, Babe and Carrie peeled away for an afternoon of girl-time, and the boys hurried to the pre-game warm-ups at the stadium, entering Gate B with the name, *ARA PARSEGHIAN*, etched above it. Jacks never got tired of the traditions: the B-2 Stealth Bomber flyover at the end of the national anthem; the stadium resounding with the "Go Irish!" cheer at every kickoff; the students raising each other in the air for push-ups after each ND touchdown and dancing an Irish jig when the band played *"Rakes of the Mallow;"* and the bombastic, crowd-rousing rendition of the *"1812 Overture"* at the end of the third quarter.

A hard-fought game that Notre Dame won with a forty-seven-yard field goal as time expired was the perfect ending to an unforgettable day. The boys stayed in their seats and watched eighty thousand people swarm to the exits, while the Irish Guard led the band in the final playing of the *"Victory March."* Finally, it always moved Jacks when the players, win or lose, gathered together arm-in-arm in front of the student section and saluted their classmates by singing the Alma Mater. He didn't say it out loud, but the boy was thinking, *"Ba-a-abies."*

On the drive home that evening, Jacks asked Gurney if they could stop at *Let's Spoon*, trying to keep the perfect day from ending. "Please, Dad!" he begged. "They've got a new flavor you'd love. It tastes just like snickerdoodles!"

"Let's see," mused Gurney. "Today's fine cuisine has included brats, burgers, popcorn, a large Dr. Pepper, roasted peanuts, nachos dripping with cheese, and giant malted milk balls from South Bend

Chocolate Factory. Your mother probably has IVs and blood transfusions waiting for us at home."

"No way! Mom would want us to go," Jacks reasoned. "We're talking frozen yogurt here. It's so good for you."

As Gurney was turning around to go back to *Let's Spoon*, Ben sat in the back seat shaking his head in wonder. *"It's amazing what words can do,"* he thought.

CHAPTER

twenty-one

Later that evening, Gurney was making his normal rounds at bedtime. After reading Carrie selections from Shel Silverstein's *WHERE THE SIDEWALK ENDS,* he turned off the light, gently placed his hand on her head, and prayed over her—as was his custom. She knew what his first words would be: *"Dear Father God, watch over my daughter in the night. Put the same hedge of protection around her you put around Job's ten children. Surround her with your angels and with your love."* After that, his words were always different, but half the time, she didn't hear them on her way to dreamland where she and Tinker Bell were "born of the same laugh" and ventured together into the magical Winter Woods.

Gurney marveled at the ease with which she fell asleep. *"Clear conscience,"* he reflected, and bent down to kiss Carrie's forehead. He pulled her covers up, whispered, "I love you, baby girl," and made his way to the boys' room. Their door was partly open, so he entered without knocking and found both on their iPhones. The instant they saw him, they simultaneously set the phones down. *"That's odd,"* he thought, but said nothing about it.

"It's been a crazy day, guys. I want those phones off in fifteen minutes." Then, as always, he knelt by their beds and, out of deference to Ben, prayed for them silently. When he finished, he quietly said, "Amen," got up, and with great warmth, added, "We love you both so much. Now get some rest. Big day tomorrow."

"We love you too, Dad"—from the bottom bunk.

When Gurney got downstairs, he found Babe reading in the family room.

"That was interesting. If I didn't know better," he thought out loud, "I'd say I caught those boys texting each other."

"Really" said Babe, smiling.

Meanwhile, Jacks finished the message he was texting when Gurney had walked in.

> Are you nervous about school Monday?

Ben answered immediately:

> Been there, done that—not too worried. Are you?

> Never been there, never done that—
> but I'm more curious than worried.

> So am I, but not about school. I'm more curious
> about you. I don't need to know who you are, though
> I have my suspicions; I need to know what you know.

> What do you want to know?

> You said you saw Katie. How
> and where did you see her?

> The best way I can explain it is I saw your whole family
> in a dream that was much more than a dream—kind of
> like seeing the ND team at the stadium today, which was
> much more than seeing them on a flat screen at home.

> I knew you'd say something like that. Where were they?

> They're all in the REAL WORLD now.

> Yeah, well, this is the only world I
> know, and they're not in it. Their
> deaths felt pretty real to me.

> You're angry with God.

> What do you think? My dad read the Bible every day of his life and was the kindest man in the world. You mean, God couldn't have given him an extra two seconds to see that hunk of metal so he could swerve around it? And why would he kill Katie? She could have changed the world.

Ben couldn't see his cousin's tears in the bed below. Jacks had waited three years for this conversation, and now words seemed futile. This was even harder than he thought it would be. Katie, the twins, Baby Rose, both parents—Ben's grief was incomprehensible; the sheer mass of it unnerving. He took a deep breath and managed to answer with:

> God didn't kill Katie.

Ben shot back:

> God didn't save Katie.

The response was swift:

> Of course He did. She's with Him now.

While Ben considered that, Jacks continued.

> Your family is alive in ways you can't imagine, and their love for you is dimensionless in every way but one.

> What's that?

> They can't be with you physically.

Why not?

Because there's a great chasm separating us. Anyone wanting to come to you is stopped at its edge, and none of us can cross over to them until the time is right.

There was a long silence, and getting no response from the upper bunk, Jacks went on:

One of the many reasons for the chasm is to protect you. Your family's senses didn't atrophy when they entered the Real World; they were engulfed. Each of them is MORE now in every way. Their gentlest touch would crush you. Their whispers would shatter your eardrums. To look on their faces would blind you and break your mind. That's why God told Moses no man could see His face and live. But there's never a moment when they're not cheering for you-- and loving you.

Even if I believed that, I would still hate God. It's not just my family. The whole world is filled with suffering and death. If there is a God and he allows that, there's nothing loving about Him. If there is a God, he must be Satan.

That's been said by others before you, and you have every right to believe it. But if you did, you'd be dead wrong. 100% of the evil in this world is caused by human irresponsibility and the evil one. Death might be the last enemy, but it's not the worst. Right now, you can't think of anything worse than death.

Of course I can. Living without my family is worse than death. And I'd have done something about it by now if it weren't for you.

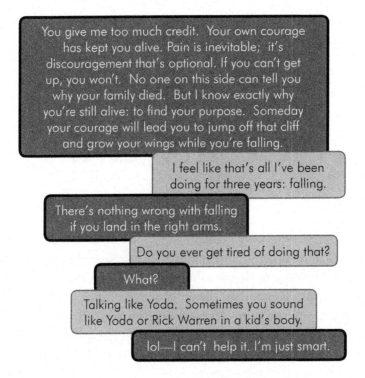

You give me too much credit. Your own courage has kept you alive. Pain is inevitable; it's discouragement that's optional. If you can't get up, you won't. No one on this side can tell you why your family died. But I know exactly why you're still alive: to find your purpose. Someday your courage will lead you to jump off that cliff and grow your wings while you're falling.

I feel like that's all I've been doing for three years: falling.

There's nothing wrong with falling if you land in the right arms.

Do you ever get tired of doing that?

What?

Talking like Yoda. Sometimes you sound like Yoda or Rick Warren in a kid's body.

lol—I can't help it. I'm just smart.

Yawning, Jacks laughed.

You're just something—that's for sure. And don't push me off that cliff. I'm a long ways from believing he cares enough to catch me. Now speaking of falling. Let's get some sleep. G'nite.

When he got no answer, Ben knew that his younger cousin had already fallen asleep. He lay there on his back for a moment, thinking. *"Even if there is a God in heaven who doesn't care, I know Jacks does."* With that thought, he felt he had possibly stumbled onto his purpose—if not forever, at least for a little while.

CHAPTER

twenty-two

It looked like an early fall in South Bend. Nighttime temperatures in the fifties and rain that would last all day. Chickadees at backyard feeders in early September. Flocks of geese already heading south. A few maple, oak and gum trees just beginning to change their colors. The days were getting shorter and the sunlight a little thinner. The summer garden was losing its battle with the weeds, which didn't seem to bother the pumpkins at all.

On Sunday, it was Babe's turn to stay home from church with Ben. She had an idea the boys were keeping late hours texting, and it was obvious things were better between them. From the porch, she waved goodbye to Gurney and the kids as they left for the early church service, and thought:

"Tomorrow's the big day, and it's supposed to rain." She looked toward the bus stop down the lane from their house. Thanks to the new GPS bus tracking app on her phone, the boys wouldn't have to stand in the rain waiting for their ride. She would monitor the bus's progress and release her scholars just in time to catch it in the vicinity of 7:15 a.m.

On the outside, she'd communicated her confidence to Jacks when he decided to enroll for fall classes at Rockne Intermediate. But inwardly, she harbored a nagging anxiety about the change. Home-schooling was the safer choice. She was losing the battle not to stress about forfeiting a huge measure of control over the boys' education. But Gurney was convinced the risks were worth it.

She walked toward the barn where she knew Ben would be saddling Pockets for his habitual Sunday morning ride around the property line, escorted by the ever-faithful Bear. In dog years, he was old enough to know he'd never catch that duck or goose, so it must have been the chase he loved.

"Fall's coming early this year," said Babe, swinging open the door. "I got stung yesterday gathering honey. It's a sure sign." Ben looked up at her thoughtfully. "Add to that," she offered, "the squirrels are acting like Wall Street pit traders on a Friday afternoon." She smiled and repeated a saying of her father's:

"Squirrels gatherin' nuts in a flurry,
winter's comin' on in a hurry."

"And we've got more acorns than grass right now," she laughed.

Ben nodded at her words and swung into the saddle. "Have a nice ride, son," added Babe, turning back toward the house. As soon as they left the barn, a distant rumble of thunder in the west caught their attention. "If that starts coming this way, dear, don't get caught in it."

Babe knew it's a myth that there's usually a calm period before the storm. Everything depends on the force and direction of the wind. For most of the day, the rains stayed to the west, but as dusk approached, the winds shifted directly toward the farm. A massive cumulonimbus cloud, strafed by lightning, came booming across the horizon, blotting out the sun like an amorphous, roiling asteroid on a collision course with planet Hightower. Just ahead of the rain, the megastorm's gust front blew in, dropping the air temperature twenty degrees in less than a minute. The family sprang into action as the rain burst upon them.

Gurney went from room to room, closing and latching windows. Ben ran to the barn with a sugar beet in one hand and a bucket for grain in the other to settle Pockets down for the night. Carrie tried to coax Mr. Meowgi and "her" four-month-old kittens out from under the front porch. Babe opened the flue and struck a match under the kindling in the fireplace to warm her wet brood when they came dripping in.

Meanwhile, Jacks was hurriedly taking down the new American flag on the pole in the front yard. Two seconds after he secured the flag and took a step toward the house, a rogue lightning bolt struck the top of the pole. The sharp crack and loud bang from the strike fifteen feet above him stunned the boy, but he was unhurt. He smelled the nitrogen in the air and realized what a close call it had been.

Jacks was aware that anyone who's ever been struck by lightning did nothing to attract the strike to them. That person was simply unfortunate to be at the exact spot a lightning strike was going to occur. Lightning is generated on too large a scale by thunderstorms several miles high and tens of miles wide to be influenced by small objects on the ground. Still, the startled boy couldn't shake the feeling that the strike wasn't completely random and that there was evil intent behind it. He decided to say nothing about it to his family.

But this was no common thunderstorm. They had no way of knowing at the time it was a precursor to the strangest winter weather the Midwest would see in more than a century.

What the storm lacked in duration it made up for with its fury: hail two inches in diameter, torrential rain causing flash floods, and winds topping seventy miles per hour knocked out power all over Michiana that evening.

Other families might have cursed the darkness or been as fearful as rabbits in a warren at the storm's rage, but Gurney would have none of it. He announced, "It's a perfect night for s'mores!" and passed out candles to everyone but Carrie, who happily got an LED flashlight. They felt like they were camping out around the fireplace for the rest of the evening, listening to Gurney's classic ghost stories and laughing at Carrie's pathetic attempts to create a dinosaur hand-shadow on the wall with her flashlight.

They all stayed up later than normal, on a sugar-high from the marshmallows and chocolate, and talking about anything and everything. Except for Ben, of course, who silently munched his graham cracker but felt more a part of this singular family than ever before. Eventually, the embers were fading when, as one, they picked up their candle stubs and headed for bed, a tiny flash mob laughing up the stairs and down the hall toward their respective bedrooms.

Without a thought about school starting the next day, Ben fell asleep quickly. Some people insist they never dream, but the truth is we usually forget what we dream. Everyone dreams every night. In fact, more than two hours of our sleep time are spent in a dream-like state.

Ben's dream that night was the only one he could ever recall. Once again he was buried under the snow and desperate for air, when he heard a dog barking.

CHAPTER

twenty-three

The following dismal morning drizzled on from the stormy night before like a wet hangover. So the school bus was moving slower on its slippery route than Babe had estimated. As a result, the boys stood for five minutes at the bus hub, huddled miserably under their hooded jackets against the bone-chilling rain. At 7:20 the bus finally appeared, sliding to a shaky stop on the road's muddy edge and throwing open its accordion door to the hapless boys.

"Abandon all hope ye who enter here!" bellowed the baldheaded, Brobdingnagian driver, whose disk-shaped face and wire rim glasses made him look more like an oversized accountant than the grizzled veteran of years behind the wheel that he was. Jacks liked the big man in the royal blue windbreaker and khaki pants immediately. "Watch your step now, fellas. That puddle looks deep," he added. Both boys leaped over the murky water and into the Twilight Zone.

"Here, guys," he said, pointing to the seat just inside the door. "Sit next to me. Everyone back there is sleeping or comatose, and I'm in a mood for conversation. The kids call me Flat Stanley; what are your names?"

"I'm Jacks," said the smaller boy, and nodding toward his cousin taking the window seat, added, "and he's my cousin, Ben. Why do they call you Flat Stanley?"

"Partly because my name is Stanley, and I own every Flat Stanley book there is, but mostly because of this," he said, turning his head sideways so the boys could see how extraordinarily level the back of his cranium was. "I guess my mother didn't roll me over enough when I was a baby," his infectious laughter filling the front half of the bus.

"Wow! You have an interesting case of plagiocephaly," said Jacks. "It's very common, but most people have hair that covers it."

Jacks' honest observation pushed the driver to another level of merriment. He slapped his right knee and roared with laughter. Now the back of the bus could hear him as well, and a few passengers opened their eyes wondering what the morning hilarity was about. All they could see was the back of their jolly driver's flat head shaking with laughter while he was grinding the bus's gear box into second and merging into the rush hour traffic.

Finally, Flat Stanley, still chuckling, took off his glasses and wiped the tears from his eyes with the sleeve of his jacket. Watching the road ahead, he spoke loudly enough for Jacks to hear him over the engine's noise. "How in the world do you know the scientific name for my beautiful head?"

"Once I read something, I usually remember it," replied Jacks, a bit embarrassed that others might have heard him.

"So you're a reader, huh? Me, too. We used to have a name for people like you when I was in school."

"What's that?" asked the boy.

"We called them students!" guffawed Flat Stanley, pleased with his joke. Jacks had made a friend.

"What's the matter with your cousin? Is he sleepy too?" asked the driver, glancing back at the boy for an instant.

"No, he's just quiet," said Jacks, an answer he would give dozens of times to people in the next several weeks, then added: "He's a thinker."

And that's exactly what Ben was doing—thinking about his recent past: his "texting-talks" with Jacks, and the way the Hightowers had taken him in and put up with his moods, and finally the emotions he was feeling last night around the fireplace.

The opposite of talking isn't listening; it's learning. And Ben had learned a lot in his three years and counting of silence. He'd learned to mind his own business and not to judge people who didn't, especially the Hightowers. Last night during the storm and by the light of the fireplace, he'd shocked himself with the realization that he cared deeply for these people. Maybe he actually loved them, a possibility that surprised him by its spontaneity. Just as astonishing was an absence of guilt for opening his heart to someone other than his real family. He was beginning to understand that there are really only two ways to go when you're up against it. One is the bad way, when you give in to the Voices and give up on life. The other is the hard way, when you start to fight back. He had decided to fight.

At least one other passenger hadn't slept for a moment on the drive to school. Even without looking in the direction of the boy, Jacks had been aware of his brooding contempt from the moment he stepped onto the bus. His classmates called him "Scary Gary," and gave him a wide berth. So he slouched alone on a seat behind the new boys, shrouded by the dark weather outside and the bus' dim interior. He hadn't missed a word of the conversation between Jacks and Flat Stanley. A notorious troublemaker, Gary Henderson, all two hundred overweight pounds of him, already loathed the driver for his cheerful spirit and for being the only one on the bus too big for him to bully. And now he had two fresh targets for his malice. For reasons he couldn't explain, he especially disliked the little curly-haired know-it-all who talked too much. "Scary Gary" would figure out a way to shut him up. He had plenty of time. After all, it was just the first day of school.

CHAPTER

---

twenty-four

If crises don't create heroes, but merely reveal them, then the awkward, confusing, hormonally charged world of middle school is fertile soil for heroism. You always wonder if other people are going through the same things as you. In middle school, all of them are. Peer pressure is stronger than gravity in her hallways, gymnasiums and cafeterias. Everything you do, or don't do, wear or don't wear, say or don't say is fair game for ridicule and judgment. And that's just the teachers.

It takes courage to be either a student or a teacher nowadays. Because kids are consumed with physical and emotional changes, finding where they fit into the school's social order, figuring out who they are and what is going on in their bodies, many teachers wonder if there's any room left in those crowded brains for geography, history and math.

The "terrible twelves and thirteens" parallel the "terrible twos." They're just not as cute. The middle school years are the time of most rapid growth in a human being, next to infancy. The bones of twelve year olds are growing faster than their muscles, so it's hard for them to sit still. At the same time, though, a middle-schooler's brain is experiencing an unprecedented growth in brain cells and connections, far more than they actually need. And what they don't use during these crucial years, they often lose by high school. Teachers who despair that nothing academic is penetrating those brains need to persevere. For the truth is the brain of a middle schooler retains what it learns better at this stage than any other in that student's lifespan. Creative, passionate teachers who are open to listening to their students will never regret choosing middle school as a profession.

Many of the negative stereotypes about middle schoolers are true. But there's another side. Middle school is when kids open up to the world. It's when they first begin to think about bigger things than themselves and become capable of self-reflection. Their honesty can be as refreshing as it can be caustic. They haven't formed their opinion on things yet. Everything is up for grabs, which can make kids that age fun to be around—less jaded and cynical than many high school students.

And no one who walked in the door of Rockne Intermediate on that first school day was having more fun than new eighth-grader, Jackson Jazz Hightower. There was nothing about the experience he didn't like. He and Ben were greeted immediately by a kid passing out flyers with helpful information to get them up to speed.

"Turn it up, juvies," the boy said. "Name's Wesley. Here's some need-to-knows for ya," holding out two flyers. "Saw ya bumpin' down the walk showin off ya new skips. Just do yourself and don't get cray-cray. Gotta bounce now." With that, he turned his attention to three girls coming through the door.

Plucking the two flyers from Wes's hand, Jacks laughed, "Looks like we're going to need some language lessons, for starters." Using the information on the flyer, the boys weaved their way through the crowded hall and found their home room, claiming two empty desks. Students of every shape, color, size and smell wandered into the room, some recognizing friends from seventh grade and trying to get desks next to them. With a reputation for being tough but fair, fun but focused, Mrs. Loretta Smalls, a gifted Reading and English teacher, stood at the whiteboard, writing out her name and e-mail address.

"If any of you need me outside the classroom this year, you can reach me via this e-mail address. I'll help you in any way I can," she said, turning around and facing the twenty-four students. At for-ty-five years old, she had a young face and bright blue eyes, in con-trast to her prematurely gray hair cut in a pixie-ish bob. Even though it meant more work, she chose to do homeroom every year because it was a way to bond with students she wouldn't normally see every day.

"We're family in this homeroom, and I take that seriously. What happens in here stays in here," she said. "You can ask or tell me anything that's important to you. Any questions?" Trace Rorie, class clown, raised his hand immediately. "Where's the bathroom, Mrs. Smalls?" Almost everyone laughed.

Without hesitation, the teacher responded, "Today, we're going to look at your class schedules, get your locker assignments to you and help the younger children find out where the restroom is. Hopefully," she said, walking over to Trace's desk and smiling down at him, "they won't confuse their locker with the restroom." The whole class erupted in laughter, and, walking back to the front of the class, she continued:

"Most of you I won't treat like children," she said, batting her eyes in Trace's direction, "because you're really not anymore, are you? It's just that your lives are unwritten so far. That is about to change. And so I've added a new element to homeroom this year." Turning to the control panel for the computer next to her desk, she announced "We're going to start each week off with a different theme song. In honor of your first day in the eighth grade, I dedicate this song to you," and she pushed the play button. A state of the art speaker system came to life as the words from the overhead projector scrolled across the screen.

> *"I am unwritten, can't read my mind, I'm undefined.*
> *I'm just beginning; the pen's in my hand, ending*
> *unplanned*

Live your life with arms wide open," sang Natasha Beddingfield, in her haunting melody, *Unwritten.*

> *Release your inhibitions; feel the rain on your skin.*
> *No one else can feel it for you; only you can let it in.*
> *No one else, no one else can speak the words on your*
> *lips.*
> *Drench yourself in words unspoken;*

Live your life with arms wide open.
Today is where your book begins.
The rest is still unwritten.
The rest is still unwritten.

When the song ended, most of her students knew they were in the right homeroom. But the two who knew that best were Ben and Jacks.

CHAPTER

twenty-five

Not everything was perfect for the boys at Rockne Intermediate. A classmate who had taken a particular interest in them was "Scary Gary". On the last day of the second school week, he was coming out of a stall when Jacks and Ben entered the bathroom. Seeing them, he decided to hang out by the sink, and, using the mirror in front of him, watched the boys take care of their business behind him. Usually he left the bathroom quickly without washing his hands, but today was different. He placed his meaty hands with their chubby fingers and splintered, prawn-pink nails under the running water, pretending to wash them while waiting for the boys to make their way to the sink. Ben got there first.

An intimidating, fleshy felon, red-headed Gary was only a few inches taller than Ben, but outweighed him by at least fifty pounds. He stuck his hands back under the water, opened his beady, porcine eyes in a feigned, crazed look, and, taking a quick step toward Ben, mocked the boy by faking sign language in his face, flicking as much water on him as he could. Ben instinctively stepped back.

"What's the m-matter, Keegan? Gonna make lemonade in your pants? Oh, sorry. You didn't understand that, did you? I forgot. I need to do deaf signs for you." He turned back to the sink to get his hands wet again.

"Leave him alone, Gary," said Jacks, coming up on the bully's other side.

"So the Halfling knows my name, huh? I know yours too, Jacksy-Wacksy. But I st-stopped playing with jacks when I became a male."

"Don't be a feckless illiterate," said Jacks, matter-of-factly.

"Th-that's how much you know, you sk-skinny, little faggot. I don't have freckles and my mother was married."

Shaking his head, Jacks said, "Ben's not deaf. He chooses to be mute."

"He's a mutant, huh?" responded the bully. "That explains a lot."

He towered over the younger boy, and raised his fist as if to strike him, surprised that Jacks didn't flinch. So with speed that defied his bulk, he pushed Jacks' books off the countertop onto the floor, then turned swiftly and drove his fist into Ben's midsection. But the silent boy, who had toned his muscles and reflexes from countless hours of drawing his compound bow and daily working outdoors for the last three years, shot out his right hand and put a vice-like grip on the striking fist. The blow still hurt him, but Ben held onto Gary's wrist and tightened his grip until the bigger boy yelled out in pain and pulled his arm away. He backed away quickly to the door, vowing venomously, "I'll t-take care of you two freaks later," he sneered. "You can count on it!"

Jacks looked over at his cousin who was watching the bathroom door in case the bully returned. "Are you okay?" he asked. Ben turned to him and nodded his head that he was.

"Good," said Jacks, "because that was awesome!"

Ben raised his eyebrows as if to say, "Are you nuts?"

His cousin smiled and said, "I think I'm getting to him!"

Ben didn't disagree.

That night in bed the boys texted about the encounter. Ben went first.

Bunk Beds

Today was just the beginning. That kid's a MANIAC! And you need to stay away from him.

I think the word's cray-cray. And you're probably right, but he's that way for a reason. He can still change.

Yeah, he can change the position of the nose on your face.

There's only one thing in this world that can't be forgiven, and that's knowing what life is, and choosing death.

What if he's choosing YOUR death, Yoda-boy? The creep factor in him is too high to run the risk.

But he lives in the dark; I can feel it everytime I'm around him. It's probably the only thing he's ever known. And the last I checked, light is still stronger than darkness. And love is stronger than death. Who's going to love him enough to tell him that when you make a deal with the devil, you're just paying the zombies to eat you last?

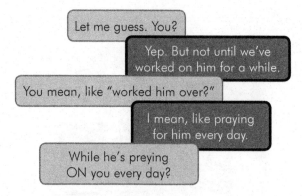

Let me guess. You?

Yep. But not until we've worked on him for a while.

You mean, like "worked him over?"

I mean, like praying for him every day.

While he's preying ON you every day?

Jacks would not be deterred, and answered:

"If your enemy is hungry, feed him; if he is thirsty, give him something to drink. In doing this, you will heap burning coals of guilt and shame on his head."

Just as deftly, Ben responded:

Let's skip the food and drink and go right to the burning coals.

You're not going to change my mind on this, Ben. Scary Gary is going to be our test case. If we can make a friend of him, then anything is possible.

It's also possible that you're the oddest kid in America. How do you plan on staying alive while you work on him?

He can't beat me up if he never catches me alone—that's where you come in. And he can't stop me from praying for him—that's where the Father comes in. I know it might take some time, but my goal is that he's eating at our table in the cafeteria before the holidays.

That will happen when pigs fly.

Then there will be pork in the trees by Christmas.

You're beyond cray-cray!

G'nite, juvie. Gotta bounce now.

CHAPTER

twenty-six

"The next day at the hour of sunset Aragorn walked alone in the woods," read Mrs. Smalls, her musical voice the perfect accompaniment to Tolkien's most famous love story. But today Jacks was having a difficult time focusing on the tale, grabbing only bits here and there.

> *"...And suddenly even as he sang he saw a maiden walking among the white stems of the birches..."*

Jacks' distraction was sitting two rows to his right and one student up in their eleven o'clock Language Arts class, where they were studying selections from J.R.R. Tolkien's, *The Lord of the Rings*. If he leaned forward at his desk, he could see most of her profile. Attentive to her teacher's voice, she held her head high, the azure triangle of her eye framed by a perfect brow and luxurious lash. Her peaches-and-cream complexion was a flawless canvas for her prominent cheekbones, petite nose, only slightly turned up, full lips and strong chin. Jacks was smitten.

> *"... Then Aragorn was abashed, for he saw the elven-light in her eyes and the wisdom of many days..."*

As much as he loved the LOTR trilogy, which he had already read twice, Jacks was more interested at that moment in the elven-light surrounding thirteen-year-old Mary Anne Wilson. The longer he gazed at her, the more his brain released a flood of dopamine, his pupils dilated, and his pulse raced.

> *"…yet from that hour he loved Arwen Evenstar, daughter of Elrond."*

Mary Anne dipped her head forward and used a pink scrunchie to tie back a glorious tumble of chestnut-colored curls. Jacks couldn't breathe and felt light-headed. *"What is happening to me?"* he thought, dropping the #2 lead pencil he'd been fiddling with in his sweaty right hand.

"And thus it was that Arwen beheld him; and as he was walking towards her under the trees of Caras Galadhon laden with flowers of gold, her choice was made and her doom appointed." Mrs. Smalls stopped reading, dog-eared that page, and asked,

"Can anyone tell me what Arwen's choice was and why it spelled her doom?"

Raising her hand, Mary Anne Wilson said, "I think I know, Mrs. Smalls." The teacher sat back in her chair, folded her arms, and replied, "You have the floor, dear."

"Well, her choice was to give her heart to Aragorn," the girl said. "And the reason that sealed her doom was because, being half-elven, she would have to give up her immortality. She must have found true love," sighed Mary Ann, "because for her to marry a human was her own death sentence."

Jacks couldn't have said it any better, and he was proud of her response. He was also wondering if Arwen could ever have been attracted to a hobbit, especially one who was younger than she was. He knew Mary Anne was almost a year older and an inch or three taller. But he was bound to grow, right?

"You're exactly right, Mary Anne" said the teacher. Standing up and turning to the whiteboard, she explained, "It's called self-sacrifice, or *sacrificial love,*" writing that term on the board. "This is a theme you will see over and over in Tolkien and the major reason I chose LOTR for us to read this semester. *Sacrificial love* is the opposite of a word I want you to think about and understand how it affects your life," as she wrote *versus entitlement* alongside the two words already on the board. *Entitlement* is a term that describes a problem with global dimensions today, and I'm hoping each of you will be a part of the solution. An entitled person is one who demands the world owes him a living; that he deserves special treatment and his rights are more important than anyone else's. Like Saruman the Wizard and the Dark Lord, Sauron, these are often the bullies of the world. In contrast, *sacrificial love* puts others first and is a trait you'll see in Sam and Frodo, Legolas and Gimli, and especially in Gandalf when he battles the terrible Balrog. So keep your eyes open when we read these passages for examples of either trait."

At that moment, the bell rang for lunch. "We'll talk more about this tomorrow, and *remember!*" she said louder, catching the last sliver of their attention. "Entitled people cut in the lunch line. Be kind to one another."

Ben noticed Jacks' eyes following a girl out of the classroom, and later during lunch was aware he looked toward her table several times.

That night in bed, Ben texted his cousin:

Has she ever spoken to you?

Good point.

Jacks thought for a moment and added:

"I love you" is just too much of a risk.

Then mime the words "Olive Juice" the next time she looks at you.

Why would I do that?

It will look to her like you're saying "I love you"—even though you're not.

Only YOU would know that.

Sure, that way, if she gets mad, you can tell her you simply said "Olive Juice," and that would be the truth.

But what if she says, "I love you too?" I wouldn't know how to handle that.

She won't. She'll probably just mime, "Elephant Shoe."

I don't get it.

"Elephant Shoe" would look like she's saying, "I love you, too"—only without the risk.

You just replaced me.

As what?

The oddest kid in America.

You're probably too late with Mary Anne anyway, you know.

Why's that?

I think she's already in love with Scary Gary.

From the bottom bunk:

> Go soak your
> head in the toilet!

From the top:

> Olive juice!

CHAPTER

twenty-seven

It was three days until Halloween, and Jacks had finally pulled together a costume to wear. He loved the original *Karate Kid* and had been tempted to go as a polka-dotted shower, but he wanted to make a statement this year, especially after his talk with Gurney on their way home from church last Sunday.

"Dad, I've got a question for you," said Jacks, seat-belted into the front passenger side of their Toyota Highlander. Gurney reached up and turned off the Satellite radio sounds of Glenn Miller's orchestra playing, *In the Mood.* "Sure, champ," he responded. "What's up?"

"My history teacher, Mr. Weathers, told us Friday there's a strong movement, world-wide, to change the calendar's designations of B.C. and A.D. to B.C.E, Before Common Era, and C.E., Common Era. He predicted it wouldn't be long before it would be illegal to use *Before Christ* and *Anno Domini,* In the Year of our Lord. What do you think?"

Gurney didn't take his eyes off the road, but Jacks could see he was considering his words before he spoke. Eventually, he glanced at his son, then turned his attention fully to his driving, and said, "It's just another example of P.C. madness. Political correctness has an appetite that will never be satisfied until it has devoured all of our Christian traditions and hijacked all of our best words."

"Define political correctness," said Jacks.

"It's an insidious frontal assault on common sense and conscience through language manipulation," answered Gurney. He was warming to the topic. "It might have started out as a movement to protect minorities, and I'm all for that, but now P.C. is out of control. In the past decade, it's become nothing short of totalitarian mind control. And so, Islamic terrorism becomes 'workplace violence,' pedophilia passes as 'intergenerational sex,' and child molesters are called 'minor-attracted persons.' It's enough to make my brain explode," he said, shaking his head and half-heartedly laughing.

"What can we do about it?" asked Jacks, knowing this was a conversation he wouldn't forget.

"The best revenge is a life well-lived," answered his father. "'Let your light so shine that men may see your good works and give glory to your Father in heaven.' We need to show the watching world that we're not going to back down from the P.C. bullies and that we can engage their illogical diatribes with reasonable, practical common sense. C.S. Lewis was right when he said, 'The Christian intellectual has so much more to be Christian with.' Historically, Christians have been the best thinkers in science, medicine, education, government, literature and the arts. And that tradition is being revived again in our world today. The church is waking up and providing the world with intellectually powerful leaders in every secular field."

"And you're one of them, Dad," said Jacks. "But what can I do? I'm just a kid."

Gurney thought for a moment and replied, "What's a dentist's favorite holiday?"

"I don't know," said Jacks, "maybe Ground Hog Day because of Punxsutawney Phil's big teeth."

Gurney laughed and said, "Nice try, son, but you're chewing up the wrong tree. It's got to be Halloween, doesn't it? The dentist knows all that candy will have him filling cavities and repairing broken teeth for most of the next year."

"You're probably right," answered Jacks, "but what's Halloween got to do with anything?"

"You can do your part, Jacks, to reclaim Halloween from the secularists who hijacked it decades ago. *Hallow* means "to make holy," and *e'en* is simply a contraction meaning "evening." So the word that's come to mean the devil's night when witches, demons and monsters rule, originally meant *Holy Evening*, a very special night when church folk prayed and prepared their hearts and minds for November 1, known universally as *All Saint's Day*. In fact, the tradition of giving out candy to children on October 31 was started by Christians who, remembering all the martyrs who literally gave their lives for the faith, wanted to give gifts to children and the poor. The church should never surrender what rightfully belongs to her. We should do our part to win Halloween back for God."

"Dad, you've just given me a great idea—if Mom will lend me the cap and gown she wore when she got her master's degree."

CHAPTER

twenty-eight

Like his parents, Jacks had read just about everything C.S. Lewis had ever written. But unlike Gurney or Babe, he was actually named after the famous author. They had decided early in their marriage that if they had a son, he would be named "Jackson," after Lewis' nickname, "Jack." It was inevitable that one year, he would create a costume that would bring attention to the world-renowned Oxford don. It would be his small way of reclaiming Halloween and remembering its origin.

So when the bedroom lights went off the Wednesday night before Halloween Friday, Jacks was excited to text Ben about his costume decision.

> Guess what? No more Spiderman or Captain America for me. I'm changing it all up this year, and you'll never guess who I'm going as.

It was Ben's habit to toss his cell phone onto the upper bunk just before he climbed the ladder. On this night, he had a hard time locating its vibrating hum in the rumpled blankets, so Jacks had to wait longer than usual for a response. When it came, he was stunned.

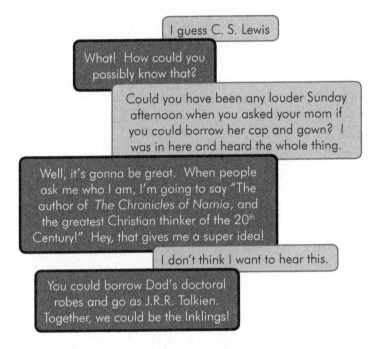

I guess C. S. Lewis

What! How could you possibly know that?

Could you have been any louder Sunday afternoon when you asked your mom if you could borrow her cap and gown? I was in here and heard the whole thing.

Well, it's gonna be great. When people ask me who I am, I'm going to say "The author of *The Chronicles of Narnia*, and the greatest Christian thinker of the 20th Century!" Hey, that gives me a super idea!

I don't think I want to hear this.

You could borrow Dad's doctoral robes and go as J.R.R. Tolkien. Together, we could be the Inklings!

Jacks heard his cousin's stifled laugh, then read:

Even if I completely understood what you're talking about, you already know my answer.

Jacks responded quickly and with as much passion as a text could convey:

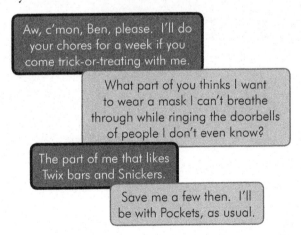

Aw, c'mon, Ben, please. I'll do your chores for a week if you come trick-or-treating with me.

What part of you thinks I want to wear a mask I can't breathe through while ringing the doorbells of people I don't even know?

The part of me that likes Twix bars and Snickers.

Save me a few then. I'll be with Pockets, as usual.

This would be the third Halloween Ben and faithful Bear would hang out with Pockets for a few hours during the annual parade of ghosts and goblins up and down the Hightower's front porch steps. Neither animal was spooked by the creepy commotion outside the door when Ben was with them in the barn.

Ben waited for a response from Jacks, and when it didn't come, he added:

> Maybe next year I'll come with you as the Headless Horseman-- IF your neighbors will let me ride Pockets on their porches.

Ben knew Jacks was disappointed in him, and that was the reason he wasn't texting back. So he wrote:

> r u ok?

Not one to hold a grudge or nurse hurt feelings, Jacks responded:

> Don't worry about me. I'll be fine. But next year, you're coming with me—even if we have to take Pockets with us. G'nite, Ben.

> Hold on. I do worry about you. It comes with the territory. Let's talk about Scary Gary.

> I know. He hasn't bothered us for two months. I think he's coming around.

> He's not coming anywhere—unless he's coming after you. You're so busy watching Mary Anne Wilson all the time you're not even aware he's always watching you. I don't want to hurt your feelings, but he really hates you. We need to be more careful than ever with him.

Why should it bother me that someone who doesn't know me hates me? It's worse to be hated by someone who was once a friend. I'll never give up on Scary Gary becoming our friend.

You're consistent; I'll say that. Just make sure you're never far away from me at school or on the bus. G'nite, Jacks.

G'nite, Ben—and I don't watch M.A.W. *all* the time.

CHAPTER

twenty-nine

The next day after school, the boys, as usual, waited for Gary to board the bus before they did. They always felt safer keeping him in front of them. Jacks took the bus steps two at a time and approached the driver for a high five. Ben slowly ascended with his head turned left, searching for Scary Gary. He found him in the fourth row, sitting by himself. Oblivious to Ben's gaze, the middle school malcontent was glaring at Jacks who was animatedly talking to Flat Stanley. Gary's eyes were like chambered bullets, steel-gray and dangerous. And Ben considered calling him out right there.

Stanley almost always had a joke for his two favorite passengers, but could see he didn't have Ben's attention yet.

"Hey, guys—I've got a question for you both," said Stanley, smiling in appreciation for his own sense of humor. "Are you ready?" Jacks nodded while Ben, keeping most of his attention on the fourth row, moved into his customary front row window seat, tossing Stanley the tan jacket he used to save that seat for the two boys.

"Okay, here goes then," and he asked his question:

"How many eighth graders with A.D.D. does it take to screw in a lightbulb?"

"I don't know. How many?" asked Jacks, to which Stanley responded, "Hey, guys, do you want to get a milkshake later?"

Jacks got it and laughed harder than Stanley deserved. Ben didn't even try and just gave Stanley his "you're so weird" look, a reaction the man took as a victory of sorts.

After Jacks slipped off his backpack and sat next to Ben, the good-natured bus driver asked, "You boys got any plans for Halloween tomorrow?"

"You bet!" exclaimed Jacks. Then catching himself: "Well, I do, anyway. Ben's got a previous commitment with a horse and a barn. But I'm going to do some serious candy harvesting tomorrow night. Now—about that milkshake."

Meanwhile, the brooding bully in the fourth row had heard what he'd been waiting for. His time had come.

CHAPTER

twenty-nine

At age fifteen, Gary Henderson should have been a sophomore at Clay High School, but there were several good reasons he was still in the eighth grade. He started kindergarten at age six because a year earlier, his waitress mother, DeeDee, left her abusive, truck-driver husband, stealing away from their apartment in the middle of the night with one suitcase and Gary in tow. She and the boy spent that year wearing out their welcome all over Memphis, living for a while with one of her co-workers, then with a variety of dead-beat men who misused her as badly as her husband had.

Finally, she talked a cousin in South Bend into letting her move in until she could land a job and get a place of her own. Working a series of minimum-wage jobs and drawing a monthly welfare check, she and Gary finally leased their own dismal apartment. It wasn't long before her son was treating her like all the other men in her life did. That's why she didn't complain when her ex-husband showed up in the summer after Gary's sixth grade year to take the boy with him on the road. "Someone needs to make a man out of him," snarled the burly alcoholic. "He's big enough to do some real work."

That plan didn't last long. After five months of not hearing a word from them, DeeDee was startled by a heavy knock on the door one nasty, wintry evening in January. Dismissing the frigid weather, Gary had hitch-hiked home from Pittsburgh starting the night before. He'd learned to stay out of sight from the state police while picking up rides at truck stops. Opening the door, DeeDee stammered,

"W-what happened? Where's your father?"

"At a rest stop in Pennsylvania."

"What did he say when you left him?"

"Not much. I hit him over the head with a tire iron after he fell asleep."

With that, he pushed past her toward his old bedroom, where the whispering darkness welcomed him home. He closed and locked the door behind him.

So the moody, churlish man-boy was fourteen in the seventh grade, a bully by nature *and* nurture, though not slow-witted like his father. He was clever and unctuous enough to get what he wanted when he knew brute force would bring punishment. Academically, they had to pass him on to Mrs. Smalls and the eighth grade, but he and the administration tacitly knew that was as far as he would go. Both of them were waiting for his sixteenth birthday, when the law could no longer require his attendance.

In the meantime, he had his eye on Jacks and Ben, biding his time and waiting for his chance to do them harm with the least consequence for himself. Almost two months had passed from the start of the school year, and daily he became more committed to hurting them.

He remembered with satisfaction the night he escaped from the cab of his drunken father's truck two years earlier. He didn't know whether or not his blow had killed the man, but he would never forget the exhilaration he felt when he obeyed the Voice that directed him to the tire iron. He was excited about the event for at least a week after, and was disappointed when he realized the man must still be alive, since the cops never paid his mother and him a visit.

Having given in to the darkness that night, he became sensitive to the light and easily offended by it—in whatever form it took. It's why he despised Mrs. Smalls as his homeroom teacher, and why he hated Flat Stanley, the upbeat bus driver. But he'd never known the kind of light that surrounded Jacks. And he wasn't the only one who noticed it.

Light had an affinity for Jacks. Sunlight coruscated from his raven black hair and accented his aquamarine eyes like a jeweler's display lamp enhances the beauty of diamonds on velvet. There were times when it seemed the light came from within the boy. It gave Gary a headache. Things got so bad that when he heard Jacks laugh on the bus, answer a question in class, or saw him score a goal on the soccer field, he would get nauseous, his anger metastasizing into dark envy.

On this particular Thursday night, one day before Halloween, he lay on his filthy bed scheming harm for the two boys who got on the bus every morning just a few stops after he boarded. Sitting behind them in homeroom, he had fantasized about what he would do to them someday. He hated the talkative one and was confused by the strength of the silent one. Surprised that neither had backed down from him in the bathroom weeks ago, he would be more careful this time. Now he would catch both of them alone.

Lately, the Voice that used to go weeks not speaking to him, never left him at night. For him, it was a single Voice that wasn't exactly a voice, was it? It came from inside him and from everywhere around him, a viscous, seductive whisper that was not made of sound but of darkness itself. It slithered through his consciousness, calling his name:

"Gary, my friend. We have work to do."

Encouraged by what he'd heard on the bus that afternoon, the sullen, lonely boy, more receptive to evil than ever, knew what he must do and the perfect time to do it.

CHATER

thirty

It was a typical fall season in the Midwest: totally unpredictable. September had been so cool the leaves fell two weeks early. Then October broke all kinds of high temperature records. Now as evening approached on the thirty-first, a biting wind came trick-or-treating down from Michigan, picking up steam as it crossed into Indiana. It shrieked through the skeletal branches of the hibernating trees, pushing their bony fingers downward, as if grasping for any unsuspecting, costumed kid foolish enough to dawdle beneath them. It was a night of mischief and mayhem, and Scary Gary Henderson, feeling anonymous and invincible behind his Jason-like hockey mask, was its voice.

"Oompa Loompa doom-pa-dee-do, I've got a perfect puzzle for you. Oompa loompa doom-pa-dee-dee, if you are wise, you'll listen to me" he half-sang, half-chanted, furiously peddling his bike down Juniper Road toward Notre Dame as the last rays of sunlight surrendered to Halloween evening. By the time he got to Jackson's house, darkness was coming quickly. Still, he steered his bicycle into the woods across the street from the farm and patiently waited for the full cloak of night.

He hadn't been there five minutes when a door across the street opened and Jackson came hurtling out, almost colliding with three grade school Disney princesses climbing the steps. "Sorry!" he laughed, neatly avoiding them while leaping off the porch, his mortarboard flying and the open-necked graduation gown billowing out like bat wings.

Standing there on the curving, red brick sidewalk, his curly, black hair aged with a baby powder dusting, lensless wire rim glasses pinching the end of his nose, and his forehead lined with faux wrinkles drawn with an eyebrow pencil, Jacks looked more like a starving refugee than an Oxford professor. But it took so little to make him happy that when he had a genuine reason for being so, as he did on this festive evening, he literally glowed with it. Trying to capture that look, Babe bustled out the front door—over seven months pregnant and both hands occupied. In one were tasty treats filling the biggest bowl she could find, and in the other she was clicking pictures rapid fire with her phone camera.

She caught one of him picking up his cap and a few more of him dancing down the driveway in a whirling dervish, while yelling, "I'll be back in an hour with twice as much candy as you've got in that bowl."

Gary waited until Jacks was out of sight, smiling behind his mask because he knew he would catch him alone on his return trip home. But first things first. Night had fallen, and it was time to deal with the silent one in the barn, who protected the shining one that offended his eyes and ruined his digestion. He would give the larger boy such a beating that he would never dare to cross his path again. The smaller one he would catch up with in the shadows between two of the neighborhood homes a bit later.

"I have very special plans for pretty little Jacksie," he thought, inadvertently reaching down to pat the right front pocket of his jeans. He felt the lump there made by a washcloth wrapped around the paring knife he'd taken from his mother's kitchen. When he was done, it would be a long time before anyone would be able to look at the boy's face without cringing. The anticipation of finally being able to harm his elusive enemies so spiked his central nervous system with adrenalin that Gary had a hard time not bursting from his hiding place with a shout. He took a deep breath and looked up at the gibbous moon, now breaking from its cloud cover, clear and bold, climbing the eastern sky.

After settling himself, he breached the woods, and slowly walking his bike, crossed the road at the Hightower driveway, stealthily maneuvering his way through the shadows of the trees on the yard's generous perimeter until he arrived at the west side of the house. There he parked the bike behind an impressive wood pile. He'd rehearsed this trip in the late afternoon the day before when, from the same woods he'd just left, he saw Ben and his golden Labrador making their rounds on the small farm. So now he fumbled through the pile of wood until he found a lengthy, heavy piece of timber that would be just right for dealing with that troublesome dog.

CHAPTER

thirty-one

Is there a literal devil? Try opposing him for a while, and you'll find out. The truth is there are two equal and opposite errors with regard to the forces of darkness. One is to deny their existence or ignore them; the other is to obsess about them. Demons are equally pleased with both tactics. The trick is to celebrate life everyday while on alert for the enemy's encroachment. Jacks had learned early on how to do exactly that. He loved the world but never forgot the evil one had a claim on it and would try to stop him if he ever let his guard down. The irony was that on this macabre night when most of the western world unwittingly opened its wallets and doors to demonic horrors and "things that go bump in the night," Jacks appeared to be blissfully unaware of the danger that had bicycled into his neighborhood.

Ben, on the other hand, was pensive and irritable, even more than usual on this, his second least favorite day of the year. Because he never spoke to Bear or Pockets, the boy instinctively knew it was important for him to give them lots of physical attention and balance his silence with music.

He'd read that low and high frequencies can cause anxiety in horses, so months ago he Googled, "Music Horses Like," and he found a CD titled, *Relaxation Music For Horses,* featuring the music and ten-string guitar of Janet Marlow. Pockets' favorite tunes were "Dreams of Fields" and "Free to Run." On this particular evening, Ben combed out her mane to the tranquil tones of "Evening Groom."

Apparently, the music worked on Bear too, because he lay curled up on the barn floor with an eccentric smile on his doggie-face.

Because his iPhone speaker was too weak to fill the barn, Ben had figured out a way to turn a regular Pringles can into a speaker booster. With scissors he cut a slit near the bottom of the can through which he could slide the phone. Then he attached two big binder clips to the ends of the can to keep it from rolling away. Finally, he stuffed toilet paper loosely and evenly throughout the inside of the can to muffle the higher end treble sounds. And *voilà*, he had a cheap but effective iPhone speaker booster especially designed for horses.

But on this night, the music did little to relieve the boy's nagging sense that something bad was about to happen. His initial thought was to go after Jacks and at least watch over him from a distance. But while trying to decide what to do, his peripheral vision caught a flash of impossibly bright light just outside the barely open door of the barn. Although he'd never seen anything like it before, he had the distinct impression someone or something was trying to get his attention.

Neither animal seemed to have noticed the light, but Bear stirred when he saw Ben set the well-used curry brush down on a hay bale and warily move toward the door. The loyal dog rose and followed the boy through the semi-darkness across the hay-strewn floor. There's nothing the mind likes better than a suspense story, and Ben sensed he was entering one. His pulse quickening, he stopped just short of the opening and peered into the darkness. The dim light from the barn's interior did little to penetrate the blackness outside. Something strange was going on out there, and he had mixed emotions about exploring it further. But a warning bell from somewhere deep within him was sounding and he knew it was in response to that odd flash of light. In fact, now that he was closer to the point of the light's origin, he felt an unusual calm come over him, and he bravely stepped into the Stygian gloom beyond the door.

With a sense of smell about a thousand times stronger than her master's, Bear was the first one aware of Gary's malignant presence fifty yards away. His head lowered while his ears flattened against his skull. A low growl rumbled within his massive chest and brought

Ben down to his ear. The boy's instinct was to speak to his dog, and if he could have, he'd have said something like, "What's the matter, boy? What are you trying to tell me?" But the words wouldn't come, and seeing no one in the shadows that surrounded them, Ben looked up toward the house. There, at the corner of a large window that opened onto the family's great room, a husky voyeur stood, wearing some kind of mask and spying on any Hightowers who were still in the house.

Ben knew intuitively that the interloper was Scary Gary and that he hadn't come for candy. Because Gurney was on trick-or-treat duty with Carrie somewhere in the neighborhood, he also knew Babe was the only one in the house tonight. Just the thought of the oversized pervert ogling his stepmother made Ben's stomach clench like a fist. The truth was that the only reason Gary chose that window was to make sure that Ben wasn't inside so he could move on to the barn to deal with him. Unknowingly, the bully had just lost the element of surprise.

With clouds covering the moon making it impossible for Gary to see him, Ben moved quickly through the dark toward the split rail fence at the back of the house. Placing both hands on the closest post, he swung his right leg up, his whole body experiencing moon gravity as he cleared the top of the fence easily, with Bear at his heels. Close enough now to call the intruder out, Ben reached down to hold the dog back—and yelled:

"Okay, Moby Dick, drop the stick now," the boy ordered, "and get the hell off our property."

Surprised, but maintaining the hubris of a predator, Gary calmly turned toward the voice that challenged him from the darkness. Knowing exactly who that voice had to belong to, and recognizing that his night vision was momentarily gone from searching the home's interior, he answered in a low, menacing tone:

"N-nobody calls me a dick and lives, little man. Why don't you step into the light so I can see you better?"

Waiting for Ben's response, Scary Gary suddenly realized something that stunned him. His beady eyes opening as wide as they could, he exclaimed,

"Hey, I didn't think you could talk!"

Slightly bent over from grasping Bear's collar, Ben stepped out of the darkness and answered,

"Moby Dick was an evil whale, just like you … and I didn't think I could either. I can't believe I'm wasting my first words on you."

"You mean your *last* words, Keegan," snarled Scary Gary, throwing off his mask and regaining his composure. But before he made his move, the ancient malice within him became aware of the translucent being just behind Ben at the edge of the shadows. The evil spirit wavered for a moment, measuring his opponent. Bear's black lips peeled back from his white fangs. There was a deadly stillness in the air and a sense that all hell was about to break loose.

CHAPTER

thirty-two

Now under the complete control of an evil that predated the creation of the planet, Gary Henderson let out an atavistic scream that pierced Ben like a three-foot icicle, paralyzing the boy for an instant. On any other evening than Halloween, that horrible cry might have drawn the attention of a neighbor or Notre Dame student jogging by the Hightower farm. But not on this night.

Growling deeply, his hackles raising the hair along his spine, the steadfast Labrador retriever jutted out his wrinkled muzzle and bared his powerful teeth. At the sound of Gary's otherworldly shriek, Ben instinctively released the dog. Raising the club above his head and lunging at the shaken boy, Gary was deterred by Bear's attack. The dog's jaws closed on the bully's left calf, just penetrating his heavy jeans, when the crazed teen swung the solid piece of hickory down like a mallet and squarely across the animal's eyes with a sickening crack. The timber snapped in two, the larger piece flying off into the darkness. Noble Bear dropped with a groan, unconscious at his assailant's feet.

"No!" cried Ben, and he sprang to his dog's side, kneeling down and stroking Bear's dense, yellow fur. Gary stood there, laughing at the two of them, and disdainfully tossed away the useless piece of wood that remained in his hands. Then the brute pivoted to the side of the boy whose complete attention was on his fallen dog and delivered a mighty kick to Ben's head that sent him skidding away from Bear and across the grass. A cloud of darkness, mingled with red sparks flew across Ben's eyes. His head was spinning like an owl on OxyContin. Not knowing whether his dog was still alive or not, the boy began shaking his head to clear the ringing in his bleeding left ear. His rage at Gary for what he had done to Bear was building like a tidal wave and fed his attempt to get to his feet.

"This is going to be easier than I thought," mused the unscrupulous thug. He decided to end it all while Ben was still down and reeling. When he saw the boy trying to stand up, Gary closed on him in an instant, and cocked his arm back to deliver a death strike to the head. Had it made solid contact, it would have knocked the thirteen-year-old senseless, maybe never to reawaken. But as if someone pushed his head down at the last moment, Ben miraculously ducked under the blow. Immediately Gary's arms were around him like a python.

Luckily, when Ben ducked, he'd thrown his left elbow forward for protection. So when the ruffian attempted to squeeze the life out of the smaller boy, he only succeeded in driving his enemy's elbow like a spear into the bones of his own chest. Gary shouted out in pain, and Ben took advantage of that instant to whirl out of his grip.

Size matters in a fight, but it's not everything. Sometimes speed and brains are more important than brute strength. When Ben broke out of Gary's hold, the bully was surprised he didn't run away. Instead, fueled by his fury over Bear's lifeless body, the boy darted in and struck Gary on the cheek with unexpected force, raising a red welt and getting the larger boy's attention. He followed that with another quick blow that cut the flesh under Gary's other cheekbone. The young villain stepped back and extended his tongue to taste the copper tang of blood trickling down the right side of his face. Gary smiled cruelly and said,

"Now you get my best, kid. You should have run away."

With a quickness that defied his bulk, Scary Gary struck at Ben with all of his significant strength. But he'd been stung, and injured fighters strike short. His prodigious blow swept just past Ben's head, and the driving arms of the smaller boy rained several more startling jabs to Gary's face. Any ordinary kid would have been stopped by

Ben's fists, but the bully's solid jaw took every hit squarely and still seemed to register only a faint shock to his demon-driven brain.

Now Gary was blind with rage. The smell of his own blood, the kinetic impact on flesh and bone, the greasy feel of sweat—all of these sensations drove the bully into a frenzy. He rushed in head down, this time to crush Ben into the side of the house. But it was like trying to corner a ghost. The boy flashed to his left and Gary succeeded only in battering himself against the house. And before he could turn, he received a powerful punch just beneath and behind his ear. This time he was staggering, and he realized he could never stand at a distance and exchange blows with this nimble enemy who had lethal hammers for fists. If only he could get to closer quarters with him.

His chance came unexpectedly. He lowered his head and plunged in, only to see the smaller boy feint again to one side, then break the opposite way. But this time as he leaped, Ben's right foot landed awkwardly on the piece of wood Gary had cast away. Down the boy went, and in that moment, the bruised and bleeding bully saw his opportunity. With a savage shout of wicked glee he threw himself onto his fallen adversary. Whining with delirious joy like the crazed devil who controlled him, Gary shoved one of his meaty arms around the body of the boy while his other hand, reaching violently upward, found Ben's throat.

Jacks' cousin was in a perilous position. His enemy was focusing all of his strength on crushing the smaller boy's windpipe. Knowing he couldn't survive Gary's viselike grip much longer, he inexorably moved his right arm up one inch at a time until he had it over the villain's wrist just beneath his chin. Using that leverage, and with a mighty effort of will, he produced a resistless pressure on the choke-hold by slowing pushing himself off the grass with his powerful leg muscles, then suddenly spinning his whole body weight into the air. In the nick of time, the death grip was torn from his throat.

Now a few feet away from his assailant, the boy stepped backward, clutching his throat and falling exhausted to the ground. Scary Gary lay in the same condition, breathing heavily. The bully was devilishly strong, but he didn't have Ben's endurance from working on the farm, his muscles as strong as whipcord. A few moments later, both boys regained their feet at the same time. They stood there swaying and trying to catch their breath. In just a little over three minutes, they had poured out all their strength. But devils don't give up their possessions readily. An inner Voice reminded Gary that he'd wrapped up something special for this occasion and placed it in his jeans pocket.

CHAPTER

thirty-three

Gary's plan to use the knife on Jacks could wait until later. He needed it now to stop an opponent he'd seriously underestimated. Ben watched him reach into his pocket and pull out the washcloth covering the knife. When the bully dropped the cloth and revealed his weapon, Ben's first instinct was to run in the opposite direction as fast as he could. It was a good plan. But at the same time, he knew Gary wouldn't leave if he simply disappeared. He was certain his enemy's priority was to hurt Jacks, and that he was the only one who could prevent it. So for the second time that night, he surprised the brute by standing his ground.

The boy who came to live with the Hightowers three years earlier planted his feet firmly, calmly raised both arms in front of him with his palms turned inward, and gestured with his fingers for the villain to bring it on. His ear still bleeding, he spoke with a rasp, softly but clearly:

"To get to him, you have to go through me. And you won't find that easy to do."

True heroes don't usually realize they are. Ben was too busy at the moment to be aware of his heroism or the aura of light that surrounded him, whereas Scary Gary was all too aware of both. Still, the demon within drove him forward. He attacked the boy with the knife held high and the blade pointing downward.

For his part, Ben wasn't about to remain upright with a knife-wielding giant coming at him. To get distance between himself and the flashing blade, he fell backward onto the grass, simultaneously thrusting out the instep of his boot to catch Gary behind the right knee. When the knee buckled, Ben kicked the bully hard alongside the kneecap with his other boot heel. Gary grunted with pain, dropped the knife into the darkness, and fell.

"You busted my knee!" he cried.

"Not even close." The boy answered. "It'll just be sore for a while." He paused, then looked over at Bear's crumpled form. *Had the dog just moved?* he wondered. But Gary got his attention again by sitting up. "Haven't you had enough?" Ben asked him, wearily.

A rattlesnake is so dumb it can think itself cornered in an open field. And so, it coils and strikes at a superior enemy instead of slithering away like most other snakes would. A lot of rattlers die who don't have to. Scary Gary was as dumb as a rattlesnake. The problem was he'd never lost a fight, so he didn't know how to quit one.

"Not even close," sneered the teen fiend, who rose awkwardly, rubbing his knee and gathering his strength for one last rush. Ben saw it coming, and a part of him wanted to pray, but he didn't know how anymore. So as the rattlesnake made one last strike, he simply thought, *Feet, don't fail me now!*

The sandy-haired boy deftly slipped to the side of the ogre's charge and met him with a thunderous blow that had more than his own power in it. It landed just beside the point of the older boy's chin. The shock of the mighty wallop sent a numb tingle through Ben's shoulder, but it stopped the possessed attacker like he'd run into a granite boulder.

Was it a screeching gust of wind, or did Ben hear a disembodied shriek escape into the branches of the nearby trees? At any rate, Scary Gary Henderson, the terror of Knute Rockne Intermediate School, toppled forward on his face and lay unconscious, immense and sprawling on the lawn by the Hightower's beloved dog.

"O, Bear, dear Bear," sobbed Ben, kneeling once more beside his faithful friend, embracing his limp body and weeping unashamedly.

CHAPTER

thirty-four

Ben's heart was beating so hard from the fight that all he could detect was his own pounding pulse when he searched for signs of life in Bear. Though he couldn't pray for himself, he was now desperate enough to try it for his dog. "I know You wouldn't do it for m-me," he stuttered, thinking it odd to hear his own voice. "So for Jacks and his family, would it be too much for you to let him live?"

At that exact moment, Gary groaned, rolled over and sat up again, massaging his adamantine jaw and looking at Ben in wonder. "Who are you?" he asked in a weak voice that only slightly resembled the one Ben was accustomed to hearing.

"Apparently someone who should be more specific when he prays," the boy replied, looking up to heaven with a frown.

Gary dragged himself a few feet over to a fencepost so he could recline against it while his head cleared. "Sorry I killed your dog," he said.

As if on cue, Bear opened his eyes and began to lick the hands that cradled his head. "Bear! You're alive!" Ben cried. Next was a joyous scene where you'd be hard-pressed to tell which of them was the happiest. For Bear, it was the first time he'd ever heard the boy speak his name. Rising awkwardly for a moment on unsteady legs, he was soon lavishing his boy's face with slobbery doggie kisses. And for Ben, well, is there any joy that surpasses the kind that erupts unexpectedly from the darkest despair?

Gary watched them frolic on the ground, waiting for Ben to look over at him. When their eyes met, the older boy said, "I think you beat the devil out of me."

"I know," answered Ben, continuing to stroke Bear's head, "and I'll do it again if you so much as look at Jacks sideways."

"No, you don't understand," replied the subdued bully. "I think you literally beat the devil out of me. He's gone."

"Who's gone?" asked the boy.

"The Voice."

"How do you know?"

"Because he stopped talking to me."

Ben remembered too well his own Voices, and asked Gary a question he'd wondered about for some time.

"Where did he go?"

Gary thought for a moment and answered honestly, aware that Bear was not growling at him anymore.

"I don't know. Hell, maybe. Anywhere to get away from your Shining One."

The boy had a flashback to the iridescent being he'd seen in his bedroom on Christmas Eve when Jacks had prayed for his healing and then taken on his sickness. While he was connecting the dots between the bully's observation and the fierce blaze of light that called him out of the barn earlier, Gary spoke again.

"You shouldn't think you beat us by yourself, you know. You're tough enough, alright, but the One with you was stronger than the one in me." The older boy sensed he had just told Ben something he'd not been aware of and now was considering. So he gave him a minute to think while he sat up a bit straighter and with the fingers of his left hand checked the cut on his cheekbone, realizing it had stopped bleeding. At the same time, he inadvertently brought his other hand up to his right eye, the target of one of Ben's jabs, as the swollen lid had almost completely cut off all sight there. He was going to have a beautiful shiner come Monday morning at school.

Eventually, Gary broke the silence. "What do we do now?" he asked.

Ben held up his hand like a stop sign and said, "Just a minute. I'm thinking." A very different Gary from the one who had biked there earlier that evening, submissively waited.

Finally, after touching his finger to his mouth, as if priming a pump that was rarely used, the boy spoke, "Alright, here's the deal. At lunch on Monday, you're sitting at our table. Whatever happens after that, as long as you behave, is between you and Jacks."

"B-but I'm the last person he'd want at that table," argued Gary.

"That's how much you know, Bubba. He's been saving you a seat for two months!" Ben could never explain later why he started calling the boy, "Bubba." He only knew he could never call him "Scary Gary" again, and, partly because of his bulk, the new name just seemed to fit.

Still, he could see that Gary wasn't convinced.

"Listen," said Ben, "hanging out with Jacks can only be good for you. He's got this crazy idea you two are destined to be friends. He told me that's the way God wants it. He's been praying for you every night and probably for part of each day. Trust me: you'll never meet anyone else like him. And besides," he added in a firmer tone, "I'm not asking; I'm telling you that you'll be there—or else."

"I g-guess if you put it like that..." Gary's voice trailed off.

For a boy who hadn't spoken in three years, Ben was already tired of talking. "Enough said," he stated. "Go home now, and I'll see you on Monday."

Before Gary could make a move though, Ben added, "One more thing, Bubba. Don't tell anyone I can talk. It will be our little secret for a while."

Cautiously pulling his large frame up on a fence rail, Gary grunted, "Uh-huh," watching to see if his movement would get any reaction from Bear. The intuitive animal sensed his master's calm and declared a truce with a wag of his tail. The bully limped off into the dark to find his bike, stepping on his mask and crushing it into the lawn. Ben heard him mumbling his new name, "Bubba," like he was trying it on for size.

Shaking his head at the bizarre events of the evening, the boy watched his adversary for a moment, then got up and went back to the barn to settle Pockets down for the night. Afterwards, he and Bear sneaked in the back door of the house and slipped unseen up the steps and into his bedroom.

Changing out of the sweatshirt and khakis he'd wrecked in the fight, the boy gathered them up and tip-toed next door into the bathroom, where he closed and locked the door. Lifting a panel in the wall, he tossed the dirty clothes down the laundry chute into the basement, certain he'd never felt this tired before. Now that the adrenaline had worn off, it seemed every part of his body ached. As quickly and quietly as he could, he took a hot shower, carefully washing the caked blood from his left ear. A few minutes later, he was in his pajamas and pretending to be asleep in the top bunk, with no one aware of the danger he'd faced that night. No one, that is, except Bear.

It wasn't long before he heard Babe greet Gurney and Carrie at the front door, back from their evening's adventure. Jacks followed about a half-hour later, never realizing the peril he'd been protected from. Ben knew his cousin well enough to predict the first thing he'd do when he got home. Sure enough, it wasn't thirty seconds later that the door of their bedroom opened a crack to check on his whereabouts. He was certain the family had noticed that the lights in the barn were turned out and the door there latched. They might have thought it was odd for him to be in bed before 9 p.m., but they respected him enough not to inquire about it. For his part, he would lie there, heal a bit, and wait for his roommate to turn in.

The next time the bedroom door opened, a small LED flashlight floated in about three feet off the floor, illuminating only those parts of the room Jacks needed to see to get ready for bed. On nights the boys didn't text each other, Jacks would habitually say, "G'nite, Ben," taking for granted that his cousin heard him, even though he never received a reply. Typically, those would be the last words spoken in the room. This night would change that.

Eventually, Ben heard the springs squeaking in the bottom bunk as Jacks fell into bed and pulled up his covers. He knew what came next: "G'nite, Ben."

Waiting until his cousin accepted the silence from above, Ben replied haltingly, "G-G'nite, Jacks," then before a response could come, added rapid fire: "Scary Gary's having lunch with us on Monday and if you try to make me talk anymore tonight I'll go another three years without speaking and if you're smart you won't test me on this 'cause I mean it and we can maybe talk about it tomorrow 'cause I've never been as tired as I am right now, so *good night!*"

If Ben had known that beneath him, Jacks lay in an apoplectic stupor, he could have spoken more slowly and worried less about any unwelcome reply from the bottom bunk. As it turned out, it was Ben who immediately fell into a profoundly restful sleep while his cousin's eyes, as big as dinner plates, as well as his open mouth, had trouble closing for what seemed to be hours.

CHAPTER

thirty-five

The first thing Jacks thought when he woke up on Saturday morning was that maybe he'd dreamed the whole thing last night. But he knew better: no one could even dream the verbal explosion that had rendered him speechless in the dark. He heard Ben flush the toilet next door and considered marching right into the bathroom to ask him what was going on. But better judgment settled in and he decided to wait for his cousin to make his own play.

When Ben went straight from the bathroom to the staircase, Jacks adroitly fell in behind him and the two descended the stairs in silence on their way to the breakfast table. Ben could feel his best friend staring holes in the back of his head, but it was obvious Jacks would have to wait until later for an explanation.

One of the difficulties of having a child who never speaks is you can't cross-examine him when he's aroused your curiosity. "G'morning," said Jacks and flopped into his chair, as usual. But Babe, dishing up oatmeal from a saucepan on the stove, noticed that Ben eased himself down with an uncharacteristic stiffness. Of anyone else in the house she would have asked, "What in the world happened to you last night?" Or noticing the redness and slight swelling behind his left ear, she'd have pressed him with, "Did Pockets kick you in the head or what?" But she was more than his aunt; Babe was his friend and surrogate mother, and her instincts told her that even if he could speak, he'd be keeping this story to himself.

Still, her penetrating gaze demanded that the boy glance her way, and when he did, Ben was glad she didn't know yet what Jacks knew about him now. *And what am I going to do about Jacks?* he thought. *How much should I tell him about last night? I need some time to think this through.*

He looked up from his hot breakfast to see that his cousin was now acting like he was more interested in the sports page than he was about the revelation that Ben could talk. But he knew better. Jacks was simply waiting for a more opportune time. And if Ben had his way, it would be a time of his choosing and no one else's. Better tonight after the family had retired and he'd had the whole day to decide what to do about this incredible development. The truth was that he was so used to being silent that a small part of him wondered if he actually would be able to talk again. *Of course I can,* he thought. *But I'm pretty sure I don't want everyone to know that.*

After serving herself, Babe joined the boys at the table. Gurney and Carrie hadn't come down yet. They'd both had trouble getting to sleep for the same reason last night: too much Halloween candy. But it was Saturday morning, so she'd let them sleep in. Meanwhile, she studied her two oatmeal eaters, heads down and much too obvious about avoiding her eyes. Ever the intuitive mother, she was as tuned into these two as she was the little one growing within her. They were up to something; at the least, they knew something she didn't. Resisting the temptation to ask Jacks what was going on, she decided to let him get uneasy with her silence and be the first to speak. Eventually, he looked up and said, "Something wrong, Babe?"

"Not that I *know* of," she replied, raising just her right eyebrow as only she could.

He caught her double-meaning and smiled warmly, then neatly steered the conversation to the events of the day.

"You don't have to worry about me today," he said brightly. "I'm biking over to Mrs. Kaufman's for my piano lesson, then swinging by Doc's office before lunch to pick up some books he's checked out of the library for me." He wrinkled up his face and did his best Doc Volheim imitation. "'I think you'll be pleasantly *challenged* by them, young man.' I love that guy! I should loan him my copy of *Diary of a Wimpy Kid.* I'll bet that would challenge *him.*"

Babe laughed, surrendering to his diversionary tactic, then added: "Just make sure you're back here by 12:30. Your dad's firing up the grill for probably your only healthy meal of the day. Then it's Bruno's pizza for dinner because Gurney and I are eating out before we take in Jay Leno at the Morris Center."

"Whoa! Date night, huh?" said the boy, standing up from the table and turning to his cousin. "The *P's* are steppin' out! So the inmates have control of the asylum all evening. Yes!" he exclaimed with a fist pump. "It looks like ice cream sundaes and moon pies for bedtime snacks!" Babe rolled her eyes and looked over at Ben, who just sat there with a dopey grin on his face. Gathering the authority that comes with motherhood, she said, "I have supreme confidence that Carrie will be secure with both of you gentlemen watching her tonight. Now before you leave, young man…" she said, pointing to her left cheek bone.

Jacks came around the table, squeezed his mother's shoulders and lightly kissed her on the cheek. His eyes were soft, and he said, "You know we love you, Babe," speaking for his cousin, as always. Then he threw a knowing look to Ben and bolted out the kitchen door, yelling: "I'll be back at 12:29. Tell Dad to make mine medium rare!" With that, he was gone, leaving Babe and her nephew staring after him.

They sat there in silence for a comfortable moment. Then Babe said, "That is one strange kid," Ben nodding his head in agreement. "But you know what?" she asked.

The boy never found out what she was going to say, because he naturally answered her question.

"He'll be back at 12:29," Ben said.

As he was speaking, Gurney and Carrie walked into the kitchen.

CHAPTER

thirty-six

That night, after Babe and Gurney had returned from their date, the boys lay in their bunks, wondering what the other was thinking. Eventually, Ben texted:

> I've got questions for you.

The reply was immediate:

> I've got questions for you.

There was a pause, then Jacks typed:

> Me first, okay?
>
> Okay.
>
> First of all, why are we texting? You can talk.
>
> First of all, I don't want most people to know that yet. And texting feels more natural to me right now.
>
> Since when am I "most people?" C'mon, you're my best friend. I want to hear what your voice sounds like.

After a moment, one word came from the upper bunk: "Doppleganger."

"What?!" whispered Jacks below.

"I said, 'Doppleganger.'"

"Why would you choose that for your first word to me?"

"Partly because it's fun to say, but mostly because it's a phantom, and ghosts are what I want to ask you about."

"Why do you want to know about ghosts?" asked Jacks.

"Because I saw one last Christmas Eve in this room."

Of course Jacks knew what he was talking about and answered, "It wasn't a ghost. There are no such things. You saw an angel, and that's less rare than you might think. They're everywhere, but few have eyes to see them."

"I thought maybe I dreamed it," replied Ben. "But something happened last night that made me think they're for real."

"And now you want to tell me what happened last night."

"No, not really. I want to ask you about…'them.'"

"Angels?"

"Yes."

"Okay, we can talk about them. But first I have a question for you. What did you mean when you said Scary Gary's having lunch with us on Monday?"

Ben leaned over the edge of his bed, looked down at his bunkmate, and said: "I meant Scary Gary's having lunch with us on Monday."

"But how could you possibly know that?" asked Jacks, enjoying this conversation more than is humanly possible.

"A wise person once said of me: 'He's not deaf. He chooses to be mute.' Or did you say 'mutant'?"

"So you're telling me that Scary Gary told you?"

"Not exactly," said Ben. "And don't call him 'Scary Gary' anymore. I renamed him 'Bubba,' and I think he likes it."

"*You* renamed him 'Bubba.' When? Where? This is amazing," said Jacks. "There's a lot you're not telling me. Okay then, *why* is he having lunch with us Monday?"

Ben rolled onto his back again and replied,

"If you learn the reason for that, it will be from him, not from me."

"Why are you being so secretive?" asked Jacks.

"Because I think it's about time I know something you don't," answered his cousin, smiling in the dark—"that is, something besides the fact that your mother and I had a nice talk this morning after you left."

"W-H-A-A-AT?!" cried Jacks, loud enough to wake up the neighbors. "When were you going to tell me? I suppose you had a pleasant conversation with Dad and Carrie too!"

"I hope they thought it was pleasant," said Ben, loving every minute of this.

"W-H-A-A-A-A-AT!?" he cried again, louder.

"Chill out, Charlie Brown! We didn't talk very long at all."

"Sorry, but I feel like I'm trying to get a drink from an open fire hydrant here. You have every right to talk to the fam. I'm just surprised you did."

"Me, too, I guess. But it felt like the right time to bring them in on it. I owe them all so much. And I know I can count on them to be cool about it."

"What are you going to do about school?" asked Jacks.

"I plan on being quiet for a while. My dad used to say, 'Even fools are thought wise if they keep silent.'"

Jacks thought it was meaningful that he'd quoted his father and decided it wouldn't be helpful to tell him that those words originally came from King Solomon. So he simply responded,

"Your dad was a wise man."

"Besides," said Ben, "when people think you can't talk, for some reason they tell you more than they would otherwise. I've learned a lot just from listening these past three years. I don't think most people really see what's right in front of them. You've got to get comfortable with silence to do that. They seem to like noise and confusion more than seeing clearly. So I have a feeling that for the rest of my life, I'll trust my ears more than my mouth. Now it's time for me to listen to you. I need some explanations."

Moved by his cousin's words, Jacks replied so softly that it was more of a thought than a whisper, "Be still, and know that I am God." Then louder: "Ben, you are a wonder."

"Ha!" retorted the older boy. "That's the blizzard calling the snowflake white. I'm just a flake. Now, can you help me or not?"

"Without knowing what happened to you yesterday, I'll do my best," answered Jacks.

"For starters, tell me about the Shining One who was with you the night I was sick in this room."

"He wasn't only with me. He was as much here for you as he was for me."

"Who is he?" asked Ben

"He's one of the Guardians."

"*One* of? How many are there?"

"That question is impossible to answer. They're without number."

"Where is he now?"

"He's always wherever you are," answered Jacks.

Ben anxiously looked around the room.

"You don't have to be scared of him; he's on your side."

"Why can't I see him?"

"The simplest way I can explain it is that he lives beyond the speed of light. The dimensions that humans are unaware of are so many. To be seen, he has to choose to slow down everything about himself. But that happens only when your need outweighs his modesty. It's an irony that the most luminous of beings are also the most humble."

"What is he here for?" the boy asked.

"As the Spirit tends to our spiritual needs, the Guardians tend to our physical ones. He's here to protect you—and to serve as a messenger between this world and the Real World. The name 'angel' means "messenger.""

"Then I'm left alone when he's on a journey between here and there?"

"You're never alone," answered Jacks—"unless you want to be. Besides, there's been more than one of them guarding you since before you were born. And don't forget that living beyond the speed of light has its advantages."

"In case I see him again, does he have a name?" asked Ben.

"Not one you could pronounce."

Ben thought about that and asked,

"Do you know his name?"

Jacks offered only two words in response:

"I do," he said.

Neither boy spoke for a while, but Jacks hoped this conversation was just beginning.

CHAPTER

thirty-seven

When the silence from the upper bunk reached a few minutes, Jacks thought Ben might have fallen asleep. He hadn't.

"Okay, then," the boy finally said. "I'm not going to push you to tell me more than you want to, but one thing you *have* to answer."

"I *want* to" Jacks replied, sensing that what was coming was not going to be easy for either of them.

"If there are countless hundreds of millions of them and their mission is to guard us in all our ways ..." he paused and thought about children who die for no good reason, "... then why are they so damn bad at it?"

"If there was a simple answer to that question," said Jacks, "it would be a lie and worse than meaningless. The answer is as complex as the reason behind the question. Here is what I know: as formidable a being as there is in the universe, a Guardian is still powerless when he gets pushed aside by the bad choices of the one he's charged to protect. A Guardian wouldn't contradict your will any more than Abba would. Love never coerces."

"How does that in any way apply to the innocent ones?" demanded Ben. "Besides boarding the plane, the only bad choice children make who die in a plane blown up by terrorists is to believe there's a God who cares about them or angels who will rescue them. I don't know how else to see it."

Jacks knew children on planes weren't the only ones his cousin was thinking about. His reply was tender and heart-felt.

"If you're searching for an answer that agrees with truth as you see it, it's never coming," he said gently. "You're looking at everything through a mist right now, but there'll be a day when you'll see face to face. The problem is until then, you live a life opposed, in a dangerous world that lies in the grip of the Evil One. And his demons are matched to you almost as particularly as our Guardians are. Before we inherit the Real World to come, we're under attack every minute of the day. The only reasons most of us are still alive and reasonably sane are *because* of angelic intervention and one other thing."

"What's that?" asked Ben.

"Our own alertness. Because angels never act alone. You were created to be a warrior. And no weapon formed against you will ever prosper, but that's only if you're in the battle. The one who chooses not to fight darkness will be overcome by it."

I almost was last night, thought Ben, *and if Bubba was right, it was a Guardian who saved me.* Still he challenged, "That's not good enough, Jacks. My parents were alert warriors for God and my brothers and sisters were walking that same path when he let them die. I can never forgive him for that."

When Jacks didn't respond, Ben thought he knew what the younger boy was thinking, so he added:

"Even if you're right," and they're in a 'better place,' the fact is I'm not. So in a way, your answer makes it worse. Do you really think I don't know I'm in a bad place right now? And if, in the end, life comes down to whether or not a person trusts in God, I don't, okay!? I can't! It would feel like I was betraying Katie and all of them. My faith in God's goodness died on the day my family died."

Jacks knew that sometimes words get in the way of healing. Just as much as the wonder of love, deep emotional pain also can break the backs of words—break them in a way that those words carry nothing meaningful and hurt more than they help. And now he figured he'd said enough—maybe too much. If it took Ben three more years—or thirty more for that matter—to find any peace, he had a right to his own counsel. If it had been anyone other than Jacks in that bottom bunk, Ben might have heard advice like: "Maybe what happens to you isn't as important as how you respond to what happens to you;" or "You don't get to choose your dark night of the soul—it's given to you. And your job is to get close to it and sift it for its gold." Words. Just words.

Shrouded by the dark, Jacks got out of bed and stood as tall as he could. Reaching over the top bunk rail, his hand found his cousin's forearm. He affectionately squeezed it and whispered, "You are a wonder. I love you, Ben."

Then he got back in his bed, fluffed up his pillow, turned over on his back, and lightly pushing with his feet on the mattress above him, said, "G'night, Snowflake."

It took almost a full minute before he heard back, and then it was barely audible: "G'night, Blizzard."

CHAPTER

thirty-eight

The next day was Sunday, and the family fell back into their normal routine. It was Gurney's turn to stay home with his nephew. Breakfast was over and, sitting in wicker rocking chairs on the wraparound porch, the two of them, along with Bear, watched the sun rise over the pond. Five Canadian geese swooped in from the north and landed gracefully on the water's mirrored surface. An annoyed muskrat swam away from the new arrivals and scurried over the shoreline into the safety of the reed grass. Meanwhile the rest of the Hightower clan was noisily getting ready for church.

To the untrained eye, nothing had changed that morning. They talked to each other, including to Ben, and he didn't talk back. But there was a tangible air of anticipation, a palpable joy in the house, each family member knowing he *could* talk if he wanted to. Still, it was obvious they were determined to let him be in control of his own mouth. Of course, Ben noticed that right away and found it humorous. Had any of them asked him a question, he would gladly have answered. But no one did, and he was fine with that, too.

Gurney got up from his rocker when he heard Babe call for him from upstairs. He pictured his wife standing as still as she could by the bathroom sink, waiting for him to come and find her dropped contact lens. It was almost a bi-weekly ritual for them. He put his hand on Ben's shoulder and said, "See you later, son." When he went into the house, the boy decided to attend to Pockets in the barn. He headed that way with Bear close behind.

Horses don't sleep for long periods of time like humans. Descended from prey animals, they are awake and moving most of the time. In fact, mature horses sleep less than two hours a day, broken into fifteen- to twenty-minute naps. That's why, no matter what time he opened the door to the barn, Ben had never caught Pockets sleeping. Usually she was eating from a slow feed hay net he'd filled in her paddock the night before. Having digestive systems that are designed to process food continuously, horses are trickle feeders and need forage available 24/7; otherwise, they often develop ulcers and colic. Pockets was healthy because Ben was her caregiver and friend.

After brushing her down, he saddled up mid-morning and exercised her with a ride along the fence line of their property. Then late morning, he let her graze in the meadow while he worked out with the bow and arrow at the target range on the other side of the barn. By the time he got back to the porch and entered the front door, the whole house was filled with the aroma of pork roast slow-cooking in the crock pot. He walked into the kitchen and found Gurney putting the burners on the gas range through their paces. Preparing the rice and stir-fried vegetables, a colorful medley of snow peas, baby corn, and water chestnuts, he looked up and noticed Ben watching. "Hi, buddy," he said, smiling. "Want to get the water for me?"

Normally, the boy would have nodded his head, but in this case, he didn't even consider silence. Besides, he was answering a question. "You bet," he replied brightly and went about the task of filling five glasses with ice and water. When the family returned from church, they found Gurney and Ben sitting at the kitchen table, immersed in a conversation about the unusually warm weather for that time of year and what they should be doing to prepare the farm for the cold that would surely be coming soon.

The three churchgoers tried to act like nothing unusual was going on, and again Ben found that humorous. They would just have to get over the novelty of hearing his voice, and he knew there was nothing he would do to diminish their buoyancy for the present. He was wise enough to realize that things would level off sooner than later.

During the meal, the boy who had never said a word at any of the hundreds of meals they'd eaten together since his arrival, was soft-spoken but at ease when he engaged in the talk around the table. Though he warmly answered when an occasional question was put to him, it looked like he was going to hold to the pattern of offering few words and never steering the conversation in a new direction. *He's still the silent one,* thought Jacks, *and probably always will be.*

Ben listened to Babe tell a story about a friend at church who found out she was pregnant on the same day the state of Indiana gave her family the authority to adopt their nine-month-old foster baby. "God has a sense of humor," she said, patting her tummy, feeling the baby move in what was becoming a smaller space daily. Aware that Gurney and Jacks hung on her every word, he thought, *Where would I be without these people? Not alive, I imagine, or locked in a psych ward somewhere.* They may not have been his immediate family, but they were the closest thing he had to one, and he loved them dearly.

The Hightowers were so verbal and spontaneous that sometimes you had to work at it to get a word in. But Ben enjoyed their banter so much it didn't occur to him until near the meal's end that Carrie had been unusually quiet. He looked in her direction and she was staring directly at him. Of course, Babe had noticed exactly that several times in the past twenty minutes, and she suspected from her daughter's wide and shimmering eyes that the word "babies" was on her mind.

When Ben's eyes met hers, the girl didn't turn away embarrassed. Instead she held his gaze and smiled. No plan survives contact with a cute kid, so he changed his pattern and asked *her* a question.

"Okay, rookie," he said to Carrie, quickly glancing at Babe before asking the girl, "What did the Mommy broom say to the baby broom?"

Delighted by his attention, Carrie giggled, "I don't know. What?"

"It's time to go to sweep!"

She should have used the bathroom when she got home from church, because the girl laughed so hard she almost wet herself. Her happiness exploded in staccato fashion that reminded Ben so much of his sister's machine-gun laughter. But he couldn't hold it against the girl—he was responsible for it. So instead, he gave in to what has become that rare and most sublime of family experiences: contagious laughter.

What started with Carrie spread until everyone at the table got a solid case of the giggles and simply couldn't stop laughing. Long after the joke was forgotten, they were still caught up in laughing at each other laughing. And just when it looked like it was over and they had mastered their mirth, one of them would snort and the whole thing would start up again.

"Enough! Enough!" cried Gurney, doubled over and wiping tears from his eyes. "It hurts," he said—which just made Babe laugh harder. And so it went until the happy hysterics finally played out and they were all a good kind of exhausted from it.

"We don't do that enough," Babe remarked to Gurney later in the day.

"It's a good thing we don't," he replied. "Otherwise, we'd never get any *sweep.*"

She wasn't even tempted to laugh at that.

CHAPTER

thirty-nine

The Bible tells a story of an evil spirit who left a person and went into the desert searching for rest. But finding none, it said, "I will return to the person I came from." So it returned and found that its former dwelling was all swept clean and vacant. Then that spirit found seven other spirits more evil than itself, and they all entered the person. And so the man was far worse off than before. This time, the evil spirits waited until late Friday night to reclaim Gary Henderson. But to their undoing, when the demons returned they didn't find him vacant.

When the fiend that had possessed Gary for years was vanquished by Ben's Guardian earlier that evening, it fled in fear, and an amazing thing happened to the broken boy it left behind. The evil spirit that seduced one moment and threatened the next; that thrived on the boy's festering loneliness and anger, had completely abandoned him.

Noise and intimacy have always been enemies. And now the Voice that had kept him perpetually distracted with all manner of loud perversions, chaos and confusion, had gone silent just long enough for him to have a chance to hear a different voice: the still, affectionate voice of hope. While limping home in the dark, leaning on his bike for support, he clearly heard someone or something say to him, "I love you."

He literally had never heard those words spoken to him before, and the stark beauty of that simple phrase stunned the boy. He stopped on the shoulder of the street and looked around to find the speaker. It would have surprised him to see someone with a sheepish grin step out from behind a tree, because he knew in his heart nothing human had made that pronouncement. A half an hour earlier, he'd been soundly defeated by a power that was greater than the darkness that lived in him. Now he couldn't help but wonder if the Source of that power had spoken to him.

A car coming up behind flashed its brights, and he steered his bike to the curb. Not ready to leave the spot where he'd been told he was loved, he engaged the bike's kickstand and sat down on the curb, inconspicuous in the shadow of a mature juniper tree. It was a perfect place to think. *What was it that Keegan said? "Jacks has this crazy idea that the two of you are destined to be friends. He told me that's the way God wants it. He's been praying for you every night…"*

Can a bad person change? There are those who think it impossible—that a bad tree could never bear good fruit. Of course they're right. But what if the tree wasn't all bad? What if it was partly bad and partly good? What if most of the problem was the grade of soil that surrounded it? And if that were true, what if the gardener unearthed that tree and planted it in good soil?

Simone Weil wrote, "Two things pierce the human heart: beauty and affliction." And Gary had experienced both on the same night. Getting whipped in the fight had humbled and shaken him badly, but it had also exposed him to a Power that now seized his imagination. With no one there, at least for the time being, to convince him that he was hopelessly evil, he had the strongest impression that someone very close by was trying to do the opposite. It felt like he was being offered a do-over by someone beautiful and kind, sitting next to him on the curbside.

He'd been given a new name by Ben earlier. Could what he was feeling now be the first blush of a new start? When you have walked intimately with evil as long as Gary had, it's only reasonable that you would recognize beauty when it came for you. The hard part is believing the invitation is for real. It just seems too good to be true. He knew he had a decision to make, and he was smart enough to know that who he'd been wasn't who he wanted to be.

"Yes," Gary said quietly to the One whose touch was so light he would have missed it if he hadn't been seeking it with his heart at that moment.

Months and years later, there would be times when he would doubt he'd actually heard a voice that told him he was loved. In moments of self-loathing, he would try to convince himself that he'd only imagined it. But he would never again succeed in believing that no one cared for him.

He made no promises to himself or to God. He had no clue what would happen next. It was simply time to get up and hobble the rest of the way home. For now, he would hold on to the three words he'd heard there at the corner of Juniper and Apache Drive and see what Monday at school would bring.

When Gary got home, he found it dark and deserted. Figuring that DeeDee, his tortured soul of a mother, was spending the night with some guy somewhere, he fell into bed fully clothed and was asleep before the springs stopped squeaking. Living in the supernatural is exhausting.

Fear is the darkroom where nightmares are developed. So the boy's dreams were usually nightmares and almost always ended in violence—either to himself or someone he was encouraged to despise. On this night the beginning of his dream was not unfamiliar. The inky, ghoulish spirits arrived at his bedroom door pregnant with malice and expecting easy entry into their accustomed haunt. More protean than smoke, they were about to pass through the door to recover the one they'd deserted earlier, when a sudden awareness aborted their advance. The house held a Presence that was to *them* a nightmare.

On the other side of that door was a magnificent being devoted to their doom. Had they still possessed the boy, they could have at least put up a decent battle with the Shining One. But in the next instant, their personal nightmare was on their side of the door as well, flooding the room with a light so intense they had to flee to avoid being unmade. As they jettisoned through the walls of the clapboard house, the stentorian voice of the Guardian accompanied them on their hasty retreat. The neighbors who were awakened by it assumed the rumbling to be late night thunder. But the spirits knew better. All the way back to hell, they were chased and bludgeoned by the words, "You have lost this one forever. The door to his heart is sealed against you. He has chosen another master!"

For Gary, the most significant difference between this dream and those he'd had before was this one wasn't a dream.

CHAPTER

forty

When Ben didn't see Bubba on the Monday morning school bus, he worried maybe he'd hurt him more in the fight than he'd thought. On the way to school, Jacks didn't mention anything about Gary's absence on the bus, but Ben noticed him turn around in home room to check out the ex-bully's empty seat. It looked like the promise he'd made to his cousin on Friday night wasn't going to happen. What neither of them knew was what Gary's Sunday night and Monday morning had been like.

At 2:00 a.m. the night before, Gary had been jolted awake by the sound of a gunshot in his front yard. He got up as quickly as he could and stumbled to the front door. Opening it, he saw a black Dodge Charger idling at the curb with the passenger door ajar. The car backfired again and Gary realized it wasn't a gun that had wakened him. He saw the driver shove a body out of the car. It landed heavily in a heap half in the street and half in the lawn. Then he floored the gas pedal, and the car bucked forward so hard the door slammed shut by itself.

Watching the car, its tinted windows hiding the driver's face, roar away laying black marks of rubber down the street, Gary had no doubt about the name that belonged to the discarded body. He hadn't seen DeeDee since Thursday after school, and even then he'd hardly noticed her. They were accustomed to not communicating and had an uneasy truce to leave one another alone. He needed her to sign the welfare checks, and as long as she worked in a local pizza parlor and could pay the monthly rent and keep the fridge full, he gave her a wide berth.

A few days ago, her current condition wouldn't have phased him. He probably would have left her on the curb. If she was dead, there was nothing he could do about it. If she wasn't, she'd eventually wake up and make her way into the house. But something was different on this night. He felt his pulse racing and knew he had to help. He crossed the yard and smelled the alcohol before he was half way to her. Fearing the worst, he bent over his mother's body. She was alive. Liquor didn't usually knock her out like this, so he figured correctly that she was probably strung out on meth as well.

Favoring his injured right knee, he struggled to pick her up, then carried her in both arms to the house. There he carefully lowered her thin, slack body to the rotting deck of the front porch, where he left her for a moment so he could prop open the front door. After transferring her safely to her bed, he went into the kitchen to put on a pot of coffee. He knew street methadone was dangerous because it works slowly without ever giving the user a "high." So it's easy to overdose, sending you into a deep sleep where you might stop breathing. Fearing this, Gary got enough caffeine in her to make it more difficult for the meth to be absorbed. Then he carried her back outside, where he stood her up on the sidewalk, put her left arm around his shoulders and forced her to walk back and forth with him in the early morning air. To make it more difficult, as she sobered up, she fought him with abandon. But compared to his bulk she was a tiny woman, and he patiently but firmly kept her on track, not once cursing her back or complaining about the pain of his own wounds.

After close to an hour of walking, he thought it was safe to return DeeDee to her bed. When they got there, she abruptly pulled away from him, filling the air with colorful invectives. But he didn't respond and wouldn't leave until he saw her get under the gray sheets and ragged comforter. Then he turned out the lights, closed the door, and limped to his own room.

He lay awake in bed for a long time, thinking about everything that had happened that weekend. He remembered Ben's ultimatum after their fight that he sit at Jacks' table during lunch the next day.

Though he was somewhat anxious about that scenario, there was a part of him that was also curious and maybe even a little eager to join them. That would be the same part of him that knew he'd not been alone walking his bike home from the Hightower farm on Friday night. That Presence was still with him here in his room. Though it had only spoken to him one time, he knew it was still very close and he felt its fondness for him. And why wouldn't the Presence be fond of him, as well as proud? Whether the boy realized it or not, he had just saved his mother's life.

CHAPTER

forty-one

"I don't know what he sees in Mary Anne Wilson," said Philomena Foster to her friend, Iggy Cunningham, as they carried their trays to their usual table in the school cafeteria. It wasn't the first time that "Phil", as everyone called her, had complained to Iggy about Jacks' obvious infatuation with M.A.W. Setting down his tray and pulling a chair up to the circular table, Iggy, probably the second smartest kid at Rockne Intermediate, responded:

"Well, for starters, besides being smokin' hot, and having major academic swag, according to Jacks, she's the most erudite girl he's ever met."

"She is not!" challenged Philomena. "I'm far more air-you-dite than she is."

"I don't want to be critical, Phil," said her friend, gently. "But do you know what erudite means?"

"No," admitted the girl, "but if I did, that's exactly what I'd be!"

"You won't get an argument from me!" laughed Iggy, just as Jacks and Ben arrived at the table.

"Hey, guys!" offered Jacks. "It looks like Mystery Meat Monday again, huh?"

"President Harry Truman created the National School Lunch Program in 1946," replied Iggy, "but he died soon after he ate one of them."

Everybody laughed, except Philomena, who was batting her eyes at Jacks and trying to smile without revealing her new braces.

But because he was Jacks, he noticed them right away and remarked, "I like the new grill work, Phil. It looks good on you." Then he did what he always did after setting down his tray of food. He walked around Ben to the only unoccupied chair and leaned it in against the table as a message to anyone interested in sitting there that it was saved for someone.

There'd been a few times when some kid would snatch the chair up and take it to use at his own table. When that happened, Jacks would quietly get up and find another unused chair to replace it. When Iggy asked him earlier in the semester who he was saving it for, he'd simply replied, "… for somebody really special. Someone you guys are going to love." Of course Philomena assumed that someone was Mary Anne. Iggy wasn't so sure, and Ben just smiled.

In the next moment, a vague shadow fell over Philomena and Iggy. It took a sizeable person to eclipse most of the ceiling light over that part of the cafeteria, but Gary Henderson was up to the task. The cousins looked up and saw the one they'd given up hope of seeing that day. Iggy and Philomena turned and looked up at the very last person they hoped to see every day: "Scary Gary!" they yelled in unison. The sunglasses the infamous bully was wearing to hide his purplish-black shiner and a band aid covering the cut on his left cheek only added to his ominous look. Philomena couldn't help herself. She let out a shriek.

"It's okay, Phil," said Jacks, jumping up and moving to the chair he'd been saving for his tormentor these many weeks. With one hand he turned the chair toward his guest. The other he placed on the boy's massive arm, looked into his sunglasses and said to everyone at the table, "He's here by invitation."

To heighten the drama, Ben grinned and spoke for the first time in public, "That invitation's from both of us. And his name's not Scary Gary anymore. It's Bubba." Philomena's and Iggy's heads jerked quickly from the behemoth behind them to Ben, whose voice they'd never heard before. Their eyes were as big as hockey pucks. "This is mega-cool!" said Iggy. Philomena was just doing her best not to pass out.

CHAPTER

forty-two

A few days later, Ben awoke with a start sometime after midnight. There was a musty, sickly-sweet, meaty odor in the room. It smelled like hamburger that had gone bad, and the boy instinctively cupped his hands over his nose to block it. When he tried to roll over to do a face-plant in his pillow, he found, to his alarm, that he was completely unable to do so. Though he still had some mobility in his hands and forearms, he felt like the rest of his body, from his shoulders to his feet, was pinned to the mattress with a force so great, had it been material, his bones would have been crushed. He could only lie there helplessly, and listen to his cousin speaking to someone whose voice Ben couldn't hear.

"I know you're there, dung god," said Jacks. "You can't hide from me."

A voice materialized from the obsidian darkness just inside the closed door.

"The stench is not my fault," said the visitor, his inhuman voice syrupy with feigned offense. "And why would I hide from you? We are old acquaintances, are we not?"

"Hiding is what you do best," replied the boy, "and the stench is your fault alone. Though you're wasting your time, say now what you've come to say."

"What else *would* I say?" he laughed derisively. Then his voice changed with his mood, now scratchy and complaining. Like fingernails on a chalkboard.

"This is my world, and I can't guarantee your safety if you insist on meddling in it. Besides, your appearances are becoming tiresome."

Jacks didn't answer.

"I've always wondered," said the disembodied voice in the dark. "What *do* you get out of all this?"

"If you could understand that, you wouldn't be who you are," Jacks replied.

Ignoring the comment and sighing, as if Jacks was unjustly testing his longsuffering patience, the obscene horror gloated,

"All is well, then. I have accomplished my purpose tonight. I came to make certain it's you."

"Any attempt you make to stop me will be turned back on you," said the boy. "That you know that and yet persist is remarkable to me."

"My, my, little one. How could I be so foolish to do that?"—the dripping sarcasm exposing his primeval hatred.

"Because you know your time is short," Jacks calmly answered.

"Short, maybe—but not without its pleasures. There is still much that I can do to hurt you. You don't fear me, but I will see what can be done to change that."

Then, sensing Jacks was about to dismiss him, the uninvited interloper, cloaked in shades of darkness, disappeared as stealthily as he had come. Immediately in the bunk above, Ben gasped when the weight that pressed down on him was released.

"Are you all right?" asked Jacks.

"I think so," said his cousin. "That wasn't a Guardian, was it?"

"He used to be," said the younger boy, "and more than a Guardian."

"Why couldn't I see or hear him?" asked Ben.

"Trust me. He was very aware of you. And I believe he thought it in his best interest that you know as little about him as possible. Take it as a compliment. He fears you."

"I doubt that," said Ben.

"Don't underestimate yourself," replied Jacks. "There are no coincidences. You're in this family for a reason, and I have a feeling we're all going to be even more grateful that you are."

"What do you mean?" asked the older boy.

"Let's just say," replied Jacks, "that from now on, we'll have to be more alert. We're about to get his best shot."

"The first fall of snow is not only an event, it is a magical event. You go to bed in one kind of a world and wake up in another quite different, and if this is not enchantment, where is it to be found?"

—J. B. Priestley

CHAPTER

forty-three

The unusual weather continued into Thanksgiving weekend. It was such a warm fall that the Notre Dame football team had to use portable air conditioners and misting fans on the sidelines all the way into November. Business was still strong at Ritter's Frozen Custard on Main Street the week before Thanksgiving, and the ducks and geese on local ponds seemed confused about when to head south. The farm's flowers were getting long and leggy with the mums on their second blooming. The meadow behind the house still needed cutting every week, although the barn couldn't hold any more hay bales. The boys had started stacking them on the barn's south side and covering them with a tarp to keep the rain off.

Soon it was Thanksgiving and the extended Hightower family gathered together around a sumptuous feast. Though Gurney's parents were on a Habitat for Humanity build in India with friends, Babe's mom and dad, the Gossmans from Nyack, New York, had made the journey to be with their daughter for a few days in the last month of her pregnancy. "Doc" Volheim was there, as usual, seated between the turkey and the dressing.

But just across from "Doc" was a newcomer to the holiday spread who merited an extra leaf being added to the dining room table: "Bubba" Henderson, who had gone to church with the family the past two Sundays. When Jacks asked him after school one day if they could pick him up for church that weekend, his answer was, "N-no th-thank you, but maybe I'll meet you there on my bike," which was a long answer for Bubba, who was even more taciturn now than Ben. Jacks correctly figured that his new friend didn't want the Hightowers to see the poverty he lived in, so he gave Bubba the church's location and the time the service started.

And there he was, waiting for them at the front entrance of the bright and burgeoning church, his overworked bike leaning against a column to the side of the front door. In fact, he'd been so excited that he left his house too early and had spent the past half hour dodging the kindly overtures of two enthusiastic volunteers on the church hospitality team and doing his best to avoid eye contact with everyone who passed him on their way into the building.

The problem was he was impossible not to notice. All frown and anxiety stretched over six feet tall, he was dressed in the bright orange shirt his dad bought him off a discount rack at a truck stop. With his coarse, tangerine hair gelled up and combed straight back, he looked like a monstrous carrot in a foul mood. To make it worse, he was in the process of convincing himself that if any of these church folk knew him, they would judge him unworthy of entering their house of worship. He was about to jump on his bike and vamoose when he heard a shout from the parking lot. It was Jacks.

"Hey, Bubba!"

He liked his new name, and offered a tortured smile when Carrie, Jacks and Gurney joined him. Entering the auditorium, Bubba didn't miss the words they passed under: *Taking Our Next Step Toward Christ—Together.* The driving sounds of the drums and bass guitar grabbed his attention, and the worship band filled the building with the numinous lyrics of Hillsong's *The Lost Are Found.*

> *"The lost are found*
> *The blind will see*
> *The lame will walk*
> *The dead will live*
> *And You are God*
> *Forever You will reign*
> *Lord of the Universe, You are near."*

By the time the four of them found seats at the front, Bubba no longer felt out of place. How could he? The Presence who found him on that fateful Friday night more than two weeks ago was everywhere here. In fact, sitting there with the Hightowers, he felt the same way he had when Jacks had grasped his arm in the lunch room and announced, "He's here by invitation!" *Chosen*, he thought, *I feel chosen.*

Is it possible to believe in God without knowing his name? This had been Bubba's predicament since Halloween. In the silence of his bedroom at night, he knew that a Person was now with him, guarding him against the familiar spirits that had made his life a living hell for as long as he could remember. He was certain that this Person was the same One who had told him he was loved. But it bothered the boy that he didn't know His name. Now he was hearing that name in the lyrics of song after song.

When the last melody ended, a man who'd been sitting only a few seats away from Bubba got up and briskly ascended the stairs to the stage. "You're going to love this guy," Jacks whispered to his friend, adding, "He's the real deal."

And, of course, he was. His silver hair framing a smiling face whose age it was impossible to tell, he opened with, "Good morning, beloved. I'm Pastor Mark and there's no place I'd rather be than here with you today. There is much I still have to learn, but one thing I am certain of is this: that no matter who you are, no matter what you've done, you are deeply loved by the only One who has the authority to forgive you and the grace to grant you a new life." At that moment, the pastor turned his head from the left side of the auditorium to the front row on his right, and Bubba was certain he looked directly at him when he declared, "No matter how dark your life has been, God can rescue you from the dominion of darkness and transfer you into the kingdom of the Son he loves. You are not your own, and you don't have to be *on* your own anymore. You were bought with a great price, the death of his Son on the Cross. Every step you've taken in your life, every scar you've received—has brought you to this moment. The Bible says that "Long before he laid the foundations of the world, he has *chosen* you to be made whole in his love."

There's that word again, thought Bubba. *Chosen.* The boy couldn't have explained how he knew every word he'd just heard was true. He knew it the same way he knew that Jacks was the first real friend he'd ever had. He knew it the same way he knew that Love was a Person and had a voice. And now he knew that Person's name.

Just before they parted ways after the service, Gurney put one hand on Bubba's shoulder and with the other handed him a blue and black book with the word *Revolution* printed across the front. Unable to return Gurney's gaze, the diffident boy looked down and opened the cover of the book where he found words that Babe had written a day earlier just under the subtitle, *The Bible for Teen Guys:*

> *To our friend, Bubba. This is the perfect Bible to help a wonderful guy like you become a spiritual warrior. It's the same Bible Jacks loves. May it be a lamp for your feet and a light for your path. —the Hightowers*
>   *P.S. Try reading one chapter a day starting with the Gospel of Matthew. WE LOVE YOU!*

The blush on his cheeks making him look even more like a gigantic carrot, Bubba raised his eyes from the book and opened his mouth to thank his friends, but no words would come. Jacks jumped to his rescue just as he used to for Ben, saying,

"It's a good thing you've got a sizeable basket on that bike, big guy. It'll be just right for your new Bible." With that, he took the book from Bubba and placed it tenderly in the rear basket. Then backing away to give the man-boy room to mount his bike, Jacks watched his quiet friend hop the curb and maneuver his way through the parking lot, calling after him, "Be careful and stay in the bike lanes!"—advice he knew Babe would have given if she'd been there.

The very next Sunday after church, Jacks walked Bubba and his new Bible out to his bike while Babe and Carrie stood back and watched them.

"Babe told me we're setting places for you and your mother at our Thanksgiving meal this coming Thursday," said Jacks. "And she was clear that if you refuse, she's personally going to drive over to your house and force you to get in the car at gunpoint. And Babe's a good shot. My advice is not to refuse."

Bubba smiled and answered, "My mom's too s-sick to come," he stuttered. "B-But my bike and I will be there. What time?"

"Any time after noon," Jacks replied. "And bring your appetite."

Thanksgiving day arrived, the grandfather clock in the Hightower dining room struck one, about five minutes late, as usual, and Bubba was about to put his appetite on display. But first Gurney explained a Thanksgiving tradition he'd borrowed from his boyhood home.

"Each of you sees two tiny kernels of corn next to your plate. One of them represents something you're thankful for today. The other stands for a special prayer request. Feel absolutely free to participate in this or not. You're a trusted member of this family or you wouldn't be here. Now we have to do this fairly quickly, or the food will get cold. I'll go first."

After Gurney thanked God for Babe, (*He does that every year* thought most of those present), he prayed for the wisdom to make an important decision at work. As this process moved around the table, it appeared that only Ben, Bubba and Carrie chose to say nothing, and that was fine. But just before Gurney was about to announce, "Let's eat," Carrie broke in with,

"I'm thankful for my two big brothers, but mostly I'm thankful that I'm getting a little sister soon." Everybody looked at Babe who removed the napkin from over her bulging abdomen, gave a quirky smile while lifting her eyebrows high, and comically pointing both of her index fingers at the baby within said, "We don't know yet!"

Carrie opened her eyes and challenged, "You may not know, Mama, but I do—and I'm not done praying yet."

Everybody laughed, then quickly bowed their heads as Carrie solemnly continued her prayer with a practicality and candor she'd heard her parents model hundreds of times.

"Okay, Lord, it's Thanksgiving and still no snow. Did you forget how? Please, please make it snow soon! We really need a White Christmas this year," she prayed, with all the passion of a newly-minted eight year old. She paused for a moment, then added—"So much snow that church has to be cancelled and we can all stay home with Ben."

While the boys couldn't repress their burst of laughter, the adults at the table responded very differently. Each of them had lived through their share of severe Midwest winters and their instincts were to knock on wood, throw salt over their left shoulder, see if they had a rabbit's foot in their pocket, and make the sign of the Cross.

Carrie didn't know what to think when she finished and looked up, only to see that everyone was looking at her. "It's not that I don't like church," she said self-consciously. "I just like snow more."

"Of course you do, dear. I feel the same way sometimes," said Babe with her fingers crossed under the table.

Years later, Carrie would wonder if her prayer had anything to do with what happened next.

CHAPTER

forty-four

If it's an ill wind that blows no one any good, then the afternoon breezes that began fifteen minutes after the family had finished their Thanksgiving meal, were getting more infirm by the minute. The horizon had gradually turned from the hue of rusty iron filings to an impenetrable grayish blue, somewhere between navy and charcoal. Crayola would never be able to match the colors on display in the sky northwest of the Hightower farm. As the family stood on the porch and watched, an eerie, sickly-yellow pall cast its spell deep within the rapidly approaching front. Whatever the source of this surreal tempest, it wasted no time hiding behind the guise of innocent looking cloud formations. Its monolithic murkiness revealed no clouds at all, but you could feel the menace of the imbedded supercells brewing behind it.

Jacks, sitting on the porch railing between his cousin and Bubba, and just out of the hearing of the rest of the group, muttered lowly: "The Prince of the Power of the Air."

"What'd you say?" asked Ben.

Lost in his own thoughts, Jacks didn't even hear the question but was aware someone had tried to get his attention. "Huh?" he said.

"I asked you what you just said," replied Ben.

"Oh, that. Uh-h-h, there's really nothing to worry about—at least not yet," he answered, still mesmerized by the advancing storm.

As the wind began to pick up, though, he turned to Ben and saw his worried look.

"I'll tell you when to worry, okay?" he said.

Just then, Gurney announced, "This is going to be a bad one, guys. Jacks, Ben—let's put Bubba's bike in the van and get him safely home before this thing breaks. 'Doc,' what do you want to do?"

"I've got some windows open at home. I'll leave with you," replied his colleague.

"Okay, then, everyone else, you'd better head for the basement. The boys and I will join you as soon as we get back."

Just as he was hurrying off, Gurney remembered something and yelled back to his wife:

"Babe darling, could you take Bear out to the barn? He'll keep Pockets calmer during the storm."

She nodded, blew him a kiss and walked Carrie toward the house.

By the time the guys returned, a full-fledged derecho that had begun on the Nebraska/Iowa border 560 miles west was now upon them. Because of the uncommonly warm weather the Midwest had been experiencing, this bow-echo line of thunderstorms had been predicted by the weather service in Des Moines a few days earlier, and was barely outrunning the first real cold front of the year.

The Hightowers and Babe's parents spent most of the rest of the day in the basement watching coverage of the storm on television. They saw video of three cars being blown sideways across a mall parking lot in Rockford, Illinois and a whole neighborhood of trees blown down in Skokie.

By ten o'clock that evening, the straight-line winds that had approached eighty miles per hour seemed to be tapering off, and everyone felt safe about returning upstairs to prepare for bed. What they didn't realize was that the oncoming cold front was pushing one last squall line directly toward them and that many trees in their area had already been compromised by the all-day assault.

Straight-line winds don't sweep across the meadows and farmlands in one, even swath of force. Rather they push harder into certain areas—like probing fingers—influenced by cities, lakes and hills that provide friction to trigger their surges.

At 2:17 a.m., a towering white pine across the street from the farm could no longer resist the windstorm's resolve and, in its fall, took out the neighborhood's power. Not usually a light sleeper, Jacks opened his eyes when he heard the air conditioning turn off. He lay in the dark listening to the cacophony outside: the shingles on the roof rippling to the rhythm of random gusts, the crack of a dead limb on the other side of the house, the wind whistling around the gables like sirens in the night, the creaking and groaning of the ancient oak that canopied his bedroom. It was as if the giant tree were warning him. He rolled out of bed immediately and reached up to shake his roommate.

"Ben, wake up! It's time to worry."

But his cousin didn't move. Jacks shook him harder without effect. Either Ben had taken a sleeping pill, which he never had before, or something more sinister was working on him. The younger boy wasn't sure what to do.

Two minutes later, the roots of the giant tree gave out and 700,000 pounds of solid oak came crashing through the roof directly over the boys' bed. The thunderous impact startled Babe and Gurney awake. She flew from their bedroom and raced down the dark hallway toward the boys' room, while he searched for the flashlight in the top drawer of his dresser.

When Babe opened the door, she could see nothing, but felt the wind blowing down from the gaping hole in their roof. Gurney caught up to her and shined his light toward the beds. What they saw were no beds at all. They were completely flattened and covered by an immense limb from the tree.

"No!" cried Babe. "This can't be!"

CHAPTER

forty-five

No sooner had Babe spoken than she heard a voice behind her in the hallway.

"Don't worry, Babe," said Jacks. "We're both right here."

"Oh, thank God!" she sobbed while turning and pulling the boys into her embrace.

"You mean, 'Thank Jacks'", said Ben. "He must have hauled me out of bed and dragged me out here while I was sleeping."

As he spoke, Carrie, in her super-hero jammies, walked toward them, rubbing her eyes and yawning. At the same time, Babe's parents came shuffling up the steps from the first floor guest room.

Ben added, "I didn't even wake up until after that ginormous tree picked us out for target practice. This is too crazy."

No, this is too uncanny, thought Jacks. *Way too uncanny.*

"Well, we can't stand in the hallway for the rest of the night," said Gurney. "The important thing is everyone's alive and well, thank God. Now we should all try to get back to sleep. I'll call the insurance company in the morning."

As he closed the door to the demolished room, his father-in-law noted, "At least it's stopped raining."

"Thank God for small favors, too," said Gurney.

Babe spent the rest of the night cuddling with Carrie in her princess bed, while Jacks and Ben shared the king with Gurney. And though all the children quickly returned to sleep, their parents lay awake until dawn; Babe thinking about the horror of what might have been, and Gurney rehearsing the steps it would take to get the damage to the house fixed.

That final storm brought with it the first winter temperatures of the season. In fact, sometime after 4:00 a.m., Gurney had to get out of bed and go down to the basement to fire up a generator so he could turn on the furnace.

You find out who your real friends are in a crisis, and the Hightowers had many they could count on in their church and at the university. While Gurney was trying to get an insurance adjuster out to the house, Babe was on her cell phone with confidants from their Bible study small group. Before noon on Black Friday, a contractor friend from the church, who had access to a huge crane, had gathered a small army of skilled volunteers to help Gurney remove the tree and patch up the roof to keep out the colder weather. By the time Babe had served up countless cups of hot chocolate, plates of turkey sandwiches and pumpkin pie, and steaming bowls of chili to the workers, the sun was fading, but the roof was secure enough to ensure the family's safety that night. The boys would sleep on cots in their bedroom until another bunk bed could be found, or they could camp out on the carpet by the basement fireplace if they wanted.

Babe's parents left for New York, "Doc" Volheim spent the day with the cleanup crew on the ground, and Bubba rode his bike over to put his considerable strength to work removing sections of the tree to the background roar of chainsaws buzzing.

That night, spooning in bed, as was their custom, Babe and Gurney were tying up the day's loose ends.

"We dodged a bullet last night, didn't we?" she said. "This could have been the worst weekend of our lives."

"But it wasn't," he replied. "Instead, we got to host a work party for some of our best friends and now have enough firewood to last us ten years."

Babe's body went rigid, and she pulled ever-so-slightly away from him.

"Is it possible to be *too* optimistic?" she asked, a bit peeved. "Doesn't anything ever rattle you?"

Gurney didn't respond to either question, and eventually she rolled back toward him and said,

"I'm sorry. That was unfair of me. It's just that when you shined your flashlight into the boys' room last night…"

"I know," he said. "I almost fainted."

They lay there quietly for a moment, dead tired but still thinking.

"Sometimes I wish we could just pack up and move our family to a lonely mountaintop where nothing could touch them."

"There are killer storms and shallow-rooted trees in the mountains," he replied.

"So now you're a pessimist, huh?"

"Maybe just a realist," he yawned, drawing her into his arms. "Life is going to happen no matter where we take them, and life can be lethal. All we can do is raise them to have the courage to face it."

"Fortune favors the brave," whispered Babe, giving in to complete exhaustion.

"Now who's the optimist?" smiled Gurney, sensing she was too far gone to respond.

CHAPTER

forty-six

U.S. Coast Guard Meteorological Station
Michigan City, Indiana
Saturday, November 30
8:21a.m.

"Hey, Stevie, put your birth-control glasses on and come see this," said Chief Petty Officer Dennis "Sparky" Cramer to his subordinate and good friend, Seaman Stephen Matteson. Birth-control glasses are standard, military-issued eyeglasses known for their lack of aesthetic appeal, i.e., ugly enough to function as contraceptives.

Putting down the sports page of the South Bend Tribune, the younger man, who had just returned from a three day leave, grabbed his coffee cup and walked over to his friend's cubicle.

"What's up, sir?" he said, scanning the computer screens surrounding the station's most gifted meteorologist.

"Captain Waltz says the brass wants a winter predictor model from us for the Great Lakes by 1500 hours tomorrow, and I don't like what I've been seeing the past few days. Three nights ago, we got a picture in from a German weather ship at the Circle, *The Laurenberg,* reporting *this* anomaly developing just north of the Chukchi Sea," said the chief, pointing to an image on the far-left screen.

Forgetting himself, the second year seaman exclaimed, "My God, Sparky! That's impossible, isn't it?" as he leaned in to take a closer look at the image.

"VIRTIS never lies," responded Sparky, referring to the prized, Visible and InfraRed Thermal Imaging Spectrometer instrument on board the German vessel. "What you're looking at is something like a gigantic hurricane with two dark, dangerous eyes. Its two polar vortices have morphed into a mega-winter storm."

"How did it happen?" asked Stevie. "Global warming?"

"Nothing like that," said the officer. "It's El Nino. For the past two months I've been concerned about the amount of warm air he's been pushing into the upper Midwest. The Kid's doing his job too well. Within hours the main force of this subtropical jet stream is going to converge with a polar jet stream containing a wind max of 130 knots. The result will probably be a *bombogenesis* event that could give us a storm of unprecedented magnitude. You can see from this image," he said, pointing to one of the screens, "that it's already begun. The whole thing is cooling and sinking into a deep, swirling atmospheric pit. And the latest pictures from *The Laurenberg* have confirmed my fears. We've got a thousand-mile-wide double polar vortex revolving wildly like a solid body and on a collision course with the Midwest. Each vortex feeds off the other one and is separated by a ring of impossibly frigid air called a 'cold collar.' That collar is about to reach the vast expanse of the Great Lakes. When that happens," he paused and leaned in to the screen in front of him. "Hell, it's already happening. The unseasonably warm waters are meeting the super-chilled, rotating system and setting up a blizzard-making machine that could last for weeks."

"A self-sustaining, atmospheric juggernaut," said the seaman. "Captain Waltz isn't going to like this at all."

"He can authorize his own transfer to the Coast Guard station at Miami Beach whenever he wants," said Sparky Cramer. "But it's you and I, and about sixty-five million other people in the Midwest who are going to have to figure out how to survive what's coming."

CHAPTER

forty-seven

"We lost a lot of flowers last night," said Gurney at the breakfast table on Monday morning.

"It was long overdue," replied Babe, looking out the kitchen window at the frost-covered scene.

"You know how you can tell we live in the Midwest?" offered Jacks, dishing up a bowl of oatmeal at the stove.

"I feel a joke coming," said his father.

"Let me guess first," quipped Ben, looking at Babe with pleading eyes. "Your parents let you skip school to go bow-hunting?"

"Nice try, kid," chuckled Gurney. "The answer is you learn there are only two seasons: winter and road construction."

"You're both wrong," replied Babe, who hadn't missed that Ben referred to Gurney and her as his parents. "It's that we actually greet people in the Midwest when we pass them on the street," she said.

"And we eat a lot of puppy chow," added Carrie, grabbing a handful of the stuff on her way to the table.

"Not for breakfast you don't, young lady," said Babe, holding her hand out to confiscate the treat.

"Are you guys done?" asked Jacks, coming close to being irritated. "I was going to make a serious observation—sort of."

"We're sorry, dear. What was it?"

"I forgot," he said, which made Ben laugh. Then he remembered. "Wait, I've got it. Yesterday outside the church, I saw a student from Notre Dame wearing a furry-hooded parka on top with shorts and tennis shoes on the bottom."

"He had tennis shoes on his bottom?" laughed Gurney.

"Sometimes I feel like the only adult around here," said Babe, shaking her head and adding, "I saw him too, Jacks. He's probably from another part of the country or world and is simply confused by our weather. It looked like he tried to dress for any contingency."

"Well, no shorts or tennis shoes on my bottom today," said Gurney. "It's twenty-eight degrees out there, and I…"

"Daddy, look out the window!" cried Carrie suddenly. "Hurray!" she shouted.

The whole family turned as one and saw the biggest, most beautiful snowflakes they could imagine feathering down from the light gray sky, spinning, dancing, swirling, sticking to whatever they touched.

It had begun.

As if the first snow of the season had reminded him of something, Gurney gulped down the last of his coffee and announced,

"Gotta run, gang. Twenty-eight freshmen are waiting to be enlightened." With that, he rose and circled the table, stopping to kiss each of the kids on the forehead and Babe on the lips.

"Stay warm today, darling," she said. "Will you be home for lunch?"

"I wish," he replied. "We've got our last departmental meeting of the year set for noon at *Doc Pierce's*. So you'll have to handle the insurance adjuster yourself if she shows up. You all right with that?"

"I'll have to be," she said. "You just be careful on those slippery roads."

He should have listened to her.

CHAPTER

forty-eight

After the lunch meeting, Gurney was rising to leave with the rest of his colleagues, when Dean Stratton approached him from the far end of the table.

"Dr. Hightower, I'd like to talk with you for a moment about your upcoming trip to Chicago."

"Sure, Dean," said Gurney, doing his best to hide his anxiety about being late for an appointment at Notre Dame that afternoon.

"I don't have to tell you what your week at Argonne National Laboratory could mean for you and the university. Alexei Abrikosov is the world's foremost theoretical physicist or he wouldn't have won the Nobel. You're going to have to be on your game, son."

"I have even higher hopes than that, sir," replied Gurney. "If my research on cold atomic systems is valid, and it is, then Dr. 'A' is the one person who can help me develop my mathematical models into actual sensors that will be able to detect all nuclear and explosive materials within a radius of ten miles. Give me one week with Abrikosov and his team, and I'll know whether or not that's possible. Then give us a year to design a defense system, and not only will airports be safe again, but no rogue terrorist will ever be able to pull off another Boston Marathon type bombing."

"Well, the fact that Argonne has invited you to spend the week before Christmas with them gives you an idea of how urgent they think your project is. I'm advising you to take a few days off for prep and rest before you leave."

"I appreciate the advice, Dean, but no one knows better than you that faculty at Notre Dame actually teach classes. Don't worry; I'll be fine. And if the snow allows, I'll be in Chicago bright and early on the morning of the eighteenth."

"All right, then," said his boss, "If I don't see you again before then, good luck, and Godspeed."

"I'll take the Godspeed," said Gurney, looking down at the time on his iPhone. "I've got to fly," he blurted, hurrying toward the restaurant door.

When Gurney crossed the wintry parking lot at two fifteen, he knew he was going to be late for a 2:30 mentoring session with a student back at the university—unless he could gain some time by making all the green lights and pressing the cars in front of him to go a little faster. It was a bad strategy that only got worse.

At the intersection of Main and Catalpa, he'd already decided to cross in the left lane half-way through a yellow light when the driver in front of him made the opposite decision. He had to slam on his brakes to avoid running up the guy's bumper. But because of the snow, braking wasn't enough and the only way he could avert a collision was to swerve into the right lane at the last second—cutting off the driver approaching the red light in that lane.

Usually drivers in Northern Indiana are wary of accidents during snow showers and customarily give each other a wide berth and a modicum of grace on the occasion of the season's first snow. But Gurney picked the wrong guy to irritate that day. Sitting behind him in a black Ford F150 pickup was manic forty-one-year-old, Robert Thrasher, who lived in an apartment above *The Kitty Litter* bar in Mishawaka. His acquaintances nicknamed him "Dusk" because he never spoke to anyone until that time of day. Only one other person, his accomplice and roommate, knew that Thrasher was one of the two "Pillowcase Burglars" responsible for more than fifty break-ins in the neighborhoods of Michiana.

In each instance, they waited in their truck down the street until they saw a garage door go up. After the owner drove away, Thrasher would get out and casually walk to the back of the house, while his accomplice stayed in the car surveilling the target and neighborhood for any possible trouble. Meanwhile, if the burglar encountered a loud alarm system or a dog, he simply hurried back to the truck and they left the area quickly. If not, he was adept at breaking in the back door or prying open a defenseless window. Once in, he sought out the master bedroom. There he efficiently snatched up jewelry, cash and any prescription drugs he could find, brazenly dumping them into a pillow case he'd taken from the victim's bed. In each burglary he was back out of the house in less than five minutes from the time he entered it. The main reason the pilfering pair hadn't been caught yet was as much a problem with muted home security systems as it was their own cleverness. Most systems are programmed to alert the homeowners first and not the police when they are triggered. By the time law enforcement arrived, the rapid robbers were long gone.

Now, as the snow continued to fall, the more unhinged one of the burglars crept forward at the red light until his 4X4 made jarring contact with the bumper of the white Toyota in front of him. Gurney was jolted by it and instinctively looked up at the rearview mirror with his hands held high in disbelief. What he saw was a wild-eyed, beefy buffoon flipping him the bird and mouthing obscene advice that would have been anatomically impossible for Gurney to accomplish. As soon as Jacks' dad looked away, hoping to defuse the situation by ignoring it, Thrasher scanned the vicinity for police cars and then laid on his horn.

His face turning red with embarrassment, Gurney could hardly wait for the light to change. When it did, he slowly crossed the intersection, careful this time not to spin out on the snow-covered road. After he built up his speed, he glanced at the mirror and saw that the truck was following him dangerously close. When the fool started blaring his horn again, Gurney knew the guy was spoiling for a fight and would follow him all the way to campus if he could. This could get very ugly fast. Shaken by the incident, his first instinct was to call and cancel the appointment at school and drive straight home where he had a gun secreted away in his den.

A few years ago, he'd thought he was going to have a hard time talking Babe into letting him purchase a weapon for home defense. But when he'd explained to her that if certain terrorist networks discovered the results of his research and the implications it would have for severely restricting their activity, they might decide to take their revenge on him or his family, she could see that having a gun at their semi-isolated farm only made practical sense. "In fact," she'd replied. "I'm going to the shooting range with you." She never ceased to surprise him.

But the last thing Gurney wanted was for this chowderhead riding his bumper to know where he lived, so as the two of them approached another street crossing, he made a dangerous, split-second decision that seemed to work. He feigned that he was passing Douglas Road when, at the last instant, he turned left onto it—too late for the thief behind to do the same.

"Dusk" Thrasher laid on his horn one more time when he saw Gurney outmaneuver him. But he wasn't too worried about it.

"Nice move, white Toyota-boy!" he yelled. "But I've got your plate number." *And my girlfriend works at the DMV,* he thought, smiling in anticipation. He had to turn on his wipers so he could see through the thickening veil of falling snow. "Merry Christmas, my new friend," he said driving past the mall. "I'll be seeing you soon. So spend a lot on Christmas presents. You've made Santa's naughty list this year."

CHAPTER

forty-nine

In 1897, when Abraham "Bram" Stoker introduced London to a race of evil beings he called vampires in his Gothic novel, *Dracula*, he got a lot of things right about The Shadows. They fear the blood of Christ more than they crave the blood of men, and therefore, they have no fondness for the Cross; they hate each other almost as much as they do those created in the image of God; they are terrified of their own dark master, and they cannot inhabit a human being unless invited in. Robert "Dusk" Thrasher, one of the Pillow Case Bandits, wasn't alone in his pickup on the day Gurney cut in front of him on Grape Road. The demon he'd invited in never left him alone. It had, in fact, been sent by the Evil One years earlier with this particular day in mind. Ever on the lookout for an opportunity to oppress the Hightower family, it recognized Gurney immediately in his car and embellished his minor offense until Thrasher was whipped into an uncalled for, meteoric rage over it. Even if he hadn't scribbled down Gurney's license plate, The Shadow would have remembered it for him. And so, the arrogant thief brooded and cursed for the next several days about how he was going to get even with the guy in the white Toyota.

Bobby Thrasher had been a good looking kid once and at times had used that to manipulate people and charm his way out of trouble. But more often than not, his acid tongue did him in. And it wasn't long before cigarettes and alcohol wrinkled his skin, stained his teeth and stole the light from his eyes. He was only forty-one years old, but with his grayish complexion and thinning hair, he easily could pass for fifty-five.

He inherited his name and size from his father, who'd been an offensive lineman for the Mishawaka Cavemen in high school. But just like his namesake, he dropped out of school after his junior year, bought a truck and half-heartedly tried to make a living with it—hauling wood in the warm months when he felt like it and plowing snow in the cold ones on the few occasions he got out of bed early enough to help people get to work. He inherited his nasty mouth and sense of victimhood from his mother who was never happy unless she was making someone else unhappy.

It says something about our world that, regardless of age or culture, most people have twice as many negative words in their vocabularies as positive ones. And if hurtful words were bars of gold, "Dusk" Thrasher would have been Fort Knox. He was a diseased and twisted bramble of a soul, and his words were always thorny and cankerous.

When the sun went down, his mouth switched on, and then he made up for not speaking during the day. On this evening, he was in the middle of a fervent diatribe against a local specialty coffee shop he frequented before the blizzard closed it and every other business in the area.

"So I said to the dopey barista: 'All I want is a large coffee. I don't want a MochaChocoLatteYayaFreeYourLadyMarmalade! Just give me a damn cup of black coffee!"

"I know, right?" replied his roommate, Rooster Barry. Late that afternoon, both men had taken the back steps down from the bedroom they shared over the bar. They went to the same scruffy rear table they always chose, where Dusk threw himself heavily into a cane-backed chair and drove his hunting knife into the pockmarked table top. They drank steadily for two hours until the sign over their heads matched their condition: *Beer is the answer, but I can't remember the question.*

Thrasher had a small following at The Kitty Litter bar where he opined loudly every evening about all manner of perceived injustices. Someday he was going to be in a position to "stick it to the man," puncture the tires of the next driver who cut in front of him, find something at the dollar store that's worth a dollar, and send every ethnic group he didn't like to the backside of Mars. He cashed his welfare check and took every entitlement he could get from the government. But it still wasn't fair that so many had so much more than he did. Federal income redistribution was just too slow and sparse for him.

Because he robbed only from those he considered wealthy, he saw himself as a kind of Robin Hood—but without the tights or the merry men or giving any of his ill-gotten gains to his poor friends. The fact was he really had no friends. Now and then, lonely women with hollow eyes would sidle up next to him at the bar. But they were usually lonelier after he had used them. He'd always had a deep-seated fear of intimacy that made it impossible for him to be in a close relationship—physically or emotionally. But he found himself in an odd Catch-22. He didn't like people enough to hear their stories, yet he had an acute awareness that life had no meaning if he was alone all the time. His answer was someday to buy a bar where people could share their sad stories all night long without him having to really listen to a single one of them.

Dusk was good at two things: never being apprehended by the law and turning his stolen goods into cash. He was always one step ahead of the authorities. Other than a few traffic tickets, he had no record at all with the police—a fact he often bragged about at the bar. He claimed to have a sixth sense for knowing when they were closing in on him. He'd also figured out a way never to risk being caught on camera with his merchandise or to have his face seen by a paying customer. He simply did all of his selling on e-commerce platforms by executing online consumer-to-consumer transactions. Of course, this required him to obtain numerous fake IDs, addresses and bank cards, but he was a gifted con man.

If he had anyone who resembled a friend, it was short but thick-set Connor Barry, who loved to drink so much he named a boy from his first marriage, "Miller Lyte," and a girl from his second, "Margarita Olympia." But he hadn't seen either of them for fifteen years. Dusk had long ago nicknamed the laconic alcoholic, "Rooster," not for the color of his hair but for the flaps of bright pink skin that hung from his fleshy neck like a banty rooster's wattle.

Barry, now in his mid-forties, had attached himself to Dusk the first time they'd met two years earlier at the South Bend Motor Speedway, where, by chance, they sat next to one another in the bleachers on Demolition Derby Night. Dusk was first impressed by the composure of the chunky little man beside him. Every time the crowd erupted over the next stupendous crash, Barry simply sat there with an inscrutable grin on his face.

After about an hour of it, Dusk finally asked him: "What are you—some kind of stupid?"

"No way, Jose. Today is opposite day for me," the purplish-nosed man said with a straight face. "I was going to attend the South Bend Civic Symphony tonight, so I came here instead."

Thrasher did a double-take. "You yankin' my chain?" he asked.

"No way, Jose. Even if I was gonna yank it, I'm doing the opposite now."

"What?!" cried Dusk, not knowing whether to laugh or thump this joker upside the head. "Are you for real?" The obnoxious bully shook his head in disbelief and held up a clenched right fist, adding: "And if you want me to chuck you onto the track, just say 'No way, Jose' one more time."

"Well," Barry answered, without flinching. "I was going to sit by the beautiful blonde three rows in front of you, but it's opposite day, so I picked someone ugly to sit by. If you're going to throw me somewhere, make it three rows down."

Dusk was stunned by the stranger's chutzpah and at first didn't know how to respond. After standing there with his mouth open for a moment, he, too, did the opposite of what he normally would have done: he decided to laugh—and much too loudly to suit the people who sat around him. "You're such a weird, little guy aren't you?" he roared. "I like that!"

And so began the oddest and most notorious burglary team ever to plague North Central Indiana. It was a marriage made in Mordor. Dusk was so dark and abrasive that no one else could stand to be around him for long, but he needed an accomplice. And Rooster was eccentric and lonely enough not to care how he was treated. After several beers and only one partly demolished car left moving on the track, the two had struck up a strange partnership.

One would supply the liquor, and the other would do whatever he was told. For Rooster, that meant planning and helping to carry out burglaries all over greater South Bend.

Within days of meeting, they'd become roommates living over the bar. Even though Rooster didn't talk much, he had developed a tic for repeating an inane phrase over and over until it drove his partner crazy. After frequently getting slapped hard on the back of the head for saying, "No way, Jose" ad nauseum, he changed to the nonword, "supposibly," and for weeks used it to answer just about every comment Dusk made to him. Recently, getting accustomed to the knots on his noggin, he'd switched to the annoying phrase, "I know, right?" and his roommate was close to needing a strait jacket from it.

What kept Dusk from strangling Rooster was the success they had at burgling. He already had more than enough cash to purchase The Kitty Litter from its disinterested, aging owner. At 20,000 dollars, the quasi-popular, southside bar was a steal of a deal—a concept with which he was very familiar. In fact, if they could pull off just a few more profitable heists, he felt he'd have ample funds to fix up the place and maintain it for years to come. And the clever thief knew exactly who his next victim was.

CHAPTER

fifty

There is a part of you in every snowflake. Water is evaporating from your skin at this moment, and finding its way into the atmosphere. You are also exhaling approximately a liter of water per day into the air, and most of this returns to the earth again within a week in the form of snow or rain. Even if you contribute only one quadrillionth of the water content in a snowflake, there are still roughly a thousand of your molecules in every snowflake that falls.

When Gurney returned home late that afternoon, he found the kids frolicking in the front yard, and Babe, in her last month of pregnancy, watching them build a snowman that had countless molecules of their own in its construction. The scene so reminded him of a classic Currier and Ives print that he decided not to disclose his unsettling experience in the car that day, and instead entered into the light-hearted activity with enthusiasm. In fact, he was so engaged that, had Babe been paying closer attention to his frenetic behavior, she might have guessed he was hiding something. But when he playfully challenged her to a contest, her complete focus turned to helping Carrie gather the snow and sculpting the shapely appendages of an unusually attractive snowwoman, so Gurney's ruse went unnoticed. What he and the boys couldn't approach in artistic panache compared to the girls, they tried to make up for in sheer size and odd proportion. Using two step-ladders and brute strength, their creation resembled a ten-foot tall cross between Shrek and a gigantic, three-layered amoeba.

By the time they had all finished dinner that evening, Gurney had, for good or bad, succeeded in putting the troubling incident with the maniacal driver that afternoon out of his head. Besides, by then, the weather had the complete attention of the whole family. The snow fell unabated, and the kids began to kindle the hope that school might be cancelled the next morning. Babe turned on the nightly news and everyone gathered around to hear the weather forecast:

"Get out your sleds and snow boots, kids," announced Jeff Murray, chief meteorologist for WGN Chicago. "The bizarre double polar vortex that has been pushing a vast low pressure front across the Canadian plains seems to have stalled over the Great Lakes, setting up an unprecedented snow-making mechanism that should keep us shoveling the white stuff through Christmas vacation. We're expecting lower temperatures and eight to twelve inches tonight, with steady accumulation every day for the next few weeks."

"Awesome," said Ben. Carrie's eyes were shining. But by morning their hopes were dashed. Even though most of the schools in the Windy City were closed that day, Chicago is not South Bend, and the Indiana students had no such luck. Michiana snow crews are experienced, crack units of "snowbusters" who take pride in keeping the roads cleared and the public schools open. And in a peculiar way, the clouds cooperated with the workers by dumping most of the day's snow in the late afternoon and early evening, then slackening off during the night when the crews redoubled their efforts. It went this way for another week, and the kids grew accustomed to their new schedule in what had become a winter wonderland of sorts. As soon as the boys got home from school, they would finish their chores quickly, then head outside with Carrie for as much winter action as they could get in before dark.

After hooking the plow up to their tractor, Ben cleared a path around the fence line so the kids could take turns exercising Pockets. Somehow, riding always seemed more fun in the snow, and the gentle horse appeared to agree. The pond had finally frozen after a few weeks of cold temperatures, so they laced up their ice skates and using three snow shovels, cleared serpentine paths all over the ice, which made for endless skating challenges.

Eventually, with a suggestion from Gurney, they discovered the most excitement they could have on their little farm. With an accumulation of at least two feet of snow on the ground, the boys plowed a small mountain of it about ten feet away from the barn under the door of the hayloft. After they attached a thick rope to the pulley hook just above the loft's opening, they had an attraction that Disney World couldn't match. Where else could you barrel down a couple of planks of squeaking wood, grab a piece of braided hemp and launch yourself fifteen feet out an elevated window, only to time the release of your swing so perfectly that you free fall through the air into a forgiving mound of fleecy white magic?

Things were going along great until they invited Bubba over after school on Friday. When he got off the bus with the boys, Babe watched them from the living room window. Her heart was moved at the sight of the brawny man-boy trudging through the snow in his beat up tennis shoes, his massive frame thinly covered by a threadbare, faded blue jean jacket. She greeted them at the front door.

"Welcome home, guys—and especially you, young man," she said, smiling warmly at Bubba, who instinctively removed his baseball cap. "There's warm oatmeal cookies for all of you in the kitchen." Then taking her winter coat from a hook in the hallway, she said. "Milk's in the fridge. You're in charge of Carrie until I get back."

"Where you goin', Babe?" asked Jacks, who knew his mother well enough to have a pretty good idea of her destination.

"I just remembered something I had to pick up at the mall. I'll be home in twenty minutes."

With that, she pregnant-waddled toward the door while her sons followed their stomachs into the kitchen. Bubba raced in front of her, his soggy sneakers slapping on the hard wood floor. When he opened the door for her, Babe instinctively hugged him.

"You have a servant heart, Gary," she said to the boy who was too bashful to look up.

Then, bending over to catch his line of vision, she articulated what her whole family felt—words that would stay with Bubba for the rest of his life:

"You're always welcome in this home, dear."

"Th-thank you, ma'am," he stuttered, following her through the door, and lightly taking her left arm to make sure she got down the icy front steps safely. On her way to the detached garage, she looked back and saw him watching.

"It's nice to know chivalry isn't dead!" she called, opening the garage door with her remote. "I'll be back in a few minutes!"

When Bubba entered the kitchen, Jacks said, "Hey, big guy. None of these cookies have your name on 'em. You'd better stake your claim."

"Sh-she called me 'dear.' I l-l-like her," stammered Bubba.

"You'll have to get in line," replied Ben. "So does everyone else."

CHAPTER

❖━━━━━━❖

fifty-one

When Babe returned from the mall, she found Bubba in the kitchen patiently waiting for her boys to put their snow boots on. Standing there with an enigmatic grin on her face, a large shopping bag from Macy's in her right hand, and a smaller one from Sear's in her left, she asked:

"Where's Carrie?"

"In her room reading another Junie B book," answered Jacks.

"Smart girl," said Babe. "Did you save her a cookie?"

Guilty as charged, all three boys looked away from Babe toward the empty plate on the table. If pathetically staring at a few crumbs had creative powers, a heaping plate of cookies would have materialized right then.

"It's okay, guys," she laughed. "I stashed a few away for her."

The relief in the room was palpable. Such was their respect for this remarkable woman.

"Now," she said. "This is 'Be kind to Preggers Week', so I need the two of you to go outside for a bit and leave Gary with me. It won't be long and he'll be swinging from the loft with you."

It was obvious what was happening, so both of them disappeared immediately.

Babe looked at the polite but uncomfortable boy and said:

"Gary, do you trust me?" she asked.

"S-s-sure, Mrs. H-H-H…"

"Mrs. "H" is all you need to say. I like that name. From now on, it's your special name for me, and you'll be the only one I'll let call me that, okay?"

He nodded.

"Now," she paused. "Do you trust me?"

Another nod.

"Then you have to let me give you your Christmas presents a little early. Why wait until Christmas day when you could enjoy them right now? Merry Christmas, dear" she said, handing him the bags containing a navy blue winter parka with gloves and a stocking cap in the pockets, and a pair of Timberland, size thirteen, water-proof boots.

"This should level the playing field for you with my boys. They need someone who can beat them at their own winter games."

"I c-c-could already do that, ma'am," he said shyly.

Babe chuckled and said, "I bought those boots extra big. If they don't fit, we can get you another pair of socks."

Sitting on a kitchen chair, he pulled the leather lace-ups over his feet and turned to her with a smile that told her they were perfect.

"Now, get out there and show those urchins of mine how to do it."

An inexpressible joy was on his face, and she urged him again.

"Get going—now! I mean it. There's not much daylight left."

Having never received a Christmas present before, Bubba burst from the house and ran to join the boys in the hayloft.

They didn't get as many swinging jumps in as normal that day because every time Bubba landed in the snow, his weight packed the mound down so far the boys had to suspend the jumping to shovel more snow and rebuild the pile. With the sky darkening rapidly, Jacks declared,

"One more jump apiece, guys! Bubba, you're first!"

The gigantic teen climbed the ladder quickly and leaped onto the loft floor. He was going to put everything he had into this jump The other boys stood on each side of the snow pile below, antici-pating something special. A charging water buffalo had nothing on their over-sized friend that afternoon. They could hear him thundering along the wooden floor planks long before he appeared at the opening. Finally he arrived, ferocious in his joy and determined to swing higher and farther than ever before. But when he grasped the rope, his substantial weight caused it to snap in two with a sound like the crack of a whip. A look of terror frozen on his face, Bubba plummeted head first into the snowy hump below and completely disappeared from sight.

Jacks and Ben didn't know what to do. Should they climb the hill and try to pull him out? Before they could decide, they heard a muffled cry from deep within the mound:

"Th-th-that was AWESOME!"

Doubled over with laughter, they did their best to scale the pile and give a hand up to the boy who had just made an unforgettable jump. He'd gone to the farm that day as just a friend. He lumbered home a legend, sporting an old pair of snow shoes the boys had found in the barn.

Two nights later, Babe and Gurney went to bed earlier than normal, setting the alarm for 5:00 a.m. so he could get to Chicago in time to put in a full day of work at the Argonne laboratory. He'd completely forgotten about the traffic incident earlier in the week and the lunatic who'd ridden his bumper. Now, taking off his glasses and setting them on the night stand, he said,

"Are you sure you're okay with me leaving tomorrow?"

"If by that, you mean, 'Do I think I'm going to have the baby this week?': no, I'm not," she answered.

"You're not okay with me leaving?"

"You know what I meant. I'm not having the baby this week, but neither am I going to have you moping around the house when your duty lies in Chicago—along with your mind and heart."

"My heart is here, though I can't always guarantee the same for my mind," he said, looking into her eyes while gently placing his hand on her ripened tummy. "And I never mope. I might skulk, or occasionally slink, but I never mope."

"That's true," she laughed, "so slink out of here without waking the kids up tomorrow, and get back to us no later than the twenty-third. You're getting a homemade Christmas present sometime this year that should weigh about seven pounds."

"Whoa, that's a heavy cherry pie," he replied.

"Try not to use the word 'heavy' around me for a while, okay? And her name's not going to be Cherry."

"Then how about Pumpkin?" he asked.

"Say goodnight, Mr. Pieman," she said, rolling over.

"Goodnight, Mr. Pieman," she heard back as he spooned in next to her for the last time in more days than he planned on.

CHAPTER

fifty-two

Plague, a gargantuan wild boar, was in a raiding mood. What's the most dangerous animal in Michigan? It's not the wolf, black bear or wolverine. Neither is it the mosquito, though the northern woods are filled with their menacing buzz in the summer. No, the most dangerous animal in Michigan is one that never stepped a cloven hoof there until a little over a decade ago. It's the feral hog.

In 1912, thirteen Eurasian wild boars were shipped from Germany and transported to Hooper Bald, North Carolina by two

American sportsmen for hunting purposes. Tracking down and shooting the often massive and always dangerous hogs became so popular that scores of privately owned, high-fence hunting preserves flourished all over the south, requiring many more swine shipments from the dark forests of Eastern Europe. But the cunning beasts often escaped their enclosures, raiding farms and mating with domestic pigs, until they eventually established wild hog populations in forty-seven U.S. states.

Even though it's a Class D felony with severe penalties to import wild hogs across state lines, at the beginning of this millennium, less than honest hunting enthusiasts conveyed clandestine U-Haul trailers filled with boars they caught in Texas. They drove north through the night and eventually released them in the forest region bordering Lake Huron in Michigan's Lower Peninsula. Some of these feral hogs were the largest ever seen in the U.S, a few of them upwards of five hundred pounds. Within five years, herds of medieval swine were the bane of farmers all over the fertile area known as The Thumb.

Digging up fields and lawns, killing livestock and spreading disease, the wild boars of Michigan are changing the eco-system. The most prolific large mammal on the face of the earth, they boast razor sharp tusks, a bottomless appetite, no natural predators, and nothing seems able to stop them. Even though hunting them is always in season and doesn't even require a license, their sows produce so many litters a year their numbers keep swelling.

Feral hogs are always on the move, searching out new sources of food. They usually travel in family groups, or sounders, made up of two or more sows and their young. Boars are normally solitary, joining a group only to breed or raid a farm. And on this night, the largest boar in the Lower Peninsula, named Plague by his sounder, was rounding up five other boars for an evening raid on a local farmer's sheep pen. While his accomplices tore up the posts with their tusks and snouts, lifting the net wire fence off the ground, Plague, smelling the fear of his victims, entered the pen and swiftly killed enough ewes for a nocturnal feast. The assault was so efficient that the six feral hogs dragged the carcasses into the shadows of the neighboring woods before the farmer could respond to the bleating of his terrified sheep.

Plague was unusually malevolent—even for a wild boar. Unlike most animals, hogs get new names from their family as they mature. The feral pig who started life as Rumblebelly, grew into an imposing hog known as Gnawbone, for the way he finished off his challengers to become consensus leader of the sounder. By the time he had grown into a gargantuan eight-hundred-pound boar that would never be challenged again, his sycophantic followers called him, Plague, which in porcine was the same word as Death. Plague, who, at fifty-six inches in shoulder height, was as big as a brown bear, and beyond dangerous for many reasons other than his enormous size. He was most perilous for the toxic bacteria that grew on his curved tusks and jagged incisors. One piercing from either diseased tusk or bite from his obscene teeth that broke the skin, and whoever opposed him was as good as dead. Pigs, in general, explore the world with their mouths. In Plague's case, the simple foraging with his noxious snout marked a tortuous trail of pestilence and extinction.

In keeping with the species' practical nomenclature, Plague's captains were known as Bristleback, Peacethief, Longsnout, Brokentusk, and, showing that even pigs have a sense of humor, though usually sarcastic, Snortwart. These six were inseparable and, not coincidentally, began their migration south from the woods around Bad Axe, Michigan on the same Halloween night Ben beat the devil out of Scary Gary.

Pigs are the third most intelligent mammals in the world, ranked just behind humans and porpoises. They showed that intelligence in Scripture when Christ sent a legion of demons into them. Smart enough to realize the depth of evil that now inhabited their piggy bodies, every last one of them rampaged over the cliff and drowned in the Sea of Galilee. Plague and his cadre of rogue boars made a different decision when the shadows of evil targeted them.

Just as intelligence in humans is too rarely attended by kindness, it is doubly so with porkers. Babe the pig notwithstanding, pigs can be an ill-tempered, mean-spirited lot—traits that dark spirits would welcome and imbue should the opportunity arise. And if any porcine would be an inviting host to one or more of *The Shadows*, it was Plague, who had made peace with his own devils early in life.

Driven by a darkness only their leader had a rudimentary understanding of, the hogs traveled an impressive number of miles in fair weather for the first three weeks. Their chief boar pushed them relentlessly, sometimes through the night. They lived off of meager foraging and an occasional coyote, fox or rabbit who unfortunately crossed within their smell radius. By Thanksgiving afternoon when the Hightowers were gathering with their family and friends around the table, Plague and his nefarious crew had reached an isolated farm just north of Ann Arbor. There, under the cover of the first real storm of the winter, they raided a cattle pen, dragging off a dairy cow and her four-month old calf.

That night, after gorging themselves, they bedded down in a deadfall with towering pines giving them some protection from the weather. Peacethief, who almost never spoke to Plague, found himself temptingly close to the giant boar stretched out in the brush next to him. Maybe it was the pleasurable feeling of a full stomach that gave him the confidence to ask: "Where are we going, Master? Will it be much further?" The silence that followed made him wish he'd said nothing. He was surprised when an answer finally came.

"Another master is here," grunted the behemoth boar. "We have been following him for some time now." And the next morning they continued to do so, through heavy sleet and snow, inexorably forging a bloody trail through the farmlands and dense woods of southern Michigan. Only Plague seemed to be aware that a malignant force within them was guiding the savage hogs around potential trouble and along backroads that offered no resistance. Even when the snow got so deep that the country roads they traveled were impassable for vehicles, they used their sheer bulk to blast through snow drifts and make steady progress every day.

Eventually they crested a small promontory west of Marcellus, Michigan. There, with a stand of birch trees behind them, they could see what looked like an abandoned barn at the bottom of the hill. It had been a hard trip, and Plague sensed they were getting close to the task for which they had been chosen. It would be good to have sanctuary for the night. Suspecting that dark deeds lay ahead soon, he calculated they would need some rest. It was December 18. One week till Christmas.

CHAPTER

fifty-three

Some of the heaviest snowfalls in the world happen just downwind of large lakes, and Lake Michigan is an excellent source of water vapor for growing snow clouds. The strong northwesterly winds had been lifting a huge amount of water from the unfrozen lake for several days and the clouds finally decided to unload their burden.

By the time the boys woke up for school on Monday morning, December 18, Gurney was still on the Indiana Toll road, slowly heading west in what had become a whiteout blizzard by the time he passed the Chesterton exit. He considered turning around, but his instincts told him the weather was even worse behind him. So a trip that normally would have taken him two hours cost him nearly six, and he didn't arrive at Argonne until after lunch.

He was greeted warmly by Dr. Steve Cassells, a research fellow at the laboratory and personal assistant to Dr. Abrikosov.

"Dr. Hightower," he called out when Gurney came through the front door of the main building. "I recognize you from your picture. We're so glad you got here safely," he said, reaching down from his six and one-half foot frame to shake Gurney's hand vigorously. "A few more hours of this onslaught, and they'll close down the toll road."

"My guess is they already have," replied Gurney, taking off his stocking cap and brushing the snow off the shoulders of his coat.

The affable and lanky scientist with shaggy blond hair looked more like a middle-aged member of the Beach Boys than the summa

cum laude graduate of Northwestern University and respected physicist he was.

"I've examined the storm predictor models for the next ten
days," said Dr. Cassells, "and you'll most likely be with us longer
than you expected."

"That can't happen," Gurney replied earnestly. "I've got to be
back for the birth of our child."

When he made that statement, Babe was a little more than six
days from going into labor.

"We'll keep our fingers crossed then," said his new protégé, "and
hope for the best. We're already in your debt and have such high
hopes for your participation in this project. You can count on us to
do everything we can to deliver you safely back to your home."

"Right now," Gurney said, wistfully looking over his shoulder
toward a window with an eastern view, "my family probably wishes
I'd done my research in weather modification."

If his eyes could have penetrated the storm that covered the
103 miles to South Bend, he'd have seen Jacks and Ben, at that very
moment, trudging out the front door of Rockne Intermediate. They
were leaning into a fifty mile per hour wind and shielding their faces
from a cannonade of blowing snow. The long line of cars with heaters
going full blast was almost invisible to them. Having been alerted
by a text message from the school, Babe, fresh from her doctor's
appointment, was waiting with Carrie for the boys to appear.

School had been cancelled for the rest of the day so all the kids
could get home well before dark. Along with increasing wind speeds
and outrageous amounts of snow fall, also predicted now were temperatures diving well below zero. Without anyone officially knowing it, no one would be going back to school until the new year.
Christmas Break had just come early.

Impossibly the snowfall thickened, and now the visibility was
so bad neither boy could detect the family's green Outback wagon.
Babe thought she recognized them through the rapid beating of the
windshield wipers so she honked her horn. But several other parents
had the same idea, so the boys were simply confused by the discor-
dant chorus of clamoring cars.

Finally, Babe yelled to the back seat, "Carrie, I have to leave the car. Stay right where you are. I'll bring the boys to you soon."

Thundersnow is a rare event but a large percentage of them happen within a fifty mile radius of South Bend, Indiana. The instant Babe opened her car door to find the boys, the sky above the school lit up with a lightning bolt that was so close to the scurrying students that its deafening peal of thunder was almost simultaneous. With the startling boom came a torrent of small hailstones called graupel pelting the boys who were about to settle for any car that would give them sanctuary.

The next flash of lightning was even closer, but Babe used it to spot them in illuminated relief against the darkness of the school building. Not wanting to move too far away from the car, she screamed against the roar of the wind,

"Jacks! Ben! Over here!"

Her voice was faint, but both of them heard her and began to tack toward the sound.

"Yes! Keep coming this way!" she shouted.

By the time they made it to her, she had both doors open, and they tumbled out of the storm into the car's warm interior—Jacks in the back with Carrie and Ben riding shotgun in the front. Keeping one hand on the vehicle for balance, Babe labored around to the driver's side.

Placing her frozen fingers on the door handle, she pulled but it wouldn't open. When she pulled harder, she lost her balance with both feet slipping out from under her. She landed on her bottom with a heavy thud. The boys jumped from the car and were at her side in a moment.

"Stay down," cried Ben over the noise of the storm. "We'll call 911!"

"Don't be silly," she yelled back. "The snow broke my fall. I'll be fine. Just give me a hand up." With Jacks behind her, and Ben grasping her wrists, they gently raised her from the snow to a standing position.

"There, that wasn't so bad," she said bravely, as together the boys pulled open her door, breaking the bond of ice that had sealed it.

But there was a grimace on her face when she squeezed her swollen tummy in behind the wheel. Jacks saw it and said anxiously,

"Babe, you shouldn't be out in this weather."

"I don't see anyone else in this group with a driver's license, dear," she replied.

Babe peered through the metronomic wipers, and, shaking her head at a foolish driver just pulling away from the school curb into an opaque wall of white, said:

"You kids might as well relax. I'm not going anywhere until I can see well enough to get you home safely."

CHAPTER

fifty-four

Snowflakes are being manufactured above you at an astounding rate—approximately a million billion crystals per second. Every ten minutes that's enough snow to make a vast army of snowmen and women, one for every human on the planet. Over the Earth's history, some ten times the mass of our world has drifted to the ground in the form of tiny, hexagonal ice crystals.

Now a significant portion of that mass was slowing life down in Illinois, Indiana, Michigan and Ohio. Record snowfalls were closing roads, schools, supermarkets and shopping centers all over the Midwest. Eventually, police were forced to ask citizens with snowmobiles to help transport doctors to the hospital. But because of zero visibility, widespread drifting and perilous temperatures, even that became impossible.

The blizzard that began on the morning of December 18 would have many names. Meteorologists called it an extratropical cyclone. A headline in The South Bend Tribune, using "second-coming" type, dubbed it *"Snowpocalypse!,"* and a few days later, *"Snowmageddon!"* But most locals would always remember it as *The Year of The White Hurricane.* The 28.05 inches barometric pressure measurement recorded on Sunday morning at the airport was the lowest non-tropical atmospheric pressure ever recorded in the mainland United States.

By the afternoon of December 21, 54 inches of new snow had fallen on Michiana with more to come, breaking the 1978 storm record of thirty-six inches. All of the Indiana Toll Road and most of the Ohio Turnpike were shut down for only the second time ever. The total effect on transportation from Chicago to Columbus, Ohio was described by Major General Scott Bennett of the Indiana National Guard as comparable to a nuclear attack.

An Amtrak train was stranded near Laporte, along with hundreds of vehicles and their endangered drivers all along the toll road. With the many stories of dramatic rescues came euphoria and hope. But reports of imperiled travelers still missing brought deep despair and anxiety.

The next morning, Governor Mike Holtgren declared a state of emergency and called out the Guard to aid stranded motorists and road crews. In a poignant plea broadcast over every available frequency, he begged Indiana residents to stay safely in their homes. "People are dying out there!" he cried. "It's not safe for you to walk to the garage in these whiteout conditions. You may not make it back into your house. This blizzard is producing winds of eighty miles per hour, deadly wind-chill temperatures of fifty to sixty below zero nearly all day, and snow drifts of twenty to twenty-five feet high."

Already clearly emotional, the governor's voice rose in pitch and intensity.

"I've never seen anything like this. Entire semi-tractor trailers are being completely buried on the sides of the toll road, and our rescue teams can't even see them to save the drivers."

The governor paused for a moment, then announced:

"Therefore I am declaring Northern Indiana a disaster area and petitioning the President for national disaster relief. In addition I am immediately invoking martial law in the city of South Bend. If anyone is caught on the streets in the next twenty-four hours without permission from the state police, they will be arrested and suffer a severe financial penalty. No one else will die on my watch this week. Stay home and pray for those who are in crisis. May God bless you all."

CHAPTER

fifty-five

The Colorado white-fir Christmas tree, festooned with silver balls, a kaleidoscope of twinkling lights and striped candy canes, filled the air around it with the fresh fragrance of a juicy orange. Beneath the tree, randomly arranged piles of colorfully wrapped presents patiently waited for the whole family to be together again. And that's exactly what had Babe worried.

With Ben tending the hissing fire and Carrie cuddling beside her, Babe sat uncomfortably on a tan sectional as close as she could get to the family room's fireplace, her feet propped on an ottoman to relieve her swollen ankles. Focusing on the Governor's impassioned plea, she absent-mindedly stroked her abdomen in a subconscious attempt to keep her baby from feeling its mother's stress. Without revealing it to the kids, she'd had three bad days since her fall at the school. But that wasn't why she was apprehensive. Mostly she was worried about Gurney. She was afraid he was going to try to make it through *The White Hurricane* to be with her.

They'd had no television reception and severely limited internet service since the harrowing experience of retrieving the boys in the storm on Monday. The raging blizzard had rendered the satellite dish useless and left them with their Bose radio and unreliable cell phones for communication with the outside world. She'd only been able to speak with Gurney three times since he left for Chicago and two of those conversations were cut short by poor reception. Last night's talk was particularly worrisome.

"Babe, darling! Can you hear me?" Gurney asked, his voice strained with tension. "Are you all okay?"

"Your voice is cutting in and out, dear," she replied. "But I can hear most of what you're saying."

"How many bars do you have on your phone?" he asked.

Looking down, she answered, "Just two for now, and the only place in the room where I seem to be able to hear you at all is one spot at the foot of the bed."

"Stay there, then," he said. "The cell towers that rely on electricity are failing us. We might only have a few more minutes to talk. I can actually hear the wind blowing outside your bedroom window. Is everyone there all right?"

Speaking faster than normal, she replied, "The governor's declared martial law in the town, but we couldn't go anywhere even if we had to. We've got snow drifts up to the roof line on the north and west sides of the house. So we can't see anything out of those main floor windows.

But the furnace is still working, and we have plenty of food and water. Please don't worry about us. And you stay there until it's perfectly safe for you to come home. Is your work going well?" she asked, hoping to change the subject.

Gurney knew her too well to be distracted. She was hiding something. Then he asked the questions she hoped he wouldn't.

"How are *you*, and how is the baby? I want the truth."

"We're going to be fine," she answered. "I don't want you to worry."

"Now I'm really worried," he said. "What is it? You have to tell me, or I'm leaving to come home immediately."

"It's probably nothing," she said. "I slipped and fell in the school parking lot on Monday." "You what?" he shouted. "Why didn't you tell me this before?"

"Because at first I didn't think anything was wrong. And I'm not sure there is now. Besides, there was nothing you or I could do about it. The hospitals have been closed for two days. No one's getting in or out of them."

"I'm on my way home," he said brusquely.

"No, you're not, Gurney. You've got it almost as bad in Chicago as we do here. All the roads are closed," she reminded him. The line went silent. At first she thought they'd lost reception again. But then she could hear him breathing.

"I know what you're thinking," Babe said with panic building in her voice. "It would be suicide for you to try it. Besides, you'd be arrested if you did."

"I'd be a lousy husband and father if I didn't," he countered. "Tomorrow, as soon as I've finished my work, I'm...." Silence.

"Gurney! Gurney!" Babe called. "Promise me you won't do anything stupid!" But her words spilled into a gusty, cellular black hole of wind and snow. The connection was broken and wouldn't return that night or the next day.

CHAPTER

fifty-six

When Romulus, the first king of Rome, invented the calendar, he so despised the winter season that he refused to give names to the sixty-one days he allotted for it. Therefore he assigned only ten good-weather months to his calendar and named most of them for the number of the month they represented. That's why the names, September, October, November and December seem so out of place in our modern calendar. Originally they were the seventh, eighth, ninth and tenth months of the Roman year. Winter just has a way of messing things up.

Not factoring in the wind chill, it was eighteen degrees below zero on Saturday the 23rd. By 11:00 a.m., Ben had gathered everything he thought he'd need to try to make it to Pockets in the barn. The blustery winds battering the newly shingled roof just outside his bedroom had awakened him in the middle of the night. Unable to get back to sleep, he climbed down the bunk bed ladder and shuffled to the window. The first thing he noticed was the utility light over the hayloft door was out so the barn was shrouded in darkness. Of course that might mean the bulb had simply burned out, but it also could indicate the electricity was off in the barn. If that were true, then Pockets was in trouble.

He hadn't seen the horse for two days because of the storm. And even though he knew she had plenty of food, he worried about her surviving the severe cold. There were blankets and a portable heater not far from her if he could get to them.

The kitchen door on the north side of the house was the closest one to the barn, so Ben started there. With their Nightcore flashlight and a trunk shovel Jacks had retrieved from a basement storage room, the boys were standing in the kitchen dressed for the elements but momentarily immobilized by the imposing vision before them. A solid perimeter of white covered every square inch of the windows on the back of the house, completely eclipsing any view of the barn. It was as if a giant had filled the town water tower with ghostly paint and turned it upside down on their house during the night.

With apprehension, the older boy opened the kitchen door. After it swung inward, a more formidable barrier rose before them. They were still contemplating their next step when Babe duckwalked into the kitchen.

"Boys! Close that door! It's freezing outside!" she exclaimed.

Jacks, standing closest to the door, calmly replied, "Above this wall of snow, you're right, and that's why we're worried about Pockets. But there's not much chance of freezing down here.

Snow is an amazing insulator, so this is more like just opening the refrigerator. The only reason we haven't started tunneling through it is a physics problem."

"I want to hear your problem, but not until you close the door," insisted Babe.

Quick to obey her, Ben closed it and asked, "How do we tunnel a straight enough line to make sure we hit the barn? We can follow the sidewalk to the fence gate, but after that it's going to be vertigo time and we could completely miss it."

Babe's lips became a thin line, her eyes narrowed and her forehead creased. *She's putting on her thinking cap,* observed Jacks.

Then his mother slowly nodded her head up and down and smiled, saying, "I've got an idea. I'll be right back."

Watching her wamble out of the room, Ben asked, "Is she going to Target to buy us new boots?"

Jacks laughed, "I wouldn't put it past her."

But Babe returned almost immediately with her car keys.

"Those won't do much good," offered Ben. "We probably couldn't find the garage either. And even if we did, we couldn't get the car out."

"I didn't bring it for the keys," answered Babe. "What you boys need is this remote." She held the black, plastic device up for them to see. "If you push this red panic button, you'll hear the car horn honk in the garage. The garage is just a little to the right of the barn and twenty feet closer to the house. When you're digging, if you keep the sound of the horn on your right at about the same volume, you can't miss the barn. Most of the time you'll hear it in front of you, and when it moves behind you, you're almost there."

"It'll work," said Ben, barely suspecting how difficult the task would be.

"You're amazing," said Jacks, beaming at his mother.

"No, I'm just a pregnant lady who loves horses. Now get going. Pockets needs you."

With a single shovel between them, the boys threw themselves into the work, one holding the flashlight while the other labored furiously, pushing snow right and left and packing it hard against the sides of the tunnel. Two adolescent moles burrowing with a purpose. Four hours later, after taking turns with the shovel and breaking for hot chocolate twice, they had drawn even with the garage. Twenty feet to go.

Both were exhausted and drenched in sweat, while a few feet above them the wind was raging and their whited out world was locked in a deep freeze. Breathing heavily and wasting no energy on words, they turned and followed the arc of the flashlight back to the kitchen. Babe heard them bump against the door, and Carrie ran to open it for them. Their ski pants swishing, they crawled into the room and rolled over onto their backs—two weary workers splayed on the wooden floor.

"You're my heroes," said Babe affectionately. "But you've both pushed it too hard. It'll be dark soon, so let's call it a day, okay? Carrie and I'll wrestle up some supper while you rest."

Ben recovered first and sat up, leaning back on his hands and shaking his head at his surrogate mother. "I'm going out again," he said slowly, a grim look on his face. "Pockets won't make it another night."

"And I'm going with him," added Jacks, who rose only to his cousin's level.

"What am I going to do with you two?" asked Babe. When both boys looked toward the door, she quickly added, "Okay, then— you're going back out—but not until I've fed you first."

CHAPTER

fifty-seven

Forty-five minutes later, with their stomachs full of hot tomato soup and grilled cheese sandwiches, the boys disappeared down the tunnel for the last time that night. Standing by the open kitchen door, Babe carefully bent to her knees to watch their progress. At intervals, they would stop, and she could hear the car horn honk from the garage. It was so muted by the snow it sounded like it might have been coming from two or three houses down the block.

When they got about sixty feet away, the light stopped moving forward and she knew they had reached the snow barrier again. Just then, her cell phone began to buzz on the kitchen counter. Carrie brought it to her as she rose from the floor by degrees and closed the door. She looked at the phone and read the words, *Argonne National Laboratories.* For some reason anticipating the worst, she went weak in the knees, but composed herself and answered.

"Hello? Gurney, is this you? Is something wrong?"

"I hope nothing's wrong, Mrs. Hightower," responded Dr. Cassells from Argonne. "Your husband asked me to keep calling until I finally got through. He tried many times before he left."

"Left?! Left?! What do you mean *left*?!" she shouted.

"He left our parking lot this afternoon at about 2:00 p.m.—and against our advice," he added. When he realized that last phrase would only increase her anxiety, the physicist apologized. "I'm sorry, ma'am. He's such a capable and convincing fellow. I mean, if anybody could make it back through this storm, it's your husband." Then it struck him that those words might have done even more harm than his first statement, so he decided to shut up and wait for Babe to speak. But the next sound he heard was a dial tone.

Meanwhile the boys were making steady progress toward the barn. The problem was they didn't know that and both feared they had missed it completely. Exhausted and numb with cold, they were just about to give up and turn back when, a little before 8:00 p.m., their shovel struck wood. Pockets' answering whinny told them they weren't too late.

"We made it!" cried Ben, feverishly shoveling snow higher than before in hopes of uncovering the door and, with Jacks' help, packing it into the sides of the tunnel. Breathing had become increasingly difficult the further they bored through the drift. Their arms and legs felt leaden with weariness and, increasing their pace, both of them were gasping for air. Eventually, the older boy dropped the shovel and began scraping the wall clean with his gloves in search of the door's latch. But Jacks' flashlight revealed nothing more than vertical boards of red wood in either direction. Without knowing it they had subconsciously tunneled slightly toward the sound of the car horn, so they ended up about halfway between the door and the barn's east side.

Now the boys had a choice to make, and at least one life hung in the balance: should they crawl back to the house to warm up and rest, or should they begin their search for the door? If they decided to continue on, that led to a second critical choice: which way should they start digging? To the right or the left? If they burrowed to their right and eventually ran out of wall, they'd know they had chosen the wrong direction and the door was somewhere behind them. If they made that mistake, their instincts told them they wouldn't have enough reserve left to start looking for the door again.

"Pockets!" Ben yelled, pounding on the outer wall, hoping a response from his horse would give them some indication of which direction to choose. "Pockets!" But there was no answer this time, and they could only guess the horse was succumbing to the cold. Having exposed even this small portion of the wall, they could now hear the roaring of the storm above them. Their first choice had been made for them. They knew if they turned back to the house, they wouldn't return—not that night. Now everything depended on them making the right second choice.

CHAPTER

fifty-eight

Having failed to find the door latch, Ben turned toward his cousin and slid down the wall, exhausted.

"It's my turn," wheezed Jacks, handing the older boy the flashlight and reaching for the shovel. That its blade was pointing to the left was the only reason he began digging in that direction. "If you keep the light on the wall," he said, feeling the effects of breathing in too much of his own carbon dioxide, we've got a 50-50 chance of saving Pockets tonight."

It turned out the blade knew what it was doing. And it was a good thing, because Jacks had little energy left. The shovel felt like a barbell with weights on it, and the weary boy moved at a fraction of the speed he had earlier. But inch by inch he uncovered the wall until eventually he heard a cry from behind, "There! A crack!" It was either a wider space than normal between two more boards or the side of the door itself.

Adrenaline is a remarkable hormone. Ben, despairing a moment earlier and close to collapse, came off his knees so quickly he knocked his flashlight hard against the handle of Jacks' shovel, shattering the lamp head and plunging the tunnel into darkness. They stood in frozen silence, the only sound their ponderous breathing.

It's one thing to be brave when you can see, but quite another to be the same when you're blind and facing what seems like an impossible task.

"I'm sorry, Jacks. Now what are we going to do?" asked the older boy, adding: "I suppose we could feel our way back to the house."

His voice rendered barely audible by the cold and his profound fatigue, Jacks' words were measured and firm. "We're gonna do what you started to do when we still had the light." He reached out in the pitch black tunnel until he found Ben's arm, and placing his hand there, squeezed it and declared, "We're gonna find that damn door."

Stunned by his cousin's word choice, Ben blurted, "Whoa! You just cussed! I didn't think you could do that!" The silence that followed told him Jacks was considering.

Ben knew his best friend well enough to recognize he was smiling when he delivered his next words in the gloom of the tunnel:

"It might not have been me," came the whispered reply. "Maybe it was a Guardian. It's dark out here. It could have been anybody."

It was exactly what Ben needed. "I know your voice," he laughed, feeling the endorphins kick in and his discouragement falter.

"If you say anything to Babe, I'll deny it," joked Jacks. "Besides, I think I feel a hinge."

"You feel a what?" asked Ben.

"A hinge—right here." He took his cousin's left hand and placed it on the spot where he'd pressed against a metal protrusion from one of the boards. Sure enough, just about waist high, Ben grasped the lower cast iron strap that allowed the barn door to pivot outward. From there he knew exactly where he would find the old black hook latch he had opened a thousand times before.

Because this was the south side of the barn, the snow hadn't drifted as high as it had against the back of the house. By standing up and poking the shovel above their heads, they were able to break through the upper level of the snow. The problem was that not only did a significant amount of snow fall down upon them, but the arctic blast they had crawled beneath with relative impunity for the last several hours was now assaulting their exposed faces. The super-chilled air, too far below zero for them even to guess at a number, hit the boys like a giant fist, stunning them and making it difficult at first for either to think clearly. But they fought through it, using the shovel and their boots to push sufficient snow away from the door to be able to open it just enough for them to squeeze through, slipping out of the gale into the darkness of the barn.

Closing the door behind them, Ben called: "Pockets! We made it! Pockets!" But once again, there was no response.

The first thing Jacks did was feel for the light switch inside the door. He flipped it once, twice, three times. Nothing. "The line must be down between the house and here," he said.

"What now?" Ben wondered out loud. "How are we going to find the heater and blankets in this darkness? I can't even see you, and you're standing right next to me."

"No, actually I'm not," called Jacks. "I'm over here near the last place I remember that stuff being. But I just realized I'm an idiot."

"What are you talkin' about? If you're anything…" but Ben didn't get to finish his thoughts, because a blinding light suddenly appeared about fifteen feet away from him.

"I forgot all about this torch light app on my phone. We could have been using it for the past twenty minutes."

"Well, let's use it now," Ben said, then haltingly added, "to see if Pockets is…"—another thought he left incomplete, and Jacks, who grabbed up a couple of blankets and turned the light toward the stall, understood why.

Was their beloved friend alive? Why was she so silent? A part of each boy didn't want to know. Jacks handed the blankets to his cousin and shined the light through the bars of the stall. There was Pockets, lying on a soiled bed of straw in the corner. Much of her still body was covered with hay she'd flung with her teeth sometime earlier that day. A magnificent animal when she was healthy, now she looked small and inanimate on the wooden floor of the roomy stall. A turn of the light to the other corner revealed the slow feed hay net that still had plenty of fodder in it.

"This is my fault," said Ben. "I should have checked on her yesterday."

"Yesterday, you thought the heating unit in her stall was working," replied Jacks, opening the stall door and reverently approaching the strawberry roan. With two long steps, the older boy whooshed past him, dropping one blanket by the horse's head and unfurling the other one to cover her as completely as he could.

Horses are like humans in significant ways. They have personalities as unique as their colors. They can be curious, stubborn, discouraged, angry or friendly, and just like humans, some of them are much better listeners than others. But horses are far more equanimous than people, and they accept their fate without whining or complaining. Self-pity, bitterness and blame are strictly human traits, and Pockets had chosen a horse's way of dealing with the killer cold temperature. After two days of shivering and moving about the stall as much as she could, she stopped eating and nestled into the hay to wait for whatever came. Her body was shutting down and she simply accepted it.

Ben blanketed her and, sitting down, lifted her noble head onto his lap. With Jacks shining his phone light on the two of them, Ben took off his right glove and ran his hand along the horse's lower jaw until he found the cordlike artery there. Using his index finger and thumb, he lightly pinched the artery and detected a weak but beating pulse. "She's alive!" he announced. "But we've got to get her warmed up."

Covering her with the second blanket, Jacks said, "Talk to her, Ben. Better yet, sing to her. She loves *you* most of all. Call her back. But you'll have to do it in the dark. I need the light for a few minutes. I saw the space heater and know where Dad keeps his generator. If I can find some gas, we'll have this stall as warm as toast in no time."

So Ben sat in the darkness, cradling Pockets' head, and gently stroked her velvet nose. With his voice trembling from the cold, he bent toward her ear and softly sang *House at Pooh Corner*, the song his mother used to sing to him almost every night when he was younger.

As Jacks set out with the light on a mission to bring heat and water to Pockets, he paused for just a moment to hear faint and familiar words from his own childhood wafting from the stall:

Christopher Robin and I walked along under branches lit up by the moon.

Ben's voice, made husky from being in the frigid air for hours, was a contrast to the boy's delicate phrasing.

Posing our questions to Owl and Eeyore as our days disappeared all too soon.

It was a holy moment, and more than one Guardian watched from the darkness, wondering at the depth of love between a boy and his horse.

CHAPTER

fifty-nine

After Jacks located the generator, he pulled it over to Pockets' stall. Finding an almost full can of gasoline and using the electronic ignition, he got it started easily, and even though the machine had a low tone muffler, he saw the horse move her head when the engine kicked in. Both boys took this as a positive sign. Then, using the heel of his boot, Jacks broke the ice in her five gallon, flat back bucket of water. He removed the male end of the bucket heater from the wall and plugged it into one of the generator's outlets. Life-giving water would be available in minutes. Finally, he did the same thing with the stall heater and turned it up higher than normal. This was a special occasion.

When it comes to recovery, horses are more like children on a beautiful summer day than any other human age group in any other circumstance: they don't fake or prolong their sickness. When they start feeling well, they immediately start behaving like it. As she began to warm, and her circulation improved, Pockets opened her eyes and insisted on standing up. And after she did that with some difficulty, she gave all her attention to the water bucket.

The boys had been watching her gather strength for several minutes when Jacks checked the time on his phone: 8:51 p.m.

"It's getting late," said Jacks, "and Babe's probably worrying about us. I'd better let her know everything's okay. You want to go back with me?"

Ben, trying to comb hay out of Pockets' mane by the ebbing light of the phone, shook his head. "Huh-uh," he said. "I'm staying here a little longer. It's going to be warm enough for me to spend the night if I have to." He paused. "But I don't really know what I'm going to do yet. I'll just see ya' when I see ya.'"

"Then I've got one more thing to do out here," replied the younger boy. With that, he found his way to the breaker box, which had been wired years ago with a plug that would reach all the way to the generator. Accomplishing that, he reset a tripped fuse, then made his way to the light switch, flipping it one more time. Three lights came on, including the one on the ceiling over the horse stall. He looked toward Ben who waved and gave him a thumbs-up sign.

Jacks turned and pushed the barn door open just enough to shine his light into the storm. If anything, the howling wind and blowing snow had intensified. *This is getting ridiculous,* the boy thought. *There's more here than meets the eye.* He glared out at the tempest, his puerile face a grim mask of defiance. Then he spoke one simple word of command:

"*Peace!*"

It was exactly nine o'clock at night, and Gurney was only seven miles from South Bend.

CHAPTER

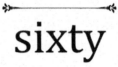

sixty

He smelled them long before finding any visible sign of their presence. Plague had been following the spoor of a pack of coyotes for more than a mile. Because of the blizzard, he and his miserable companions hadn't eaten anything for two days. That was two days longer than he normally fasted. For too long they'd been living off the metabolic water stored in their own fat reserves, but now they desperately required the preformed water they could get only from consuming their prey.

An hour ago, he seriously considered slaughtering Peacethief with his razor-sharp tusks. But then he picked up the scent and later rumbled upon the tracks of a rabble of scavengers who regularly marked the surrounding woods with evidence of their own territorial claim. He had tasted coyote before, but then, there was little he hadn't tasted. And these dogs would do nicely if he could figure out a way to slow them down.

From a long line of predators, Plague knew the difference between the tracks of a coyote and any other animal in that region. Unlike the deer or wild turkey, the coyote leaves a track longer than it is wide. And the hunter can always tell what direction it's moving in because the front of its heel pad has only one lobe, whereas the rear has two. This killer pack of five wild dogs was moving southeast through the woods, paying close attention to dying or dead standing trees called snags, where they might stealthily come upon a sleepy family of red squirrels or raccoons. Normally, they would leave the raccoons alone because they counterattacked with such ferocity. But today they were hungry enough to risk anything, even if it meant trying to bring down a migrating bobcat or a battle-tested badger.

Being upwind from the coyotes, Plague knew he and his marauders had the element of surprise on their side. Besides, even if any one of the boars found himself alone against the dogs, he would have little to fear. Each of them carried ten times the weight of the largest of the wretched curs, and their thick, prehistoric hide covered with hair as coarse as the bristles on a wire brush made them almost impervious to the snapping teeth of their intended prey.

From long experience, the feral hogs knew how to track as silently as their bulk allowed. Now their chief brought them to a halt. Even in this storm, his acute senses of smell and hearing told him their prey had stopped moving. He lifted his snout and focused on the distinctive sounds ahead. From the spitting and hissing that cut through the wind to his ears, he surmised the dogs had discovered an unsuspecting opossum—most likely in the hollow of a dead tree. He would allow them their meager find and knew it would give him the time he needed to make his own plans.

The massive beast scanned his surroundings. The peculiar bumps and snowy mounds indicated the area was littered with buried deadfall and piles of brush. It was a perfect place to set a trap. From the beginning of the hunt, he'd understood he and his captains had a problem: their brute strength was more than offset by the speed of the coyotes. He couldn't kill them if he couldn't catch them. Now he saw a way to nullify the dogs' advantage—if he could lure them into this area. Plague decided to play on ancient traits deeply imbedded in their canine DNA: hunger, greed and curiosity.

He gathered his evil comrades around him to give them the plan. His tail bristling with excitement and his ears moving like semaphore paddles on the deck of an aircraft carrier, Plague grunted,

"We have finished our journey. Now we must feed well to have strength for the task ahead. Do exactly as I say, and you will sleep with full bellies tonight." The other five swelled with anticipation but muffled their enthusiasm to keep their prey from detecting them. Plague turned clockwise to glare at each hog in turn.

"While the dogs are eating their kill," he growled, "the snow will cover most of our tracks. But one overgrown rat won't be enough to satisfy them for long. We will give the scabby thieves reason to come to our party. And when they do, we will be ready for them." Pigs, even domestic ones, are notorious for their cursing. What followed was a string of muttered swears from his comrades that would startle a rogue wolf.

"Here is what you must do," he continued. "Four of you will come up behind these mounds and burrow beyond the brush just short of breaking through the snow. You will wait for two sounds. The first sound," he snarled, turning to the hog on his right and staring down at him, "will be Snortwart here, death-squealing loud enough to draw our meal to us."

When they come, the second sound will be me killing the pack leader. When you hear that, all of you must escape your snowy graves and keep the rest of the dogs from running. I want them in a tight circle with me in the middle. Now move out and get in position. Snortwart, you stay."

Plague hadn't chosen this hog because he was his least favorite. The chief had no favorites. He despised them all, but they were useful to him, so he tolerated their presence. He chose Snortwart simply because he had unusually large ears.

CHAPTER

<hr>

sixty-one

<hr>

With the others disappearing behind mounds of snow, the two boars waited patiently as the flakes fell around them. Finally, the malignant chief asked his inferior a question:

"Are you afraid, insignificant one?"

"N-not at all, master," came the trembling reply.

"You should be," grumbled Plague, "because if you fail me, we will feed on you instead of the dogs."

"I will not fail you," answered Snortwart, reading his chief's deadly mood and not daring to raise his head. Not hearing a response, he bowed lower still and added: "I will act like I am dying in great pain to draw all of them to us."

With no warning, Plague launched himself onto the unwitting boar and, with his mammoth bulk, pinned him to the snow, his hideous mouth against Snortwart's ear. Whispering, "You will not be acting," he bit deeply into the base of his victim's sizeable ear, and with a jerk of his neck, tore the entire organ from his head.

Blood spurted everywhere and the hapless hog's terrible shrieking echoed through the woods. But Plague maintained his position on top and spoke firmly to the squealing pig beneath him:

"This bite will not kill you—today," he grunted. "But *I will* if you don't stop whining immediately. And I'd rather not, because we might need you for our task tomorrow."

Fearing the present wrath of Plague more than his impending demise, Snortwart obeyed and stifled his cries.

"Good," observed the vile bully. "Your noise has worked. I can hear them coming. When I release you, move behind those trees over there," he motioned with his snout. "Then join in the slaughter when you hear my signal."

Snortwart got up and lumbered away, shaking his head and whimpering under his breath, while Plague, his face mottled with his minion's blood, lay down on his side next to the macabre, mangled ear.

Moments later, the first coyote cautiously padded up through a copse of beech trees and stopped some thirty yards from the fallen boar. Even from there he could smell the blood of the enormous animal. His comrades joined him, and together they crept toward the mountain of swine flesh rising from the snow, all the time scanning the area for signs of the one or ones who had brought the beast down. Their thinking clouded by their gnawing hunger, it didn't occur to them to wonder why the victor would leave such a prize. And having no natural enemy in these woods, they were less cautious than they should have been.

The alpha dog and his mate were the first to approach the imposing carcass. His large, triangular ears erect, he lowered his long, narrow muzzle and sniffed at the bloody ear on the snow next to the silent hog. He licked it once, then picked it up with his teeth and laid the gift at the feet of his female. He was aware of the impatience of the rest of the pack, mewling with anticipation several steps away from the circle, waiting for their leader's judgment that it was safe for them to move up.

Darkness was coming and there was work to be done. They had to get as much of this meat back to their den before the blizzard covered it and other animals claimed their share. So the alpha dog threw back his head, flared his nostrils and, his eyes smoldering with a moony madness, howled out his claim to this carrion offering from the wolf gods.

It was all the other coyotes needed to hear. Accustomed to starvation rations of mice, rabbits and squirrels, they approached the incomprehensible feast without their usual vigilance. And it was their undoing.

The coyotes had a problem: where do you start feeding on an animal of this magnitude? Waiting for the leader of their pack to make that choice, two of the other males watched him pace back and forth, prodding the boar's viscera with his black nose. The third looked enviously at the alpha female chewing on the ear she'd been given. Finally, the alpha male, standing on his sinewy hind legs, chose the softest area he could find just above the hog's right shoulder. A low growl rumbling in his throat, he thrust out his rough-hewn jaw and sank his stiletto-sharp teeth into Plague's ample neck.

Screeching in triumph, the boar rose to his full height in an instant, pulling the coyote up with him. The helpless dog hung there for a second, his back feet dangling in the air while Plague's horrific scream froze his blood. The other coyotes, stunned by the spectacle, were immediately surrounded by five more monstrous hogs that seemed to materialize miraculously from the snow. Then Plague simply fell onto the cursed pack leader, crushing him to death, and in so doing, pushed his four doomed companions into the tusks and teeth of their executioners.

A few hours later, evening settled into the woods, and each boar burrowed back into the shelter of a large brush pile, dragging his share of meat and bone with him. Plague, who had never experienced anything like joy, was uncommonly sanguine. The closest he had ever come to being happy was perhaps a sense of conquest and the absolute devastation of anyone that stood in his way. But on this particular night, his belly filled with the ill-fated one he had killed that afternoon, he felt something completely new for him. It was a buoyancy that came from pleasing the dark master who had driven him this far south.

He was a pig of many thoughts and few words, and his captains were glad of it. Whenever he did grunt a command, it almost always made their lives more difficult and dangerous. So they were stupefied to hear him chortle out what amounted to the only joke he had ever told:

"A mangy dog once ate a possum that filled him
to the brim. And now a pig that played a possum,
has finished eating him."

Pleased with his verse, feeling invincible and more possessed than ever by an unspeakable evil, he lay on the lee side of a deadfall and reflected on his recent accomplishments. After leaving their last refuge, an abandoned barn to the north, he and his band of hogs had steadily rutted and blustered their way through the treacherous storm until they reached these woods just a few hundred yards north of the Indiana Toll Road. This, he knew was their destination, and his inner guide confirmed it.

In less than two months, Plague had led his captains on an unthinkable journey that covered 297 miles, foraging and slaughtering their way across the countryside. And here, in the woods due west of Notre Dame, among the beech and sugar maple, black ash and blue spruce, white cedar and basswood trees, the wild boars of Battle Axe would take shelter from The White Hurricane and wait for their human targets to appear.

It was exactly 9:00 p.m., and Plague noted that the wind had died and the snow had stopped falling.

PART FOUR

"A great sign appeared in heaven: a woman clothed with the sun, with the moon under her feet and a crown of twelve stars on her head. She was pregnant and cried out in pain as she was about to give birth....Then the dragon was enraged at the woman and went off to wage war against the rest of her offspring—those who keep God's commands and hold fast their testimony about Jesus" (Revelation 12).

CHAPTER

✦————✦

sixty-two

The day before he left for home in the blizzard, Gurney stood over a couch packing his clothes in the lab office he'd been using as his sleeping quarters for the past two nights. The White Hurricane had hit Chicago with such force on Wednesday that there was no way he could even make it back to his room at the Argonne Guest House in the evening. A young lab assistant named Jason had braved the storm to retrieve Gurney's personal items and a couple of blankets from his room and delivered everything to the office adjoining his research laboratory.

As it turned out, the gale force winds and drifting snow had kept Dr. Abrikosov and two other key team members from making the commute from their homes in nearby Bolingbrook and Romeoville. Consequently, Gurney's high hopes for the project were temporarily dashed. Still, he labored into the late hours of the night on his own, seriously distracted by the concerns he had for Babe and the kids. After his last talk with her, he knew he had to get home sooner than later. And yet, that seemed unlikely in this blizzard.

Dr. Cassells, who also was stranded at the Lab by the weather, had kept him apprised of the storm's ferocity and the impassable condition of the major highways between him and his family. He had originally planned to leave for home late Friday afternoon, but the whiteout conditions made that impossible. So instead of being with his loved ones two days before Christmas Eve as planned, he spent Friday night alone in his makeshift bedroom, packing his duffel bag and feeling helpless. He'd always been a look-for-the-worst, hope-for-the-best kind of guy, and on this night, he couldn't shake a preternatural sense that Babe was in trouble and needed him. When a man like Gurney Hightower reached that state of mind, no power on earth was going to stop him. By the time he turned off the light and stretched out on the couch, using his folded winter parka for a pillow, he'd decided even if the blizzard intensified, he was making the trip to South Bend the next day.

He was restless during the night, praying and worrying in equal parts. And even though he got almost no REM sleep, he awoke early, anticipating what lay before him. After he washed for the day in the facility's closest bathroom, he sought out Dr. Cassells, whom he found in the otherwise empty cafeteria, a cup of coffee in one hand and a half-eaten apple on the table in front of him.

Easy going and affable, the lanky scientist kicked the chair across from him out from the table and with a smile said,

"Have a seat, Hoosier," using the nickname he'd given his guest soon after his arrival. "I see you couldn't sleep either."

"Steven," replied Gurney, "the next time I sleep will be in my own bed. I'm leaving today."

Slow to respond, Dr. Cassells shook his head thoughtfully. He waited for his colleague to sit before he said,

"That would be madness, my friend. Stay with us a little longer and see if this storm breaks."

"The baby is coming. I can feel it in my bones. And with the hospitals closed in South Bend, my wife's going to need me."

"Your wife needs a husband who survives this blizzard. That's the important thing."

"My wife is the important thing," countered Gurney, getting tired of this conversation.

Dr. Cassells saw his discouragement and added,

"Granted, things are a little better on this side of the lake, and they've already started clearing emergency routes in the city. In fact, just before you came in, I called for a pickup truck with a plow to work on our parking lot at noon today." When he saw Gurney's eyes spark with a bit of hope, he warned him.

"But that doesn't mean I think you'd have the slightest chance of getting home. Even if you could make it to the east side of Chicago, the Toll Road will be closed for days. The state police would arrest you before you got started."

The good doctor's last comment gave Gurney an idea. He excused himself and went back to his room. He picked up his freshly-charged android, highlighted the blue phone icon, and scrolled down his contact list until he found the name he was looking for: Russ Lawley, his occasional golf buddy and a member of his small group at church who also happened to be a lieutenant in the Indiana State Police. Because the storm had rendered cell service almost non-existent in South Bend, Gurney knew he had a better chance of reaching Russ if he was at his post as Commander of the District 21 station on the toll road near Bristol, Indiana.

He walked to the window and observed the surreal white-on-white world outside. From his office he could just see where he had parked his car. It looked like the giant Stay Puff Marshmallow Man from *Ghostbusters* had exploded on that end of the parking lot, burying the stranded cars in ivory ectoplasm. If the snowplow didn't show up at noon, the scene appeared to be hopeless.

Still, he typed his friend's number on the touch tone key pad and hit *Send*. But he heard no ring, and his screen announced, *Error/No Such Number Exists*. He tried a second time and got the same result. Dispirited despite his resolve, he looked out the window again. Was it his imagination or was the snowfall lighter than a minute ago? He took it as a sign and googled District 21's phone number. A moment later, a weary female voice answered:

"Indiana State Police," she said. "To whom may I direct you?"

Surprised he got through, Gurney was briefly flustered and almost lost his opportunity. But before she disconnected, he managed to ask, "Excuse me, Miss, but is Lieutenant Lawley in this morning?"

"Everyone's in this morning," she replied with a comic sigh. "No one could get home last night, so we're all still here," sarcastically adding—"and we're having a *WONDERFUL* time!" Then back to her business voice: "The next sound you hear will be the lieutenant's phone ringing."

He picked up on the second ring.

"Commander Russ Lawley speaking."

"Russ!" Gurney exclaimed. "I can't believe I got you."

Recognizing the voice immediately, the trooper answered, "Gurney, what's going on?"

"I'm stuck in Chicago and I'm afraid Babe's going to have the baby with no one there to help her," the expectant father replied, his words coming so fast his friend could hardly keep up with them. "The hospitals are locked down, so no one's getting in or out, including the doctors. I've got to get home today."

"Hold on there, professor," said the officer. Phlegmatic by nature and accustomed to crises, the lieutenant's words were thoughtful and unhurried.

"Do you know for certain that Babe is in labor?"

"No, but..." was all Gurney could get out before his friend cut him off with authority.

"That's what I thought. Now let me get this straight. Her situation may not be critical, and if it is, she has the boys there to help her. Am I right?"

"You're not going to talk me out of this, Russ," answered Gurney firmly. "If you guys can't get to her, with God's help I will."

CHAPTER

sixty-three

The commander of District 21's State Police station knew his friend well enough to recognize he was going to lose this argument. Still, he had to make one more try.

"*Nobody* can get to her, Gurney—including you. You can't even imagine how bad this storm is. Nothing, I mean *nothing*—not on wheels or skis—is moving in St. Joseph County today. Give me your word you'll stay in Chicago, and I'll use our digital radio here at the post to reach District 24 down in Bremen. They've had less snow. Maybe they can get an emergency vehicle up to Babe in the next few days."

"I don't know how I know it, Russ," answered Gurney, in a more measured tone. "But that's too late. I'm heading home today if I have to rent a truck and plow my way there. I appreciate you worrying about me, buddy. I really do. But I'm going. Now I'll just say '*adios*' and you get back to your ..."

"Don't hang up," interrupted the trooper. "I need a minute to think about this." If it had been anybody but Gurney, he'd have kept to himself what only he and a few other commanders knew. He was convinced that his friend would make the mad attempt with or without his help and knew his chances of survival were infinitesimal even if he could reach the eastbound toll road. So against his principled nature, and with a mountain of misgivings, he decided to tell Gurney about an emergency operation that Chicago Rush Hospital, in conjunction with SECAH (the Second City Association of Hospitals), had initiated late the previous night and that the Ohio, Indiana and Illinois State Patrol had already set into action.

"Gurney, are you still there?" asked the lieutenant.

"I'm here. What are you thinking?"

"Two things, actually: that you're an idiot for putting your life in danger, and that I'd probably do the same thing in your place. Now, pay close attention because I think I can increase your odds of making it."

"Whatever you say, Russ. And thank you," replied Gurney.

"Don't thank me yet. You may be cursing me before this day is over."

"Anything's better than sitting on my hands in Chicago."

"That's probably been said by a lot of Chicago Cubs managers over the last hundred years or so," answered Russ.

"What are you talking about?" asked Gurney.

"You'd know if you were a Cub fan. But nobody's perfect, so never mind that. Let's just get you into a situation where you at least have a chance. Here's the plan: Sometime today and again tomorrow two tankers from a refinery near Cleveland are going to be hauling dedicated diesel fuel to Chicago to run the emergency generators for several city hospitals. To that end, we've enlisted twenty volunteer snow plow teams to clear a *single* westbound lane for just thirty-two hours from Exit 148 in Tinley Park on I-80 all the way to…uh"—he paused, looking down at a printout on his desk—"the Great Lakes Petroleum Company at Exit 165 on the Ohio Turnpike. The teams began their plowing at 1:00 a.m. last night all along the route."

"The trick will be," continued the commander, "getting you on that westbound lane *after* the first truck gets to Chicago and *before* the second one passes South Bend. I've already done the math on the lead tanker. It left the refinery at three this morning. It figures to average about twenty-five miles per hour in this storm, so it should be off the toll road by two o'clock this afternoon. As soon as it makes the city, I'll hear about it from one of my troopers. Be sure your phone's charged because that's when I'll call you immediately with permission to enter the toll road. You'll need to make fairly good time because the second truck is scheduled to leave Cleveland some-time after midnight. By the way, what will you be driving?"

"My white Toyota Highlander," replied Gurney.

"Oh, *that's* going to be easy to see in this whiteout. But just in case one of my guy's has x-ray vision, I'll pass the word to let you go if they spot you. Their instincts will be to arrest you and lock you up for life if they see you out in the blizzard going east in the westbound lane. Also I'll notify INDOT to let their plough trucks know you're out there. If this storm dissipates, they might finish their job and be home before you leave. But if not, you should see their flashing lights in plenty of time. Keep your lights on and get to the side as far as you safely can. They should be able to plow around you with no problem. That's all I can do."

"Thanks, friend. I won't forget this."

"Just do me a favor, okay? Don't go and die on me. On the same day I'd lose my job and the only guy I can take money from on the golf course."

"If you lose your job, maybe the Cubs would hire you in the front office," said Gurney, sounding more lighthearted than he felt. "They're getting new owners next year anyway."

"What are you talking about, crazy person?" laughed the lieutenant.

"Yeah, a group of businessmen from the Philippines are buying the Cubs so they can rename them *The Manila Folders.*"

"Maybe *I* should arrest you and lock you up for life," groaned Gurney's friend. "Now, seriously, be careful out there today. Got it?"

"I got it," said Gurney, adding: "Just one more thing, Russ, okay?"

"What is it?"

"Pray."

CHAPTER

sixty-four

Gurney checked the volume on his phone as he walked back to his room. He grabbed the sleeping bag he'd brought and the blankets he'd been using from the guest house, his briefcase and his duffel with a week's worth of laundry in it and proceeded to the facility's main entrance. After dropping everything in a chair by a window with a full view of the parking lot, he backtracked to the vending machine area by the bathrooms. Using his credit card, he selected a wide variety of snacks and drinks in case he needed them en route to South Bend. Finally, he settled into a teal armchair that looked like it had been bought at IKEA and someone had given up trying to put it together. But comfort was the last thing on his mind.

He spent the next few hours waiting for the snow plow to arrive, praying for his family, and unsuccessfully trying to call Babe to tell her he would be home that night. Shortly after 11:00 a.m., Gurney looked up from his phone and noticed that both the snowfall and the wind had decreased significantly. In fact, the view was so clear by noon he spotted the red pickup truck more than a block away on South Cass Avenue approaching Argonne. Surely this was a sign he'd made the right decision.

An hour and a half later, the Dodge Ram had cleared enough of the lot that Gurney could leave. But first he had to find Dr. Cassells to ask a favor of him. He found the likeable scientist in his office.

"Steven, I'm leaving as soon as I say goodbye to you."

"Then don't say goodbye. Just because you might make it out of Chicago now doesn't mean you'll reach your destination." Turning away from Gurney and looking out the window, he continued. "Much of the weather we've gotten here is from an extraordinary system that appears to be weakening. But that could change momentarily."

"Add to that," he said, pivoting back to face his colleague, "forty miles east of here you're going to be blasted by the lake effect snow that has buried Northern Indiana. It's just too risky. If, for some reason, you were caught in that trap".... His voice trailed off.

"Goodbye, Steven," said Gurney firmly, but with softness in his eyes. "Even though our work was interrupted, this trip was worth it for me to find a friend like you."

The physicist rose from his chair, and, towering over his companion, grasped Gurney's outstretched hand and pulled him in for a warm embrace. When they separated, Gurney said,

"I just have one favor to ask before I go."

"Name it."

"Even though you probably won't succeed, keep calling my wife, okay? You might get lucky and catch a reception window. I want her to know I'm on my way. Here's the number," he said, handing Steven a slip of paper.

A minute later, Babe's cell phone number in hand, Dr. Cassells opened the front entrance door and was shocked by the blast of cold air that rushed into the lobby while Gurney awkwardly exited with his belongings. Though the wind and snow had diminished, the glacial air from outside pierced him like an icy dagger thrust. He later told friends he'd never felt that degree of cold before in his life. So not having braced himself for it, he instinctively recoiled and let go of the door, which then unceremoniously bumped his friend's posterior on the way out.

Feeling guilty he was standing in a relatively warm lobby watching a good man battle arctic weather, he regretted not putting more pressure on him to stay. He stood by the same chair Gurney had sat in earlier and watched its last occupant unload his gear in front of the second in a row of peculiarly shaped mounds of snow. While Gurney, wearing a bulky, hooded winter parka, used his gloves and coat sleeves to wipe away great swaths of snow from his vehicle, Steven had a flashback to a classic movie called *Nanuk of the North*. It was a silent film he liked about a beleaguered Eskimo who had to uncover his dog sled and team of huskies after they'd been buried the night before by a tremendous blizzard. *There is nothing new under the winter sun,* he thought. *Did Nanuk survive?* He couldn't remember.

Eventually, Gurney and his cargo were inside the SUV, and Steven wondered if it would start. Sure enough, a thin cloud of white vapor exploded from the tailpipe and dissipated into the frigid air. He hoped his friend's GPS was working but figured he knew the way without it. Slaloming around moguls of freshly plowed snow, Gurney skillfully pulled out of the parking lot and turned east. Steven, his hands and the tip of his nose against the frosty window, earnestly watched him until he disappeared from sight. Even then, for several minutes the physicist continued looking in that direction—as if his intense focus was willing Gurney forward. *He just might make it,* he thought—*especially if he uses the main expressways to reach the toll road. Surely the Chicago crews have been working on them since the weather improved a few hours ago.*

Gurney's four wheel drive got him to I-55 South. It was slow going but obvious that some brave civil servant had recently been at work clearing that stretch of the interstate. Still, as far as he could see, he was the only one on the road, a reality that seemed ominous to him. It was Saturday morning, just two days before Christmas, and the city was eerily silent. Crawling through the canyon of skyscrapers, hearing only the crunch of his tires on the snow, he felt like he was Will Smith in a winter version of *I Am Legend.*

In the hour it took him to navigate his way to the 80/90 Tollway, he had seen only two cars, and both were the police. The first was being driven by one of "Chicago's Finest," who must not have noticed Gurney pass in his white vehicle. The second was a state trooper sitting at the toll road's exit. Gurney's heart sank, figuring this was the end of his attempt to reach Babe. But the officer made no move to stop him from heading up the exit ramp and driving east on the westbound side. In fact, it appeared he nodded when Gurney drove by. Commander Lawley had kept his promise.

After he negotiated the steep ramp and his wheels found the single plowed lane, he felt a rush of adrenaline. *This is going to work!* He drove the first ten miles averaging almost thirty miles per hour. Once he got it up to forty, but after fishtailing out of the cleared lane and almost getting stuck in a drift, he slowed down significantly. He knew if he got stuck on this barren snowscape, it would probably be fatal.

During the next hour, he found that his greatest danger was monotony. There literally was nothing to look at, nothing he could focus on. At least the ice planet, *Hoth,* had an occasional *tauntaun* passing by. But with no sunshine to provide perspective, it was as if everything had been covered with a flat, white-grey blanket. There was no distinction between the earth and the sky. They had simply frozen into one lifeless, hoary canvas. And with no horizon to hold his eye, he tended to drift and eventually could detect the narrow, safe path only by feel.

To add to his problems, it was rapidly getting darker. By the time he turned on his headlights, the snow gleamed silver under a churning, gunmetal sky. He glanced at the clock on the dashboard. It was still set for Eastern Standard Time and read 5:02 p.m. In a half an hour it would be pitch black outside.

But as darkness encroached, and with his lights on, he found he could distinguish the lane better, and with the improved vision his hopes began to rise again. Each new mile added to the odometer was a boost to his spirit. He could see Babe's face in his mind. She was smiling and relieved to have him at her side. The kids leaped up from the floor by the cozy fireplace and ran to meet him at the door when he came in just in time for Christmas. He was so caught up in the vision that he hardly noticed the first few flakes of snow on his windshield.

CHAPTER

sixty-five

With no warning but the snow that started to fall again, a gale-force wind directly out of the east struck Gurney with such power he felt his engine kick into another gear as if it was suddenly navigating a steep hill. Now the snow wasn't just falling; it was assaulting him head on and limiting his vision to zero. He immediately braked the car and switched off his brights, giving him a few feet of forward visibility. And he sat there for several minutes just thinking. Stopped in a fierce storm at night in the middle of the westbound lane heading east, and all he could do was sit and think.

I can't be more than twenty miles from South Bend. I can still make it. I don't have to worry about oncoming traffic. No fool would be out here but me.

Staring ahead, it seemed to him that all the snow in the world was being directed at his windshield, like the sky was filled with machine guns using snow pellets for ammo and most of them were aimed at him. *And what's with this east wind? It's been blowing out of the northwest for three weeks. This isn't just lake-effect snow.*

It was the first time since he left Argonne that it occurred to Gurney that someone other than God might want him on this toll road. That thought sent a chill up his spine, but instead of discouraging him, it simply made him angry and more resolved to get home. He squeezed the shift knob from park into drive and began to inch forward. Seemingly in response, the intensity of the wind and snow increased. *Greater is he that is in me, than he that is in the world,* thought Gurney, slightly pressing on the gas pedal.

The next hour of driving was a battle and he had no trouble staying awake. With each passing minute, it was getting harder to discern the plowed lane. One false move and he would lose it, with little hope of getting back on. And he tried everything he could think of to get an advantage. He turned his wipers as well as the window defroster on high. He lowered the driver's side window periodically, thrusting his head out to get a better view while awkwardly trying to keep the car on a straight line. He even considered turning around on the chance he could see the lane more clearly going east in reverse. But he didn't trust he could make that move without getting stuck.

Unable to see any kind of a road sign or highway mile marker, he had to rely on his odometer to give him an idea of how far he had left to go. But he didn't like taking his eyes off the road even for an instant, so he disciplined himself to drive a full ten minutes before checking the mileage. And being a guy, he made a game out of it by trying to cover exactly three miles every ten minutes. To do that, he had to average eighteen miles per hour, and accomplishing that in this blizzard was all he could handle—especially because every time he lowered his eyes to check the mileage, he cut his speed in half to lessen the risk of driving out of the safe lane, which was far less safe than it had been an hour ago.

Holding the steering wheel with his left hand, Gurney reached down for his half-filled water bottle. After taking a drink, he pulled a nutrition bar out of the plastic bag on the passenger seat. Moving his left hand to the bottom of the steering wheel, and gripping it with the three left fingers of that hand along with pressing up on it with the top of his upper left leg, he was able to keep the car on track. Meanwhile, he used the remaining index finger and thumb of his left hand and those same digits on his right to open the breakfast bar. But just as he raised it to his mouth for a first bite, he thought he detected a slight difference in the opaque wall of snow before him. Was it his imagination, or was there a yellowish light deep behind it?

Stan Wolff, veteran of fifteen years with the Indiana Department of Transportation, was in his muscular, ten-wheeler International

Workstar truck replowing the toll road about five and one-half miles west of the Notre Dame exit. He was one of twenty volunteers trying to keep a single lane of the road open for two diesel fuel tankers to deliver their load to the Chicago hospitals. He had volunteered for the dangerous mission partly because he was a good guy and partly because of the overtime check he'd be getting at Christmas time.

But Stan had received no warning to be on the alert for a man who might be coming his way in a desperate attempt to get home to his pregnant wife. If he had, he might have slowed down, but as it was, he was driving a little faster than he should have been for the whiteout conditions he found himself in. And the reasons for that were two-fold: when you've spent most of the previous night and all of that day shoveling snow on the portion of the highway assigned to you without seeing another human being, you tend to get too comfortable with the danger. Add to that the knowledge you are only a few miles from the salt dome where you will get some much-needed food and rest, and you have incentive to press the gas pedal too hard.

Meanwhile, Gurney had a decision to make. He knew at his present speed he was approximately fifteen minutes from his home exit, and a part of him wanted to press on no matter the risk. But a stronger instinct told him he hadn't imagined the yellowish light. The problem was his own lights reflecting off the furiously blowing snow effectively blinded him to anything that might be coming behind it. So he decided to slow down and turn off his headlights to see what could be seen. That instinct gave him one second to swerve to the left and saved his life.

The snow was so dense and the truck driver so focused on the cut of his v-blade down the center of the highway that he never even saw Gurney's vehicle with its lights turned off. For Gurney's part, at first he saw only an immense, orange blur burst from the storm, and in that split second did everything he could to avoid it. And he might have succeeded if Stan Wolff hadn't been using his wing blade as well that night. The blade clipped the back end of Gurney's car which threw its front into the side of the passing truck. The truck driver felt a slight jolting near the rear of his vehicle but passed it off as storm debris and kept his focus on the road in front of him. The collision was far more serious for Gurney.

He heard the sickening crunch of metal on metal. Instantly, a small switch in the passenger side airbag igniter sensed the crash force and sent a signal to the inflator system. The inflator set off a chemical charge producing an explosion of nitrogen gas, filling up the air bag. As the bag inflated, it burst through the dashboard panel and invaded the passenger side space, showering it with a cloud of talcum powder. All of this happened in twenty-five milliseconds, the time it takes you to blink or sneeze.

But Gurney's brain was in turbo mode and the world had slowed down for him. It was as if, for an instant, he was seeing things with the eyes of God. He could distinguish individual snowflakes on his windshield, each with its unique, six-sided pattern. He could read the lettering and the number of the orange truck as it crawled past him: *INDOT 60568*

And he could see Babe clearly at that moment. Or at least he could see her from behind. With Carrie sitting at the kitchen table eating a bowl of Lucky Charms, a green and a blue marshmallow coloring her spoonful, Babe was bent over, looking out the open kitchen door and down what appeared to be a tunnel through the snow.

In the next millisecond, the driver's side airbag exploded from the panel behind the steering wheel. Though it deployed at two hundred miles per hour, he watched it slowly expand and observed the suspension of powder in the air around him, noting its acrid smell of burning dust. As the car careened away from the massive snowplow, turning upside down then upright again into a deep snow drift at the north side of the highway, he was surprised by two things: that the bag was much larger than he expected it to be, and that his glasses stayed on when it pinned them to his face. The bag, however, failed to push his right fist downward and out of the way. Instead, with the surreal, slowed-down ringtone melody, *Cheer, cheer for old Notre Dame,* coming from the phone in his pocket, Gurney involuntarily raised his arms to protect himself, and the erupting bag drove that fist into his forehead, knocking him unconscious.

In the two hours that followed, *The Notre Dame Fight Song* played many times in Gurney's car while the eighty-mile-per-hour winds and freakishly heavy snow worked to bury most of it from sight. Those same punishing gusts shrieked like demonic laughter across the four hundred yard open tract that lay between the comatose man and the noisy woods, where they masked the disgusting sounds of a gruesome band of enormous wild boars feasting on their evening kill.

CHAPTER

sixty-six

The crisis in the barn had passed. Lying next to Ben, who was hand feeding her bits of hay and grain, Pockets playfully nudged the boy's ribs with her nose. She was going to recover fully and fast. Jacks remained just outside the barn door for a moment. After the storm had been silenced at his command, the thirteen year old looked up and observed the clouds breaking for the first time in weeks. The few stars he could see were as bright as ice chips flung across the sky. He smiled, reached back and pulled his parka hood up, then bent down and entered the snow tunnel. A few minutes later, still on his knees, he knocked on the bottom of the kitchen door.

Having just put Carrie to bed, Babe opened the door and exclaimed, "Thank God you're all right!" Jacks scrabbled into the kitchen, stood up and closed the door.

After she embraced her son, holding on to him longer than he expected, she eventually let go and asked, "Where's Ben? Is Pockets alive?"

When the boy gave her the good news, she still seemed disturbed, so he asked, "What's wrong, Babe? What do you know? Is it Gurney?"

Her soulful eyes hooded with concern, her lips a tight, thin line, she nodded slowly, then answered, "I got a call from Argonne more than an hour ago, and they said your father left for home at 2:00 p.m. Chicago time. Even allowing for the time change and the blizzard, he should have been here by now. Unless…"

"Don't even think that," replied the boy. "He's got to be okay." The two of them sat down at the kitchen table and waited in awkward silence. Jacks checked his phone for any missed calls and turned the volume up as loud as it would go. Another hour passed and still no word. Finally, putting her phone down and rising in stages from the table, bracing both sides of her swollen tummy with her hands, Babe said,

"I don't think sleep will be an option tonight, so I'm gonna make a strong pot of tea. Want some more hot chocolate?"

"No thanks. Tea's fine. Milk and honey in mine, okay?"

She nodded and started filling the kettle with hot water when they heard a light rap at the back door. Jacks jumped up and ran to let Ben in. The older boy was weary but happy that Pockets was warm and resting peacefully in her stall. The last thing Jacks wanted to tell him was the predicament their father was in. But before he could speak, Ben sensed something wasn't right.

"It's late. What are you two doing up? I could have gotten in that door by myself as long as you left it unlocked." Jacks had an enigmatic look on his face, and for him that was tantamount to being clinically depressed. And Babe sat at the table staring into her cup of tea.

"What's the matter?" he asked. "Were you *that* worried about me and Pockets?"

Babe looked up. "Of course we were, dear."

"It's not that," interrupted Jacks, trying to carry a part of his mother's load.

Ben felt a gnawing uneasiness in the pit of his stomach. "Then out with it," he said, impatiently. "What's happened?"

"It's Dad," answered Jacks.

"Bloody hell," said Ben, from watching too much *Sherlock* on the BBC. "Where is he?"

"We don't know," Jacks replied. "He's somewhere between Chicago and here. He left at 3:00 p.m. Eastern time, and that was," he glanced at his phone, "over eight hours ago."

The older boy stood there immobile, trying to take in the meaning of what he had just heard. And then, "No!" he shouted.

"Not again!" Furious, he stormed past Jacks in his hurry to leave the kitchen. A moment later they heard the bedroom door slam. Again.

"He's thinking the worst," Jacks said softly.

"He has a right to," replied Babe. "Poor kid. He's had too much loss."

"Dad's not lost," the boy countered. Then he walked over and laid his hand on Babe's shoulder. She reached up and grasped it with her own. "We need to pray," she whispered. They sat at the table long into the night, silently praying and hoping one of their phones would ring. Eventually Jacks laid his head on his arms and fell asleep.

He awoke in the dark, with only the tiny bulb above the stove still on. Babe must have turned off the overhead light and gone upstairs to bed, probably slipping in next to Carrie. He checked his phone for the time: 4:17 a.m. Other than his neck hurting a little from the awkward sleeping position, he actually felt refreshed and knew exactly what he had to do.

CHAPTER

❧———❧

sixty-seven

Dad's not lost, Jacks thought, *and I've figured out how to find him—if his phone has any juice left.* The boy walked into the den and recognized his mother's laptop charging on a side table by her favorite chair. After he opened it with her password, which she had never attempted to conceal from him, he went directly to the *Verizon Family Locator* app. There he found Gurney's profile and simply scheduled an e-mail alert to be sent to Babe's computer with Gurney's location at 4:30 a.m. Six minutes later, the alert came through with a comprehensive map to his father's whereabouts—along with detailed turn-by-turn directions. He had almost made it home, and even now was only six miles away on the Indiana Toll Road!

With his heart rate maxing out, Jacks read the directions—and then read them again. *There must be some mistake,* he thought. *This says his car is on the west-bound lane. How can that be? Well, I'll worry about that when I get there. I've got a lot to do first.*

The boy knew that if Ben somehow discovered what he was up to, his cousin would stop him—even if he had to use force. The embittered older boy was convinced Gurney had died in the blizzard and simply wouldn't allow Jacks to risk doing the same. Realizing he would need Bear and that the dog wouldn't know whose side to take if Ben woke up, the boy left the light off in the hallway and stole quietly into their shared bedroom.

Ben and Bear were both sleeping soundly, but Jacks took no chances. He waited for his eyes to adjust to the darkness, then stealthily crept toward the dog, reaching down to hold his tail so it wouldn't wag against the bed post when the boy led him out of the room. When they reached the staircase, Jacks bent down and whispered, "No barking, boy. We can't wake anyone up. Okay?" Whether the dog shook his head involuntarily or actually nodded it in agreement, the boy wasn't sure. But he was confident the yellow lab would keep his excitement in check.

When they got to the kitchen, Jacks used only the light from the open refrigerator door to find everything he needed for both of their breakfasts. "It's going to be a long day," he said to Bear. "We'd better fill up the best we can."

Fifteen minutes later, after he'd bundled in layers for the severe weather, Jacks and Bear were in the snow tunnel and headed to the barn. Once there, the boy flipped the light switch and walked over to check on Pockets. Though the heater in her stall was doing little to bring warmth to the rest of the barn, she seemed comfortable enough, so Jacks set his plan into action.

First he found the snow shovel just inside the door. He took the woolen scarf from his neck and tied it around his face. Then, pushing the barn door open as far as it would go—less than two feet—he slipped out into the frigid air and attacked the snow in front of the entrance. His goal was to be able to open the door just far enough to drive the tractor out. Two furious, ten-minute-shoveling sessions with a middle trip to Pocket's stall for warmth and rest did the trick.

Next, at the end of the barn furthest from Pockets, he grabbed a few tools from his dad's work bench, after which he pulled the old blue tarp off the John Deere tractor. Then he set about removing the brush hog they'd used that fall to clear the pasture. He'd seen his dad do the same thing many times and found it to be a fairly simple operation. But disconnecting the three point hitch from the back of the tractor and attaching it to the front proved to be slow and tedious. The subzero temperatures that had assaulted the barn after the electricity failed caused the bolts to hard-freeze into place. It was all the thirteen-year-old could do to force them loose. He labored so long and hard over the job that tiny streams of sweat vapor were escaping from under his parka and mixing with the white puffs of water vapor he exhaled with every breath. More than once he wished he had Ben to help him.

Also, his waterproof, leather mittens were making it difficult for him to use the wrench, but being that far away from the heated stall, he feared contact frostbite if he took them off. At ten below, touching metal of any kind can cause serious damage. And now the chore was taking him so long that he began to worry about Bear and eventually had to lead him over to Pockets and close him into her stall while he worked.

After connecting the hitch came the hard part: lifting the NorTrac snowblade with its quick-attach mount into position while simultaneously lining up the proper slots and dropping the two lynch pins into place to secure it. But it's remarkable what you can do when you have to, and after three failed attempts, he heard the two clicks he was listening for. Breathing heavily, he collapsed to the floor for a moment to rest. It's strange what comes to your mind when you least expect it. Sitting there rubbing his aching biceps, he remembered a phrase in a recruiting commercial he'd seen on television. Two marines were dropping out of a helicopter onto the deck of a moving aircraft carrier when a voice offscreen declared, "A marine does more before breakfast than most people do all day."

Jacks rose from the floor, retrieved the ignition key from a hook on the wall and climbed into the cab of the tractor, thinking, *I'd make a pretty good marine.* "Semper Fi!" he yelled when the faithful, sixty-six-horsepower machine started up on the first try, its four-cylinder, shrouded diesel engine quieter than most tractors. Still, hoping not to awaken anyone in the house, Jacks was careful with the gas pedal for the next hour as he steadily cleared a path from the barn to the driveway and from there to the road. The snow had begun to fall again, adding to the five feet already on the ground. But the wind had increased as well, covering some of the noise of Jacks' plowing. His purpose wasn't to clear the whole drive, because he knew even if he did, the family station wagon wouldn't be able to go anywhere on the roads in their present condition. The only chance he had of getting to Gurney was on the farm's snowmobile.

CHAPTER

sixty-eight

Restless in his upper bunk, Ben writhed about in the grip of an old nightmare, from which he simply could not awake. It kept replaying with a different ending every time—each one more grotesque than the last. If he heard the diesel tractor engine in the driveway outside his window, it simply merged into the highway sounds in his grisly dream—a dream that always started the same way: he was following the van with his parents and siblings inside when their gas tank exploded. Only he wasn't in the back seat looking over his grandparents' shoulders at the horrific sight. In this dream, he was always alone at the wheel and had a decision to make when his family crashed into a final ball of flame.

In one dream sequence, he simply followed them into the concrete embankment and exploded alongside their own inferno. Another time, he chose to screech to a halt behind them, jump from his vehicle and begin the insane process of entering the car and pulling each screaming victim from the raging hellfire—his own face melting along with theirs. The worst version, though, was when he chose to keep driving, turning his eyes from the scene and speeding away riddled by guilt.

Ben had no idea how long this nightmare held him in its grasp. It could have been hours or seconds. But he was aware that just before he woke up, a different kind of familiar dream replaced it. He knew this one so well. Once again, he was buried under the snow. But this time, there were more details. He realized that none of the snow was touching his body because he was in some sort of protected space. Though he couldn't see anything, he sensed he was partly covered by a peculiar kind of blanket. He brought his hands up to push it away, and that's when he discovered that at least two of the fingers on his right hand were broken. Using only his left, he removed the covering, which felt like a heavy, deflated air mattress coated with a powdery substance.

He instinctively moved his arms and legs in the dark, and they seemed to be fine. But what grabbed his attention was a raw, throbbing in the front of his skull. When he explored it with his fingers, he was shocked by the stabbing pain and the size of the protrusion in the middle of his forehead. It was torturous to touch, and he instinctively jerked his hand away from it, knocking his glasses onto his lap. After finding and carefully putting them back on, he sat in the darkness for what seemed to be many hours. Eventually, he was having so much trouble breathing that panic began to set in. With just a trace of oxygen left, he heard a dog bark very close to him.

This is when he always woke up, and nothing changed this time. But when he rolled over and looked toward the window, seeing that dawn had already broken, he heard the dog bark again!

Confused, he wondered if he was still dreaming. So he swung his feet over the side of the bunk and slid down to the floor, his feet touching the cold wood simultaneously with the sound of another dog bark. He rushed to the window and looked down to the driveway. There he saw his cousin coaxing Bear to join him on the back of the snowmobile, its rumbling engine causing her to hesitate. *You crazy fool!* thought Ben. But just as he raised his hand to pound on the storm window, the yellow lab leaped up behind Jacks and the two of them roared out of the driveway and onto Kintz Road.

The older boy was a jumble of mixed emotions. He was angry with Jacks for leaving, frightened by the risk his cousin was taking for a lost cause, and profoundly disturbed by Bear's barking. It reminded him of something else. What was it? He sat down on the chair by his desk and thought. The only thing that came to him was the odd version of the otherwise familiar dream he had lived with for so long. The new details of the dream were troublesome. What was that peculiar covering with the powder coating he pushed away in the dark? How did he get that painful swelling in the middle of his forehead? It hurt so much that when he touched it, he'd knocked his glasses off. Wait a minute! Glasses! I don't wear glasses!

More puzzled than ever, Ben had a nagging sense that the answer to this riddle was more important than anything else in his world. In fact, he somehow knew that the answer was the key to everything. And suddenly, like sunshine breaking through a thick layer of clouds, he got it.

Gurney wears glasses, he realized. *This dream isn't about me. It's never been about me!*

Trembling on the wire of this new awareness, a part of the boy wanted to push it away and return to his accustomed way of seeing the world. But now he had a pretty good idea about the identity of the dog who barked in his dream—a dream that had haunted him for many months. Often he'd been sick with worry when he woke up from it, because he always assumed it was a portent of an evil that waited for him somewhere in the future. Now he was faced with the only conclusion that made any sense to him. The God he had hated since the death of his family more than three years ago had been preparing him all along for this very moment.

Parting with your familiar demons and changing your mind about the nature of God are almost impossible tasks for most sons of Adam and daughters of Eve. It often takes something like a near-death experience, or a blinding light knocking you off your horse when you're traveling to Damascus to persecute first century Christians, or in Ben's case, a harrowing dream coming true for someone else. But there was no time for wondering if he'd been wrong about God.

What he knew for certain was that he was right about the dream, and that meant that Gurney had been buried in his car under the snow for many hours already. He also felt confident now that the desolate man was somehow still alive and that Jacks and Bear would reach him with little time to spare.

"What am I going to do?" he said out loud, as if there was someone in the room with him. *Is there someone in the room with me?* he wondered. His spine tingled and the hairs on the back of his neck stood up. Rising from the chair, he listened in silence for a long moment. He could feel his heart beat quicken. "Who are you?" he asked. Though he neither heard nor saw anything in response, the boy had an unshakable sense that there was a presence in the room with him.

It wasn't simply an aura that filled the air around him. This felt like there was a person there, actually taking up space in the corner nearest to the door—a person watching him and listening to him. And it was nothing like the evil one Jacks had confronted that night months ago when Ben was pinned to his upper bunk in a catatonic state by the fear that went before it. In fact, this time, he felt like he was being encouraged to speak. So he took one tentative step toward the corner and asked, "Are you him?"

The boy had never forgotten the incandescent, serene face he'd seen in this same room exactly one year ago today—specifically on the night Jacks had taken on the sickness that initially held him in its grip. At first he thought the incident might have been a vision conjured by his delirium. But he'd stopped believing that after a conversation with his cousin about the Shining Ones. Now he was faced with the real possibility that he was in the presence of one of Them. Jacks's words came back to him:

> *"He's here to protect you—and to serve as a messenger between this world and the Real World."*

"Is there something you want to tell me?" Ben asked of the darkness. "I'm listening."

Instantly, two words formed in the boy's mind. They weren't audible, but they were definitely there. "Go, now." It was all he needed. "Thank you," he said, politely, and five minutes later, he was in the kitchen, making a ham sandwich and heating up hot chocolate for his thermos, when Babe shuffled in.

Ben looked up. "Jacks is gone," he said.

"I know, dear. He's going to bring his father home," she replied, handing him the note Jacks had scotch-taped to her bathroom mirror just before he left.

> *Babe, don't worry, I believe Dad's alive. And thanks to his phone app, I know where he is—only six miles east of here on the toll road. I'll try to call you after I find him. Maybe our phones will work again by then. If you need anything, Ben will help you. Pray for all of us. I love you.*
>
> *—Jacks*

"He's absolutely right," said Ben.

"About what?"

"Dad's alive." And then he told her about his dream and the Shining One in the bedroom upstairs.

CHAPTER

sixty-nine

It was the cold that woke Gurney up. He instinctively gasped and opened his eyes. He could see nothing in the darkness and his first thought was that the French doors on the balcony to their bedroom had blown open again, filling the room with an arctic blast. And then he remembered where he was and what had happened to him: the snow plow exploding out of the storm and brushing him aside like he was driving a Matchbox car, turning upside down during the crash and thinking he was going to die. *Maybe I am dead,* he mused. *I don't know how the dead could be any colder than this.*

He felt something frigid and heavy covering his chest and touching his chin. But when he raised his hands to push it away, a stabbing pain shot up from his fingers, and he realized at least a few of them were broken. So with just his left hand, he removed what he figured had to be the deflated airbag. It probably had kept him from slamming his head into the steering wheel. Or had it? He felt a throbbing pain in his forehead and impulsively touched it—a mistake he wouldn't make a second time. His agony was exquisite.

Jolted by the severity of the angry swelling, he'd knocked his glasses off and searched for them in the dark. When the pain diminished, he continued the inventory of his body parts. Nothing else seemed to be broken or injured. But the cold was pinching at his earlobes and creeping through his woolen pants like frosted metal along his skin. Unable to control his shivering or the chattering of his teeth, he knew he was in trouble if he didn't get warmer right away.

He had no doubts now about where he was: buried in his car under the snow just off the toll road and not far from home.

Using his good hand, he tried to open the driver's side door. When it wouldn't budge even after he put his shoulder to it, he knew he wasn't going anywhere. He was trapped by a few tons of snow and ice and his only hope was that someone would find him. He had no idea what time of night or day it was. He guessed that it was daytime and that he had spent the entire night entombed in his Toyota.

Thank God for the insulating properties of snow, he reflected. *Still, if I'm going to keep this car from becoming my refrigerated coffin, I'd better do something fast.* Then his thoughts ran to Babe and the kids at home. He didn't know how many of them were praying for him, but he had a bedrock certainty that at least one of them was at that very moment. A sense of calm settled on him and an inner courage took root in his heart. He spoke defiantly to the darkness that enveloped him: "You'll have to try again another time. This will not be the day I die!"

He pulled out his cell phone and saw he still had ten percent of his charge left. But when he tried to call 911, it wouldn't connect. He got the same result when he punched in Babe's number. Then he reached through the bottom of the steering wheel with his off-hand and found the keys still in the ignition. He understood that if the car's tail pipe was buried along with everything else, he could die of carbon monoxide poisoning by trying to get warmth from the running engine. But that risk became moot when he got no spark from the starter. He immediately turned clockwise in his seat and reached behind it, feeling for the blankets and sleeping bag. The bag had fallen onto the floor during the rollover, and when he found it, he proceeded with difficulty to move into the back seat. In doing so, he inadvertently knocked his right hand against the side of the driver's seat, and the jagged pain of his broken fingers brought tears to his eyes.

Before attempting to climb into the sleeping bag, he found the duffel with the food and water he'd put in it. Shaking like a politician under oath, he covered himself with a blanket the best he could. For the next five minutes he carbon-loaded on bags of baked Lays, mini-pretzels, Peanut M&M's and two chocolate chunk granola bars, washing it all down with half-frozen orange Gatorade. Next he exercised his arms and legs the best he could in the back seat, trying to work up a little body heat. By the time he shoved himself into the waterproof, mummy-style sleeping bag, he knew he was not going to die from the cold in the car—at least not for a while. His job was to stay alive as long as he could. But he knew the odds were against him. Who could possibly find him in this blizzard?

That's when he remembered some advice a friend gave him years ago after a doctor had told Babe that she could never get pregnant. He'd said, "Whenever God wants to do something good, he starts with something difficult. But when God wants to do something extraordinary, he starts with the impossible." Through the years, that advice had become like a permanent message thumbtacked onto the notice-board of Gurney's mind. *Nothing is too hard for Him,* he thought, closing his eyes and zipping the fur-lined bag over his face. What he had was hope. What he needed was a miracle.

CHAPTER

seventy

Like the GPS receiver and the aerosol can, the snowmobile has its origins in military technology. The army needed something that could move over soft and unstable terrain where a wheeled vehicle couldn't gain any traction. A snowmobile's tracks and skis spread the sled's weight over a greater surface area, allowing it to travel just about anywhere. Even so, Jacks and Bear hadn't gone five blocks on their sled before the depth of the snow and poor visibility almost made them turn back.

The wind picked up again, and the clouds above him shed millions of tiny, twirling wheels—each one with six rounded, semicircular teeth—biting at his eyes under the ski mask. The boy throttled down and braked his machine almost a mile from the Toll Road entrance near Notre Dame. Bear, the perfect travel mate, sat behind him on the Sherpa dual-track sled, his snow-covered head turned away from the bitter wind that quartered them out of the northwest. Now that they had stopped, he stood and shook off the accumulating powder, restoring the insulation of his furry coat.

As the four-stroke engine idled, its emission cloud streaming away like the condensation trail from a jet plane, the boy heard a raucous sound and looked up to see a murder of crows swimming briskly in the high, icy currents of the storm. Because of the cold, he decided to put on his helmet—even though he felt he could see farther without it. The visor on the helmet had an anti-fog coating so that when the cold, moist air outside it met his warm breath on the inside the resulting condensation wouldn't impair his vision. After flipping the front of the helmet down, he looked up again to see if the crows were still there. They weren't. He couldn't help wondering if the scavenger birds were wheeling, even now, toward a frozen, human body several miles down the highway.

"Don't give up, Dad," he said grimly, his words scattered by the howling gale. "We're coming for you." He turned to his dog and yelled, "Get down, boy!" The yellow lab obediently curled into a ball behind Jacks, who shouted against the wind, "Good Bear! Good dog!" Then, his instincts telling him he needed some speed to move through the deep powder, the boy hit the throttle with too much force. The sled leaped ahead awkwardly almost throwing Bear off, but the dog dug his claws into the leather to stay on the seat. Before Jacks could regain control he burrowed his machine partway into a monolithic snow drift three times the height of him and the sled.

As he began the arduous task of digging out, the snow began to fall even harder. "This is just great!" he complained to Bear. He realized he was in more trouble than he'd figured on.

Now that they were out of the neighborhoods and in the open, they had a bigger problem than the others they first encountered.

Besides there being dangerous moments when he was moving forward without being able to see five feet past his windshield, the new difficulty was that the snow wasn't uniform in its depth. There were places where the wind had blown it into drifts fifteen feet high and other spots where the blizzard had done the opposite, sweeping away what would have amounted to several feet of standing snow and leaving only a few inches on the surface. Negotiating these treacherous variations made the ride difficult and slow.

Since he couldn't really distinguish any roadways because of the blizzard, he looked for traffic lights and signposts to approximate the location of the road he was attempting to travel. Still, in spite of his best guesses, too often he slid off to the side and down the steep grades of more than one roadside ditch. Once he sank so far into the soft powder that he completely buried the sled.

How am I ever going to find Gurney like this? thought the boy, the machine beneath him and the snow up to his chest. Time and again he was forced to dig out with the shovel he'd attached to the sled with two bungee cords. He had to do it so often that he was getting skillful at the process. Each time, he would first clear much of the snow from around the machine. Then he used the shovel to tamp down the ever-deepening drifts in front of the sled. Finally, stomping with his boots, he packed down the pathway ahead so the snowmobile would get some traction on it.

After a few hours of "three steps forward, two steps back," the snowfall lessened so much he could see far enough to throttle up and keep the machine floating on top of the snow for a while. As he got more experience riding through the powder, he learned that a little track spin could go a long way, so he began to work the throttle with more finesse. Whenever he was on the throttle too hard and started trenching, he would back off and feel the sled surface to the top of the powder again. Once that happened, he rolled into his throttle with more confidence and moved forward—until the whiteout conditions caused him to bury his sled in another drift that rose up before he could avoid it.

And so it went for him all the way to Interstate 80. He continued to fight the same problems he had from the start, only more so when he came to the toll road entrance. Once there, he found the wind much fiercer with no buildings and few trees to thwart it. Still, after wiping off his visor, he made decent time negotiating the four lane access road that took him to the toll booths. And that's where Bear and he paused to make a crucial decision.

Should he choose the east or westbound lanes to begin his search? He assumed the locator app had been wrong about what side of the road Gurney was marooned on. He just had to be six miles down on the eastbound lane. Nothing else made sense to him. So that's the lane he chose. But before he started up again, he got off the sled and checked the straps on the cargo platform to make sure the things he'd packed were still secure. The wood for a fire was still in place, along with a hand axe he added in case he needed to gather more. So was the camp cooler, filled with a large thermos of hot chocolate, five bottles of water, a box of crackers, an empty plastic dish, some leftover hamburger patties and hot dogs in a Tupperware container, and assorted breakfast bars. He noted the poly tarp and four, extra-long driveway reflector poles he'd added in case he needed a temporary shelter from the snow. Finally, he patted the red cross sign on the metal, winter survival kit that never left the snowmobile—not even in the summer. Along with many other helpful things, it included first aid supplies and a few packages of disposable hand warmers, two of which he removed from the kit to replace the ones he'd been using for the past several hours.

As he and Bear finished their descent of the curving, Notre Dame exit ramp and found themselves moving into the teeth of The White Hurricane, Jacks stopped, and his eyes searched north toward the westbound lanes. From where he sat on his sled, peering through the storm with a mittened hand acting as a shield to keep the snow off his visor, he couldn't see that a single lane had been plowed only on that other side. In fact, when he looked in that direction, he could distinguish no surface irregularities at all in the snow. The problem was that, even at midday, the light was so diffused no shadows were cast. There wasn't even a visible horizon because the white cloud layer appeared to merge with the white snow surface. He knew then his only chance of spotting his father would be if he was out of the car and his parka appeared dark against the blizzard. But even as he thought it, he understood if he found him outside the vehicle, he would not find him alive.

Fighting the temptation to despair, he forced himself to refocus on the difficult task of covering the next six miles.

CHAPTER

seventy-one

Babe had no trouble believing Ben's story about the Shining One in his bedroom or the certainties that he knew Gurney was alive and that his dream had been about her husband all along. Her biggest problem with the argument for the Supernatural had always been that an argument should be needed at all. If there is a God engaged in his creation, shouldn't there be evidence of him in every breath we take and in the birth of every child? If anything as breathtakingly beautiful and formidable as angels and as unspeakably depraved and menacing as demons existed, shouldn't their existence be as obvious as the sun in the sky? It's a fact of life that people don't see what they don't want to see. Babe harbored no such prejudice, so she quickly grasped the truth of her nephew's story on several levels.

First, Ben had given her at least some hope that Gurney could be rescued. In the darkest moments of the anxious night before, it crossed her mind more than once that the infant in her womb might never see its father. In fact, when she'd awakened that morning, even before discovering that Jacks was out in the blizzard with Gurney, a pall of discouragement had settled on her like nothing she'd ever known. Now a part of her was tempted to hold onto Ben's conviction that a thirteen-year-old and his fourteen-year-old cousin were going to find him.

She also realized that the boy had to leave as soon as possible to help Jacks. When the Guardian had told him to "Go now," she didn't even consider questioning the wisdom of that instruction or complain that she would be left without the boy's considerable assistance. She had only one question for him, and it was a simple one: "How will you get there?" she asked.

"Pockets," he responded. "It'll do her good to get out of the barn and she's a lot more trustworthy than any snowmobile."

"Of course," she said. "Now put on some layers and then get her ready for the trip. But before you start tacking up, bring me her saddle bags as soon as you can. I'll fill them with plenty of food and water." Then a thought came to her, and she said, "While you're getting the bags, I've got something else you're going to need. Let's meet back here in a few minutes." She left the kitchen and returned a moment later with plenty of hand and foot warmers from the mud-room closet, where she'd noticed that some of them had already been taken. When the boy returned, she said, "Here," and handed him two of the packages. "Put these on now before you go back to the barn and I'll stuff the rest into your bags." Her brow creased, and she added, "I feel like we're forgetting something else important."

"We are," replied Ben, in his terse style: "You and the baby."

"No, that's not it," she responded. "Even if you stayed, I couldn't get to the hospital in this blizzard. Besides, if things go well," she said brightly, hoping he couldn't sense the growing apprehension she was forcing down, "the three of you will be back tonight and I'll have all the help I need. Hey, I know what we're forgetting." She turned and opened the cabinet door above the microwave oven, pulling out a can of non-stick cooking spray. Handing it to the boy, she said, "Spray each of them liberally with this stuff, and it'll keep the ice and snow from sticking to her hooves. Now, get a move on." The boy headed upstairs to put on his thermal underwear and two pair of woolen socks.

Five minutes later, sitting at the kitchen table nursing a steaming cup of tea, she watched her nephew open the kitchen door and enter the snow tunnel to the barn. It wasn't lost on Babe that something remarkable had happened to the boy. He was on a desperate mission now and was smart enough to know that the One sending him was the same One he had hated for so long. Rubbing her hands over the firm but tiny back of her daughter who stretched the skin of her tummy to its limits, she whispered, "Heavenly Father, watch over him," and then louder, "And while you're at it, there's a little girl in here who's going to need her dad and big brother very soon."

No sooner had she spoken those words than Babe was seized by a brutal contraction. It began in the middle of her back and slowly moved around to the front. There had been signs for two days this might be coming. Besides the spots of blood on her underwear, she hadn't been sleeping well at all, had to pee all the time, and this morning woke up hardly able to breathe because the baby's foot was pressing so hard against her ribs. But whereas with Carrie her first contractions felt something like cramps, this one was in a league of its own. It felt like her body was being punched, twisted and wrung from the inside out and that every organ beneath her heart was experiencing catastrophic failure. The pain was so intense she slipped into a state of shock for the thirty seconds it lasted.

When it subsided, she was sweating and panting heavily. Her first thought was, *Dear God, what was that? How many sadistic little gnomes are in my abdomen squeezing it with hot vices?* Her second thought was, *whoever said every pregnancy is different was right. Is every contraction going to hurt as much as this first one?*

A sense of dread and anxiety took further hold on Babe's mind—mostly because she didn't know what to expect next, and because she feared Ben would reappear when she was in the middle of being battered by an oncoming freight train, which was probably due soon to tear through her insides again.

CHAPTER

seventy-two

When Ben opened the door to the barn, he saw that Pockets was already on her feet—as if she knew they were about to leave on a trek together. The first thing the boy did was give her a quick but thorough grooming, paying special attention to the areas where the equipment would touch her. He brushed the hair on her back in its natural direction to keep her from developing saddle sores later in the day. Next he got down on his knees and lifted each of her legs in turn, using a pick to clean her hooves before treating them with the cooking spray. Then he put a waterproof, wool cooler over her shaggy winter coat to wick away perspiration so she wouldn't feel damp from the strenuous exercise she was about to get. He knew she would naturally adapt herself to the cold weather if he could keep her sweating under control.

After he'd gently cinched the saddle and slid the bridle over her head, Ben buckled the throat latch and spoke softly into her ear, "You're such a good girl," he cooed, stroking her withers with his right hand. "You wanna help me find Gurney now?" She rubbed her silky jowl lightly against his cheek and shook her head up and down as if she'd understood the question. Even though Pockets went more than three years without hearing Ben's voice, she'd always had a special affection for the boy. But since he started speaking to her seven weeks ago, she was as tightly bonded to him as a horse could be. He could ask anything of her and she would give him her all.

He took a clean sponge from the shelf above the saddle rack and dipped it into the slightly heated water bucket. After squeezing the water out leaving the sponge only damp, he used it to carefully clean the matter from her eyes. Her vision was going to have to be at its best to navigate the snowy terrain that stood between them and Gurney's car.

After he finished cleaning her up, she lowered her magnificent head which always meant she wanted him to hug her. The boy kissed her on the top of her muzzle and reached his arms around her neck, drawing him close to her ear. "This won't be easy, girl," he whispered. "It's crazy cold out there. Once we leave here, we might not make it back."

It didn't matter to Pockets. There is no temperature bar to riding a horse that trusts its rider. If it wasn't too cold for him, the weather wasn't even a consideration for her. She was an Appaloosa trail horse in the prime of her life and would take him anywhere he wanted to go—or die trying.

As for Ben, he had no illusions about the challenge he and his beloved friend were taking on. Still, he was so convinced the dream was a sign that he had to risk it. He wasn't certain whether it was a part of that dream last night or not, but he'd heard the eerie howl of a coyote or young wolf in the woods across the street from the farm. It reminded him now to retrieve the scabbard holding his compound bow and arrows from its hook on the wall across from Pockets' stall.

Because he was wearing convertible mittens with a lockdown zipper, he could move his hand through the opening and use his fingers without them getting too cold thanks to the inner glove. Now, with the top of the mitt off, he took the soft, blue scabbard and tied it behind the saddle on the right side of the horse so it would give him easy access to his weapon if the need arose and wouldn't interfere with his riding.

It was time to leave. Jacks and Bear had a sizeable head start on him, but who knows what difficulties they were facing on that snowmobile. He had an inner conviction that he and Pockets, by steadily plodding forward through the blizzard, could reach them in time to help Gurney. But first he had to pick up his saddle bags from Babe.

CHAPTER

seventy-three

After filling the saddle bags, Babe called Gurney's number and 911 a half dozen times, but got no results. The White Hurricane had finally knocked the regional cell phone towers completely off the grid with no functioning back up system. Now she had a decision to make. The second contraction had arrived ten minutes after the first and again was thirty seconds of stunning agony. She knew the baby was coming, and that she could use Ben's help in delivering it—especially in light of the signs that this was going to be a grueling childbirth with real risks for her and the infant. She considered waiting to see if his return from the barn occurred during a contraction or between two of them. If during, she would ask him to stay and see her through the ordeal. If between, she would do her best to act like everything was okay and send him on his way. But on a deeper level, she believed the boy was probably the key to any chance, however slight, of rescuing her husband from his own peril. There was no decision to make. She would have to face whatever was coming on her own. So even though she couldn't shake the sense of dread that was on her, Babe haltingly took a path that at least was familiar to her:

"Lord, I've never been this scared in my life," she prayed out loud, visibly shaking in fear of the next contraction. "I don't think I can do this—not without Gurney." Just verbalizing his name brought back all the worry that had tormented her through the night. The further possibility that both Jacks and Ben were profoundly putting themselves in harm's way as well was simply too much for her at that moment. Her eyes spilled over with tears, and, crossing her forearms on the table before her, she threw her head down and wept with abandon. Had Ben walked in on her then he never would have left to look for Gurney, dream or no dream.

Instead, what happened next reminded Babe later of a scene in the Gospel of Luke. The Son of Man was facing extreme physical torture and began sweating drops of blood from the emotional turmoil. Suddenly, an angel from heaven appeared to him in the garden and strengthened him for the cross that lay ahead. That is what guardians do best.

As Babe sat at the kitchen table, her head in her arms, her face a melt of tears, anticipating the next bolt of pain, she felt a warm, firm hand on her right shoulder. Gurney had done that very thing to her so many times through the years when she needed encouragement that her instinct was to reach her own hand up to place it on his. Then she remembered the situation she was in and figured Ben had caught her unawares. But when she lifted her head and turned to look at the boy, there was no one there! Though she had never seen one of the Guardians, she'd been aware of their presence enough in her life to know what had just happened. God was in her kitchen.

And it was all she needed to bring her back. She sat up as straight as she could and took a deep breath, both arms wrapped around her belly. She wasn't alone, and now it didn't matter when Ben returned. Babe knew what she had to do.

Soon the boy appeared back at the kitchen door. Pale and exhausted, she greeted him with a genuine smile, still wondering when the next contraction would strike.

"Are you sure this is the right thing to do, dear?" she asked, knowing what his answer would be.

"It's the only thing," he replied, too focused on his mission to notice her weakened condition.

His youthful courage and unwavering purpose were breaking her heart with pride for him, but she maintained control and, handing him the saddle bags, said, "There's plenty of food and water in here for you and Pockets to share. Keep changing your hand and foot warmers whenever you need to; if you have to dismount for any reason because of the blizzard, don't let go of your horse's reins; and above all, *look for help when you least expect it.*" She wasn't even sure where that last thought came from, but it had already escaped her lips, so she let it ride.

Ben wanted to catch up to Jacks with daylight to spare, but the intensity of Babe's gaze held him where he stood. "Promise me this," she said, her honey and hazel eyes swimming with fierce emotion. The boy dutifully nodded up and down.

"Bring my boys home to me," she said.

"Yes, ma'am," he answered softly.

Babe hugged him the best she could in her condition, kissed him gently on the cheek, and then he was gone—back in the snow tunnel taking the saddle bags with him. She had no time to watch him crawl away. Because when the pain struck again, she had to grab the back of a table chair to keep from crumpling to the floor. But this time, she was determined to master it. "Is that all you've got?" she shouted at the pain. As it turned out, it wasn't. She was going to need Carrie's help to survive this day.

CHAPTER

seventy-four

Jackson

Riding in powder is more physically demanding on both the rider and the snowmobile. And the powder was so deep on the toll road that Jacks was forced to boondock for long periods. In fact, the only times he sat down on the machine were when he got so tired from standing that he had to rest. When that happened, he would circle back and stop on his own track so he would have traction when he started up again.

Only twice had he gotten stuck on the straightaway, and both times were because of poor visibility. When the wind shifted slightly and was more out of the west than the northwest, it was directly into his face, and he could see nothing, so essentially he was riding blind. That's when his fear of steering off the road and into a ditch caused him to throttle down and sink into the powder. Tired from all the shoveling he'd done just to get to the toll road that morning, he learned he could clear enough of the snow from under the front of the sled using his legs and feet. Then, like earlier, he'd simply stomp a path in front of the machine, climb back on, brush the snow off the blanket that covered Bear, feather the throttle and ride the new track back up to the surface.

The relentless wind was coming out of the northwest again, so visibility was slightly better. Once he built up some momentum, he took an athletic stance and got into the rhythm of picking his line and transferring his weight from side to side so he could control the sled by counter-turning through the deep pockets of powder. Eventually, his stomach told him it was way past lunch-time, so he started looking for a safe, level place to brake on.

His choice was random, but when he circled back on his track and stopped, he looked downwind and saw something behind him and just off the highway that made his heart jump. It was a great wall of snow rising from the ditch at the side of the road, and it vaguely resembled a semi-tractor trailer.

What if it is a truck? thought the boy. He turned away from it and looked ahead down the highway through the driving storm. He thought he recognized the overpass that spanned the toll road at Interchange 72. He brushed his coat sleeve across his visor and held his mitten over the front of his helmet to ward off the flakes. *Yes, that's Highway 31!* He was sure of it. *I'm less than a mile from Dad.* He glanced back at the ghostly wall of snow, his sled idling in the middle of the buried road. *It might not even be a truck. Maybe it's just a weird drift created by the wind. I've got to get to Dad before it's too late. What should I do?*

What Jacks did was get off the snowmobile, walk around it to the cargo platform, unstrap and open the camp cooler, and pull out of it a plastic dish, a Tupperware container and a bottle of water. He took a long drink of the water and poured the rest into the dish, which he laid, along with two hamburger patties, on the seat in front of Bear's nose. "Here, boy. You need some fuel." The dog sniffed the burger but stayed under his blanket, stretching his tongue and jaw out to pull the meat into his mouth. "A little cold, huh?" Jacks said. "Me, too." Then the boy grabbed the snow shovel, turned away from the sled and walked into the ditch, throwing snow left and right until he came to the wall rising before him.

He turned the shovel around and, poking its handle through the snow, he heard it strike metal. The truck was there! Could a driver be trapped inside? Even though it meant a risky delay in reaching his own father, Jacks had to do whatever he could for whoever was in there. Minutes later, he had cleared enough of the door that he could open it and gain entrance to the cab. Jacks paused, preparing himself for what he might find. If the driver was dead, he would leave him and let the weather preserve his body until a state trooper found him. If he was still alive, he had a tough decision to make, knowing it might mean giving up on finding Gurney in time. His heart racing, he opened the cab door.

The cab was empty. He grabbed the steering wheel and pulled himself into the driver's seat. A meaty odor came up from the floor behind him. *A bad sign,* he thought. He turned, apprehensively, fearing what he would find in the sleeper cabin. He stood up between the two front seats and turned toward the back of the cab. Then the boy took off his glove, reached into his ski pants pocket and pulled out his cell phone. Engaging the flashlight app, with a trembling hand he raised the phone to the darkness, and there it was in the middle of the driver's bunk—an Arby's bag turned on its side with a half-eaten, beef 'n cheddar sandwich spilling out of it.

In another situation, he might have laughed out loud from comic relief. Now, he was just glad he hadn't found a corpse. His thoughts were a rapid-fire stream of consciousness: *That could have been a lot worse... Whoever was in here must have tried to walk to safety; I hope he made it...I wonder if Dad tried the same thing.*

Picturing his father stumbling through the snow in the night, he leaped down from the cab into a deep drift, and extricating himself from it, high stepped his way back to the sled. He'd been fighting the storm for several hours and the cold had long since been affecting his ability to think quickly. But now a clarion bell was sounding in his heart that this was the last round of the fight. It had come down to this: he had to find Gurney soon and then figure out a way to get them both to warmth. Even if his mind hadn't been numbed by the subzero temperature, the alternatives were still unthinkable.

CHAPTER

seventy-five

Ben took Pockets' reins and walked her from the barn to the driveway. There he mounted her and followed the path Jacks had plowed that morning to the road. The cold was brutal, and even with a thick ski-mask on, he could feel the damp surfaces of his nostrils beginning to freeze. He reached into his parka pocket and pulled out a red, woolen scarf and tied it over his mouth, nose and ears. In a real sense, he was more at risk than his shaggy-coated horse, who would maintain a measure of warmth by the constant exercise of her muscles.

The surrounding woods muted most of the wind at that hour, and as they followed Jacks's snowmobile track out of the farm and down the road, Ben was struck by the silence. It was as if a giant, winter spider had spun a gossamer web of white in the night, soundproofing anything capable of making a noise. There were no cars, trucks, snowmobiles, or horse-drawn sleighs to be seen or heard. Nothing. All flights had been cancelled at the South Bend Airport, so there wasn't even a plane in the sky. The only sounds were his horse breathing and her hooves crunching along the trail that had been left before her.

When Jacks had negotiated this same road earlier on the deafening snowmobile, he'd been so focused on slaloming around mega drifts without sliding into a ditch, he paid almost no attention to his surroundings. Now, Ben, who was giving Pockets her own head to follow Jacks' clear route, was awestruck by the otherworldliness of the snowy scene he was riding through. Under the gloom of a turbulent sky, almost nothing looked familiar to him. After another night of high winds and heavy snowfall, several single-story homes he knew well and expected to see had completely disappeared. Here and there, he detected the dark patch of a roof peak that had been swept clean by the capricious wind, but most of the small homes he approached from the north were entirely buried on that side. Only a thin curl of smoke from a chimney gave some of them away. He had to turn and look at them from behind to see any signs of life in the charcoal grey shapes, their back windows like curious yellow eyes watching him pass.

Each time Pockets came to a place where Jacks had gotten his machine stuck, she would paw the snow-covered ground and blow out through her nostrils. Ben wondered if she was marking the spot so he would notice, or simply showing she could balance better on three legs than the snowmobile could on its skis and tracks. Whatever her reason, she wouldn't move on until she had lowered her head and thoroughly sniffed the area around the trench made by Jacks and Bear.

When she apparently had paid ample homage to the snowmobile's mishap, the determined horse resumed her trek along the path that climbed out of the ditch. Resolute in her course, she didn't even shy when Ben was startled by a sudden movement on their left. It turned out to be one of the middle branches of a pine tree dumping enough powder to spring back into position. The boy looked around and saw that most of the evergreens were so heavy with snow their lower branches were crushed to the ground and buried under a heavy shroud of white.

As he got closer to the main road that connects South Bend to Michigan, he could hear the wind crying shrill in the tops of the oak trees. Otherwise, the eerie silence and complete inertia that met him when he rode up to the notoriously busy thoroughfare was even more striking than what he'd experienced in the neighborhoods. Stopping there for a moment, he had the sensation that the world lying before him hung in suspended animation, and he was disagreeably interrupting it.

Before they walked onto the road that would take them to the I-80 entrance, Ben unzipped his left parka pocket and pulled out one of the carrots he'd stored there. "Here, good girl, take this" he said, reaching around the horse's head and offering the treat. She picked it off his glove while he stroked her neck with his other hand. "Now it begins," he said. "This is gonna be wild."

The wind was far stronger in the open, but the horse leaned into it and before long they reached the spot where Jacks had made his critical choice. Even though the drifting snow made it harder here for Ben to read his cousin's trail, there were enough signs left for him to see the choice the younger boy had made. It wasn't a path suited to a horse. The snow was so deep in places he doubted Pockets could manage to get through them.

It's a good thing horses see differently than humans. Because they are a prey species, horses have eyes with rectangular pupils that are designed to scan the horizon. Pockets stood there with a large panoramic field of view. Using both of her eyes, she could see virtually 350 degrees—almost a complete sphere of vision. While Ben was intent on finding Jacks' route down the eastbound exit ramp, his horse was picking up an interesting reality beyond the median of the highway. She balked when her rider, loosely holding the reins, tried to steer her onto the trail he wanted to follow. The boy tightened his grip and tried again. She refused to budge.

He knew his horse well enough to trust her instincts, so he gave control back to her. "It's all yours, girl!" he shouted to be heard over the wind. "Let's go get Gurney." She immediately turned away from the eastbound ramp and headed toward the opposite side. A few minutes later, though The White Hurricane punished them for their daring, they found the single-plowed lane going west.

CHAPTER

seventy-six

Later, Babe came up with her own categories for the grades of contractions she experienced that afternoon. The first ones she called *the hammer and sickle* variety. The next level was the *mortar and pestle* medley and the last hour introduced *the boulders with teeth* category. This was to be the hardest day of her life.

When Carrie finally came down for breakfast, she entered the kitchen but no one was there. *That's odd,* she thought. *I'm not that late, am I?* She looked at the clock over the stove and realized she was. Still, it seemed peculiar that she didn't hear a sound in the house. She wandered into the family room and found Babe sitting alone on the couch staring at the phone in her left hand. In her right, she held a pen poised over a TV tray supporting a white envelope with what appeared to be lines of numbers scribbled on the back of it. When she looked up, her face was lined with worry and pale as the egg-shell colored wall behind her.

"What's wrong, Mama? Are you sick? Where are the boys?"

Babe smiled weakly, "They've probably found your father by now and are in the process of bringing him home. And me? I'm just timing my contractions."

The girl's eyes opened wide. "What? You're having your baby? Now? Here? Without a doctor? Without Dad?"

"Guilty on all counts, dear," she replied, returning to her phone screen. When the next one hit, she groaned involuntarily and dropped the phone, turning toward the arm of the couch and gripping it with both hands. Carrie rushed to her side, sitting close and patting her back. "Oh, that's good!" gasped Babe. "Press both of your fists into the middle of my back and push down hard." The girl did as she was told, and forty-five seconds later, the pain had subsided.

"Eight minutes," Babe panted. "That's too far apart." Seeing her daughter's concern, she added, "Thank you, sweetie." She took a shallow breath and wheezed it out. "You really helped me get through that one."

Carrie noted the beads of sweat on her mother's brow. "Mama, what are we going to do?"

Babe drew her daughter close and embraced her, gently kissing her on the forehead. Then she looked into her questioning blue eyes and said, "Together we're going to bring your baby sister into this world."

Can we do it, Mama?" asked the girl.

"We have no other choice, darling. Now here's what I need you to do."

For the next few minutes, while Babe was in the basement storage room rummaging through their camping equipment, Carrie went to the main floor laundry room, pulling a load of towels and bed sheets out of the dryer and folding them the best she could. Babe found the small space heater she was looking for, a plastic tablecloth and the LED lantern they used for camping. She had a good use in mind for all three of them. But no sooner did she have everything in hand than another contraction hit. She endured it bravely while throwing her weight back into an old mattress leaning cockeyed against the concrete block wall. Less than a minute later, her brow dripping with sweat, she slowly pulled herself erect, gathered her articles, and trudged up to the kitchen. Glancing at the clock over the stove, she noted, 11:11 a.m.

Babe waddled with her load to the foot of the staircase. Her legs trembled from exhaustion, and she said out loud, "Lord, I can't get up there unless you help me." One minute later, she set the lantern by the side of the bed, covered the mattress with the plastic cloth and plugged the heater into an outlet under the bedside table. She knew she was racing the contraction clock and moved as quickly as possible.

Shuffling across the hallway to the bathroom, she washed her hands and cleansed her underbelly area. Opening the medicine cabinet, she hurriedly pulled out a package of dental floss, a sturdy pair of scissors, one bottle of hydrogen peroxide and one of isopropyl alcohol. With her hands full, she returned to the bedroom just as Carrie reached the top of the stairs with a stack of towels and bed sheets in her arms.

"Do me a favor, sugar," Babe said. "Put those things on the bed and go down to the kitchen to fetch me two of the smaller cereal bowls. The ones I'm thinking of are dark green, and I think they'll be perfect."

"I know the ones you want," the girl replied eagerly, dropping her load off and heading back to the stairs where she rushed down them two at a time.

I wish I was as excited as she is, thought Babe. When Carrie returned to the room, she held the bowls out to her mother. But before she could take them, Babe sat down abruptly on the bed. "Ugh!" she grunted, gritting her teeth and grabbing a bedpost. The little gnomes were back with their hot vices. Along with the oppressive wave of nausea, it was like being pressed in an old-fashioned laundry ringer. With her head down and her eyes closed against the pain, she still had the presence of mind to ask Carrie, "What time is it, dear?"

The girl looked at the alarm clock on the bed stand. "11:17, Mama," she answered.

"Six minutes," Babe panted. "They're getting closer. Come put your fists against the middle of my back again and press as hard as you can."

When the contraction had passed, Babe turned to Carrie who was sitting on the end of the bed behind her "I'm so sorry you have to be a part of this, sweetheart."

"But I want to help you," the girl replied.

"I know you do, and I appreciate it so much," Babe said, taking her daughter's hands in hers. "But no eight-year-old should have to see what you're going to see today."

Carrie looked closely at her mother's face, in a way family members seldom do. The long pregnancy had hollowed Babe's cheeks and eyes, and exaggerated her full mouth. "I'm tougher than you think, Mama," the girl answered.

"Yes, you are, my darling. And I'm pretty sure you're going to need to be."

CHAPTER

seventy-seven

Jacks was getting anxious. He was boondocking now exclusively on the snowmobile, scanning both sides of the road for anything that resembled a buried vehicle. The sled's odometer told him he had traveled six miles from the Notre Dame exit, the exact point where the locator app had marked Gurney's phone. The boy knew he should be seeing some indication of his father's car, and his stomach was twisted in a knot because he didn't. He braked the machine and dismounted, the muscles in his legs aching from his tense riding stance.

"Stay, Bear!" he ordered, and, detaching the shovel from the side of the sled, proceeded to plant it like a flag in a drift as a six mile marker. Then he waded into the ditch to confirm that nothing but snow was there. He did the same thing on the opposite side of the two-lane, eastbound road before climbing back onto the Sherpa and riding it another quarter mile to the west. When he was certain there was nothing buried along either side of the road, he turned and came back to the shovel. He sat there with his back to the wind, his thoughts swirling around him like the blowing snow. *Where is my dad? He has to be right here!*

Jacks knew he was running out of time. Holding the instinct to panic at bay, he bowed his head and, with lips cracked by the cold, prayed the ancient words of 2 Chronicles 16:9—"*For the eyes of the Lord search back and forth across the whole earth, looking for people whose hearts are fully committed to him, so that he can show his great power in helping them.*" Then, with his shoulders slumped and his eyes still closed, he shook his head and cried out, "Where is he, Father?!"

He opened his eyes and obeyed an impulse to look toward the north. He sat for a long moment, trying to see what couldn't possibly be seen through the blizzard at that distance. With the storm and the idling engine providing a clamor of white noise, the boy was now desperate to figure this puzzle out. For hours he'd been stumbling along the edge of Occam's Razor, believing that the simplest solution is always the right one, when suddenly it struck him that simplicity can work in the opposite direction as well. *As much as it doesn't make any sense,* he thought, *Dad has to be on that westbound lane!*

He pulled out his phone and looked at the time: 1:04 p.m. *He's spent all night and half of this day buried alive!* Immediately, the boy throttled up and turned left toward the median of the highway, which was hidden some five feet below the powdery surface. By standing near the back of the sled to keep the front of the machine a little higher, he repeatedly pivoted the skis in the opposite direction he wanted to turn and so power-waggled his way across the median to the far side of the westbound lane. There he stopped, his eyes sweeping the shoulder of the road and beyond. Through a veil of spiraling snow, he thought he detected an unusual form in the otherwise empty white flat scene about fifty yards to the east, so he gave his vehicle some gas and carved his way toward it.

As the sled neared the mysterious shape in the ditch, Bear leaped off, barking like he'd picked up the scent of something interesting that now had all his attention. The yellow lab threw his powerful chest toward the looming formation of powder and began digging furiously into it. Soon whining frantically, he used his forepaws to jettison huge amounts of snow between his hind legs until his burrowing was stopped by an unmovable barrier. When Jacks heard the dog's nails scraping metal, he came in behind with the shovel and began clearing the front side of the entombed vehicle. "It's him, Bear! It's him!" the boy cried out, gradually uncovering the pearl-colored Toyota and silently praying that his father was still alive.

Eventually Jacks tossed the shovel and began brushing away the snow from the edges of the driver's side door. He pressed his face against the window, and his hope sputtered when he saw there was no one in the front seat. With the inside back of the SUV too dim to tell if anyone was there, he yelled out, "Dad! Dad! We're here!" Then the boy tried the door latch, but it was locked. "Dad, if you're in there, unlock the doors!" There was no response. Jacks pushed down his worst fears and grabbed up the shovel again.

After clearing the rear side of the car, he anxiously peered in the frosty back window. His first take was that nothing was there. "No!" he shouted, wiping the glass the best he could with his right mitten and looking again. This time he could make out a shadowy rumpling of blankets and the irregular, lumpish contour of what appeared to be a body. His heart leaped and he turned back to the sled. There was no time to debate the pros and cons of smashing the back window and gaining access to that seat.

Instinctively, he ripped off his helmet and grabbed the hand axe from the snowmobile. The cold slapped his bare face and squeezed tears from his eyes. Bounding through a drift back to the car, he swung the butt end of the axe head with all his might into the middle of the back side window. The tempered glass exploded into thousands of harmless round pieces of crystal, most of which disappeared into the snow. A moment later, Jacks was in the back seat, pushing away a blanket to reveal a sleeping bag arranged in a fetal-like position, containing the still figure of a man with the unconscious, pasty-white face of his father.

CHAPTER

seventy-eight

There is no exact core temperature at which a human dies from cold. Nazi experiments at Dachau's cold-water immersion baths revealed that death usually arrived at seventy-seven degrees Fahrenheit. By the time Gurney stirred in his sleeping bag late on Sunday morning, Christmas Eve day, his body core temperature had gradually plummeted from 98.6 to 85 degrees. He had crossed the thermal boundary into profound hypothermia, and his blood had thickened like crankcase oil in a frozen engine. During the previous night, the activity of his heart and liver, along with involuntary shivering, had produced most of his body heat. But as his core cooled, he stopped shaking, and these organs, in essence, shut down to preserve heat and protect his brain.

The lower body temperature had made his breathing so shallow and his heart rate so slow that when Jacks took off his glove and touched his father's pallid, blue face, he feared he was dead. In haste, the boy unzipped the bag and pulled him part way out, preparing to perform CPR. But first, he opened Gurney's coat, drew up his layers of clothing and threw his head onto the man's naked chest.

The cold remains a mystery to most cold science researchers. To date no one can predict how quickly or on whom hypothermia's icy fingers will place its death grip. It appears the cold is more likely to kill men than women, more deadly to the slender and athletic than to the two thirds of us with avoirdupois. But severe cold is most prone to dispatch people who are arrogant and unaware of its lethal capacity. Gurney had been neither arrogant nor unaware.

Jacks' breath rolled out in short, frosted puffs, in contrast to the stillness shrouding Gurney's face. The boy noticed the ugly bluish-yellow bump in the middle of his father's forehead, and anxiously pressed his ear against his cold chest. His skin felt waxy and as stiff as old playdough. At first he heard nothing, but that only made him focus harder. Seconds passed like minutes, and just as he was about to give up, he thought he detected a slight sound—a single thump, so insignificant that initially he assumed it was the blood pumping through his own ear. But then he heard another thump—and another.

As temporary illness sometimes leads to better health by offering its victims the opportunity to lose debilitating weight because they're too sick to eat, so extreme and deadly cold sometimes offers those who suffer from it a peculiar salvation. At absolute zero, molecular motion stops abruptly, and that includes body metabolism. The heart pumps less blood, and the lungs inhale little oxygen. Under normal temperatures, that would cause brain damage. But the super-chilled brain, having slowed down its own metabolism, requires only a fraction of its usual oxygen-rich blood, and can, under the right circumstances, survive intact. Maybe it's God's way of making up for blizzards. And so, Gurney had remained in this cold stasis, his brain undamaged, for many hours.

Jacks pulled the layers of clothing down to cover his father's torso and removed his own parka, blanketing the coiled exposure victim with it. Then he opened the sleeping bag and crawled into it, drawing the man's tortured figure into his arms and spooning him from behind. After thirty minutes, he felt Gurney stir slightly. Fifteen minutes later though, the boy sensed that this process was too slow and he needed to change tactics. He remembered the wood and the tarp on the sled.

Adroitly, Jacks freed himself from the bag, leaving his parka with his comatose father and instructing Bear to nestle up next to him. Though exhausted, he took up the shovel again and doggedly worked to clear a rectangular area from the car to the side of the ditch. Every few minutes, he would stop and rest, leaning on his shovel and turning his gaze to the woods just north of them. When he had the ground prepared, he retrieved the tarp and poles from the sled, and using yellow, nylon tie lines, he anchored the poles to support the tarpaulin. By the time he shoveled and packed snow around each pole, he'd established a sturdy little shelter against the storm.

With a PK12 lighter and two starter logs, he ignited the kindling and firewood he'd specifically brought for this occasion. It wasn't long before a robust fire was reflecting its heat back from the ditch's incline into the shelter. The boy stood before it for a moment, breathing hard and absorbing its warmth. He anxiously looked toward the woods again. It was time to bring Gurney out.

He returned to the car to grab the three blankets from the back seat. Two of them he dropped on the lee side of the fire and would use them to cover his father. The other he spread out a safe distance from the life-giving blaze. Then, retracing his steps, he reclaimed his parka, putting it on quickly, and yelled to the dog, "Okay, boy! I'm going to need your help now!" Bear jumped down beside him while Jacks used gravity to slowly pull the sleeping bag with Gurney in it out of the back seat, being careful to lay his head gently on the ground. Bear joined in, taking a toothy grip on the corner of the bag, and helping Jacks drag the unconscious body to the blanket by the fire.

Meanwhile, standing at the edge of the woods, a foot taller than his eager captains, Plague had watched the boy's fire flame into life. He chortled when he saw him and the dog labor to remove the man from the car and tow him to the blaze. *"Take them now!"* commanded the Voice within him. The great boar smiled, his obscene teeth jagged and yellow-green with disease. *This will be easier than taking corn from a piglet,* he thought. His guttural roar rose above the blizzard. "Go, my dark children! Your other Master runs with you. Through wind and storm, through fire and snow, destroy them—bone and marrow! Take them now, and bring me their hearts and heads!"

Jacks knew they were coming. He'd been aware of the evil in the woods from the moment he arrived at Gurney's car. Now, out of a finger of timber the length of four football fields away, the wild hogs came. Jacks turned from the fire and saw their dark forms against the snow.

CHAPTER

❧————————❧

seventy-nine

Babe remembered that when the last ultrasound revealed that her baby was a bit underweight for a full-termer, she'd been disappointed and concerned, even though the doctor assured her everything was going to be fine. Now she saw the child's size as a possible advantage for what lay ahead of her that afternoon. Although she was anxious about delivering her own baby without professional help, she believed she was as ready as she possibly could be. Ever since Gurney left for Chicago and the blizzard hit, she'd known she had to prepare for this eventuality. Calling on her own past experience and reading every article she could find on her laptop about emergency deliveries, she'd gathered the materials she would need and readied two rooms on the second floor of their home for the birth of her baby.

Babe was grateful she wasn't alone and had Carrie with her. Even though the girl was proving to be an invaluable help and wise beyond her years, Babe felt guilty for asking so much from her eight-year-old. When she'd explained earlier that day what was coming and what she would need her daughter to do, Carrie was unflappable. "No problem," she'd responded. "Remember, I'm the one who helped 'Mr. Meowgi' have her five kittens—so I'm already sort of a veterinarian."

Now it was early afternoon, and Babe knew it was time to tell her daughter something that had been worrying her for hours.

"Everybody's different when they're hurting," she explained, while sitting uncomfortably on the edge of the guestroom bed, her feet on the floor supporting part of her weight, and her hands on the mattress behind her, bracing her upper body. Across from her on the bed, Carrie listened intently.

"Some people get quiet and withdraw," she went on. "That's not me. I get mad at the pain and yell at it. Do you understand what I'm saying?"

The girl nodded soberly, and Babe's heart filled with pride for her, even as she measured her next words and prepared for another jarring contraction.

"There's a good chance this afternoon I'm going to yell some words you've never heard your mother say before. Try to remember I was raised by a cop from Pittsburgh and sometimes that side of the family slips out when I'm under stress. You'll probably need counseling someday if I let it fly when the pain is at its worst. But I've got a plan."

"Don't worry about me, Mama. What's your plan?"

"When I start feeling like a lemon being crushed in a juicer, I'm gonna try to shout out my favorite Psalm."

Before Carrie could answer with, "That's a good idea," Babe's eyes crossed, she gripped down on the tarp covering the bed and cried out:

"*He-E-E-E-E*" *who dwells in the shelter of the Most High*," she gasped, the wave of pain taking her under before she had a chance to grab a breath, "*will rest in the shadow of the Al—might—te-e-e-e-egads, that hurts!*"

She had re-entered that hurtful red and orange tunnel, and it was closing fast. Carrie slid across the bed and quickly moved in behind her, balling up her fists and applying counter pressure to the muscle spasms in Babe's back.

"*I will say of the Lord, he is my refuge and my fortress, my—sweet fancy Moses!*—this is a bad one!" she exclaimed—"*my God in whom I trust.*"

It went like this for another hour, Carrie faithfully taking instructions from her mother, pressing against her back with all the force she could muster when the contractions peaked, recording the duration of each of them, bringing her ice chips in a damp cloth when Babe rested between them, and using her unique sense of humor to keep her mother's spirits up.

"What does it feel like, Mama?" she asked once during a lull in the action.

"It's impossible to explain, darling," replied Babe. "But it will all be worth it when it's over."

"I've been watching you. I think it feels like throwing up in reverse," she stated matter-of-factly.

Babe towel dried the sweat from her forehead and laughed for the first time that afternoon, responding weakly: "You're right. That's exactly what it feels like."

Although she wished she could have spared her daughter all of this experience, Babe was aware that the two of them were bonding in a way few parents and children could in these modern times. Just feeling her little girl's tiny hands on her back had a calming, spiritual effect on her, and she knew she would never look at Carrie the same again. While she was contracting, riding the painful waves, and quoting Psalm 91, she could hear her daughter quietly praying, "Help her, Jesus. Help my mama now"—over and over again.

So with Carrie establishing a direct connection to heaven, Babe simply concentrated on the miracle of bringing a new life into the world. When anxiety about Gurney and the boys or the next contraction came, she forced herself to channel all her attention on birthing this baby girl. If she'd had her choice, of course it would have been safer and better in a hundred ways to be with attentive health care professionals, but she had no choice. So while her daughter prayed that God would help her, Babe discovered a remarkable truth: her body knew how to do exactly what it was supposed to do.

As if her mind no longer controlled the process, she could feel her body shifting into its own rhythm and preparing for the grand finale. It was like driving your car onto the moving track at the automated car wash only a lot more painful. At one point earlier in the afternoon, when the contractions were still ten minutes apart, Carrie had helped her to the shower, where she allowed the hot water to soothe her aching back while the contraction peaked. But suddenly, just after 4:00 p.m., they were coming one after another—only two or three minutes apart. That's when she told her daughter that if she needed to use the bathroom for any reason, she'd better do it right away, because Babe was going to need her full attention very soon.

Babe had read somewhere that going on all fours and rocking back and forth could alleviate some of the back labor pains. So she returned to the guest bedroom, climbed up on her bed and did exactly that. At first, she felt a little relief, so she kept it up, rocking right and left for a few minutes—until her water broke. She was caught off guard by the flood of fluid. Carrie walked in just then and seeing a surprised look on her mother's face, asked, "What happened?"

Babe's eyes were two huge hazel circles with big black dots in the middle, and from just behind her curious smile came the whispered words, "It's time, dear. She's coming."

CHAPTER

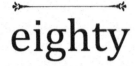

eighty

Ben realized that if Pockets hadn't led him to the single plowed lane on the eastbound side of the toll road, they would never have had a chance of catching up to Jacks. Trying to travel through the deep powder on the other side of the highway would have exhausted his horse beyond her capacity to get to their goal, let alone to make the return trip. Though the snow was gathering again on the plowed lane, it wasn't nearly as deep there, and Ben was a good enough horseman to keep Pockets well collected, with her weight back over her hindquarters. That way, she was more agile and could walk through the snow with less effort. At the same time, the boy gave her enough rein so she could use her head and neck for balance.

After the first few miles, they were making such good time that Ben started thinking he might actually reach Gurney before Jacks did—especially if his cousin had trouble getting his sled stuck in the drifting powder. Then two things happened that made him change his mind. First, a macroburst of high-velocity, electrically charged air, as if hurled directly at them by an angry wind god, exploded twenty yards in front of the rider and his horse. It stunned the boy and stopped Pockets in her tracks. At the same time the winds from the downburst were spreading out radially and muddling their sense of direction, the falling snow thickened into what seemed to be an impenetrable wall. The battle was on, and Ben knew exactly who the opposition was.

With the wind and snow came a heavy shadow that descended on that section of I-80 like a black fog, turning the day into a grainy twilight. Ben felt Pockets shaking beneath him and knew it wasn't just from the cold. He stroked her frozen forelock, gathered himself and spoke to the shadow that enveloped them:

"You won't paralyze me this time, dung god," he said grimly, remembering Jacks' name for the evil one. "I'm not alone anymore." The boy bent down to his horse's ear and said softly, "Don't be afraid, girl. Most of his strength is in our fear of him. We've got to keep going." He lightly tapped her flanks with his boots, and Pockets moved forward. Immediately a preternatural growl filled the air, and the spectral face of an immense gray wolf materialized from the swirling snow. Impossibly suspended before them, the snarling visage blocked their path, and the horse's courage faltered. She stood there trembling, unable to take another step.

Ben reacted instantly. He unknotted the long scarf from around his neck and chin and used it to cover Pockets' eyes, tying it off at her upper cheek. Then he patted her neck and bent over again. "It's gonna be okay, friend. Trust me now. I'll get you through this," he said. He kissed her cheek and shortened the reins. Sitting up tall, he gently squeezed his legs and, with his hips, he pushed down and forward on the saddle, saying, "I love you, Pockets. Now, *let's go!*" And out of a reciprocal love that was literally blind now, she began to walk forward again. Though she could see nothing, the savage growling had never ceased. Added to that, now, were the unearthly howls of a whole pack of ghostly wolves. The boy felt her caution and knew she was paying a price for her faith in him.

Because his own vision was so diminished by the storm, he set a slow, steady pace for them, constantly searching out a path that would keep them on the road. To compete with the howling, he decided to try to encourage Pockets by singing songs he remembered from the years he'd spent at his father's church. But no sooner had he begun to sing than new apparitions appeared out of the storm, only this time they were rushing toward him and sweeping across his face. The first two were the distorted images of his anguishing parents burning in flames, followed by the tormented faces of his siblings.

Though they caused him to tear up under his ski mask, their unintended effect was to put more steel in his resolve to reach Gurney.

He forced himself to focus on the man he was risking his own life for, trapped in the buried car and waiting to be rescued. And, as if on cue, the bluish-gray death mask of Gurney's face suddenly loomed in front of him. *"You lie!"* he shouted, startling the unseeing horse beneath him. When the grotesque likeness dissolved, others followed, most of them repeat performances. It was a depraved hour of macabre madness, but, singing one song after another, Ben rode on, chasing the sounds and shadows for the next four miles.

After what seemed an eternity, the boy sensed they were getting close to their objective. *Was Gurney still alive? For that matter, did Jacks and Bear survive this storm?* As he pondered these questions, the black fog that had surrounded them lifted, and he watched it sail swiftly toward a dense stand of woods he could barely make out far ahead on his right. Although he felt he could breathe more easily and his head was less muddled, he observed that the dark cloud was moving with purpose against the strong wind currents and thought, *That can't be a good thing. I wonder what he's up to now?*

CHAPTER

eighty-one

Due to high mortality rates from predation, the average lifespan of a feral hog is four to eight years. This was the fourteenth winter of Plague's long life, and his beady red eyes were bright with anticipation. With his size and vicious temperament, he was born to kill and had commanded many a slaughter through the years. But the massacre unfolding before him now would be his crowning achievement. His malevolent soul was in perfect concert with *the shadow* that lived within him, and he anticipated an evening of feasting on that rarest of prizes: human flesh.

He monitored his five captains as they rumbled through the deep snow toward their two human targets. Bristleback and Longsnout, younger and hastier than the others, were at the front of the attack by a wide margin. *It doesn't matter,* thought Plague. *There's no need to keep them together against these furless weaklings who will probably not even put up a fight.*

Jacks felt them coming before he saw them. A tremor ran up his spine, and he turned away from the fire to see the five enormous beasts headed toward his shelter. There was no time to think. He knew he couldn't get Gurney back inside the car in time, so he did the most counterintuitive thing he could do. He decided to take the fight to them.

His instincts told him to flee and at least try to save his own life. But his heart took over before his mind could talk him out of it. He snatched the hand axe from on top of the feeder pile of wood, and yelling, "Let's go, Bear!," he and the yellow lab leaped onto the snowmobile. He turned the key, released the choke and the machine roared to life. In a few seconds he had it turned and moving toward the charging menace. The cottontail rabbit was chasing the fox now, and it was the last thing the oncoming boars were expecting.

Jacks didn't want to die. But more than that, he didn't want Gurney to die. In a space of fifty yards, he had the sled breaking to the top of the snow at forty miles per hour and steered it directly at the lead hog. He'd been subconsciously hoping that the sight and raucous noise of the machine would scatter the horde and frighten them away. But as he got nearer to them he realized that wasn't going to happen. Now, throwing a wake of powder at sixty-five miles per hour, an irresistible force was about to meet an immovable object.

Bristleback heard the roar of the metallic monster coming toward him, but he had no fear of it. If anything, its appearance only stoked his mania. The furious boar put his head down, thrust his tusks out and charged the intruder, meaning to destroy it as he had anything that had ever opposed him.

Jacks saw the collision coming with the monstrous hog that seemed to be purposely challenging him. Just to its left was the other beast out front that looked like it would pass him on that side. Streaking over the snow on the sled, he turned and shouted to Bear on the seat behind him, pointing to the hog on their left:

"When I yell, *'Jump!'* you take Porky Pig there. Hogzilla is mine!" Turning back to face the charging brute, he throttled up the sled with one hand and brandished the hand axe firmly in the other. When they were twenty yards away, he cried, *"Jump!"*, bracing himself for the impact he knew was coming.

Because Bear's leap got unbelievable air from the side propulsion of the speeding sled, he overshot his target, and that probably saved his life. Had he landed in front of or on top of the stampeding swine, it surely would have savaged him like it did the coyote in the woods the day before. But leaving the boy on the metallic monster for Bristleback to handle, Longsnout's undivided attention remained on his human target by the fire. So Bear found himself pursuing the crazed animal from behind.

Meanwhile Jacks on the snowmobile hit his wild boar head on with such force that the boy, who had been leaning a bit to the right, flew a good distance in that direction while the sled and the screaming hog shot several feet straight up into the air. The sound of metal on bone and the bellowing of the boar was so loud that even Gurney, his body core temperature rising back by the fire, rolled over and looked toward the noise.

The machine landed almost straight up on its rear in the snow and toppled over onto its back, the engine sputtering. The stunned hog lay quivering on his side, both tusks snapped off at their roots, his right eye socket empty, and a horrible gash across his face from the pointed hood of the snowmobile that almost severed his snout from the rest of his hideous head. Jacks was spread out on the snow, dazed from his own fall but still clutching the hand axe. Gathering his senses, he could feel the ground beneath him shake as the three trailing assassins thundered past his prone form on their way to finish the job at the fire.

Lying there, the heroic boy assumed that the stupendous crash had eliminated one foe, but he could hear Bear still engaged in a deadly battle with the other boar. His head clearing, he didn't know whether to help his dog or try to get back on the sled and pursue the killer hogs. He pulled himself up to a sitting position and looked around just in time to see the impossible. The beast he had run into was bearing down on him from ten yards away!

CHAPTER

eighty-two

Driven by an ancient evil, Bristleback rose from what should have been his snowy grave and lumbered toward the boy who was lying face down. At twenty yards, he saw Jacks roll over, sit up, and look around until their eyes met. At first the boy was mesmerized by the frightful sight before him. The hog's snout, only partially attached to his upper jaw, and his lunatic face a mask of blood, made for a ghastly image that Jacks couldn't turn away from.

At the same time, Longsnout was having his trouble with Bear. The great hog had barely passed his fallen companion when the courageous dog attacked from behind. The golden Labrador retriever bit into the back right leg of the depraved animal who screamed in anger and turned as fast as he could in the deep powder. But there was nothing there. Bear was already behind him, sinking his teeth into the knee joint of the same leg as before. He felt the muscles tear and the bone crack as the furious hog turned on him again.

A few paces away, the other beast was on Jacks before he could react, pushing the boy over with its intact lower jaw, which was snapping grotesquely against its misaligned upper teeth. His intent was to throw his bulk onto his prey and crush him to death. But as Jacks toppled backwards, he used the momentum of the fall to roll toward the pig's blind side. Standing up quickly, he lifted the hand axe high in the air above the villain, and before it could find him with its one good eye and knock him over again, the boy drove the weapon deep into the creature's massive forehead.

Shocked by what he was seeing, Plague heard the death cry of one of his captains, and the black Shadow's shriek when it abandoned its host, leaving the mammoth pig to collapse onto the snow. Disgusted, he turned his attention to Longsnout's battle with the blur of yellow that circled him like a fast-orbiting killer moon. Bear wanted nothing to do with his enemy's teeth or tusks, so he bet his life on trying to stay behind it, and the deep snow had, so far, made that possible. When the crippled hog recognized it wasn't even going to get much of a glimpse of its elusive adversary it decided to make an awkward break for Gurney and the fire again.

Plague was ashamed of Longsnout for running. He watched the dog seize his opportunity and move in to latch onto the back left leg of the fleeing hog. But this time, before Bear could snap the knee joint, the pig managed to turn and savage his opponent's ear. Still, the dog wouldn't let go until, with a mighty twist of his wounded head, he heard the leg break, rendering the killer useless.

Enraged at the spectacle before him, Plague was about to storm in from the woods to destroy the upstarts who had taken two of his best fighters out of the fray, when he was distracted by strange noises coming from the snow-covered highway. Plague wouldn't have known what to call the sounds, but he knew he hated them. On the other hand, Jacks was very familiar with them. Trumpets, hundreds of them breaking out of the blizzard from the east were resounding up and down the bleak road.

The boy saw that the three hogs that had gotten past him were just a hundred yards from Gurney, a small, dark figure huddled by the raging fire. He knew he didn't have time to turn the sled upright and try to rescue his father from the onslaught. He whistled for his dog to come to him then turned toward the fanfare on the highway.

For his part, Ben heard no trumpets, only the steady, heavy panting of Pockets and the violent storm around them. He knew he should be seeing something, anything by now. And suddenly he did. He thought he detected a light just ahead.

But Jacks saw something totally different. Bear had not returned to him, and the boy looked toward the highway just in time to see Ben explode from the storm, followed by more than five hundred *shining ones* with trumpets to their lips, mounted on supernal steeds pushing his cousin along in front of them.

Ben could see the light clearly now. It was light from a fire, and it looked like a body was crumpled on the ground to the side of its blaze. And three large animals were headed toward it. *Are they bears?* he wondered. Of course he knew the body by the fire belonged to either Gurney or Jacks, so the boy kicked Pockets hard and together they vaulted off the road and over the ditch, charging through the snow to fend off the attackers.

Ben recognized now that they were gigantic wild hogs and that this was going to be a close call. They were less than forty yards from reaching their target. While they were rushing in on a southwest trajectory from the woods, he was riding due west toward the fire. The boy stood up in his stirrups, and did a quick assessment of the situation. If he was lucky and perfect, he might be able to stop two of them, but all three? Not likely. Flapping open the tops of his mittens, he reached down to the scabbard just over Pocket's right flank. Matching his movements to the thundering horse beneath him, he took up his bow, notched an arrow to it and aimed eighteen inches in front of the lead hog who was about to arrive at the makeshift shelter. *Zing!* He let it fly.

Instantly, he took another arrow and aimed two feet in front of the second boar. *Twang!*

The first arrow covered thirty yards in one-sixth of a second. The force of it knocked Peacethief off his feet and drove the large broadhead through the pig's shoulder and directly into its heart. Just behind came Brokentusk, who started to swerve away from his foul, fallen comrade when the second arrow penetrated his skull with such velocity that it turned the hog around and threw him against the backside of the half-buried car.

But the fact was that both shots might have been for nothing if Bear hadn't left Jacks a few minutes earlier. He chased down the hapless, one-eared boar who had been savaged the day before by Plague. Running slightly slower than the others because of his condition, Snortwart still would have reached Gurney if the dog hadn't jumped him just short of the shelter. Feeling Bear on his back was the only motivation the wounded creature needed to change direction and run toward a nearby cornfield. To make sure that it wouldn't turn back, the dog followed the fleeing hog for several minutes across the frozen field—where Snortwart would perish on its far side the following morning from the effects of Plague's toxic bite.

Trudging back to the shelter, Jacks saw his dog disappear into the blizzard in its pursuit of the lumbering boar. Before he bent down to tend to his father, the boy yelled a greeting to Ben, who rode up on his beleaguered mount, her senses dulled by the bone-chilling cold and by her profound exhaustion. Both horse and rider seemed dazed by the crazy heroics they'd just participated in. If Jacks hadn't been singularly focused on stoking the flames and helping Gurney, and if the steady roar of the blizzard hadn't covered all other sounds, surely he and his cousin would have realized that the battle wasn't over yet.

For wicked Plague, terrible in his fury, had burst from the woods the moment Ben and Pockets jumped over the ditch. So, shrouded by the storm, he wasn't that far behind Jacks when he reached the flames. A moment later, eight hundred pounds of satanic vengeance with tusks down blindsided the spent horse at the point of her hip and bowled both her and the boy over. The massive boar would take care of the two by the fire in a minute. But first, he must annihilate this intruding bowman and his worn-out nag.

CHAPTER

eighty-three

When Plague hit Pockets at full speed, it was like a battering ram bringing down the inviolable gate of a fortress. The unsuspecting horse was driven to the ground hard enough to catapult her rider over the culvert and up to the edge of the highway, where the boy lay face down in the snow. The hideous beast knew the horse was no longer a danger to him and that the blow he gave her would mostly likely be fatal. Now it was time to finish off the human who rode her.

Pockets was completely played out. She lay on her left side, her eyes wild with shock, trying to get some sort of purchase on the slippery surface with her scrabbling hooves. But there's very little blood flow in the lower half of a horse's leg and virtually no muscle, so as hard as she tried, the valiant steed could not even roll over or sit up. Plague ignored her and focused on the boy who was slowly attempting to rise from his own fall.

The hog from hell drooled with anticipation of his kill. He would especially savor the taste of this troublesome prey and leave the others that he would soon massacre as generous gifts for the local predators. He glared at the boy from the sides of his eyes as he circled the area to gain momentum for his death charge up the slope of the ditch. He was so intent on timing his run to strike the target at the moment he stood erect that he paid no attention to anything else around him. The rumbling of an approaching vehicle on the highway didn't even register on his consciousness. Neither was he aware of Pockets finally rising from her knees on his right.

From his sitting position, Ben saw the mad hog begin its attack. He knew in his heart he couldn't escape what was coming. He was like a prizefighter who had expended all of his energy and could no longer lift his arms so that his only defense was to stand in the corner of the ring and take a beating. The only decision he had left was whether or not to stay down and present a smaller target or to stand and face the assault head on. Even as he made himself as small as possible, words that Babe had spoken in the kitchen that morning came back to him: *"Look for help when you least expect it." I least expect it,* he thought grimly.

By the time Plague completed his circle and began the demonic dash up the incline, Pockets had recognized his intent and, with astonishing strength of will, pulled herself up to a standing position, her hindquarters toward Ben. Then just as the raging hog passed her, the 1700-pound Appaloosa braced herself with her front legs and gave out with a mighty kick of her hind legs squarely into Plague's ample rump.

With a prodigious squeal that caused Jacks to turn his attention away from his father, Plague went sailing into the air. What occurred next happened so fast that the two people who saw it would forever have a difficult time recounting it clearly. Ben, who just a moment before had resigned himself to his death and had chosen to remain as low as he could get to the ground, was first distracted and then frightened by a deafening sound coming up quickly behind him.

What the two boys saw was the front end of a massive tanker with a load of diesel fuel bound for the hospitals of Chicago. It thundered out of the storm, air horn blaring, just as the murderous hog flew over Ben's head and directly into its path. For years to come, the driver of the Kenworth five-axle B-train tanker swore that pigs actually *could* fly, but nobody believed his story. He said that a monster hog came hurtling through the air out of nowhere into his lane, and that before he hit it, the pig snarled at him, brandishing its teeth in a furious death cry. In fact, he was so shaken by the image that he never even slowed down, hearing and feeling the beast pass beneath his rig and under at least half of his eighteen wheels.

After he reached his destination later that evening and delivered the fuel that was critical for keeping the hospital generators going, he got out of his cab for a closer inspection of the front of the truck. The memory of the gigantic, airborne wild boar still fresh in his mind, he shuddered when he saw that most of his radiator grille was crushed, along with extensive damage to his front right fender and bumper. His flashlight revealed blood and bits of bristle and fur imbedded in the grille work. Little did he know that he had saved lives that day even before he got to Chicago.

CHAPTER
eighty-four

GurNEY & Babe
'Baby Bump'

Gurney and Babe had settled on the baby's name the night before he left for Chicago. Lying in bed in the dark, they had disclosed their preferences. As usual, she'd been working for weeks on first names while he continued the tradition of choosing unusual middle names that most people would remember after hearing only once.

"I think I've got it," she offered.

"Me, too," he replied, not noticing she'd used a singular pronoun. "You're going to love both of mine. But you first."

"Her name will be Rosalie, and we'll call her Rose to honor her cousin who never got to have a first birthday."

"How do you know it's going to be a girl? We purposely never found out."

"For lots of reasons," she answered. "I crave chocolate all the time, I'm carrying this baby awfully low, I've been extra moody lately, my face is rounder than usual"…she paused…"and I had an ultrasound done two days ago at the doctor's office."

"You what!?" he blurted out. "Why didn't you tell me?"

"Because you so badly wanted it to be a surprise."

"Then why tell me now?"

"You're surprised, aren't you?" she giggled.

Gurney was quiet for a moment, thinking about them having another daughter.

"Are you angry I didn't tell you?" Babe asked, wishing she could see his face.

"I think I'm a little disappointed," he replied, "but I know you don't like surprises, and you had every right to find out. And I actually love the name, but shouldn't you have checked it with Ben first?"

"Ben is the reason I chose the name," she said. "Still, you're probably right. Now, what have *you* got?"

"Okay, but you have to use your imagination. Are you ready for this?" he asked, obviously enthused about his choice for a girl's middle name. "First, I have to ask you another question. What do we save to eat last at almost every meal?"

Gurney couldn't see in the dark that Babe was already rolling her eyes.

"I don't think I like where this is going," she said.

"No, you're wrong this time. Look, we've both decided this will be our last baby, and everyone knows you always save the best for last, so I was thinking…"

Babe cut him off with, "*Dessert* is not going to be our baby's middle name."

"But everybody loves dessert, and people would remember it," he argued, "and how did you know what I was thinking? Was that a lucky guess?"

"I know *you*, darling," she laughed. "And you just lost your chance to name this baby. Her middle name will be *Blessing.*"

They were silent for a moment. Then, her lids growing heavy, Babe yawned, "By the way, what was your middle name for a boy?"

"*Honor,*" he answered.

"I love it," she whispered, drifting off to sleep.

"Of course you do," Gurney said softly, following her lead into slumber.

That conversation took place six days earlier, and now Babe sat on the edge of the bed doing her best to resist an overpowering urge to push the baby out.

"Carrie," she said, "I forgot something important. Go fill the small bucket under the mudroom sink with warm water and bring it to me quickly." The girl obeyed without question, and by the time she returned, found Babe pushing hard with her bottom on the bed, her legs propped up on the desk chair and the baby's head crowning.

"I can see her!" cried Carrie, as the head emerged. "What do you need me to do?"

"Just set the bucket there, get down by the chair and be ready to catch her when she comes," gasped Babe.

"This is great!" exclaimed the eight-year-old.

Great for YOU maybe! thought her mother.

Now that the head was visible, Babe placed her hands down there and gently guided it out. That's when she realized the umbilical cord was loosely wrapped around the infant's neck.

Remarkably calm, the mother simply hooked a finger under it and eased it over the baby's cranium. With the next contraction, the child's shoulders turned and passed through, followed immediately by the rest of her little body.

"Here…she…comes!" cried Babe. "Catch her!"

And Carrie did just that, grasping the slippery infant and exclaiming, "I did it! I did it!"

In awe, the girl handed the slippery, dusky blue newborn, with the umbilical cord trailing, up to her mother, who was weeping and laughing at the same time. First, Babe towel-dried the child and placed her on her chest so that the skin-to-skin contact would keep her warm and calm. Then, to stimulate breathing, she ran her fingers down the outsides of the baby's nostrils from the corners of the eyes to help drain the amniotic fluid. She vigorously rubbed the infant's back up and down the sides of her rib cage, making sure to keep her head a little lower than her feet, until she started breathing on her own. Finally, she put the baby to her breast to release a hormone that would ensure that the placenta would be expelled a bit later.

Babe looked up from her duties just in time to see Carrie mouth the word, "*babies*," the girl's eyes glistening with adoration.

"You were wonderful, darling," said her mother. "I couldn't have done it without you."

"No, Mama. I just made a good catch. *You* were wonderful! Can we name her now?"

"Her name is…" then Babe paused, remembering the warm hand on her shoulder that morning.

"Her name is Angelica Blessing Hightower, and we're going to call her Angel."

CHAPTER

eighty-five

It was 4:30 P.M. on Christmas Eve, and both Pillow Case Bandits sat drinking by the ambient light of a *Goose Island* beer sign. The White Hurricane had closed The Kitty Litter bar for most of the week, so the two of them had the run of the place. They could talk freely about Dusk's latest scheme, an idea Rooster had disliked from the moment he'd heard about it several days ago when his roommate returned in a rage from a traffic run-in that day.

Fueled by a fulminating darkness, Thrasher had stomped up the back steps and kicked the bedroom door open, yelling, "He thinks he got away with it. Well, now he's gonna pay!"

"I know, right?" Rooster responded absently, without looking up from a game of solitaire he was playing on the ratty, cardboard table in the middle of the room. "Where you been?" he asked.

"Finding our next sucker," Dusk replied. He told his accomplice how some pin-headed jamoke had almost hit him at a stoplight and then cleverly escaped by turning too quickly to be followed.

"But I got his plate number," the scoundrel sneered. "And by tomorrow, I'll know where he lives. Then this Bad Santa's gonna pay him a visit."

The week before Christmas had passed slowly while the unprecedented storm brought the world outside the bar to a standstill. Christmas Eve had finally arrived, and Rooster, who'd had plenty of time to think about Thrasher's scheme, still didn't like it. Now, as the light faded to darkness outside the windows of the bar, he watched

Dusk mindlessly drive his hunting knife into the top of their table and then pull it out—over and over again. He swallowed nervously and decided to try to change his confederate's mind.

But before he could speak, he had to wait for Thrasher to finish another one of his weird talks with himself. These had been happening more often lately, and Rooster could never make any sense of them. This one was particularly unsettling to him. What he couldn't hear was the Voice inside his partner giving him sinister instruction.

"Your path has been cleared, favored one," *the Shadow* announced in a husky female voice.

"You mean you plowed the roads for me?" answered Dusk.

"No, lover," she laughed affectionately, hiding her disdain for this half-witted human. "You will accomplish that with your own truck and superior skills. What we have done was to remove anyone in the house who could have given you trouble—not that you wouldn't have handled them with ease," she added.

"So the house is empty then, right?" he asked.

"It's better than empty," the sultry voice replied. "There are three Christmas bonuses there for you—an attractive, helpless woman, her newborn baby and a golden-haired little girl."

"What do you want me to do with them?"

"You're a red-blooded male, darling. After you've stolen their presents, you'll figure something out. Just make sure that when you're done, you take the baby with you."

"What in the world am I going to do with that?"

"We'll sort that out later, lover. Just don't leave the house without that baby. And if your idiot partner gives you any grief about it—well, you've got a knife. Leave him under a deep snow drift somewhere. Now it's time to go. I am with you always."

Dusk smiled cunningly and looked up at Rooster who was just opening his mouth to speak. The villain was pleased that he appeared nervous.

"I'm…I'm not sure we should do this job, Dusk. It could be a really bad idea. I don't have a good feeling about it."

"I don't feel so good about you right now either," the thief snarled. "Look, moron, the road to life is paved with flat squirrels who couldn't make up their minds. I've made mine up: we're going."

"But we're going to get caught if we target everybody you don't like," Rooster challenged.

Staring his partner down, Dusk didn't answer. If he didn't need him for this job, he might have dispatched Rooster right then. The wicked man was in a foul mood and the last thing he wanted to hear was criticism of his plan. Blizzard or no blizzard, he was going to steal Christmas and a great deal more from the guy in the white Toyota. Thanks to Google Maps he knew that the house they would burgle that night was isolated just enough to give him a good chance of keeping his record perfect for not being caught. No one but a lunatic with four-wheel drive and a snow plow would be out in this weather anyway.

"We leave in an hour," he announced, surrendering completely to *the Shadow* within him. "This is one house where I won't mind finding someone at home," he said, pulling his knife out of the table and sliding it into the custom leather sheath on his belt.

CHAPTER

eighty-six

Cold can kill, and Gurney's life hung in the balance for a while. A human being is not designed for polar weather, but the heat of the sheltered fire had done wonders for his body core temperature. After they ran out of the firewood Jacks brought, both boys kept the blaze going by trips on the snowmobile back and forth to the woods. There was plenty of deadfall under the snow, and using the hand axe, they pared it down to throw on the fire. Their biggest problem was keeping the flames at a height that wouldn't burn through the plastic ceiling of the shelter.

Late afternoon gave way to early evening and the weather changed. Although the wind still cried shrill in the branches of the oak trees, the snow had abruptly stopped falling. The sky began to salt with stars, and out from the circle of the campfire, the snowy landscape floated off into darkness. With Bear curled up next to him for warmth, Gurney opened his eyes and spoke for the first time that day.

"Water," he croaked. Kneeling down to his surrogate father, Ben helped him get a drink from his canteen. The parched man grabbed the flask and forced it to his shaking lips.

"Easy now," the boy said. "Not too much at first."

When he'd had enough, Gurney sat up the best he could and asked, "Did…did she have the baby yet? Are they okay?"

Jacks looked at Ben who answered, "When I left this morning she was fine. She maybe looked a little tired, but I don't think she's close to having the baby."

"You're wrong, son," Gurney said, shaking his head slowly. Then he took another drink from the canteen and his brow furrowed deeper. "I feel it in my bones. Your mother and our baby are in danger."

"What do you mean, Dad?" asked Jacks, now worried about something besides the ugly, discolored bump on his father's forehead.

"I'm not sure," he said, putting his arms around Bear's neck for balance. "It's just that ever since I told her on the phone that I was coming home, something or somebody has been trying to stop me from getting to her."

Jacks thought about the unreal experiences all of them had been through in the past few days: the crazy mega-storm, Gurney's almost fatal wreck, the trouble he had finding him, the surreal battle with the monstrous hogs, and finally Ben's story of the evil black fog that had descended and the ghostly figures that had materialized from it to try to stop Pockets and him.

Finally, the boy spoke: "I think we'd better get home right now."

Ben, who'd walked over to feed Pockets some carrots he'd brought in his saddle bags, looked up. "What's wrong?" he said.

"Babe's at home with no one but Carrie to help her. That's probably not a coincidence."

"What do you mean?" asked Gurney.

Jacks held his father's gaze for a moment and answered, "Maybe this whole thing was a distraction. Maybe somebody wanted all of us to be away from the house when the baby comes." He paused, turning his eyes from Gurney, then beyond the fire toward South Bend, as if straining to see what was going on inside their home just six miles away. Finally he rose from his seat by the blaze and announced, "We need to go." Looking down at his father, he said, "I think he wants the baby. It wouldn't be the first time he's done something like this."

CHAPTER

eighty-seven

Babe had already turned the thermostat up to seventy-five degrees earlier that afternoon. Now she held the blanket-covered baby to her breast while Carrie helped her scoot back into the pillows she had propped up against the headboard. There she cradled the newborn in her arms, allowing her to recover most of the blood that was still in the placenta and umbilical cord. After about five minutes, she could no longer feel a pulse in the cord. Then laying the baby on her lap, she followed the instructions she'd read on Web M.D.

Babe reached over to the bedside table where Carrie had placed everything she needed. First, she took a piece of dental floss and dipped it in the bowl containing a small amount of hydrogen peroxide. Then she tied the floss firmly but not too tightly around the cord about two inches up from the baby. The second piece of floss she tied the same way two inches further up the cord. Finally, after dipping the blades of the scissors in the bowl of isopropyl alcohol, she confidently cut through the cord between the two knots. It surprised her that it felt like cutting through a piece of tough rubber. Carrie looked on with her eyes and mouth wide open.

Exhausted from the whole experience, both mother and daughter were speechless for a while. Eventually, Babe broke the silence.

"Come sit by me, dear. Here's a pillow for you," she said, reaching behind her and shifting one of her own pillows to Carrie's side of the bed. The girl cuddled in close to her mother, enjoying her front row seat to the baby's first real breastfeeding.

"That doesn't look like milk, Mama," Carrie said when the infant withdrew her tiny mouth for a moment.

"No, it doesn't, darling. It's a rich cream called colostrum, and it's filled with important nutrients for little Angel until my milk comes in."

The girl watched a while longer until her eyelids grew heavy and she began to drift off. Babe noticed and said, "Carrie, wake up, dear. I'll be done here in just a minute. Before we both fall asleep, let's go downstairs and set up on the couch. I want to be there with you and the baby when your father and the boys arrive." Because of the hand she'd felt on her shoulder that morning, she still had an inner conviction that God was somehow going to bring all of them back to her. But now that it was dark outside, that conviction was beginning to waver.

Babe turned off all the lights downstairs except for the lamp on the end table by the family room sectional. She covered Carrie with an afghan on one end of the couch. Then she settled in with the baby at the other end. Turning the lamp off so the three of them could get some rest, she began to sing her favorite lullaby, *Baby Mine*, from the movie, *Dumbo*.

> *"Baby mine, don't you cry.*
> *Baby mine, dry your eyes.*
> *Rest your head close to my heart,*
> *Never to part,*
> *Baby of mine."*

After a while, sitting there in the dark, Babe heard a sound at the front door. "Gurney," she whispered. Overcome with relief, she couldn't express it because of the sleeping children. She assumed her men had made it safely home and must have decided to work their way through the snow to the front porch instead of entering the barn and crawling through the snow tunnel to the kitchen. Her heart pounding with anticipation, she turned on the lamp and waited.

320

CHAPTER

eighty-eight

Dusk Thrasher hated Christmas. And having to engage his snow plow and clear a driving path from the Kitty Litter Bar to the Hightower farm across town gave him almost an hour to complain to Rooster about his least favorite holiday. Bargain shoppers, holiday traffic, messy live Christmas trees, sappy, predictable movies, the same songs looping over and over again, amped up, unbearable children out in droves. "There's not enough coal in the world to fill their stockings," he groused. But as they neared their destination, he changed the subject.

"We're about a block away," he said, plowing north on Juniper Road. "When we get there, we're gonna park on the side of the street just west of this guy's house. Whichever part of the main floor that's got no lights on, that's where we break in."

"I heard you back at the bar say something about the house being empty. But what if it's not?" offered Rooster.

"As usual you don't know what you're talkin' about," snapped Dusk. "There's people there all right, but no one we need to worry about—'specially since nobody's phone's workin' anyway." Rooster wanted to ask him how he knew who was at the house, but he couldn't work up the courage. So they scraped along in silence for the next few minutes.

Because there are no street lights on Kintz road, when the burglars arrived at the farm, the neighborhood was shrouded in darkness. It was a good night for a felony. When they looked toward the house, the only light they could see, and it was dim at that, came from a back side window. It was the light over the kitchen stove that had been accidentally left on all day. Otherwise, the home appeared lifeless.

"We're goin' in the front," snarled Thrasher. "Bring that roll of trash bags for the presents."

The sound that Babe had heard at the front door and assumed to be Gurney and the boys, was actually the two Pillow Case Burglars, one with a set of mole grips. Thrasher took the grips and forced them over the lock barrel of the door knob. Then, with a powerful turn, a bump and a snap, he shattered the bolt in the lock, rendering it inoperative. He opened the door. Within one minute of reaching the porch, the thieves had slipped into the dark front hallway of the house.

Even from the family room, Babe felt the air pressure change and heard the wind howling when the front door opened. She expected to hear voices and see ambient light filter into the room from the hallway or living room, and when neither happened she knew something was wrong. *Someone* was in the house! She was tempted to set down the baby to go find out who had come in. But her maternal instinct told her to hold onto the child and wait. In retrospect, she probably should have turned the lamp off again. But fear froze her in place.

A moment later, she heard whispering in the hallway, followed by the click of a flashlight being turned on. While its fitful beam searched for the open doorway of the family room, she unconsciously tucked the blanket tighter around the baby and inched closer to Carrie beside her. Her heart hammering within her chest, Babe watched the door and listened to the approaching footsteps. She couldn't breathe. Suddenly, the flashlight clicked off and two men in parkas entered the faintly lighted room. For a fleeting instant, Babe hoped they might be travelers seeking refuge from the blizzard.

The first man was taller and powerfully built. His left hand hung at his side, but his right stayed in his coat pocket—as if he were grasping something there. *A gun perhaps?* she thought.

"Well, well, what do we have here?" he asked with a leering grin. His beefy, mottled face was insolent and uncultured; the wild, brown eyes took her in with a gleam of appetite. His gravelly voice grated on her ears, and any hope she may have had disappeared with his next words. "So what's a beautiful woman like you doing without male companionship on a cold night like tonight?"

Behind him, the shorter one stepped out of the bigger man's shadow, and Babe saw that he held a shiny black cylinder of some sort in his right hand. He was staring at her very differently from his companion, with a look that she thought might have been fear. "Leave her alone, Dusk. We're here for the merchandise."

"*You're* here for the merchandise, *ROO-O-O-OSTER*," bellowed Thrasher, drawing his accomplice's name out, then adding, "Or should I say, Connor whatever-your-middle-name-is Barry? Now she knows both of our names, you moron. Maybe we came for the merchandise, but you telling her my name kind of changes things, doesn't it? Now I need to have bigger plans."

"But, Dusk, she's got a baby, and..."

"Strike two, little man!" the bully shouted, cutting Rooster off and pointing his finger at him. "One more and you're out!" he growled. "Now get over to that tree with those trash bags and start loading up our Christmas presents, or I'll add you to tonight's casualty list!"

Babe saw what was coming, and her mind raced to figure a way out of this nightmare.

CHAPTER

eighty-nine

DeeDee Henderson didn't know what to think of her son anymore, but she was pretty sure she liked him more before *The Change.* They used to leave each other alone. Now it seemed like he was always around, and she hated the concerned look in his eyes when she caught him observing her. "Stop looking at me, you freak!" she screamed one day after getting home from work. "Why don't you go play with your new little, sissy friends? Maybe *they* want you staring at them!"

Despite the constant verbal abuse, Bubba didn't want to leave her alone anymore. He figured if he was there, she wouldn't be able to hurt herself like she had before. Whether DeeDee liked it or not, she was stuck with a bodyguard for a son now. But the way she saw it, this kid was constantly sticking his nose into her business. It got to the point that she could never find her cigarettes, booze or dope anymore. So she'd taken to hiding her stash in places he'd never look— like under her lingerie in the bottom drawer of her dresser, or taped beneath the toilet seat in her dingy, half-bathroom.

Still, his vigilance was probably the reason she was drinking and "using" less these days—simply because she didn't want him taking her outside in the blizzard to walk her unconscious stupor off again. And her pathetic "love life" was almost non-existent now because of his over-protectiveness. One night last week, she'd tried to slip out after thinking he'd gone to bed. But when she quietly opened the front door, she saw her ride, the black Dodge Charger, peeling away from her house, and her massive son standing at the curb with his powerful arms folded across his chest, making sure the car with the tinted windows didn't come back.

Because they didn't rely on a satellite dish for reception, DeeDee had been spending a lot of time lately watching television and sneaking a drink when she didn't think Gary was watching. It was during one of those moments, after the sun had gone down on Christmas Eve, that he walked into the dreary room where she was watching a rerun of *Cajun Pawn Stars* on the History Channel. He casually picked up the remote resting on the shabby arm of the couch next to her and turned the TV off.

Without taking her eyes off the plasma screen, she hollered—not realizing what she was saying about herself: "Hey, I was watching that, you stupid son of a b—." But DeeDee didn't finish her imprecation, because out of the corner of her eye she saw the young giant raise his arm in the air. Instinctively cowering, she covered the back of her head with both hands. More than once, she'd had that head almost knocked off by a man's fist thrown in anger. But Bubba would never be one of those men again. Instead, he harmlessly tossed the remote toward a ramshackle, faux leather chair at the side of the room. It bounced on the cushion and landed on a large rip there held together by an ancient strip of grey ducktape.

Next, the laconic man-boy did something he'd never done before. He rested his hand tenderly on the doubled over back of the woman who had given birth to him and now expected him to strike her, and he awkwardly repeated the words that had changed his life several weeks ago: "I-I love you," Bubba said softly.

DeeDee Henderson didn't believe in miracles because she didn't believe in God. Maybe there'd been a time when she had as a little girl, but that was buried under an avalanche of misfortune and abuse. All she felt at this moment was that she'd escaped a beating, and she was enough relieved at that to turn in her chair and look up into her son's eyes. *Who is this person?* she wondered, as if he had dropped in on her from another solar system.

Bubba's disk-shaped face was pinched with emotion, but he was determined to fight through his recent inhibitions to ask his mother a question that had haunted him for many days. "W-would you—cc-could you forgive me," he paused, and squeezed the next words out with difficulty: "for b-being such a bad son?" There. He'd done it. He'd finally asked her to do for him what he'd done for her, without being asked, almost two months earlier.

DeeDee wasn't so drunk that she didn't recognize that the boy had stammered out a stunning question. It's just that no one had ever asked her forgiveness for anything, and she simply didn't have the wherewithal at that moment to verbalize an answer for him. Instead, she nodded her head so slightly that if he hadn't been looking for it, he surely would have missed the gesture. Then she reached up with both hands and touched his arm with one of them while weakly pushing him away with the other. Bubba got the message and turned back toward his room.

Once there, he reflected on what had just happened. It wasn't everything he'd wanted to say to his mother or the only question he'd wanted to ask her, but for now it was enough. Maybe tomorrow or the next day, he'd get a chance to ask her to go to church with him when the blizzard allowed it to open again. And even though he knew what her answer would be, he also knew that he couldn't keep what he'd found to himself. That the One who had spoken to him on Halloween night would love her as well was a given. That the Hightowers would find a place for her in their hearts as they had for him was also beyond doubting. The only thing he doubted was his ability to bring her to them. Well, there was nothing more he could do about that tonight. Tomorrow was another day. Tomorrow was Christmas.

CHAPTER

ninety

His shimmering feet planted firmly just inside the bedroom door, the towering Guardian who never left Bubba's side and heard everything he'd said to his mother, smiled down on the boy sitting on the edge of his bed. *For good or bad, the sons of Adam never cease to amaze me,* he thought. *I wouldn't trade this job to serve on the Holy Mountain or to walk through the middle of the Stones of Fire.*

Though Bubba hadn't seen anything paranormal since his fight with Ben, he was aware that he was never alone anymore. The One who loved him now lived within him. Having spent so much of his life by himself, he'd become something of a connoisseur of loneliness. It was his observation that many lonely people withdraw and become insular. Others overcompensate and become soft targets for predators. But ever since he was a little boy, he'd always been frightened when he was alone, and without fail, that fear morphed into anger. It was predictable that, given his size, constant loneliness and anger issues, he would become the bully he had been.

But things were different now. Not perfect, but different. He knew that he and his mother were poor compared to most of his classmates. He didn't have any of the stuff other guys his age had: a cell phone, an iPad, a pair of Chuck Taylor Converse sneakers or a Darkstar skateboard. And most of his clothes came from Goodwill. But for the first time in his life he had friends. Ben and Jacks had even invited him over for Christmas. And Mrs. "H" said she was making him his favorite dessert: banana pudding with a graham cracker crust. Just the thought of being with the Hightowers the next day brought a smile to the boy's face. *I hope I can get there in this weather,* he thought. *I may have to use the snowshoes those guys gave me.*

Bubba moved back on the bed and sat against the wall. It was time to keep his promise to Mrs. "H." He plucked the Bible she'd given him off the drab pillow to his side and opened it to the first page, going right to her P.S. to read the words he'd already committed to memory: *Read one chapter a day starting with the Gospel of Matthew. WE LOVE YOU!* He knew Jacks' mother had written those words forty-one days ago, and he had faithfully obeyed her instructions ever since—whether he felt like it or not. So that put him in Mark 13 tonight. He loved the main character of these stories, who'd become more than a superhero to Bubba, but the boy didn't always understand everything he said. Tonight was no different.

This story opened with people asking his hero about things that would happen at the end of the world. He read the verses before him like he did every night: looking for things that seemed to apply to his situation and passing over those that didn't. But for a reason he couldn't comprehend, the fifteen-year-old stopped cold when he reached the fourteenth verse.

"Be ready to flee when you see the monster of desolation standing in a place where it does not belong," he read. His mind ran immediately to an image of the wicked dragon, *Smaug,* in the movie, *The Hobbit.* The boy knew something about monsters from past nightmares, and for some reason the mention of this one put him on high alert. The Guardian beside him was looking over his shoulder with intense interest. Bubba read on.

"You who can read, make sure you understand what I'm talking about. If you're living in Judea at the time, run for the hills; if you're working in the yard, don't go back to the house to get anything; if you're out in the field, don't go back to get your coat." He lifted his eyes from the page, looking at the warm winter parka Babe gave him, flung over the back of a chair in the corner—the coat that he wore everywhere now with pride. But when he got to verses seventeen and eighteen, he was so startled that his head snapped back and banged against the wall behind him. He knew immediately who these words in the Bible

were about: "*Pregnant and nursing mothers will have it especially hard. Hope and pray this won't happen in the middle of winter.*" The meaning was so clear to him that he yelled out his conviction loud enough for his mother to hear in the other room: "M-Mrs. 'H' is in trouble!"

If the Guardian beside his bed had materialized and spoken to him face to face about Babe's perilous situation, Bubba couldn't have been more motivated to get to the farm as quickly as possible. But first, he had to find those snow shoes.

CHAPTER

❧━━━━━━━❧

ninety-one

Dusk Thrasher, his eyes like sleet, was *standing in a place where he didn't belong*, ogling Babe's spent body and amaranthine face. His accomplice, Rooster Barry, had just dragged four heavy trash bags, filled with the Hightower family's Christmas presents, out to the front porch. From there, he would carry them, one at a time, through the deep snow drifts all the way to the pickup parked on the road alongside the farmhouse. When he had finished that task, he would return to the family room to gather one more load.

He knew it was Thrasher's job to find a pillowcase and fill it with the family's prescription drugs, jewelry, and any other small valuables he could find in the upstairs master bedroom and en suite. But he had a sick feeling this time that his partner had far darker plans, and that if he tried to stop him, he might wind up on the wrong end of the villain's hunting knife. Dusk had been getting moodier and harder to be around for the past several weeks, so much so that Rooster was beginning to doubt his sanity. The little man regretted having ever hooked up with him, but feared he had waited too long to be able to make his escape. Thrasher would track him down and take his life without a second thought.

And now a major part of Rooster wanted to leave the gifts on the porch and disappear in the truck before the psychopath raped the woman and hurt her children—or worse. Maybe he could call the police anonymously, and they could rescue the family before any-thing bad happened. But then, Dusk would finger him as well, and he'd go to jail for a long time. He didn't know what to do, so he began carrying the first bag to the truck.

With his partner doing the hard work out in the cold, Thrasher knew he had time to toy with his prey. He casually sat down in a navy blue, high-backed chair with only an area rug separating him from Babe and her daughters. Pulling his considerable knife out of its leather sheath and absently running his thumb up and down its spine, he cast his crooked, vulgar grin across the room before speaking.

"You don't have to look so scared, little lady. I'm more interested in you than I am your brats. And if you're nice to me, I might even leave them alone."

Babe knew he was lying. Alarm bells were going off inside her, and she had to come up with something fast. *Dear God!* she thought. *What am I going to do? After what I've been through today, I have no physical strength left to fight him.* On top of her anxiety about Gurney being in danger and the boys looking for him in this blizzard, now she was faced with the responsibility of protecting her newborn and Carrie from this madman. Some people would have gone to pieces in her position. Thrasher saw the tears in her eyes and wondered if she was about to do exactly that.

What the thief didn't know was that "Babe" Holly Dawn Hightower had a resource beyond his understanding. After noticing her purse sitting near her feet at the end of the sectional, she did the only thing she could in her predicament. She held her baby close, bowed her head and prayed. At first, the predator simply observed her. Then he mocked her.

"Really?" he taunted. "You think that's going to help you?"

Eventually Babe opened her eyes. She had a daring idea now, and it gave her a semblance of hope—even though she had no delusions about it being a dangerous plan. Still, trying something—anything—was better than passively waiting for the fiend to make his next move. But first, she gave Thrasher his chance.

"If you walk out of here right now, you can keep the presents, and I promise you I won't call the police." Suddenly, Carrie stirred on the other end of the couch and sat up. Rubbing her eyes and looking at the scruffy stranger across the room, she asked, yawning,

"Who's that, Mama?—and what's he doing here?"

"Carrie, darling, I want you to go up to your room right now and lock the door behind you. Please obey me immediately." she said. The girl was up the stairs before the intruder could react.

"That was pretty slick," he offered. "I'm impressed, but do you really think there's a door in this house that can keep me from getting to her when I feel like it?"

"You're not going to get away with any of this, you know. If the law doesn't catch up to you, God eventually will."

"How do you know God didn't send me?" he quipped profanely.

"The God I serve didn't send you here," answered Babe.

"The god *I* serve did," he replied quickly, as if he'd been waiting for the opportunity to say that.

"You've had your chance, Dusk," she said. "It's on your own head now."

"The only thing on my head, pretty lady, is a brain too quick for the cops," he said with a sarcastic smile that changed instantly to an ugly frown. "Now, put the baby down and stand up," he barked. "You're beginning to bore me, and I want to get a better look at you."

Babe knew it was now or never. So with a silent prayer that went something like, "*Okay, Lord—here goes!*" she put her idea into action. First she set the baby down as he'd ordered. She wrapped her snugly with a blanket and placed her gently on Carrie's end of the couch.

"Now, stand up!" he demanded. Instead, she calmly reached over to the lamp and turned it off, throwing the room into darkness.

"What the hell are you doing?" yelled Thrasher, jumping up from his chair. Sheathing his hunting knife, he paused for a second, waiting for his eyes to adjust, and that gave Babe her opportunity. She reached down to the purse at her feet and deftly withdrew her car keys. Meanwhile, the thief moved unsteadily toward the sectional, groping in the dark to feel for her. When his grimy left hand touched her knee, he threw his bulk forward, pinning her to the couch. His leaden weight hurt every part of her body; his sour breath offended her nostrils while his mouth searched for the side of her face.

"Gotcha!" he finally hissed, his lips pressed heavily against her ear. She felt like vomiting. Then he made his mistake. He backed off of her just enough to fumble for the knob on the lamp socket. After he switched the lamp on, he turned back toward Babe, who emptied a small canister of key-ring pepper spray directly into his wide open eyes. The beefy burglar fell backwards onto the rug, clawing at his eyes and screaming in pain.

Babe was all motion. "Carrie, come down here!" she cried at the bottom of the stairs. The girl was there in an instant, taking in the surreal scene before her, then focusing on her mother's words. "Take Angel upstairs with you and lock the door again!" With that, Babe was off to the den, which also served as Gurney's office, before the girl could reply.

Her heart beating out of her chest, she reached under the middle desk drawer and pressed a hidden button that unlocked the bottom drawer on the right. There she found the small security safe where Gurney had concealed their home defense weapon. She nimbly worked the combination and was back on the couch a moment later watching Thrasher writhe and rage like a petulant child while gradually regaining his vision. The first thing he could see clearly was a Glock 19 semi-automatic pistol pointed at his chest.

CHAPTER

---

ninety-two

When Dusk's vision improved enough for him to see Babe sitting on the couch holding a gun on him, he instinctively reached for his knife. She simply smiled in response, shaking her head back and forth. Then she leaned forward, leveled the barrel directly at his head, and asked,

"Do you know what people say who bring knives to gun fights?"

He didn't respond, giving all his attention to the ebony firearm aimed between his eyes.

"Why, they don't say anything, you foolish man," she continued, answering her own question, and then added, "Because they're all dead."

Thrasher was shaken by her smile and confidence. They were unearthly and unnerving, and he began to wonder if he'd met his match in this strange, praying woman. But his bluster and bravado had always carried the day for him, so he decided to try to restore his swagger before the situation got out of hand. Rising slowly from the floor to his full height, he looked down at her from just six feet away and mocked her with a contemptuous laugh.

"Who do you think you're kidding, lady? We both know you don't have what it takes to shoot me. Besides, that gun's probably not even loaded."

Her response was immediate. Babe professionally braced her right wrist with her left hand under and around it, and steadily lowered the gun barrel from his head to the middle of his chest while stating matter-of-factly: "Mothers protect their children, and I can't miss you from this distance." She watched the conflict behind his eyes and knew he was considering bull rushing her to test her resolve.

"If you don't drop that knife immediately, and if you move one step toward me," she warned, "there's a hollow point bullet in this gun with your name on it. It will blow a hole in your chest big enough to see hell through. Think of it as me arranging a meeting between you and the god who sent you here tonight." With that, she depressed the trigger safety and stuck her tongue slightly out of the right side of her mouth the way she always does just before she pulls the trigger at the range. Dusk heard the gun's characteristic click and knew his time was up.

"All right, all right!" he yelled, letting the knife slip through his fingers onto the rug. Besides, he knew he still had an excellent chance to turn the tables on her. Rooster was due to return any minute from the truck. The way he figured, when his accomplice re-entered the room, this difficult woman would be distracted. And he only needed an instant to jump her and take the gun away. Just then, he heard the front door open, and it was his turn to smile.

CHAPTER

---

ninety-three

By the time Bubba got to the Hightower farm, the stars were low and plain as candles in the sky. Though the snow clouds were scattering toward the east, the wind still rifled across the drifts of powder and worried the skeletal branches of the trees. It was the first night in two weeks there was enough moonlight to cast shadows on the snow. Buoyed by his snowshoes and hidden by one of those shadows, the boy was particularly interested in the scene before him. He'd spent the last few minutes watching a short, pudgy man laboring to carry what appeared to be a heavy bag all the way from the Hightower's front porch to his pickup truck.

Bubba had no way of knowing how many previous trips the man had made, but, in fact, it was his fourth and final load. When Rooster reached the truck this time, he set the bag down for a moment to rest before he worked up the strength to fling it up and over the tailgate. As it turned out, he should have bought a higher-rated brand of trash bag. Because when he lifted it by its drawstring and went to hurl it onto the truck, the thin layer of cheap plastic stretched like taffy and burst, throwing Christmas presents every which way out of the bottom of the compromised bag.

If the circumstances were different, the boy might have laughed at the image of the chubby thief cursing the innocent bag while scrambling around in the snow trying to recover the gifts that were being chased here and there by the wind. But Bubba was on an urgent mission, and all he could feel for the burglar was outrage. He moved quickly through the shadows of a grove of stately pines as quietly as his bulk would allow. Soon he was standing undetected over the prone form of the frustrated little Grinch who was attempting to steal his friends' Christmas. The thief was doing his best to get stuck under the back of the pickup while trying to secure a package that was just out of his reach.

"Hey, you down there," yelled Bubba in the most menacing tone he could work up. Rooster froze in place. "If you're not Santa Claus, you'd better have a really good reason for coming out of that house."

Suddenly, the chubby crook felt strong hands grab his boots and pull him face down through the snow and out from under the truck, and then toss him effortlessly headfirst and deep into a mound of powder. The giant of a boy considered leaving the burglar there, his head and shoulders stuck in the drift while his lower torso flopped about like a plump catfish out of water. But a moment later mercy set in, even though he was still angry when he plucked the man out of the drift and stood him up to ask him a question. Unfortunately, when brushing the snow off Rooster's face so he could answer, the boy slapped more head than snow, knocking him silly and back down into the drift again. So he picked him up like a rag doll and stood him on his feet one more time.

"I know you're not Santa," Bubba finally said, towering over the miserable burglar. "So who are you?"

But poor Rooster was so afraid that the hulking teen was going to try to clear the snow off his face again, that he instinctively turned to escape. Bubba's right leg flashed out, tripping the wretched man who, of course, plunged head first back into the same mound of snow. Giving up on any chance at interrogation and remembering his original mission, the sturdy boy lifted Rooster from the ground one last time, bopped him on top of the head, and transferred his unconscious body up to his massive shoulders. It was time to find Mrs. "H."

CHAPTER

ninety-four

When Dusk heard the sound of the front door opening, a malignant smile revealed his assumption. He expected Rooster to come walking into the family room any second. In a way, he was right about that. His accomplice did come directly to the room where Babe's gun, safety off, held Thrasher at attention—but Rooster wasn't walking. When Dusk saw his partner, he immediately lost all hope. He was being carried like a sack of potatoes on the shoulders of a rugged, young giant who, tossing his burden heavily to the hardwood floor, announced, "I found this one, ma'am, stealing your Christmas presents." Even in his senseless state, Rooster groaned when his body hit the unforgiving surface. Then, nodding toward the thief she was focused on, Bubba asked, "Do you need any help with that one?"

Never moving the barrel of the gun from Dusk's chest, Babe, feeling that she could breathe again, replied with deep gratitude: "Why, yes I do, Gary. How thoughtful of you to come out on a night like this. And with your help, I'm going to give both of these unruly boys a timeout in the den."

"What do you want me to do?" asked the boy.

Babe sighed and thought about it. "Well, first things first. There's packaging tape in the den—lots of it. Would you be a dear and bring it to me, please? It's on the small end table in there with rolls of wrapping paper leaned against it. When you get back, I'll tell you what to do with it."

Ten minutes later, both burglars, with even their mouths covered with layers of tape, looked like they were ready to be shipped to places unknown. All they lacked was sufficient postage. After securing them with more tape than he needed, Bubba carried each man just loosely enough to bang his head on the occasional door frame or open desk drawer before depositing them rudely on their keisters in a corner of the den.

Satisfied that the burglars were harmless now in their shiny, new cocoons, Babe put Bubba on guard duty to watch them. But before she left the room, she handed over Thrasher's hunting knife in its sheath to the boy. "Early Christmas present," she said. "Be careful with it." Finally, she couldn't resist turning to the almost mummified miscreant brooding in the corner and announcing, "By the way, Dusk, you were right." His eyebrows raised in a question mark. "It wasn't loaded," she revealed.

After calling for Carrie to bring the baby back downstairs, Babe turned on every light in the room, including the overhead ceiling fan light. The adrenalin that had carried her through the past harrowing hour was wearing off, and by the time she and Carrie had a cheery blaze going in the fireplace, she was having a hard time keeping her eyes open. She had never felt so tired. But there was the baby to feed and her men to pray for. So she put the infant to her breast, settled back into the couch and closed her eyes, listening to her eight-year-old pray for the safe return of her father and brothers.

CHAPTER

ninety-five

Babe opened her eyes when she heard the sound of a snowmobile turning into their driveway. She shook Carrie's arm gently to wake her.

"Your prayers worked, darling. I'm sure this is them. We've still got a few minutes. They'll be taking Pockets and the snowmobile to the barn first. Then they'll come through the snow tunnel to the kitchen. Let's get some hot chocolate ready for them."

But before she could pull her weary body from the couch, she heard heavy footsteps on the front porch.

"Carrie, run to the front door, and see if they're coming in that way." She turned to go when Babe stopped her. "And Carrie—don't tell them anything about our 'guests.'" She winked at her mother and took off.

Sure enough, when the girl got to the door, in tramped Jacks and Ben with Gurney in between them—his arms around their shoulders for support. Just behind them, Bear shook the snow from his fur and padded immediately to his doggie bowls for food and water. At first sight of the four of them, Carrie was ecstatic. She clapped her hands and shrieked with joy. Then they got closer and she grew quiet. All of their eyes were bloodshot and teared up from the severe cold; their lips were cracked and their faces gaunt and ashen. Small icicles hung from their eyebrows and larger ones from Gurney's beard. They looked like they'd just walked back from the Russian front—after losing the battle. Then her father raised his head higher, and she saw the ugly, discolored bump on his forehead.

"Daddy, are you okay?" cried the girl.

"Yes, sweetie, I'm still just a little dizzy. How's your mother?"

"That was the first thing I wanted to tell you. She had the baby! And I helped!"

Gurney was so excited that he broke away awkwardly from the boys, found his balance and made his way down the hallway toward the family room. Jacks and Ben started to follow him, but remembered that they weren't quite done with the cold.

"Listen, Sis," Jacks said. "We've got to take care of Pockets and put the snowmobile in the barn before we can warm up. We saw the smoke from the chimney. We'll meet you by the fireplace as soon as we can. Got any hot chocolate and real food?"

"I'll have it ready when you come in," she answered.

As the boys started out the door, Ben mumbled something to Jacks. Then both boys turned, and the younger one asked his sister a question.

"Is it a boy?"

"Nope," she replied.

Then Ben gave her that crooked, wry smile she loved and asked, "Is it a girl?"

Even though she was concerned about both of them going back into the cold, Carrie couldn't help but giggle. "Very funny," she answered, her hands on her hips while rolling her eyes at her cousin.

The boys pulled their ski masks down and headed outside, even as Jacks fired off one more question:

"So what's her name?"

And just before the door closed, she yelled back:

"Angel!"

"H-m-m-mm," muttered Ben, grinning. "That's perfect."

CHAPTER

ninety-six

Gurney & Babe

When Gurney saw Babe holding their baby girl, his heart melted along with the icicles in his beard. Despite the fire radiating warmth, he wasn't ready yet to take off his parka. Heck, he might never take it off again. Babe watched her husband walk unsteadily toward her. Her compassion spilled over to her eyes, and she patted the cushion next to her. He collapsed onto it, and not saying a word, put his arm around her and stared at the tiny infant. "Merry Christmas, darling," she whispered, turning and kissing his rough, still cold cheek. They sat there in silence for several minutes, nestled as close as they could get, simply looking at the sleeping baby.

Carrie waited in the kitchen until the boys crawled through the snow tunnel and joined her. They gathered food and drink and brought them into the family room. Babe looked up and smiled, but her husband kept his eyes locked on the child. Finally, he spoke to no one in particular: "She looks like me—beautiful, but a little rough around the edges." The kids laughed. Gurney was back.

While Jacks and Ben huddled near the fire, Babe described her emergency home birth, bragging about Carrie helping her deliver Angelica Blessing. "She was a real trooper through the whole thing. I simply couldn't have done it without her," she said. Then she skillfully changed the subject and began asking the boys questions about how they had found Gurney. At first, their answers were short and a bit vague—almost as if saying too much about the trials they'd faced would bring some of the fear and dread back. But as the fire and food began to warm their bodies, so the growing realization that, by God's grace, if not altogether miraculously, each of them had survived only a little the worse for wear, began to loosen their tongues.

And some of the tales the boys told were news to each other: like Jacks choosing the wrong side of the toll road to search, and coming upon the completely buried eighteen-wheeler, and almost giving up hope only to have Bear pick up Gurney's scent and dig through the snow until his claws struck the entombed car; and Ben urging Pockets on through the assault of ghostly spirits that tried to stop them after the evil, black fog had descended around them. Even Gurney entered in a bit by telling a brief rendition of his frightening drive home through the blizzard and how he was knocked off the highway by a massive snowplow just as he was about to reach his goal. Babe shuddered and pulled him closer as he spoke. But each of the guys stopped short of recounting the tale of the attack of the monstrous wild boars. Babe sensed that they were holding something back, but accepted that there would be more details later and some stories better left for the future.

Meanwhile, the girls were so caught up in the narratives that they forgot about poor Bubba and the captured thieves in the adjoining room. What made them remember was something Gurney said at the end of the story-telling time. "Well, everybody, the past twenty-four hours have been pretty crazy for all of us. Maybe we should take a moment and thank God that we're safely back together again. Did anything else happen to you girls today that we should be thankful for?"

Jacks noticed a look pass between mother and daughter that told him there was more to their story too than they were telling. While Babe was considering her answer, Gurney pulled the couch pillow out from behind him to hold it to his chest as he often did. When he did that, he leaned back against something hard and metal. "Ouch!" he said, and Babe, realizing what the object was, quickly reached over and grabbed up the empty Glock 19 she had inadvertently left there earlier that evening.

"What the heck?" exclaimed her husband.

"Mother! What was that doing there?" shouted Jacks.

"Kinda gives new meaning to the phrase, 'Baby Photo-shoot,' doesn't it?" laughed Ben.

"Tell them, Mama," begged Carrie.

"Tell us what!" the three guys yelled simultaneously.

"It would be much easier just to show you," said Babe, getting up and motioning the boys to come with her. "Besides," she added, "it's time to give Bubba some help."

"What!" said Ben, the first one to jump up and follow. "Is Bubba here?"

"Yes, dear," answered Babe, reaching the door to the den. "And he's not the only one," she said, turning the knob.

CHAPTER

---

ninety-seven

When the snow stopped falling and the White Hurricane began to dissipate, cell phone service was restored and snow crews began clearing the major thoroughfares. Consequently, two South Bend police cars pulled into the Hightower driveway a little after 9:00 p.m. on Christmas Eve. When the officers in those vehicles radioed in that they were about to take into custody The Pillowcase Burglars, two more squad cars, a prisoner transport van and a WSBT-TV mobile news truck showed up within ten minutes. Nabbing these notorious bandits was a big deal in this city.

When the arresting officers arrived, they'd already been told to come to the front door. Even so, they had to high step through the snow to get to the porch. When Ben let them in, he saw that they had their handcuffs ready and their weapons drawn. He couldn't keep from grinning because he knew what they were about to find: the two suspects totally immobilized and thoroughly encased in layers of packaging tape. All that was missing were two big red bows. In fact, the police's biggest problem was cutting away just the right amount of the tape to get the dejected burglars unwrapped enough to walk to the van under their own power.

After the police had retrieved all the presents from the back of the pickup and returned them to the Christmas tree, the last officer to leave their home was Sergeant Butch Whitmire, who was sensitive to the family's need for privacy. At the door he tipped his cap to Babe, shook Gurney's hand and said, "I'll take care of the reporters outside and make sure they leave when I do. I mean, it's Christmas Eve for heaven's sake," he declared. "You all deserve some family time now."

The truth was that, more than family time, this beleaguered band of adventurers needed healing sleep. The baby was doing fine, and Gurney appeared to be recovering well, so they all decided to head to their respective bedrooms and not expect anyone to come out until noon the next day. Then they could find something to eat and get on with keeping Christmas. So Babe holding Angel baby, and Gurney at their side, climbed the stairs with great care, followed by Carrie who was leading Bubba to the guest room. The bunk bed boys brought up the rear.

Fifteen minutes later, Ben was on the top bunk, listening to James Blake's LP, *Radio Silence*. Ear buds in, he'd just heard the words, "I'll swim to you while I'm sleeping," when a text message came through.

There was a moment of silence, and then:

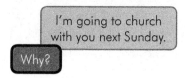

Because I was wrong about God.

What made you change your mind?

Lots of things. Bubba, for one. And a dream I kept having that came true. But mostly just living in this crazy house.

There's a name for spaces like this. They're called 'thin places,' a Celtic term for a spot where the distance between heaven and earth collapses. The most famous one is Bethel, where Jacob saw the Guardians. But most thin places are homes where God is loved, and those are all over the world. This home is just one of them.

You're doing it again, Yoda-boy. But you can't help yourself. You just know too many things. After what happened today, there's only two things I want to know.

What's the first?

I'm willing to help you in any way I can. In fact, I think that's why I'm still alive. And I know who the enemy is now. What I don't get is why he's trying to kill you. What's in it for him? What's his game?

He's the first of *The Shadows*, the Fallen One who won't be satisfied until the whole world has fallen with him. He's a cancer that won't stop growing until the entire body is dead. More than anything else, he wants to be worshipped and knows that can't happen until he defeats me. I don't plan on letting that happen. What's the second thing?

Why are you here in the first place?

I'm always here—in one way or another. But if you mean: "Why am I in this town at this time?" It's because The War is coming—a war like the world has never seen, and I want to be with this family at the epicenter when it comes.

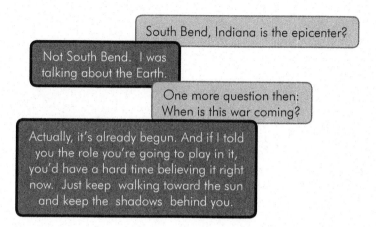

Lying there in the dark with his hands tucked under his pil-lowed head, Ben thought about Jacks' words and the battle between heaven and earth that he'd already been a part of for months without knowing it. He knew that a dangerous enemy beyond his compre-hension had targeted him and that he might someday have to lay his life down to stop him.

"I'm in," he whispered, his face fixed in a smile that could have been seen from the moon.

ABOUT THE AUTHOR

Bob Laurent has been speaking and writing full-time, all over the world, since 1972. His communication style is both humorous and hard-hitting, encouraging and provocative, geared to reach youth and adults. As president of Good News Circle, Inc. for fifteen years, he spoke in hundreds of high school assemblies, city-wide crusades, prisons, youth rallies and churches and published seven books. He has been the keynote speaker at hundreds of national and regional conferences.

Bob has served as chapel speaker for a number of major league baseball teams including the Chicago White Sox and Minnesota twins. As a college professor, where he also served as head coach for tennis and softball, "Dr. Bob" received the "Sears Roebuck Teaching Excellence Award," the "Outstanding Faculty Member Award", and two "Coach of the Year" awards.

Bob has for the past fifteen years been a teaching pastor at Granger Community Church in Granger, Indiana, and is now fulfilling a lifelong dream as a free-lance writer. He and his beloved wife, Joyce, remain close to their four children and nine grandchildren.

"Bob Laurent's ability to communicate is his gift. I met him as a teen, and it changed my life forever. Bob's sense of humor, his caring spirit, and his passion to communicate Christ have impacted thousands of people. While many have influenced the style of music I play--Bob Laurent influenced the content." --Michael W. Smith, Musician and Songwriter.